最生動、最實用的**英文文法大全**，
讓你的英文突飛猛進！

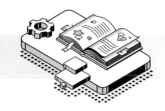

User's Guide

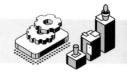

使・用・説・明

學習重點一 ▷ **認識英語**句子的基本組成，**從此學習無障礙**

本書從介紹英語句子的基本概念開始，逐一介紹主詞、謂語、賓語、表語等句子的成分，也介紹英語句子的基礎句型，如主詞＋動詞的SV結構、主詞＋動詞＋狀語的SVA結構、there句型等。熟悉這些基本知識，學習後續文法才能更輕鬆！

學習重點二 ▷ **參照**劍橋英語語料庫，**例句最實用**

本書的所有文法重點皆有例句輔助說明，而本書的例句都參考劍橋英語語料庫，不只豐富又專業，還相當實用！例句都是母語人士實際會使用的句子，保證讓你學到最道地的英文！

學習重點三 ▷ **易混淆用法要小心，容易錯誤的地方提供**貼心小提醒

在出現不規則用法、特殊用法，或者易混淆、易犯錯誤的地方，本書都會特別撰寫「注意！」的貼心小提醒，即時釐清文法概念，才能避免出錯，講出一口漂亮英文！

學習重點四 ▷ **文法句型各自搭配的單字大不同，**列表說明**最清楚**

不同的文法句型會搭配的單字都不太相同，而單字本身也會有所有格、單複數、時態等不同的變化。本書不只介紹文法重點，更會適時提供適用的單字清單以及單字變化表，讓你一目瞭然，學習更輕鬆！

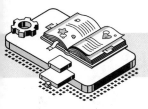

Preface

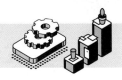

前・言

英語學習中常常涉及兩個層面：一個是感性層面，另一個是理性層面。在語言的實際應用過程中，學習者通常會接觸到各種各樣的語言現象，但是如果不對其加以理性的分析、整理、歸納和總結，很難對語言有理性層面上的認識，也就不能深入地瞭解語言或掌握語言的規律性，從而不能更好地運用語言來達到交流的目的。

學習文法的目的正是為了把對語言的認識從感性層面提高到理性層面。通過學習文法，將豐富多樣的感性素材分析歸類，進而形成理論系統和概念。這樣，學習者才能恰當地理解文法規則並實際運用，從而提高自身對語言的掌握和運用能力。本文法書正是基於以上目的而編寫的。

本書的編寫原則是追求科學性、系統性、全面性、創新性和理論性。在體系編排、內容取捨與表達方面體現了科學性。編者力圖準確、系統、全面地向讀者呈現英語知識，反映英語在真實語境中的應用。全書以標準英語特徵為編寫準則，書中的例句選取自劍橋英語語料庫，來源於真實生活，貼近現實，並呈現多種語體和不同語境，給讀者提供了豐富的英語語言素材，便於讀者理解語言規則和概念。這也是本書最大的特色。

英語學習注重實踐，除了聽、說這種口頭交際形式以外，讀、寫、譯也是不容忽視的交流方式，恰如其分的書面表達和得體的言談都會起到事半功倍的效果。就此而言，本書正是一本不可多得的工具書。

為了便於讀者查找相關資訊，本書主要包含文法規則、概念、基本用法等內容，同時還包含了用法提示（如不規則用法或特殊用法）、應引起讀者特別注意的資訊（如易混淆、易犯錯誤之處）、用法比較等。凡遇到結構需與詞彙結合的地方，補充一個適用於該結構的單字表，幫助學習。

祝各位讀者學習順利！

編輯團隊

寫在本書之前：
學英文一定要認識的重要構成

怎麼說出完整的句子？——認識句子的成分

想要學好英文，就要先認識句子的成分。在句子中，主詞和謂語通常作為句子的直接成分，構成句子的主體；受詞和補語作為謂語的下位成分，進一步補充和說明動作的物件和結果；定語和狀語作為句子的附加成分，限定人和物的性質、特徵和範圍，表明動作的程度和方式等。

主詞

主詞（Subjects）是句子評述的對象，常由名詞片語或相當於名詞片語的成分組成。

❶ 名詞充當主詞。例如：

▶ **Mexico** bans the cultivation of biotech corn. 墨西哥禁止栽培轉基因玉米。

❷ 代名詞充當主詞。例如：

▶ From every outcome, **they** expect perfection.
他們對每個結果都力求完美。

❸ 定冠詞the＋形容詞充當主詞。例如：

▶ **The poor** aren't strangers, and they're the folks you meet every day.
這些窮人並不陌生，你每天都會遇到他們。

▶ **The young** and **the educated** flooded into this metropolis.
年輕人和受過教育的人蜂擁至這座大城市。

❹ 動詞-ing形式充當主詞。例如：

▶ Increasingly, **smoking** is regarded as an anti-social habit.
吸煙越來越被視為一種反社會的習慣。

❺ 不定詞充當主詞。例如：

▶ **Not to change** is to die. 拒絕改變就是坐以待斃。

❻ 名詞片語充當主詞。例如：

▶ **The failure of an energy policy**, however, has made the price of gas go up.
但是，能源政策的失敗刺激了油價的上漲。

▶ **The spread of civilization and the taming of the land** wore hard on the native fowl,however. 然而，文明的傳播和土地的開墾讓原本生活在當地的禽類備受騷擾。

❼ 子句充當主詞。例如：

▶ **What happened to her** is anybody's guess.
她發生了什麼事誰也說不準。

❽ it充當主詞

這裡所說的it主詞句型是由非人稱代名詞it作主詞的三種類型。

• **it 泛指天氣、時間和距離等。例如：**

▶ Last year **it** rained an awful lot. 去年雨下得很多。

▶ **It** was 7 p.m. 那是晚上7點。

▶ **It** must be within five miles or something. 距離肯定在大約5英里之內。

• **it 作先行主詞（Preparatory Subjects），而真正的主詞移到後面，避免主詞過長，前後失衡。例如：**

▶ Perhaps **it**'s easier to save someone else.
也許救其他人還來得更容易些。

• **it強調句型，即分裂句，一般結構為「It＋動詞be＋強調部分＋that/who(m)子句」。例如：**

▶ **It** is Ellen that/who will fly to Paris. 是艾倫要飛往巴黎。

🎯 謂語

謂語（Predicates）是對主詞進行的評述，常由動詞或動詞片語充當。

❶ 單一動詞充當謂語。例如：

▶ They **create** government-sponsored health care.
他們建立了由政府贊助的醫療保健制度。

❷ 動詞片語充當謂語。例如：

▶ A postmodern nation of historical amnesiacs must **seek for** other types of hero.
一個遺忘歷史的後現代民族必須要尋找其他類型的英雄。

▶ Miller's bias-free approach **has enabled** him to succeed in all kinds of markets.
米勒採用的無偏見策略使得他在商場上戰無不勝。

🎯 表語

表語（Predicatives）位於連綴動詞之後，用來補充主詞的意義，通常由形容詞或名詞充當。表語也叫做主詞補語（Subject Complements）。

❶ 名詞充當表語。例如：

▶ I mean I am a really keen **environmentalist**. 我是說我是一個相當熱衷於環保的人。

❷ 形容詞充當表語。例如：

▶ When they were roused to outrage, the damage they could do was **appalling**.
他們一旦被激怒，產生的破壞力是令人震驚的。

❸ 副詞充當表語。例如：

▶ I told Mr. Kenyon and Mr. Abramovich that we must be **together**, to think as a team.
我告訴凱尼恩先生和阿布拉莫奇先生，我們該團結一致，從團隊的角度出發去考慮問題。

❹ 不定詞充當表語。例如：

▶ When mothers experience stress, male embryos are more likely **to perish**.
當母親經受壓力時，男性胚胎往往更容易死亡。

❺ 子句充當表語。例如：

▶ The big problem is **that Paige did have a lot to offer, but he didn't get a chance to offer it**. 問題是佩奇的確有很多東西可提供，但卻沒機會這麼做。

受詞

受詞（Objects）是位於及物動詞或介係詞後，表示動作的對象和結果的成分。受詞通常由名詞、代名詞、動詞-ing形式、不定詞、子句等來充當。

❶ 名詞充當受詞。例如：

▶ She hates **lazy people**. 她討厭懶惰的人。

❷ 代名詞充當受詞。例如：

▶ If battery runs out, doctors can replace **it** with minor surgery.
如果電池的電量耗完，醫生用個小手術就能更換。

❸ 定冠詞the＋形容詞／動詞-ed形式充當受詞。例如：

▶ The old hate **the young**. 上年紀的人不喜歡年輕人。

▶ And I want to thank you for that because I strongly believe the future belongs to **the educated**. 我真想好好謝你，因為我一直堅信未來屬於受教育的人。

❹ 動詞-ing形式充當受詞。例如：

▶ I just don't like **complaining**. 我只是不喜歡怨天尤人。

❺ 不定詞充當受詞。例如：

▶ And his parents pretended **to be distracted**. 他父母裝出一副心煩意亂的樣子。

不定詞作受詞時，it可以放在受詞位置充當形式受詞，後面跟不定詞充當真正的受詞。

▶ Holes in the state's ocean monitoring system make **it** impossible to say whether it's safe to swim or fish along the Jersey shore, an environmental group said Wednesday.
週三某環境保護組織宣稱，國家海洋監測系統中存在的漏洞使它無法對人們在澤西海岸從事游泳或垂釣等行為的安全性作出正確的判斷。

不定詞前還可以加疑問詞，如when，what，which，how，where等，與不定詞一起充當受詞。例如：

▶ I was so afraid the cancer would come back and I didn't know how to deal with it.
我很擔心癌症復發，對此束手無策。

❻ 子句充當受詞。例如：

▶ I endeavored to calculate how much longer I could stay in the Custom-House.
我努力計算著還能在海關大廈待多久。

有些及物動詞後面會跟兩個受詞，動作的直接對象稱為直接受詞（Direct Objects），動作的間接對象（多在介係詞後）稱為間接受詞（Indirect Objects）。例如：

▶ In 1990, after the fall of Mrs. Thatcher, he offered it to John Major as the base for a successful leadership campaign. 1990年柴契爾夫人下臺後，他把它提供給約翰‧梅傑作為成功進行競選的基地。

補語

補語（Complements）是用來補充說明主詞和受詞的成分，補充主詞的是主詞補語（Subject Complements），補充受詞的是受詞補語（Object Complements）。表語是在連綴動詞之後的主詞補語，本章中我們將表語和補語分開介紹，但也有學者把這兩類合二為一，統稱為補語。

以下介紹的是受詞補語，通常由名詞、形容詞、動詞-ed形式和-ing形式等充當。

❶ 名詞充當補語。例如：

▶ His Hall of Fame baseball career made him a hero to the state's sports fans, and his 17 years in the House and Senate have made him a political icon.
他榮登棒球名人堂的職業生涯使他成了全國體育迷心中的英雄，而參眾兩院17年的從政經歷又使他成了政壇上的偶像。

❷ 形容詞充當補語。例如：

▶ He'd think she was an imbecile, anyway, so why not tell him and prove him right.
不管怎樣他都會認為她是個傻瓜，那幹嘛不告訴他，並證明他是對的？

❸ 動詞-ed形式和-ing形式充當補語。例如：

▶ Everybody on the flight was trying to get themselves photographed next to a plane that would soon cease to soar. 機上的每位乘客都爭著和即將停飛的飛機合照留念。

▶ As she rang the bell, she heard a child crying somewhere inside the house.
她按門鈴時，聽到屋裡某個地方傳來孩子的哭聲。

定語

定語（Attributives）是對名詞或代名詞的性質、特徵進行說明，起修飾作用的成分，通常由形容詞、名詞、代名詞、分詞、不定詞、介係詞片語、副詞、數詞和子句充當。它們可以單獨作定語，也可以與其他詞一起作定語。

❶ 形容詞充當定語。例如：

▶ But even his fiercest opponents do not question his intelligence and his almost fervent commitment to children and their educational achievement. 即使是他最激烈的反對者，也不得不承認他的智慧和他為孩子們及孩子們在學業上的進步所付出的熱情投入。

❷ 名詞充當定語。例如：

▶ In fact, a sort of mini oil crisis is developing and the price of a barrel of crude topped $37 a barrel in London yesterday, the highest for 13 years.
事實上，一場小型的原油危機正在醞釀，昨天倫敦市場的原油價格已高於每桶37美金，為13年之最。

❸ 代名詞充當定語。例如：

▶ He put up his hand and began to massage his temple. 他把手放在太陽穴上，開始按摩起來。

❹ 動詞-ed形式和-ing形式充當定語。例如：

▶ Her pioneering efforts to encourage the study of Asian and Pacific music and dance paved the way for future generations.
她為推動亞太音樂和舞蹈的研究所進行的開創性的工作為後人開闢了道路。

▶ The problem discussed at the meeting yesterday was what to do with radio active waste. 昨天在會上討論的是如何處置放射性廢料的問題。（動詞-ed形式作後置定語）

❺ 不定詞充當定語。例如：

▶ There were other cultural and linguistic chasms to bridge, as well.
也有其他文化和語言上的分歧要逾越。

▶ If that's true, efforts to prevent teen smoking could become even more urgent.
如果情況屬實，那麼防止青少年吸煙的工作將變得更加緊迫。

❻ 介係詞片語充當定語。例如：

There is plenty of water in the tank at the back of the house. 屋後的蓄水池裡還有足夠的水。

❼ 副詞充當定語

充當定語的副詞常位於名詞之後。例如：

▶ Last year alone, however, the NTSB documented at least five instances in which the CF6 engine failed because of cracks, causing several near-crashes.
然而，僅去年，美國國家運輸安全委員會記錄顯示至少有五次CF6型飛機因裂縫而導致引擎無法運轉的情況，幾乎引發數起事故。

❽ 數詞充當定語。例如：

▶ More than **600 million** people in the country flew last year, and that number is expected to reach 1 billion in 10 years.
  在這個國家，去年有超過6億人次乘坐了飛機，而且這個數字在未來10年裡將達到10億。

❾ 子句充當定語

　　充當定語的子句即定語子句（Attributive Clauses）可分為限定性定語子句（Defining Attributive Clauses）和非限定性定語子句（Non-defining Attributive Clauses）。前者與被修飾的句子成分關係密切，可由that，which，who(m)，whose等關係代名詞引導。例如：

▶ Dreaming may also fulfill many functions **that** we don't yet understand.
  做夢或許也能實現很多我們現在還不知道的功能。

▶ A policeman **who** drove a schoolgirl to the brink of suicide with sick text messages missed out on a possible jail sentence yesterday—because he is away on holiday.
  一個員警因曾經向一個女學生發下流簡訊幾乎導致對方自殺，而可能面臨牢獄之災，但他卻因為休假而缺席了昨天的審判。

▶ A sensuous performer **whose** sultry vocals had taken her to the top of the pop charts, she already had two Grammy nominations to her credit and two platinum albums.
  她是一位性感歌手，她那迷人的嗓音使她一躍登上流行音樂榜的榜首，現在她已經獲得兩次葛萊美提名和兩張白金唱片。

　　限定性定語子句也可以由when，where，why等關係副詞引導。例如：

▶ Concerns over new competition are part of the reason **why** officials from Jamaica and other small Caribbean countries want a few conditions included in the new free trade agreement. 牙買加和其他加勒比海小國的官員要求在新的自由貿易協定中附加一些條件，部分原因是出於對新一輪競爭的擔心。

　　非限定性定語子句與被修飾成分的密切程度不高，書寫時常用逗號相隔，通常對被修飾成分起補充說明作用。例如：

▶ Oil revenues, **which** provide $30 billion a year, also fell, along with the price per barrel.
  每年約300億美元的原油收入也隨著每桶原油價格的下降而下降。

▶ He said a balanced assessment program, **which** allows us to assess our students' progress, is appropriate. 他說為了讓我們能評估學生的進步，得有一個公正的評估方案才行。

▶ Officials estimated that 3,000 people died in the city, **which** has a population of about 240,000. 官方估計城裡有3,000人喪生，整個城市大約有240,000人。

▶ The study season runs from October through mid-July, **when** the grasses get so high it's difficult for researchers to see the coyotes. 對於草原狼的研究從10月一直持續到次年7月中旬，這時由於草長得太高，研究者很難發現它們的行蹤。

> **注意！**
> 關係代名詞that 一般不用在非限定性定語子句中。

🎯 狀語

　　狀語（Adverbials）是修飾動詞、形容詞、副詞、介係詞片語以及子句的句子成分，可由副詞、介係詞片語、形容詞、不定詞、分詞或子句充當。

❶ 副詞充當狀語。例如：

▶ But recently, the firm has launched a complete overhaul of its fund business.
但最近，這家公司對其基金業務進行了一次澈底的改革。

❷ 介係詞片語充當狀語。例如：

▶ But no one, besides her family, knew Roukema was leaving until she faxed an announcement Thursday. 在魯克瑪週四發來傳真之前，誰都不知道她要走了，包括她的家人。

❸ 形容詞充當狀語。例如：

▶ The journey is more than 1,900 kilometers long and will take 16 days.
這次旅行的行程將超過1,900公里，耗時16天。

❹ 不定詞充當狀語。例如：

▶ Standard helmets are made to prevent bleeding in the brain and skull fractures, not concussions. 標準的頭盔能起到防止顱內出血和顱骨骨折的作用，但無法防止腦震盪。

❺ 動詞-ing形式和-ed形式充當狀語。例如：

▶ The locks will be closed for about two weeks so that cracks can be repaired, forcing the goods to be transported by other means.
為修復裂紋，閘門將關閉大約兩週時間，所以不得不用其他方式運輸貨物。

▶ Their paydays are still pale, however, compared with those of top-paid CEOs elsewhere. 然而，與其他高薪的公司執行總裁們相比，他們的發薪日仍然顯得相形見絀。

❻ 子句充當狀語

　　子句充當狀語可分為時間、地點、方式、原因、條件、讓步、目的和比較等狀語。也可統稱為副詞子句。

・時間副詞子句

　　時間副詞子句（Adverbial Clauses of Time）多由when，as，as soon as，whenever，before和after等詞引導。例如：

▶ My wife took some time off after we had our first child.
我們的第一個孩子出生後，我太太便休息了一段時間。

・地點副詞子句

　　地點副詞子句（Adverbial Clauses of Place）多由where和wherever等詞引導。例如：

▶ It's become a rock-star-like scene wherever she goes.
她到哪裡，哪裡就像搖滾明星造訪一般轟動。

• 方式副詞子句

　方式副詞子句（Adverbial Clauses of Manner）多由as，like等詞引導。例如：

▶ Her name is Sugar, **as** she says in the autobiographical novel she writes in her spare time. 就像她在閒暇時間寫的自傳體小說中提到的，她的名字叫「甜心」。

• 原因副詞子句

　原因副詞子句（Adverbial Clauses of Reason）多由because，as，since等詞引導。例如：

▶ Caricom has little authority to enforce agreements, **because** its members are sovereign. 加勒比共同體在促使協議的生效上沒有多少權力，因為其成員都是主權國家。

• 條件副詞子句

　條件副詞子句（Adverbial Clauses of Condition）多由if，even if等詞引導。例如：

▶ **If** they aren't consumed by the desire to know what happens next, they simply stop reading the book. 如果不是非常想知道接下去發生了什麼事，他們就不會再讀下去。

▶ **If** anyone calls, just say I'll be back in the office at four o'clock. 如果有人給我打電話，請告訴他們我4點鐘回辦公室。

• 讓步副詞子句

　讓步副詞子句（Adverbial Clauses of Concession）多由though，although，no matter how，in case等詞引導。例如：

▶ Rose also believes that she can improve sales, **although** the timescale for this is as elusive as ever. 儘管一如既往地難以把握所需的時間，蘿絲仍然相信她能提高銷售額。

▶ The richest clubs have been winning for years, **in case** you hadn't noticed. 也許你沒注意到，這些年贏得比賽的總是最有錢的俱樂部。

• 目的副詞子句

　目的副詞子句（Adverbial Clauses of Purpose）多由so that，in order that，that等詞引導。例如：

▶ Powell will meet the Iraqi politicians on whom the United States is pinning itshopes for a peaceful transition **so that** Washington can start cutting the high costs of the occupation. 鮑威爾將接見伊拉克的一些政治家，美國期待他們能實現伊拉克權力的和平交接，這樣政府才能減少美軍在伊駐守的高額支出。

• 比較副詞子句

　比較副詞子句（Adverbial Clauses of Comparison）多由than引導。例如：

▶ That's about 135,000 more students **than** for the 2003–2004 school year, or an increase of less than half a percent. 與2003至2004學年比，學生人數增加了約135,000人，增長不足0.5%。

🎯 插入語

插入語（Parenthesis）是句子的修飾語，是插入句中、對句子的理解作說明或注解的語句，通常由片語、分句、副詞、動詞-ing形式和不定詞等構成。

❶ 片語充當插入語

可作插入語的片語有as a result，for example，for instance，in other words，in all，on the whole等。例如：

▶American fashion is extremely commercial, while in the UK people are willing to die for their art, **in other words**, eat potatoes and look glamorous.
美國人追求極其商業化的風尚，但英國人則為了捍衛藝術不惜一切代價，換句話說，即使是吃著馬鈴薯，他們也要讓自己看起來極其優雅，魅力十足。

❷ 分句充當插入語

可以作插入語的分句有 I think，I know，it seems，it is true等。例如：

▶They had, **I think**, a very good exchange and it was a very productive meeting.
我想這是一次卓有成效的會面，他們進行了良好的交流。

❸ 副詞充當插入語。例如：

▶But **unfortunately**, we could not get away from it—this is the cost we had to pay for the visit. 很不幸的是，我們沒法逃避──我們必須為此行付出代價。

❹ 動詞-ing形式充當插入語。例如：

▶The lower long-term rates, **generally speaking**, reflected investors' growing confidence in the Fed's ability to keep inflation under control.
總的來說，較低的長期利率反映了投資者對美國聯邦儲備局控制通貨膨脹的能力越來越有信心。

❺ 不定詞充當插入語。例如：

▶And so what I suggest is that while they might be teasing you, **so to speak**, and holding a carrot out in the form of credit card offers, it's up to you to say, "No."
我的建議是，儘管可以說他們可能在戲弄你，用信用卡作誘餌來誘惑你，你仍然可以決定說「不」。

🎯 同位語

名詞或相當於名詞的成分組成兩個相鄰的並列結構，後者對前者作補充說明，起修飾作用，後者就是前者的同位語（Appositives）。名詞、代名詞和子句等都能充當同位語。

❶ 名詞充當同位語

大多數的同位語都由名詞或相當於名詞的成分來充當。例如：

▶Against Barrada, **one of the most deceptive and attacking players in the world**, Power had all the options and read him like a book. 針對當今世界最能迷惑對手的攻擊型（足球）球員之一的巴拉達，鮑爾有著各種應對的招數，而且非常清楚他的想法。

❷ 代名詞充當同位語。例如：

▶ The issue came up between the two and they both spoke about the need to resolve it.
他們之間談起了該問題，兩人都認為有必要解決。

❸ 形容詞或形容詞片語充當同位語。例如：

▶ Every computer studio, big or small, still faces the same technical problem.
每個電腦工作室，無論規模大小，都面臨同樣的技術難題。

❹ of + 疑問詞 + 不定詞充當同位語。例如：

▶ He will later tackle the question of whether to take water away from agriculture.
是否限制農業灌溉用水是他隨後要解決的問題。

❺ of +名詞充當同位語。例如：

▶ No one who has not lived for some period in the city of New York, I think, could quite understand the venom with which most New Yorkers treat politicians.
不在紐約待上一段時間是無法理解為什麼大部分紐約人對政客如此深惡痛絕。

❻ 子句充當同位語（同位語子句）。例如：

▶ Detectives have been consulting health professionals amid growing fears that the attacker is being treated for serious mental health problems.
由於越來越擔心襲擊者正因為嚴重的精神疾病接受治療，警探們不斷詢問醫護人員。

▶ What happens in a case like this is that a court will have to consider at some point early in the process the question whether an injunction should be issued.
在審案初期遇到像這樣的案例，法庭就必須考慮是否要頒發強制令。

　　同位語與被修飾成分之間有時存在插入語，常見的插入語有：that's，that's to say，especially，mainly，in other words，namely，for example等。例如：

▶ Tom said he wanted to spend more time with his family, namely his 14-year-old son.
湯姆說他想花更多時間和家人——14歲的兒子——在一起。

　　同位語有限定性同位語（Restrictive Appositives）和非限定性同位語（Nonrestrictive Appositives）之分。非限定性同位語前用逗號或破折號與前面所修飾的成分隔開，大多數的同位語是非限定性同位語，如上述例句所示。限定性同位語與前面所修飾的成分關係緊密，沒有用逗號或破折號隔開，形成了一個整體。例如：

▶ Swedish media pumps out a picture of the American President Bush as being an uneducated, fumbling politician with the "wrong" views.
美國總統布希被瑞典的媒體刻畫成一個毫無教養、笨嘴拙舌、觀點「荒謬」的政客。

母語人士常用的基本句型有以下幾種：

❶ 主詞＋動詞（SV）結構

主詞＋動詞是基本句型，V一般是不及物動詞，這個結構可以看作是回答「某人在做什麼事」的問題。例如：

The little girl	cried.	小女孩哭了。
S	V	

❷ 主詞＋動詞＋狀語（SVA）結構

如果對SV結構中的V進行修飾，就產生了狀語A，即SVA結構。狀語A可以是時間狀語、地點狀語等。

Tea	arrived	in Russia from Mongolia.	從蒙古來的茶葉已運抵俄羅斯。
S	V	A（地點狀語）	

❸ 主詞＋動詞＋表語（SVP）結構

V代表連綴動詞，如be，seem和smell等，表語也稱作主詞補語，是對主詞特徵的表述。

They	are	American tourists.	他們是美國遊客。
S	V	P（表語）	

❹ 主詞＋動詞＋受詞（SVO）結構

V為及物動詞，O為受詞，通常是動作的承受者。

Each picture	told	a story.	每幅畫都講述了一個故事。
S	V	O	

❺ 主詞＋動詞＋受詞＋狀語（SVOA）結構

如果對SVO結構中的V進行修飾，就產生了狀語A，即SVOA結構。

I	will pay	that	as soon as I get paid.	我一拿到錢就會付帳。
S	V	O	A	

❻ 主詞＋動詞＋間接受詞＋直接受詞（SVO$_I$O$_D$）結構

V為及物動詞；O$_I$為間接受詞，是動作V的間接對象，多為人；O$_D$為直接受詞，是動作V的直接對象，多為物。

My mama	taught	me	that song.	那首歌是我媽媽教我的。
S	V	O$_I$	O$_D$	

❼ 主詞＋動詞＋受詞＋受詞補語（SVOC）結構

　　動詞V主要是使役動詞，表達「把……造成某種狀態或效果」，最常見的使役動詞是make，let和get等。

Her blue skirt and jacket	made	her eyes	look like azure pools.
S	V	O	C

在藍色的外套和裙子襯托下，她的眼睛就像是蔚藍的池水。

　　感覺動詞如see和hear也能用於SVOC結構。

I	saw	him	come through the windows in the drawing room.
S	V	O	C

我看他從客廳的落地窗外走進來。

❽ there句型

　　there句型表示存在的意義，there只作為形式主詞置於句首，而真正的主詞卻置於謂語動詞之後。there句型的謂語中最常見的是be動詞，受時和數的制約，如is，was，are，were等。

　　be動詞還可以與助動詞或情態動詞搭配，如has been，have been，will be，must be，might be等。例如：

▶ In 1999, there were 58 alcohol-related crashes during the July 4 holiday.
　1999年7月4日（美國）國慶期間發生的車禍中有58起是因飲酒而導致的。

▶ If the leader is dead, there might be no hope for the war.
　如果領袖死了，那麼贏得戰爭的希望可能就沒有了。

　　there句型中的be動詞也可以是表示存在的其他動詞，如come，remain，follow 和seem等，這些動詞通常是不及物動詞。例如：

▶ From the enemy there came a sudden clamor of shouts.
　敵軍那裡突然傳來了大聲的呼喊。

▶ But there remained one big, unresolved problem in his life, the hole left by the suicide of his sister, Kay, 15 years ago.
　15年前姐姐凱的自殺給他造成的陰影，至今還困擾著他的生活，揮之不去。

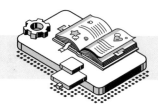

Contents

目·錄

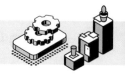

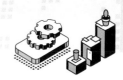

名詞

名詞概說

　　名詞是詞的分類之一，用於表示事物（Thing）、人物（Person）或地點（Place）。在文法範疇裡，名詞有數和格（Case）的變化。名詞分別有單數和複數形式。名詞的格表示名詞與句中其他詞語之間的文法和語義關係。

　　英語名詞在意義上有性別（Gender）的表達形式，也反映在與名詞有指代關係的人稱代名詞上。在句法功能上，名詞可作介係詞和及物動詞的受詞，也可作句子的主詞、表語、副詞、補語和同位語等。名詞在名詞片語中作中心詞。

名詞分類

　　名詞可分為普通名詞（Common Nouns）和專有名詞（Proper Nouns）。按詞彙意義劃分，普通名詞可分為個體名詞（Individual Nouns）、集體名詞（Collective Nouns）、物質名詞（Material Nouns）和抽象名詞（Abstract Nouns）四類。

　　依據意義和文法表現，普通名詞還可以分為可數名詞（Countable Nouns）與不可數名詞（Uncountable Nouns）。可數名詞與不可數名詞均能與單位名詞（Unit Nouns）搭配，表達數量、品質和度量的概念。

普通名詞

　　普通名詞表示人或物的名稱。除了專有名詞外的名詞基本上都是普通名詞。普通名詞還可以分為個體名詞、集體名詞、物質名詞和抽象名詞。普通名詞還有可數與不可數之分。可數名詞表示可分的、個體的、可計數的實體，可用單數和複數表示。

❶ 個體名詞

個體名詞通常是作為個體存在的人或事物，如boy，artist，friend，tiger，insect，house，accident，case，game，smile，dream，week等。個體名詞通常指具體的人或物，是可數名詞，有單數和複數形式。例如：

▶ At the age of 16, I was living in a shared **house** in Oxford with a group of **friends**.
我16歲那年和一群朋友同住在牛津的一棟房子裡。

▶ I'm not going to buy **houses** or **cars** or anything, but I'll probably try to start saving money when I get older.
我並不打算購買房子、車子或別的什麼。不過，隨著年齡的增大，我或許會想辦法多存點錢。

▶ More than half of college-age **adults** who drink have reported being drinking at least once recently.
大學年紀的成年飲酒者中，有一半以上被回報說近期至少有一次飲酒狂歡。

▶ More than half of **women** think of themselves as overweight.
一半以上的婦女認為自己過重。

▶ Josie still felt as if she were in a **dream**, as if her mother was alive and merely away on holiday somewhere, about to return next week.
喬茜仍然覺得她彷彿在夢裡一般，彷彿母親依然活著，只是在別處度假，下個星期就要回來。

▶ The teenager was described as a talented **sportsman** with a "zest for life" who excelled at most sports, particularly **football**, **rugby** and **judo**.
這位少年被形容是一個「對生活充滿熱情」、很有天賦的運動健將。他擅長大多數運動項目，尤其是足球、橄欖球和柔道。

❷ 集體名詞

集體名詞是指一群人、動物或一組東西等的集合體名稱，如committee（委員會），family（全家），government（政府）都是集體名詞。

由於人們在使用集體名詞時的視角不同，用於互指集體名詞的代名詞既可以是單數又可以是複數。常見的集體名詞有：army，audience，board，club，committee，crew，family，government，jury，public，staff，team等。例如：

▶ Not everyone was enthralled with the **committee**'s plan.
並非人人都對這個委員會的計畫感興趣。

▶ At this point, the **audience** erupted, shouting and clapping.
此時此刻，觀眾們沸騰了，他們一邊歡呼，一邊鼓掌。

▶ Last week, **police** announced the arrest of the two military police officers and a third man, all of whom allegedly belonged to a clandestine security group that provided protection for drug traffickers.
警方上週宣佈逮捕了兩名憲兵軍官和另一名男子，據說他們都屬於一個保護販毒分子的祕密安全組織。

▶ He and his **crew** are the first Europeans in Texas, and claim it for Spain.
他和他的船員是第一批到達德克薩斯的歐洲人，並聲稱西班牙擁有這塊土地。

▶ He was arrested but the government were reluctant to put him on trial in case it came out in court that he'd been simultaneously training the National Guard and the death squads. 他被逮捕後，政府不願對他進行審判，以免在法庭上公開他在訓練國民衛隊的同時也一直在訓練敢死隊。

❸ 物質名詞

　　物質名詞指不可以分為個體的物質，如air，snow，bread，rice，beer，salt，milk，iron，ink，sugar，wool等。物質名詞一般是不可數的，但是可以與單位名詞和量詞搭配來表示量的概念。例如：

▶ One person needs at least a gallon of water a day.
一個人每天至少需要一加侖水。

▶ A lot of money has been spent on teacher training or in compensating staff for extra work. 大筆資金花費在教師培訓和職員加班補貼上。

▶ After a certain period of time people are going to be so mentally and physically exhausted that they want to get away for a few days.
經過一段時間，人們就會在精神和體力上感到非常疲倦，想要離開幾天。

▶ He configures classroom spaces so that furniture can be rearranged easily, and he provides separate areas for small-group meetings.
他安排了一下教室的空間，讓家具可以輕鬆地重新擺放，也為小組會議留出獨立空間。

▶ Their equipment is available now, which gives them a head start.
現在有了設備，這使他們處於領先的地位。

❹ 抽象名詞

　　抽象名詞指用以命名非實物、品質、狀態或動作的名詞，主要指一些抽象概念的名稱，如happiness，stability，establishment，glory，honesty，failure，education，faith，pleasure，truth，love，luck，growth，patience，beauty，violence，work等。抽象名詞一般是不可數的。例如：

▶ I was impressed by the beauty and warmth of the people.
我被人們的美德和熱情打動了。

▶ Deacon held on to his patience with difficulty.
迪肯費力地保持著他的耐心。

▶ One senses the pleasure in his achievement at having come so far by the age of 40.
人到四十能有這樣的成就，會從中感到快樂。

▶ Democracy depends on majority rule, but—without quite admitting it—our elites have lost faith in the wisdom of the majority. 民主取決於少數服從多數的原則，但是精英人物已經不相信大多數人的智慧，儘管他們不太承認這一點。

▶ The Russian interpreter appeared to be having difficulty translating his master's words.
這位俄語翻譯似乎在翻譯自己雇主的話時遇到了困難。

> **注意！**

英語中有的名詞具有可數與不可數的雙重身份（Dual Class Membership），即既可作可數名詞又可作不可數名詞，但在語義上有區別。例如：

- a beauty（美人），beauty（美麗，漂亮）
- a difficulty（難點，難事，麻煩），difficulty（困難性，困難程度）
- experiences（經歷），experience（經驗）
- a light（燈），light（光）
- a lamb（羊），lamb（羊肉）
- times（次數），time（時間）

▶ Foreign travelers in **difficulties** have the option of throwing themselves on the mercy of their nearest national consulate.

外國遊客遇到麻煩可以到最近的本國領事館尋求幫助。

▶ When you think about the bad **experiences** again and again, the negative memories begin to join up so that there is no space between them for the feelings of love, yearning and regret.

如果你老是一遍遍地想著種種不幸的經歷，各種消極記憶就會聚集在一起，這些記憶之間就沒有慈愛、嚮往和遺憾等情感存在的餘地了。

▶ A former fund manager has more than 20 years' fund management **experience**, having graduated with a degree in politics from New York University.

從紐約大學獲得政治學學位的前基金主管具有二十多年的基金管理經驗。

專有名詞

專有名詞一般指人名、地名、月份、星期、節日、書名、雜誌名、作品名稱、組織名稱或某些事物和事件的名稱等。例如：

- 人名：Charles Dickens, George Bush, Sam, Jones
- 地名：Washington D.C., Beijing, America, Asia, Wall Street
- 月份、星期、節日名稱：April, Sunday, Thanksgiving, Christmas
- 書名、雜誌名、作品名稱：Vanity Fair, News Weekly, La Marseillaise
- 組織名稱：the World Trade Organization (WTO), Congress, Parliament
- 某些事物的名稱：English, Muslim, Ford, Kleenex, the Renaissance
- 稱呼：Father, Mother, Uncle, Aunt, Grandpa

▶ My father knew every line of **Shakespeare** by heart, and I still have great chunks of it in my head.

我父親能背誦莎士比亞的所有詩句，對此我仍保留著大部分記憶。

▶ The case has attracted widespread attention in **England**.

這個案件在英格蘭引起了廣泛關注。

▶That facility is undergoing a $1.3 million renovation and isn't expected to be ready until January.
該設備的革新要耗資130萬美元,而且到1月才能完成。

▶On summer Sunday mornings the park is the site of a giant flea market, selling genuine Swedish antiques alongside general tat.
夏天每逢禮拜日上午,這個公園就變成了一個大型的跳蚤市場,舊貨中有真正的瑞典古董。

▶Christmas spending over the Internet is set to top 2 billion pounds this year, according to research published today.
據今天公佈的調查,今年耶誕節網路購物消費有望超過20億英鎊。

▶Time magazine came out with an article saying Philip Johnson and I.M. Pei are the leaders of architecture in America today.
《時代》雜誌刊登了一篇文章,說菲力浦・詹森和貝聿銘是美國當今的建築設計大師。

▶If Africa's efforts to deal with the crisis fail, the United Nations will come under renewed pressure to act.
假如非洲在處理這次危機中所做的努力失敗,聯合國又將重新面臨採取行動的壓力。

　　專有名詞與普通名詞的不同之處在於,專有名詞的首字母必須大寫,使用時一般不帶定冠詞,比如Taipei前不能加定冠詞。即使帶定冠詞也不構成對比關係,比如the United States不能和United States形成對照。又如The Hague(海牙)這個地名本身帶有定冠詞,是一種固定的表達形式,不能用不定冠詞來代替,也不允許中間插入修飾詞。

注意!

①專有名詞通常只有一種本義,首字母必須大寫。專有名詞被其他詞修飾,或專有名詞修飾其他名詞時,在所構成的複合名稱中,修飾詞或被修飾詞的首字母也要大寫,如:Senator Kury, Dallas Road, President Bush。

②專有名詞可以用作普通名詞,比如某些人名或地名的專有名詞已經轉化為普通名詞。例如片語to keep up with the Joneses,人名Joneses不是特指某個人,而是指任何其他人,the Joneses在片語中可以指鄰居。又如片語to meet your Waterloo,Waterloo(滑鐵盧)不再是一個地名,片語的意思是「遭受毀滅性失敗」。

◎ 單位名詞

　　單位名詞也稱單位詞(Partitives)或量詞,指與可數名詞或不可數名詞連用的,用來表示事物的數量、品質和度量衡的詞。英語的可數名詞可與單位名詞搭配表示「一組,一群,一幫」等意思。不可數名詞沒有單、複數區別,不能以個數計量,但對其計量時仍需要用單位名詞。

單位名詞結構表示整體中的部分意義。這種意義含有質與量的概念，如：a kind/ type/sort of paper（一種紙）和a piece of paper（一張紙）。

英語有三種單位名詞：度量衡單位名詞、特定單位名詞和一般單位名詞。

❶ 度量衡單位名詞

常用的度量衡單位名詞（Measure Partitives）有：表示長度的，如一英尺、一公尺、一碼電纜線（a foot/ meter/ yard of cable）；表示面積的，如一英畝、一公頃土地（an acre/ a hectare of land）；表示容量的，如一加侖汽油（a gallon of gas）、一品脱或夸脱牛奶（a pint/ quart of milk）；表示重量的，如一盎司黃金（an ounce of gold）、一磅奶油（a pound of butter）、一公斤柳丁（a kilo of oranges）、一噸礦石（a ton of ore）。此外還有inch，liter，gram，ton/ tonne等度量衡單位名詞。

▶ In this small village, half **a meter of** snow settled at village level after a 48-hour fall.
這個小村莊連續下了48小時的雪，平地上積雪達半公尺深。

▶ The cost of growing **a hectare of** winter wheat in the northeast is estimated at 77 pounds, compared to 71 pounds in the southeast.
據估計，在東北部種一公頃冬麥要花費77英鎊，而在東南部需71英鎊。

▶ Yesterday, **a gallon of** regular gasoline was selling for $1.88 nationally.
昨天，一加侖普通汽油售價全國都是1.88美元。

▶ The company produced more than 2.9 million **tons of** steel in 1997 with a payroll of $230 million. 1997年，該公司生產了290多萬噸鋼材，所付工資總額為2.3億美元。

❷ 特定單位名詞

特定單位名詞（Typical Partitives）與特殊的名詞搭配，要求兩者在形狀、狀態、數量和容積方面有密切聯繫。表示形狀，如一滴水（a drop of water）、一片麵包（a slice of bread）、一粒沙（a grain of sand）；表示狀態，如一陣怒火（a fit of anger）、一線光明（a flash of light）；表示數量，如一雙鞋（a pair of shoes）、一群大象（a herd of elephants）、一群魚（a shoal of fish）；表示容積，如一杯水（a cup of water）、一瓶酒（a bottle of wine）等。例如：

▶ To the local boys of summer, heaven is **an ear of** barbecued sweet corn in one hand and a beer in the other.
對於當地的男孩，夏日的天堂就是一手拿著一根香噴噴的烤甜玉米，另一手端著一杯啤酒。

▶ His hand was indeed plunged into **a bucket of** water—**a bucket of** cold water.
他的手確實伸進了一桶水裡——一桶冰冷的水。

▶ She shows **a flash of** humor when she talks about her 15-year-old son, Christopher.
每當説起她那15歲的兒子克里斯多夫時，她總帶幾分幽默。

▶ The firm plans to release **a swarm of** new products in the next five years.
該公司計畫在下一個五年裡推出一批新產品。

常見的特定單位名詞搭配有：

(1) a head of cattle, a bar of chocolate, a bundle of firewood, a drop of water, a loaf of bread, an ear of corn, a lump of sugar, a flight of stairs, a spiral of incense, a grain of sand, a slice of meat, an atom of truth, a blade of grass, a block of ice, a speck of dirt, a stick of chalk

(2) a bottle of ink, a cup of coffee, a bowl of porridge, a bucket of water, a bushel of rice, a gallon of oil, a truckload of iron ore, an armful of hay, a jar of beer

(3) a fit of temper, a peal of thunder, a flash of hope, a display of force

(4) a pair of glasses, a school of thought, a group of people, a bench of jurors, a pack of wolves

> **注意！**
>
> 有些物質名詞既可以是可數名詞，也可以是不可數名詞。因此，這些名詞當可數名詞使用時，可以直接用不定冠詞限定，也可以與單位名詞搭配。例如：a beer，a pint of beer。a beer 通常表示a glass/cup/bottle of beer。

❸ 一般單位名詞

　　一般單位名詞（General Partitives）的用法不受特定名詞的限制，表示名詞的「個，件，條」等意義，常用的有：a piece of，a bit of，an item of，an article of 等。

　　一般單位名詞可與不可數名詞搭配，如：a piece of paper/news（一張紙／一條消息）， a bit of cloth/cheese（一小塊布／乳酪）；也可與可數名詞搭配，如：a piece of a loaf（一塊麵包）， a branch of a tree（一根樹枝）， a section of a newspaper（一段報紙內容）， a verse of a poem（一句詩）。

　　另外，表示部分、局部的單位名詞（Fractional Partitives）也可以歸為一般單位名詞，如：half /all /whole of +名詞。例如：

▶ People have to start behaving like consumers: you want to know what you can do, how to go about getting your money back if the product's not very good, as you would if you were in a restaurant or buying **an item of** clothing.
人們不得不開始表現得像消費者：想要知道能做些什麼，如果東西不好，如何設法把錢要回來，就像在飯店吃飯，或買了件衣服，不滿意要求退錢一樣。

▶ It's become **an article of** faith that sports build character, that they teach universal virtues.
體育能培養性格，能灌輸人類共同的美德，這已成為一條信念。

▶ I always said he was a good boy and just needed **a bit of** time.
我老是說他是個好男孩，只不過他還需要點時間。

▶ Scientists seeking the perfect steak have created the world's first cloned cow from **a piece of** meat. 尋找完美牛排的科學家已經從一片肉中成功地創造世界上第一頭複製牛。

▶ Coldplay's Chris Martin shambled on to sing **a verse of** their Man in the Moon.
酷玩樂團的克里斯・馬丁拖著腳走上台，唱了一段他們的《月上人》。

▶ The sudden collapse of **a section of** the mountain would be harder to predict and would render the telephone alert system less useful.
局部山體突然坍塌會更難預測，也會使電話警報系統派不上太大用場。

▶ I don't know **half of** these people.
這些人裡有一半我不認識。

▶ In three months, **half of** these businesses will close.
三個月之後，這些企業將有一半會關門。

▶ Measles cases so far this year already top **the whole of** last year's total.
到目前為止，今年的麻疹病例數已經超過去年全年的總數。

名詞的數 ▷

　　英語名詞的數由單數和複數構成，單數（Singular）表示「一個，單一」的意思，複數（Plural）表示「兩個以上」的意思。英語名詞的數看似簡單，但在語言形態上比較複雜，涉及名詞的分類、規則、不規則現象以及外來語的數的特殊表達形式。

◎ 個體名詞的數

　　英語的個體名詞一般指作為個體而存在的人或東西，個體名詞通常是可數名詞。可數名詞單數是無標記的形式，與詞典上詞彙條目的形式相同，此類名詞之前可加定冠詞the、不定冠詞a(n)，或加數詞one，如：the/a/one book, the/a/one man等。

　　名詞的複數形式可分為規則的和不規則的，規則複數一般在名詞原形後加-s或-es，如：desks, books, benches, boxes等。不規則名詞的變化是通過名詞內部的母音變化或在名詞後加上別的複數標記而構成，如：foot→feet, woman→women, ox→oxen等。

❶ 規則複數的拼寫

　　規則複數的字尾大多以-s的形式出現，包括以不發音的-e結尾的名詞也只加-s表示複數。但因英語名詞系統比較複雜，例外的情況較多。

(1) 以不發音的-e結尾的名詞直接加-s，凡以-s，-z，-x，-ch，-sh結尾的名詞都加-es。例如：

- purpose → purposes
- overpass → overpasses
- buzz → buzzes
- bench → benches

(2)以-o結尾的名詞，變複數時加-s或-es。

a. 以母音（或母音字母）+-o（包括-oo）結尾的名詞，加-s。例如：

- zoo → zoos
- portfolio → portfolios
- cuckoo → cuckoos
- studio → studios
- kangaroo → kangaroos
- bamboo → bamboos

b. 某些以-o結尾的專有名詞和某些以子音+-o結尾的名詞，加-s。例如：

- Filipino → Filipinos
- Eskimo → Eskimos
- kilo → kilos
- photo → photos
- Euro → Euros
- solo → solos
- memo → memos
- piano → pianos

c. 某些以子音+-o結尾的名詞，加-es。例如：

- domino → dominoes
- hero → heroes
- potato → potatoes
- echo → echoes
- embargo → embargoes
- veto → vetoes

d. 某些以-o結尾的名詞可加-s或加-es。例如：

- archipelago → archipelagos或archipelagoes

　　類似的名詞有：banjo，buffalo，cargo，grotto，halo，innuendo，manifesto，motto，mulatto，tornado，volcano。

(3)以-y結尾的名詞，複數形式變化如下：

a. 以子音+y結尾的名詞，將y變為i，再如-es。例如：

- spy → spies
- study → studies

b. 以母音+y結尾的名詞，加-s變成複數。例如：

- way → ways
- day → days

c. 以-quy結尾的名詞，複數變化與以子音+y結尾的名詞形式相同。例如：

- soliloquy → soliloquies

d. 以-y結尾的專有名詞變複數時，可直接加-s。例如：

▶The book deals with the relations between the two (West and East) Germanys.
這本書論述了兩個德國（東德和西德）的關係。

▶Which Mary? There are two Marys in our office.
哪個瑪麗？我們辦公室有兩個瑪麗。

(4)末尾子音雙寫時，加-es。例如：

- fez → fezzes
- quiz → quizzes

(5)拼寫以-f或-fe結尾的名詞，其複數形式變化如下：

a. 通常直接加-s。例如：

- safe → safes
- roof → roofs
- chief → chiefs
- cliff → cliffs
- belief → beliefs

b. 有的需要變-f、-fe為-v，再加-es。例如：

- calf → calves
- elf → elves
- half → halves
- knife → knives
- leaf → leaves
- life → lives
- loaf → loaves
- self → selves
- sheaf → sheaves
- shelf → shelves
- thief → thieves
- wolf → wolves

c. 極少數名詞既可直接加-s，又可變-f 或-fe為-v，再加-es。例如：

- dwarf → dwarfs 或dwarves

其他名詞如hoof，scarf，wharf 變複數的情況也是如此。

❷ 不規則複數

　　不規則複數的形式不能從名詞原形中預測到，只能像記單字一樣學習掌握。有的外來語名詞的複數變化與英語名詞不同，可歸為不規則複數，但有其自身變化規則，例如analysis的複數是analyses。由此可類推：thesis → theses，basis → bases，crisis → crises等。

　　當然，詞源不是唯一的標準，因為一種外來語本身也有例外，例如larva（幼蟲）的複數是larvae或larvas。

　　不規則複數可分為三類，即英語不規則名詞複數（複數通過名詞內部母音變化構成）、外來語名詞的複數（根據外來語自身的規則變複數）及外來語複數形式和英語複數形式兩者兼用。

(1)英語不規則名詞複數。例如：

- child → children
- foot → feet
- goose → geese
- louse → lice
- mouse → mice
- woman → women
- tooth → teeth

(2)非英語詞源的外來語名詞，其單、複數與一般英語名詞的單、複數變化規律不同。例如：

- alumna → alumnae
- alumnus → alumni
- criterion → criteria
- datum → data
- hypothesis → hypotheses
- parenthesis → parentheses
- stratum → strata
- phenomenon → phenomena

(3)外來語名詞原形、複數與英語複數

　　有些外來語名詞已經英語化了，因此複數有兩種，即外來語複數形式和英語複數形式，兩者可兼用。有的英語複數的意義有所變化，如antennae指「觸角」，而複數

antennas還有「天線」的意思。一些常見外來語名詞的原形、複數與英語複數形式如下表所示（外來語複數與英語複數意思相同時，僅在英語複數下標注中文意思）：

外來語	外來語複數	英語複數
antenna	antennae（觸角，天線）	antennas（天線）
appendix	appendices（附錄）	appendixes（闌尾）
cactus	cacti	cactuses（仙人掌）
corpus	corpora	corpuses（語料庫）
curriculum	curricula	curriculums（課程）
focus	foci	focuses（焦點）
fungus	fungi	funguses（真菌）
formula	formulae	formulas（公式）
memorandum	memoranda	memorandums（備忘錄）
medium	media	mediums（媒體）
plateau	plateaux	plateaus（高原）
radius	radii	radiuses（半徑）
sanatorium	sanatoria	sanatoriums（療養院）
syllabus	syllabi	syllabuses（教學大綱）
terminus	termini	terminuses（終端）

(4)單、複數同形的名詞

　　單、複數同形的名詞主要是一些動物名稱、運輸工具名稱和某些國家名稱，還有一些以-s結尾的單、複數同形的名詞，如：antelope，fish，flounder，herring，reindeer，sheep，shrimp，woodcock，craft，aircraft，spacecraft，hovercraft，barracks，headquarters，means，works，series，species，Chinese，Japanese，Portuguese，Swiss 等。例如：

▶ The fish lay in a puddle and he told the youngster to pick it up.
魚兒躺在水坑裡，他讓小孩去抓起來。

▶ There are old fishermen in the village who talk about the time when fishing was one of our proudest industries, when a man went out knowing there were limitless fish to catch and no one to fight. 村裡有老漁民談論往事，當時，捕魚是我們最值得自豪的行業之一，男人出門就知道有抓不完的魚，沒人爭鬥。

▶ Space officials said the craft had entered Earth orbit without incident.
航太官員說，太空飛行器已安全進入地球軌道。

▶ This figure assumes two craft in use, each running for 2,000–3,000 hours a year over an average 19 km route at 55 km/h.
這個數據假定，兩架投入使用的飛機，在平均19公里的跑道上，以每小時55公里的速度，每年滑行2,000至3,000小時。

▶We don't have a means of bringing everyone together to concentrate energies on the city's future.
我們沒有辦法讓所有人團結起來把精力集中在這個城市的未來上。

▶The dictionary and drug are both means of escaping from reality—for a short while at least.
字典和藥都是逃避現實的手段——至少短期內有效。

▶The fish have their own chef who prepares daily specials for each species.
每天有專門的廚師為每種魚配製特別的食料。

▶Searchers found 302 species of vascular plants and 94 species of fungi.
檢查員發現302種維管植物和94種真菌。

集體名詞的數

集體名詞的數比較複雜，原因是這類名詞有的可以計數，如a government，a family，而有的不能計數，如machinery，arms，poetry等。

可以計數的集體名詞本身可以作為單一的概念來處理，如作主詞時其謂語以單數形式出現；也可以看成是由多個個體組成的單位，因此作主詞時可與複數形式的謂語保持一致。常見的可計數集體名詞有：

> army, association, audience, bacteria, board, cast, clan, class, club, college, commission, committee, community, company, corporation, council, couple, crew, crowd, data, department, enemy, faculty, family, federation, firm, flock, gang, generation, government, group, herd, institute, jury, majority, media, minority, navy, nobility, opposition, party, public, staff, team, university

例如：

▶HSBC's audit committee met up to eight times a year, for 10 hours each time.
滙豐銀行的審計委員會成員一年中碰面8次，每次長達10小時。

▶Meanwhile, a committee to represent Enron's creditors is being created.
與此同時，正在籌辦一個代表安隆公司債權人的委員會。

▶After fighting for five days, the Dutch army yielded.
戰鬥了5天之後，荷蘭軍隊投降了。

▶He said he had enough ammunition to take an army to war.
他說他有足夠的彈藥讓一支部隊投入戰爭。

▶ Personally, I think that Mary's methods are the correct ones and the majority agree with me.
我個人認為，瑪麗的方法是正確的，而且大多數人也同意我的觀點。

▶ In the majority of cases, employers ignored, downplayed or misjudged the threat, according to a USA Today analysis of 224 instances of fatal workplace violence.
根據《今日美國》對224起工作場所致命暴力案例的分析，在大多數情況下，雇主們忽視、低估或錯誤判斷了暴力的威脅。

▶ As the rest of the jury began to compromise on a life sentence, Juarbe insisted on parole after 30 years.
儘管陪審團其他成員開始傾向判決無期徒刑，但華爾布堅持30年後給予假釋。

▶ A jury took six hours to decide the Hollywood star went on a shoplifting spree "for the sheer thrill of it".
陪審團花了6小時判定這名好萊塢明星是「為了尋求刺激」而在商場瘋狂行竊。

▶ The crowd were chanting and holding up banners.
人群在高舉著旗幟，呼喊著。

▶ A crowd of Bush supporters greeted his motorcade at the hotel, chanting "four more years".
一群布希的支持者在飯店門口迎接總統車隊，反覆喊著：「連任四年。」

集體名詞與個體名詞在語義上有時構成上下義或抽象概念與具體事物之間的關係。

集體名詞	個體名詞
clothing	jacket，sweater
cutlery	knife，fork
mail	letter
clergy	priest
foliage	leave
machinery	motor，generator
furniture	wardrobe，cupboard
weaponry	cannon，gun，artillery
baggage	suitcase，bag

例如：

▶ All the different dishes had to go in their allotted places and the cutlery had to go in with knives on the right, forks on the left, spoons in between.
所有的碗盤要放到規定的地方，餐具擺放時刀在右邊，叉在左邊，湯匙在中間。

▶ I threw away innumerable pieces of **furniture** (**bed**, **bedside tables**, **old stuffed chairs**, **laundry baskets**), and put every item of clothing inside its own carrier bag—but to no avail.
我扔掉無數件傢俱（床、床頭桌、老式的填充椅、洗衣籃），還把每件衣服放到各自的袋子裡——但這一切都毫無作用。

▶ Despite being amply prepared with **weaponry**, including **rifles**, **pistols** and **sabers**, the Warrior was never challenged and she did not even fire a **cannon** in her 22 years at sea.
儘管勇士號艦艇上武器配備齊全，包括步槍、手槍、軍刀等，但它在海上22年從來沒遇上敵人，一炮都沒放過。

物質名詞的數

物質名詞用於指稱物質實體，通常為不可數名詞，沒有單、複數之分，如water，milk，soil，silver，hydrogen等。這些物質名詞所指稱的實體本身沒有界限，即它們不是由一個個單一的個體組成的，例如從河中舀一勺水，勺中的水與河裡的水仍然是同一物質。

但是，有些物質名詞可作個體名詞，因而成為可數名詞。不過，當物質名詞作可數名詞時，其語義就發生了變化。例如rubber（橡膠），stone（石料），lamb（羔羊肉），onion（洋蔥）等物質名詞作可數名詞使用時，分別就有「橡皮擦」、「石塊」、「羔羊」、「洋蔥頭」等意義。（參見P022〈物質名詞〉）

抽象名詞的數

抽象名詞的數比較複雜，一般可分為可數與不可數兩類，如triumph和experience都是既可作可數名詞，又可作不可數名詞。

同時，由於英語的一詞多義現象較為普遍，原本不可數的抽象名詞在用於表達具體事物的意義時，又可以當作可數名詞使用，如：relation → relations，youth → youths，business →businesses 等。（參見P022〈抽象名詞〉）

反之，有些名詞原本是表示實物的可數名詞，但在一些固定搭配中卻成為抽象的不可數名詞，如：family，room，ear，fool，man，coward，coquette，politician，sportsman，scholar，poet 等。例如：

▶ A troupe of foreign dancers is one of the leading **attractions** in the festival.
國外的舞蹈團是慶典裡最引人關注的焦點之一。

▶ I hope there's going to be enough **room** in the fridge.
希望冰箱裡有足夠的空間。

▶ I'm moving to Detroit because I have some **family** there.
我就要搬到底特律了，因為我在那裡有些親戚。

有些不可數的抽象名詞有與其對應的可數名詞。

抽象名詞	個體名詞
baggage	bag，suitcase
clothing	coat，jacket
correspondence	email, letter
cutlery	knife
fun	joke，joy
homework	assignment，exercise
laughter	laugh
music	song
photography	photo，picture
permission	permit
work	job

例如：

▶ There was some laughter from the audience accompanied by an uncomfortable shuffling of feet.
從觀眾中傳來了陣陣笑聲，伴隨著一陣不安的腳步聲。

▶ Maria's only flaw is she has a truly horrible laugh.
瑪麗亞的唯一缺點是，她笑起來真的太可怕了。

▶ The treaty also requires exporters to secure permission from target countries before importing "living modified organisms" such as genetically altered seeds.
該條約同時要求，出口商須得到進口國的許可才能進口「基因改造活體」，例如基因改造種子。

▶ The program requires a permit for any source discharging pollutants into the water—from fish waste to sewage, oil to pesticides.
此方案規定，任何污染物排入水中——不論是魚類排泄物還是污水、油污或是農藥——都必須取得許可證。

▶ It is well worth doing your homework and shopping around a bit before deciding on which carpet to buy.
先做點「功課」，再逛逛店，最後再決定買哪條地毯，這是很值得的。

▶ I did all the exercises in the lovely grammar book.
這本文法書很有趣，裡面所有的練習題我都做了。

專有名詞的數

專有名詞除原本帶有複數詞綴外（如the United States，the Philippines，the Netherlands），本身均沒有複數形式。

當專有名詞轉變為普通名詞時，就可帶名詞複數的詞綴。這種情況通常見於表示某一家人中兩個以上的成員，或同姓同名的人物。例如：the Grays，two Miss Smiths，Misses Smith。

▶ Hitching is generally possible in Belgium, the Netherlands and, especially, Germany, but notoriously bad in Scandinavia itself.

在比利時、荷蘭，尤其德國，搭便車通常行得通，但是，眾所周知，在斯堪地納維亞行不通。

▶ At independence from America in 1946, the Philippines was one of the richest nations in southeast Asia.

1946年從美國獨立出來的菲律賓，是東南亞最富裕的國家之一。

▶ Are you looking for the Misses Mackintosh?

你在找麥金托什家的小姐們嗎？

▶ Henry represented himself as an old friend of the family of the Misses Selsdon.

亨利聲稱自己是塞爾斯登小姐們一家的老朋友。

專有名詞，如人名前也可以加不定冠詞，表示「一個叫……的人」。例如：

▶ A Mr. White called a moment ago.

一位姓懷特的先生剛才打來電話。

單位名詞的數

單位名詞的功能之一是將不可數的事物分為各個部分，再來指稱各個單一的成分。這種指稱方式可以通過數量計算，可以通過形狀計量，可以通過體積計量，可以通過動作狀態來描述，也可以用「雙」、「組」或「群」等單位來計量。

儘管單位名詞可以與不可數名詞搭配，但它本身是可數的，因此單位名詞有單複數之分。

❶ 表示個數的單位名詞

表示個數的單位名詞通常是a piece of，an article/item of等。由於此類單位詞本身是可數的，所以它們也有單、複數形式。例如：

▶ I ask if they have a piece of bread and a piece of cheese and if so, could they please put the two together.

我問他們是否有麵包和乳酪，如果有，就請把它們夾在一起。

▶ The envelope was addressed in neatly printed block letters and also contained a sketch, an article of the woman's clothing and a piece of jewelry.

信封上的地址是用大寫字母工整列印的，裡面裝了一張草圖、一件女裝，還有一件首飾。

▶ Frank suspected that the boy had stolen an item of merchandise.

法蘭克懷疑那個男孩偷了一件商品。

▶The chewing gum market has nearly trebled in size during the past decade and there are now an estimated 28 million regular chewers in the UK buying more than **13 million pieces of** gum every day.

過去的10年中，口香糖市場擴大了將近三倍，據估計，英國現在有2,800萬人經常嚼口香糖，他們每天要買超過1,300萬片口香糖。

▶My mother stooped over the carrier bags, flinging tissue paper and **articles of** clothing over her shoulder.

我母親在購物袋前彎下腰，把衛生紙和一件件衣服朝身後扔了出去。

▶She said that a number of **items of** property belonging to Laura believed to be in her possession when she disappeared had yet to be recovered.

她說，據信蘿拉失蹤後名下留有幾筆財產，還有待找出這些財產的下落。

❷ 表示形狀的單位名詞

表示形狀的單位名詞與物體的形狀有關。常用的表示形狀的單位詞有：chip of，chunk of，grain of，loaf of，lump of，scrap of，sheet of，slice of，strip of，heap of，pile of，stick of，wedge of等。例如：

▶The extreme drought is also across the entire northern **strip of** the state extending east from the southern portion of Yellowstone National Park.

嚴重乾旱也影響了這個州的整個北部地帶，由黃石國家公園南部向東蔓延。

▶Every few thousand years, **a pile of** volcanic rock becomes unstable and collapses into the sea.

每隔幾千年，一堆火山岩就變得不穩定，隨後坍塌墜入大海。

▶I ask what she plans to do for the remaining **scrap of** her weekend.

我問她週末剩餘的一點時間打算做什麼。

▶Though, generally, despite what people say about a marriage license being just **a scrap of** paper, when a couple don't get married, there's usually a reason for it.

不過，一般情況下，儘管人們說結婚證書只不過是一張紙，可如果一對情侶不結婚通常都是有原因的。

▶In the same way **a lump of** iron will sink in water, but an iron ship will float.

同樣，一塊鐵在水裡會下沉，而一艘鐵制輪船會漂浮。

❸ 表示容積的單位名詞

表示容積的單位名詞由各類容器擔任，主要用於表示物質或實體的數量。常見的有：barrel of，basket of，box of，crate of，cup of，keg of，pack of，packet of，sack of等。

有的容積單位詞可加-ful，構成量詞，如basketful，spoonful，bowlful 等。例如：

▶The Government would give schools "**a full package of** support and advice on the best ways to get parents involved".

政府會給各學校「許多支援和建議，提供最佳辦法讓家長能參與」。

▶ She was standing on a crate of oranges.
她站在一箱柳丁上面。

▶ Since the 1980s, the cost of discovering a barrel of oil has dropped from $20 to less than $5, according to the U.S. Energy Department.
據美國能源部統計，自1980年代以來，每桶原油的探勘成本已由20美元下降到不足5美元。

▶ Perhaps a spoonful of sugar would help this slightly bitter medicine go down.
或許一匙糖可以幫助你吞下這種略帶苦味的藥。

❹ 表示動作狀態的單位名詞

　　表示動作狀態的單位名詞有：act of，fit of，slip of，collection of，selection of，display of，flash of，peal of等。例如：

▶ The very act of writing was implicated in an encounter between tradition and innovation.
寫作本身促成了傳統與革新的相遇。

▶ The joint moves were an unusual display of emerging U.S.-Mexican cooperation against drug traffickers.
美國與墨西哥的聯合行動，是雙方在反毒品走私方面進行初期合作的一次非同尋常的展示。

▶ A flash of light in the night air could be anything.
夜空中的一道閃光可能意味著任何事情的發生。

▶ Carlotta looked up at her rival with a flash of pure hatred.
卡洛塔抬頭用充滿仇恨的眼光看著對手。

▶ He instructed that on his death his collection of 38 paintings would be sold to the British Government for 57,000 pounds, forming the nucleus of what is now the National Gallery.
他指示，死後把他所收集的38張畫，以57,000英鎊的價格賣給英國政府。這些畫後來就成了國家美術館的核心收藏。

▶ Most frequently, according to homicide statistics, it's a parent with a history of domestic violence who kills in a fit of rage.
根據謀殺案件資料統計，在大多數情況下，有家庭暴力史的家長會一氣之下殺人。

❺ 表示成雙、成組、成群的單位名詞

　　表示成雙、成組、成群的單位名詞常用於某些固定搭配。

• 指物：a pair of binoculars/scissors/shoes，a set of cutlery，a suit of clothes。

• 指人：a group of people/soldiers，a troupe of actors，a bench of judges，a gang of four。

• 指動物：a flock of birds，a swarm of bees，a school of fish，a pack of wolves，a litter of kittens，a herd of elephants。

例如：

▶She walked to the counter and picked up **a pair of** scissors, sliced neatly through the top of the envelope.
她走到櫃檯，拿起一把剪刀，整齊地把信封的上緣剪開。

▶Now, he can't fly anywhere without **a flock of** fans waiting for him, autograph books thrust out in supplication.
他現在飛到哪裡都有一群粉絲等著他，把簽名本推向他，懇求他簽名。

▶She has just witnessed **a herd of** elephants strolling past her bathroom window on the way to the nearby watering hole.
她剛才看見一群大象經過她的浴室窗前，向附近的水坑走去。

▶Flames engulfed **a swarm of** firemen and bystanders who dashed to help when the train came off the rails.
火車脫軌時產生的火焰吞噬了一群沖上前去救助的消防員和過路人。

▶They opened the door, and in came **a troupe of** students, who chanted through the house.
他們一打開門，一群學生就湧了進來，叫喊著進了房子。

▶The more you empower the grass roots activists, the more the grass roots develop a vision and develop **a bench of** candidates for the future.
給予草根社運人士的權力越大，草根民眾就越能開闊視野，越能培養一批未來的候選人。

複合名詞的數

複合名詞指由兩個以上自由語素合成的名詞，如farmland，matchmaker，seafood，seaman，teamwork，go-between，in-law，arm-chair，passerby，woman driver，war game，prison camp等。複合名詞也有可數與不可數之分。例如：

▶We want to encourage good **teamwork** and communication.
我們想鼓勵良好的團隊精神和相互溝通。

▶Then wash up, change your clothes, and come greet your future **in-laws**.
去沐浴更衣，迎接你未來的親家。

可數的複合名詞有單數與複數形式，複數形式通常是在字尾加-s 或-es，如go-betweens，in-laws，girlfriends，letter-boxes，grown-ups，forget-me-nots等。

但有些複合名詞將-(e)s字尾加在主體名詞後，如：passersby，parents-inlaw，editors-in-chief，lookers-on，runners-up 等。例如：

▶The cat jumped to the floor, darted through the legs of several **passersby**, and disappeared into the bar.
貓跳到地板上，從幾個過路人的腿間竄過，消失在酒吧裡。

某些由man，woman構成的複合名詞，兩部分都變作複數。例如：

- woman doctor → women doctors
- woman artist → women artists
- woman writer → women writers
- woman president → women presidents

但是有的同類複合名詞只是將man和woman變作複數。例如：

- seaman → seamen
- chairwoman → chairwomen
- policeman → policemen

名詞的格

名詞的格的分類

在古英語中，英語名詞主要有主格（Nominative）、受格（Accusative）、與格（Dative）和所有格（Genitive）。每一種格都有特別的含義。名詞作句子的主詞和表語時為主格，作動詞的直接受詞時為受格，作間接受詞時為與格，名詞用於表示所屬關係時為所有格。

但是在漫長的發展演變中，英語的名詞已經失去了格標記。在現代英語中，名詞的主格、受格和與格都是無標記的，即名詞的形式不變，通常稱為通格。

名詞所有格

名詞所有格（Genitive Nouns）是名詞的一種文法變化形式，由「名詞+'s」構成。名詞所有格適用於表示人物、有生命生物和作為有生命生物的名詞，也適用於表示地理、天體、時間、度量和價值等概念的名詞。

❶ 名詞所有格的構成

名詞所有格的構成有以下幾種情況：

(1)單數名詞和不以-s結尾的複數名詞，在名詞後面加's，如：teacher → teacher's，children → children's。

▶Under the system, a new teenage driver may obtain a learner's permit by first passing a written exam and vision test.
根據這個系統，十幾歲的新駕駛員首先得通過筆試和視力測試，才可以拿到實習駕照。

▶For Ferial Radha, 62, the doctor's wife, the worst thing is the constant worry.
對於這位醫師62歲的妻子費裡亞爾・拉達來說，最糟的事就是那沒完沒了的擔心。

▶Andy's parents divorced when he was young, and he spent summers with his father in Ann Arbor, Mich., and the school year with his mother, Trudy, in the suburbs of Boston.
安迪小時候父母就離了婚。每年夏天，他和父親住在密西根州的安娜堡。上學時，他和母親特露迪住在波士頓的郊區。

(2)如果名詞有複數字尾-s，就直接在名詞後加「'」。但在比較正式的情況下，要在該複數後面加-'s，如：Mr. Jones' ill-treatment→ Mr. Jones's ill-treatment。但其他的人名只可加-'s，如：Ross's，Marx's。

▶Mrs. **Jones's** son Tony was too distressed to attend the press conference but issued a statement saying: "I am devastated by the loss of a marvelous woman and mother."
鐘斯夫人的兒子東尼過於悲傷而不能參加記者招待會，但他發表了這樣的聲明：「我因失去一位了不起的女性和母親而萬分悲痛。」

(3)並列名詞表示共同享有的關係時，在最後一個名詞的字尾加-'s；表示各自享有的關係時，在每個名詞後面加-'s，如：my mother and father's room（一個房間），my mother's and father's rooms（兩個房間）。

▶**Jason's and Patrick's** advisory groups include soldiers who have gone through rehabilitation.
傑森和派翠克各自的顧問團包括一些已經完成康復的軍人。

▶**Mary and Mark's** most memorable Christmas was two years after separating.
瑪麗和馬克兩人最難忘的聖誕回憶是離別兩年後的那個耶誕節。

(4)在表示「店鋪」、「某人家」的名詞所有格後面，通常要省去它所修飾的名詞，如：the barber's，the tailor's，the doctor's，the Smith's。

▶He had his hair cut every second week **at the barber's** near the market square.
他每隔一週要到購物廣場附近的理髮店去理髮。

▶I went to drop something off **at Mom's** and I stayed to chat.
我去母親那裡放點東西，隨後就待著聊天了。

(5)由複合名詞或一個名詞片語構成的所有格，-'s要加在最後一個名詞的字尾上，如：Virginia Tech's tragedy，an hour and a half's discussion等。

▶It commemorates Canadian **Steve Bauer's** silver medal at the 1984 Los Angeles Olympics.
這是慶祝加拿大的運動員史蒂夫・鮑爾，在1984年洛杉磯奧運會上獲得銀牌。

❷ 名詞所有格的功能

　　名詞所有格主要表示名詞與名詞之間的關係，即被修飾名詞與修飾名詞的所屬關係，所以稱為「所有格」。但英語中的所有格不只限於所屬關係，它的意義要根據參與此結構的名詞性質來確定。

(1)特指所有格

　　所有格最重要的功能是具有特指意義，即像限定詞一樣特指某一名詞，同時被修飾

名詞又屬於所有格片語中名詞的一部分。例如：

- a/that/the boy's eyes
- a/that/the horse's hoofs

上述例子中的eyes和hoofs 分別屬於the boy和the horse。

特指所有格可用帶of的片語來解釋，例如the horse's hoofs可解釋成the hoofs of the horse。

▶ A deadened look came into **the girl's eyes**.
女孩的雙眼顯得呆滯。

▶ One technique that may, in the future, be a major weapon against drug abuse is the extraction of illegal substances, using high-performance liquid chromatography, from a hair of **a horse's tail**.
使用高效液相層析從馬尾巴毛中提取出非法物質，這一技術將是未來對付吸毒的主要武器。

▶ There was a jingle of harness and the rhythmic suck-slurp of **a horse's hoofs** crossing muddy ground.
泥地上響起馬具的叮噹聲和馬蹄有節奏的咕嘟聲。

▶ The majority of low-income parents whose children attend private schools selected by choice say they are very satisfied with the academic quality of **their children's schools**.
大多數將子女送到自己選擇的私立學校上學的低收入父母表示，對孩子們所在學校的教學品質非常滿意。

(2)類別所有格

有的所有格表示類別而不表示特指，如a bird's nest，children's clothes。特指所有格要回答的是「誰的？」，而類別所有格回答的是「哪一種？」。

類別所有格可由限定詞和整個名詞片語修飾，如a new bird's nest，而不只由bird's 修飾。所有格與後面的名詞之間不能插入別的修飾成分，如a bird's new nest是錯誤的。

類別所有格可用帶for的片語來釋義，而不用帶of的片語，如：men's shoes = shoes for men，而不是shoes of men。

類別所有格通常與人稱名詞複數連用，如：boys' camp，a girls' school，boys' jackets，a men's team，the oldest women's club，women's magazines。

但是，類別所有格的拼寫形式多樣，目前還沒有完全統一的寫法，例如：a bird's nest，a birds' nest，a bird nest，birds' nests。這些形式基本都可接受，但a bird's nest 最為常見。

▶ **Women's income** as a whole, which includes benefits and money from investments, is only 49 percent of men's.
婦女們的總體收入，包括福利和投資收益，只有男人的49%。

▶ Iraq loses semifinal match to Paraguay in Olympic **men's soccer**.
伊拉克隊在奧林匹克男子足球的半決賽中輸給了巴拉圭隊。

(3)時間所有格

　　時間所有格用於表示時間點，例如：last week's meeting，Friday's talk，this autumn's statement。此類表達多用於媒體對某事件發生的時間的報導。一些時間名詞的通格可替代時間所有格，如：a winter's day = a winter day。

▶ If this spring's dip in growth to a 3 percent rate proves to be more than just temporary, it will postpone further rate increases in the fall.
如果這個春季增長率降至3%不是暫時的，那麼，秋季的增長率就會推遲。

(4)度量所有格

　　度量所有格包括時間、距離長度以及價值的度量。例如：three days' leave, a month's holiday, a minute's delay。

▶ This cheerful hotel is well-equipped and a stone's throw from the beach.
這個敞亮的旅館設施齊全，而且離海灘又很近。

▶ He has been fined a maximum two weeks' wages for breaching the club's code of conduct last month.
他上個月違反了俱樂部的行為規範，為此，被重重罰去兩週的工資。

▶ In her excitement, switching from Greek to broken English, she held him at arm's length before kissing him soundly on both cheeks.
她非常激動，從希臘語轉到不流利的英語，伸開雙臂抱住他，然後親熱地吻了他的雙頰。

❸ 名詞所有格的用法

　　名詞所有格作為特指所有格時，它在名詞片語中的作用相當於限定詞和前置修飾語。作為限定詞時，名詞所有格的作用相當於所有格代名詞。例如：

- a girl's face = her face
- a horse's hoofs = its hoofs
- a dog's tail = its tail

　　上述例子都是名詞的特指所有格。但是，當名詞所有格作為類別所有格時，其作用相當於形容詞和名詞性前置修飾語，因為這時要回答的問題是「哪一種？」或「怎麼樣的？」。例如：

▶ a boys' school = a school for boys

▶ the oldest women's club = the club for the oldest women
　　（參見P040〈特指所有格〉和P041〈類別所有格〉）

❹ 名詞所有格的分類

　　根據所有格與名詞中心詞的關係，可將名詞所有格分為獨立所有格（Independent Genitive）、雙重所有格（Double Genitive）和組合所有格（Group Genitive）。

(1)獨立所有格

　　名詞所有格充當限定詞或修飾語來修飾名詞中心詞時，中心詞因上下文的作用可以被省略而不影響意義表達，此時的名詞所有格就是獨立所有格。獨立所有格也稱省略所有格。例如：

▶ Her memory is like an elephant's (= an elephant's memory).
　　她有驚人的記憶力。

　　許多獨立所有格已經逐漸被規約化，因此，即使中心詞沒有在上下文中出現，意思也明瞭。規約化的獨立所有格主要用於表示家宅、教堂、學校、店鋪或公司等。例如：

▶ From the age of 35 he drank a bottle of Jack Daniel's every day, but still lived to 82.
　　從35歲起，他就開始每天喝一瓶傑克‧丹尼爾威士忌酒，但依然活到82歲。

(2)雙重所有格

　　雙重所有格是一種特殊結構，其中的中心名詞之前可加一個不定冠詞，在中心名詞之後帶一個含of 結構的特指所有格。例如：an idea of Johnny's 相當於one of Johnny's ideas。

　　雙重所有格的中心名詞之前通常不帶定冠詞the，因為修飾名詞片語的特指所有格相當於定冠詞的作用。所以，a friend of my father's不能說成the friend of my father's。

　　雙重所有格可以帶諸如this，that等指示限定詞，例如this car of her father's，that clever idea of Mr. Davis's。另外，a portrait of Mr. Smith和a portrait of Mr. Smith's的意義也有不同。前者是「一張史密斯（本人）的肖像」，後者是「一張由史密斯畫的或收藏的肖像」。

▶ Haber approached his superiors with an idea of his father's.
　　哈伯帶著他父親的想法與上司接洽。

(3)組合所有格

　　組合所有格是指所有格的中心名詞與所有格字尾-'s 之間插入了其他成分。例如：

▶ the father's face → the father of five's face (the face of the father who has five children)

▶ her mother's house → her mother-in-law's house

▶ the clerk's decision → the clerk of the course's decision

▶ My son-in-law's brother has confessed to his wife that he has been having an affair.
　　我女婿的兄弟向他妻子承認他有風流韻事。

▶ Professor Ball will give a lecture today at the University of London's Institute of Education to mark its centenary year.
　　鮑爾教授今天將在倫敦大學教育學院發表演講，以慶祝該校百年校慶。

❺ **-'s所有格與of所有格**

　　帶-'s的所有格（S-genitive）和of 所有格（Of-genitive）跟中心詞的關係分別是前置修飾和後置修飾的關係。

　　-'s所有格與中心詞的關係在結構上比較緊湊，但意義比較含糊；而of所有格修飾中心詞在句法和意義上則比較清楚。例如：John's portrait可以理解為「John畫的肖像」和「John本人的肖像」，John在前者充當主詞的角色，在後者是起受詞的作用，即這個帶-'s所有格的結構可理解為a portrait by John 和a portrait of John。不過在許多場合，兩種表達意思一樣，例如：the car's owner 與the owner of the car。到底採用哪種形式，取決於多方面的因素。

(1)所有格中的名詞種類

　　人物指稱，尤其是專有名詞，更多地與-'s所有格連用；無生命物的指稱、集體名詞和複數則多與of 所有格連用。

(2)中心名詞與所有格的語義關係

　　如果中心名詞與所有格是所有關係（the family's car）、屬性關係（a man's voice）、來源關係（Shelly's poems）、主謂關係（Henry's arrival）時，多採用-'s形式。

(3)所有格的資訊狀態

　　已知資訊常在-'s 所有格中出現，新資訊常在of 所有格中出現，因為表示人稱、事物或現象的名詞往往是已知資訊，而後置修飾往往是被介紹到話語中的新訊息。

(4)具體搭配關係

　　某些類別所有格和度量所有格往往是固定搭配，例如：life's work，nature's way，for heaven's sake，for old time's/times' sake等。

▶ I've been forced to pay a high enough price for the goods, for heaven's sake.
　　天哪，我被強迫以昂貴的價格購買這些東西。

▶ You know she said all this feeling tiredness is just nature's way of keeping you at home to look after the baby.
　　你知道，她說所有這種疲勞感不過是上天安排讓你待在家裡看孩子。

▶ They are the product of the failure of the American dream for many poor people in this country.
　　對這個國家許多窮人來說，它們是美國夢破滅而產生的後果。

▶ Since the death of her husband, Heinz Kerry has kept tight control over family documents.
　　自她的丈夫去世以來，海因茨・克麗一直牢牢控制著家族檔案。

名詞性別的表達 ▷

英語名詞的性別與被指稱物件的自然性別有著密切的聯繫。指稱有生命事物的名詞性別分為三類，即男／雄性／陽性（the man）、女／雌性／陰性（the woman）和雙重性別（a doctor）。指稱非生命事物的名詞多為中性，如a bridge，a school等。

🎯 陽性名詞與陰性名詞

名詞性別的表達主要通過區分不同性別對應的詞語來實現，這種對應關係一般體現為家庭關係、社會角色關係和動物的雌雄。如grandpa – grandma，father – mother，brother – sister，king – queen，lord – lady，bull – cow，cock – hen。

常見的表示人的性別的名詞：

陽性	陰性
man	woman
boy	girl
brother	sister
uncle	aunt
bridegroom	bride
emperor	empress
king	queen
prince	princess
actor	actress
waiter	waitress
master	mistress
host	hostess
heir	heiress
hero	heroine
duke	duchess
landlord	landlady
fiancé	fiancée
widower	widow
nephew	niece
monk	nun
sir	madam
steward	stewardess

常見的表示動物性別的名詞：

陽性	陰性
lion	lioness
tiger	tigress
bull	cow
stallion	mare
cock (rooster)	hen
dog	bitch
boar	sow

陽性名詞與陰性名詞分別有對應的代名詞he和she與之互指。（參見Part3〈代名詞〉）這兩類性別名詞從形態上看可分兩種，一種是詞彙上無標記的，另一種是詞彙上有標記的。

1. 無標記陽性名詞

英語中常見的無標記陽性名詞有bachelor，boy，brother，emperor，father，god，hero，host，king，man，Mr.，monk，nephew，prince，steward，uncle等。

2. 有標記陽性名詞

英語中只有極少數的有標記陽性名詞，例如bridegroom，widower等。

3. 無標記陰性名詞

英語中常見的無標記陰性名詞有aunt，bride，girl，Mrs.，Miss，Ms，mother，niece，nun，queen，sister，spinster，woman等。

4. 有標記陰性名詞

英語中常見的有標記陰性名詞有hostess，waitress，princess，heroine，stewardess，usherette，goddess，empress等，其中多數以-ess結尾。

🎯 雙重性別名詞

雙重性別名詞（Dual Gender Nouns）指可以用who，he或she與其互指的名詞詞類，例如：artist，cook，doctor，enemy，friend，guest，performer，person，professor，scientist，teacher，tutor，writer等。

使用此類雙重性別名詞時如果有必要說明某名稱的性別，就可在名詞前加male或female，如male/female teacher。雙重性別名詞的使用日趨普遍，但名詞有何種性別的含義取決於該行業中從業人員以哪種性別為主，如有特殊情況就需要在名詞前加上性別標記。例如，男護士要說a male nurse，而女護士就是a nurse；男工程師是an engineer，女工程師就是a female engineer。

隨著時代的演進，某些帶有性別特徵的名詞，如chairman，出現了與其並用的chairwoman來表明女性特徵，或者用沒有明顯性別特徵，即無性別歧視的中性名詞chairperson來作指稱。雙重性別名詞也稱為中性或通性名詞。

名詞的句法功能

名詞在句子中的功能比較多，通常能擔任主詞、受詞、表語、副詞、前置修飾語以及同位語等角色。

❶ 作主詞。例如：

▶ **The books** are intended to help provide Afghan women in particular with basic health and nutrition information.
這些書特別針對阿富汗婦女，旨在向她們提供基本的健康和營養資訊。

▶ **Advertising executives** are hoping the scenario will stimulate amusement rather than anger. 廣告經理們希望，這種情景能激發樂趣，而不是憤怒。

▶ At the same time, **a national economic slow down** curtailed sales tax collections.
與此同時，全國經濟發展的速度減緩導致了銷售稅收的縮減。

▶ **Experience** has taught that manager that weekly kick-off meetings stimulate discussion and hopefully energize everybody for the week ahead.
經驗告訴了那位經理，每週一次的開工會能引發討論，而且有望給大家的下一週工作鼓勵。

❷ 作受詞

名詞在句子中可作直接受詞、間接受詞和介係詞受詞。

(1)作直接受詞。例如：

▶ He ran **a gas station** down in St. Louis for two years.
他在聖路易斯經營過兩年加油站。

▶ He gave his commanders **90 days** to resolve the problem.
他給了指揮官們90天時間來解決這個問題。

(2)作間接受詞。例如：

▶ You seem to have sent this letter to **all the friends** you can think of.
你似乎把這封信寄給了所有你能想到的朋友。

▶ He bought **his mother** some flowers.
他給母親買了些花。

(3)作介係詞受詞。例如：

▶ You can't go to Los Angeles without confronting the fact that wages **for native born African Americans** are being bid down daily **by desperate people from Mexico**.
到了洛杉磯，你肯定會遇到這樣的情況：不顧一切的墨西哥人與土生土長的非洲裔美國人競爭，使其工資每天都在下跌。

❸ 作表語。例如：

▶ Harris is **a tremendously productive lawman**, but his moral compass is woefully bent.
哈理斯是一位卓有成效的執法官，但糟糕的是，他的道德準則被扭曲了。

❹ 作受詞補語。例如：

▶ The reason we are bringing this study out is that we consider it **a crisis situation** that requires a national conversation.
把這一研究公佈於世的原因是，我們認為這是一個有待全民參與對話的危機局勢。

▶ Some experts had considered him **a possible successor** to Bin Laden.
有的專家曾認為他可能是賓拉登的接班人。

❺ 作副詞。例如：

▶ I would like to have a retirement **some day** and not work until I'm 75.
我想將來某一天就退休，而不想工作到75歲。

❻ 作前置修飾語。例如：

▶ There were six **women** soldiers who were mothers.
有6名做媽媽的女兵。

❼ 作同位語。例如：

▶ I met the band for the first time when we rehearsed at the Bull's Head, **a famous jazz pub** in Barnes.
我是在巴恩斯一個叫「牛頭店」的著名爵士樂酒吧裡彩排時與這個樂隊首次相遇的。

小結 ▷

名詞是語言中重要的詞類之一，用於指稱人、事物和地點。名詞在文法上有數、格和性別等範疇。在句子中，名詞可以作主詞、受詞、表語、補語、副詞、修飾語和同位語等，是構成句子的重要成分。

Part 2 限定詞

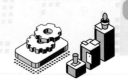

限定詞概說 ▷

　　限定詞是名詞片語的一部分，位於名詞中心詞之前，用來限定名詞中心詞所指的人或物。部分限定詞還可以充當代名詞或副詞，這些用法分別在代名詞和副詞兩章討論。

限定詞的分類 ▷

◎ 特指和泛指限定詞

　　名詞片語有特指和泛指兩種不同用法，它們常常是通過限定詞來體現的。鑑於此，人們通常將限定詞分為特指限定詞（Specific Determiners）和泛指限定詞（General Determiners）兩類。

　　特指限定詞主要包括定冠詞the，指示詞this，that，these，those和代名詞限定詞my，your，his，her，their等。泛指限定詞則由不定冠詞a/an和量詞many，much，few，little等組成。例如：

▶There's **the** student who kicked his friend for throwing a football into a tree.
　那位學生就是那個因為朋友把足球扔到樹上，就踢他的人。

▶We are tracking down **a** murderer with blood on his hands.
　我們在追蹤手上有血跡的兇手。

◎ 前位、中位和後位限定詞

　　一個名詞片語可以有一個以上的限定詞，有時甚至有四個限定詞，例如：all the many such possibilities。按照限定詞與限定詞之間的相互搭配關係，限定詞可分為三類：前位限定詞（Predeterminers）、中位限定詞（Central Determiners）和後位限定詞（Post Determiners）。

　　前位限定詞包括all，both，half，倍數詞和分數詞等。中位限定詞包括冠詞、指示限定詞、代名詞限定詞、不定限定詞、疑問限定詞和名詞所有格等。後位限定詞包括基數詞、序數詞和量詞等。下面就這三類限定詞各舉一個例子：

★前位限定詞：

▶Fresh water, after all, makes up less than 3 percent of **all** water on Earth.
畢竟，地球上的淡水只占全球水體總量的不到3％。

★中位限定詞

▶Looking back on **my** career has made me realize that the most important moment in **my** life was the day Coach Seymour walked into it.
回顧我的職業生涯，我意識到，西摩教練的出現是我人生最重要的時刻。

★後位限定詞

▶Ray said rent will be charged after the **first** few months to give residents time to get used to monthly bills.
雷說先過幾個月後，再開始收房租，以便讓住戶慢慢適應按月付房租。

　　若前位、中位和後位三類限定詞同時出現在名詞片語中，它們的先後順序為：前位＋中位＋後位。例如，在all the three persons中，all 是前位限定詞，the是中位限定詞，three是後位限定詞。

　　兩個前位限定詞或兩個中位限定詞無法同時修飾同一個名詞中心詞，但兩個後位限定詞卻可以。如我們可以說the last few days，因為last和few均為後位限定詞，可以同時使用。但不能說my this English teacher，因為my和this都是中位限定詞，不能同時使用。

中位限定詞 ▷

冠詞

　　冠詞（Articles）有定冠詞（Definite Articles）和不定冠詞（Indefinite Articles）之別，分別為the和a/an。除此以外，還有零冠詞（Zero Articles），一般不寫出來，但可標記為ø。

　　在名詞片語中，冠詞總是位於名詞中心詞之前。若名詞之前有形容詞修飾，冠詞一般位於形容詞之前，但也有例外的情況。當形容詞之前有how，so，too和as修飾時，a/an應置於形容詞之後。例如：

▶His new house was **as** comfortable **a** place as you could imagine.
他的新房子要多舒適有多舒適。

▶It is difficult to express **how** great **a** loss her death is for her family and friends.
她的去世對她家人和朋友來說都是一個無法估量的大損失。

❶ 不定冠詞

1. 形式

不定冠詞有兩種形式a和an，可以與單數可數名詞連用，泛指人或事物中的一個，屬於泛指限定詞。a/an的選用取決於它所限定的名詞的第一個音節，如果是母音，用an；如果是子音，則用a。例如：

- 母音開頭：an egg, an engineer, an orange, an X-ray
- 子音開頭：a sandwich, a knife, a problem

注意！

有些單字以母音字母開頭，但讀音是子音，必須用a，例如：a European country, a university student 等。但是，有些縮略語以子音字母開頭，但讀音是母音，必須用an，例如：an MP，an RRC member，an SOS。

以h開頭的某些單字如hour，honor和honorable 中，h不發音，所以用an，例如：an hour，an honourable guest，an honest person。

2. 用法

不定冠詞通常用於以下幾種情形：

(1)用於個體名詞前

不定冠詞用於個體名詞前通常表示「某個」、「有一個」或修飾不確定的人或物，類似a certain的意義。在敘述過程中涉及首次談到的人或物時，多用不定冠詞來限定。例如：

▶ One day **a** driver made a fast, illegal turn, and knocked me down.
　一個司機開車時突然違規轉彎，把我撞倒。

▶ Three years ago, Reed found **an** apartment in this 1880s building and immediately bought it.
　三年前，理德看中了這幢19世紀80年代建築裡的一間公寓，立刻買了下來。

(2)與名詞片語結合充當表語或者受詞補語

當不定冠詞所修飾的名詞片語作句子的表語時，通常泛指一類人或物。例如：

▶ I think luck is part of **a** player's career.
　我覺得運氣是運動員職業生涯的一部分。

(3)用於專有名詞前

不定冠詞的這種用法表示某個人、像某人似的人、某家的人、某個人的作品或產品。例如：

▶ In February 2003, his father was cared for at home by a Marie during his battle with cancer.

2003年2月，他父親正患病在家，與癌症抗爭，那時一個叫瑪麗的人在照顧他。

▶ I hope, with all my heart, the young man may be a Weston in merit, and a Churchill in fortune.

我衷心希望那個年輕人能擁有溫斯頓的美德，邱吉爾的財富。

▶ The name Wontner, from a family who had been inn-keepers, had been brought in several generations previously by a lady who married a Smith.

旺特納這個名字來自一戶經營旅館的人家，最初是幾代前由一個嫁到史密斯家的女子帶來的。

▶ He once spent 18 million pounds on a Picasso.

有一回，他花了1,800萬英鎊買了一幅畢卡索的畫。

(4) 與單數名詞連用

不定冠詞用在單數名詞前，表示某類人或事物都有的性質，類似any的意義。

例如：

▶ An adult can be more manipulative, but people my age—and I can't do it either— can't hide their motives.

成年人更善於擺佈別人，但是像我這個年紀的人——而且我也做不到——不會隱藏自己的動機。

(5) 與表示數量的詞連用

當不定冠詞和數量詞連用時，可以表示one（一個）的意思。例如：

- a mile or two = one or two miles

- a day or two = one or two days

- a dozen = one dozen

▶ Do you remember I phoned you a week or two ago about some books I wanted?

一兩個禮拜前，我打電話告訴你我想要的書，你還記不記得？

(6) 用於單位名詞前

不定冠詞用在單位名詞如價格、時間、速度等名詞前，通常表示類似per或each的意義，但語氣較弱。例如：8 hours a week，80 miles an hour，20 pounds a kilo，once a month等。

▶ Father and son talk on the phone about twice a month and never run out of things to say.

父子倆一個月大概要通上兩次電話，總有說不完的事。

(7)與動名詞連用

不定冠詞與動名詞連用表示一種行為、一個事件等。例如：

▶ She hears **a** beating of wings and sees the approach of the swan.
耳邊傳來了拍動翅膀的聲音，然後，她看到天鵝過來了。

(8)與抽象名詞連用

不定冠詞用在抽象名詞前，表示「一種」的意思。例如：a good knowledge of English，a great love of rock and roll等。

▶ The last few months had taught him quite clearly that **a** good knowledge of writing, reading and arithmetic was no longer enough.
過去的這幾個月，讓他瞭解了只掌握讀、寫和算術這些技能不再足夠了。

(9)與表示種類、性質的物質名詞連用

不定冠詞的這種用法表示一類或一種。例如：

- a nice wine 一種不錯的酒
- a different tea 一種不同的茶葉

(10)與single連用

不定冠詞與single連用可以起到增強語勢的作用。例如：

▶ In **a single month** leading up to Christmas, Barbie Fashion Designer sold over 200,000 copies in the US and sales are now approaching the 500,000 mark.
光在臨近聖誕的一個月，「芭比服裝設計師」就在美國狂售20多萬件，而現在這個數字正在向50萬靠近。

(11)在一些數量詞中使用

不定冠詞與數量詞連用表示量的概念，有些用法是固定搭配。例如：a few，many a，a great many，a good many，a little，a large number of，a great deal等。

(12)用於一些固定片語中

在這些片語中，習慣上要加a/an，並形成了一種固定的搭配。例如：

as a matter of fact	as a result	as a rule
at a deadlock	at a halt	at a loss
for a moment	for a while	in a hurry
in a moment	in a sense	in a way
in a word	keep an eye on	on a large/small scale

once upon a time	quite a few/little/bit	make a difference
make a habit of	make a fool of	make a fortune
make a fuss	make a living	make a mockery of
make a profit	make an attempt	take a chance
with a will		

當兩個並列的單字被看成一個整體時，a/an 用在第一個名詞前。例如：

• a cup and saucer 一套茶杯和杯碟

• a knife and fork 一副刀叉

❶ 定冠詞

1. 形式

定冠詞只有一種形式the，可以放在普通名詞、集體名詞、抽象名詞、物質名詞前，特指人或事，屬於特指限定詞。例如：

▶ For a start, I'm not sure Glover is the man for the job.
打從一開始，我就不太確定格洛弗能否勝任這份工作。

2. 一般用法

(1)前指

定冠詞與名詞連用，特指上文已經談到的人、事物或群體。這種用法稱為前指，前指又分為直接前指（Direct Anaphora）和間接前指（Indirect Anaphora）。

直接前指是指the所限定的名詞或名詞片語在前文已經出現過，兩個名詞或名詞片語指的是同一個人、事物或群體。例如：

▶ He bought her a book called The Lives of the Great Composers for her seventeenth birthday. However, she thought the book was boring.
他買了一本《偉大的作曲家傳記》作為她17歲生日的禮物，可她卻覺得這本書挺無聊的。

常用的表示前指的片語有：the latter，the former，the rest，the remainder等。

間接前指是指所指的人、事物或群體要從交談雙方已知的資訊中推斷得到，並不能直接獲得。例如：

▶ The couple fixed the wedding day, the guests were invited, the dress and the cake were brought to the house.
夫婦倆敲定了婚禮的日子，請好了來賓，也把禮服和蛋糕拿到房裡了。

在上述例句中，the wedding是事先約定的，而the guests，the dress，the cake都是與the wedding相關聯的資訊，均為特指。

(2)特指交談雙方都知道的事物、自然界的現象或日常生活的一部分。

如下表所示，在以下指稱中通常用定冠詞表示特指的關係：

天體	自然界	方向	日常生活
the sun	the sky	the north	the city
the moon	the wind	the east	the country
the earth	the rain	the south	the traffic
the stars	the sea	the west	
	the snow	the left	
	the weather	the next	
		the last	

例如：

▶ Most of **the station**'s functions can be controlled from IBM laptops running Windows 95.
車站的大部分功能都可以透過裝有Windows 95系統的IBM筆記型電腦來操控。

注意！

當上面列舉的這類詞前面出現形容詞作定語，表示一種狀態時，用a/an修飾。例如：a full moon滿月，a new moon新月，a cold wind 寒風。

(3)與複數名詞或集體名詞連用

表示一個階級、一個群體。例如：the public，the working class，the lower class，the middle class，the upper class，the ruling class等。

(4)用於某些片語中

定冠詞可以與表示人的身體部位或服裝部位的名詞連用，常用結構是：動詞＋ sb.＋介係詞＋ the＋身體部位或服裝部位。如下所示：

- catch sb. by the arm 抓住某人的手臂
- grasp sb. by the collar 抓住某人的衣領
- give sb. a pat on the back 在某人背上拍一下
- hit sb. on the head 打中某人的頭
- hit sb. in the face 打中某人的臉
- kick sb. in the stomach 踢中某人的肚子

• pat sb. on the shoulder 拍某人的肩膀

例如：

▶I felt raindrops hitting me in **the** face.
我感到雨點打在我的臉上。

(5)用於某些名詞前

　　定冠詞可以與某些表示傳媒、娛樂、樂器的名詞連用，形成一種固定的表達形式，表示特指。如下表所示：

the radio	the mail	the papers	the press
go to the theater	go to the cinema	play the guitar	play the piano
play the violin	play the flute		

例如：

▶A year later, White got a surprise check in **the** mail from his friend, repaying the debt plus $20 interest.
一年後，懷特意外地收到了朋友寄給他的一張支票，不但還清了欠他的債，還支付了20美元的利息。

▶Now Harry is a handsome boy, speaks pretty, and plays **the** violin like an angel.
現在哈利變成了個小帥哥，說話好聽，而且拉小提琴時的樣子就像個天使。

注意！

定冠詞與press連用時，表示新聞媒體的總稱，有特指的意義，謂語動詞可以用複數形式。但是，當定冠詞與television或者TV連用時，the也可以省略。

　　3. 特殊用法

(1)與專有名詞連用

a. 加定冠詞的專有名詞

　　在某些專有名詞前一般要加定冠詞，表示特指。例如：

• 海洋：the Pacific (Ocean) 太平洋，the Dead Sea 死海

• 沙漠：the Gobi (Desert) 戈壁（沙漠），the Sahara (Desert) 撒哈拉（沙漠）

• 河流：the Nile 尼羅河，the Yellow River 黃河

• 群島：the Aleutian Islands 阿留申群島

• 山脈：the Alps 阿爾卑斯山，the Caucasus Mountains 高加索山脈，the Himalayas 喜馬拉雅山脈

- 運河：the Suez Canal 蘇伊士運河，the Panama Canal 巴拿馬運河
- 海峽：the Bristol Channel 布里斯托爾海峽，the (English) Channel 英吉利海峽
- 政治組織和機構：the Central Intelligence Agency (CIA) 中央情報局，the Department of Defense 國防部，the Ministry of Agriculture 農業部，the United Nations 聯合國
- 報紙：The Daily News《每日新聞》，The Economist《經濟學人》，The New York Times《紐約時報》
- 人名：the Johnsons，the Browns等；定冠詞與姓氏的複數形式連用時，表示夫婦或者一家人，例如：the Smiths 史密斯夫婦或史密斯一家

b. 不加定冠詞的專有名詞

有些專有名詞前不加定冠詞。例如：

- 山峰：Mount Ararat 阿拉臘山，Mount Vesuvius 維蘇威火山
- 單個海島：Long Island 長島
- 湖：Lake Michigan 密西根湖，Lake Ontario 安大略湖
- 海角：Cape Hatteras 哈特勒斯角，Cape Coral 佛羅里達州珊瑚角
- 大洲：Africa 非洲，Antarctica 南極洲
- 國家：Brazil 巴西，China 中國

> **注意！**
>
> 美國五個湖組成的五大湖區則要用the：the Great Lakes。例外的還有：the West Lake 西湖。

> **注意！**
>
> ①專有名詞+普通名詞構成的國名，要加the。例如：the United States美利堅合眾國，the United Kingdom 聯合王國（英國）。
> ②如地名結構為the +普通名詞+ of +專有名詞，the不能省略。例如：the Sea of Japan日本海，the Cape of Good Hope好望角，the Mount of Olives橄欖山。
> ③有些國家和地區名稱之前要加定冠詞，這是一種固定用法。例如：the Hague 海牙，the Netherlands 荷蘭，the Vatican 梵蒂岡，the Middle East 中東地區，the North Pole 北極。

- 州：Washington State 華盛頓州。
- 城市：London 倫敦，Hangzhou 杭州。

• 城市中的公園、廣場、橋樑、著名建築：Central Park 中央公園，Madison Square Park 麥迪森廣場公園，Red Square 紅場，Times Square 時報廣場，Golden Gate Bridge 金門大橋，Buckingham Palace 白金漢宮，Westminster Cathedral 西敏主教座堂

注意！

有些市區的建築物則要加定冠詞。例如：the White House白宮，the Pentagon五角大樓，the Forbidden City 紫禁城。

• 以人名、地名命名的大學：Harvard University 哈佛大學，Massachusetts Institute of Technology 麻省理工學院，Peking University 北京大學

注意！

①英國有些以地名命名的大學的正式名稱表達為the University of XX，例如：the University of Cambridge劍橋大學，the University of London倫敦大學。這時片語前要加定冠詞。但是，這些大學也可以表達為XX University，例如：Cambridge University，London University。這時則不加定冠詞。
②美國的州立大學一般用the University of XX，例如：the University of California 加利福尼亞大學。私立大學一般用XX University，例如：Yale University 耶魯大學。

• 雜誌：Time《時代》，National Geography《國家地理》，Fortunes《財富》。雜誌名稱或標題常常不加定冠詞。

(2)與形容詞、分詞連用

定冠詞可以與某些形容詞或分詞連用，表示某種特定的意義。

a. 表示集合名詞的意義

定冠詞與形容詞或分詞連用表示一類人或一個群體，相當於集合名詞的意義。例如：the rich，the poor，the young，the old，the learned，the deaf，the disabled，the abused，the oppressed。

定冠詞也可以與表示國家或地區的形容詞連用，指全體人民，用作複數名詞。例如：the English，the French，the Chinese。

b. 表示抽象名詞的意義

定冠詞與形容詞或分詞連用表示一種抽象的意義。例如：

▶ Sydney was in the grip of Steve Waugh fever and believed in his ability to produce **the incredible**.
對史蒂夫・沃的狂熱席捲整個雪梨，人們堅信他能創造出奇跡。

(3)與數詞或限定詞連用

定冠詞通常與數詞或限定詞連用，構成固定搭配的形式。如下所示：

- 與序數詞連用：the first，the second，the first day，the first two，for the first time
- 與限定詞連用：the other ones，the other two，one of the few buildings

(4)與時間名詞連用

a. 與表示晝夜時間的名詞連用

在一些表示晝夜時間的名詞如morning，evening，daytime前要加the，例如：in the morning，in the daytime等。

但是，如果這些時間段前面有yesterday，tomorrow，next，last，this，that等詞限定，一般不用介係詞也不用定冠詞，例如：yesterday morning，next morning，this morning。

如果這些時間段前面有表示星期幾的名詞修飾，一般不用定冠詞，但要加介係詞on，例如：on Sunday morning，on Wednesday evening等。

> **注意！**
>
> ① night 前的介係詞用at，而且不加定冠詞。
> ②在next morning，last morning 等時間片語前面有時加定冠詞，有時不加，但整個句子的意思會有些不同。試比較：
>
> ▶ William had been told to pack, tidy up and return the keys to the landlord when he left **next morning**.
> 威廉被告知明早走的時候要把東西打包，房間整理乾淨，並把鑰匙歸還房東。
>
> ▶ The maid-servant woke me **the next morning**, shaking my shoulder and urging me to get up.
> 第二天早晨，女傭不停搖著我的肩膀，催我起床。
>
> 在第一句中next morning是以現在為起點的明天早上，而第二句中the next morning具體是指哪個早上，要根據句中的意思，有可能是以現在某個時間點為起點，也可能是以過去某個時間點為起點的下個早上。

b. 與其他表示時間的名詞連用

定冠詞與其他表示時間的名詞連用構成名詞性片語，例如：the past，the present，the future。還可以構成介係詞片語，例如：in the past在過去，at the moment在此刻，for the present暫時，in the future在將來。

注意！

在有些表示時間的片語中，帶定冠詞和不帶冠詞表示的意思有所不同。

① at present表示「現在」、「目前」的意思，一般不用定冠詞，與for the present 意思不同。後者表示「暫時」、「暫且」。

② in the future 表示「在將來」，而in future 表示「從今以後」、「今後」。比較 以下例句：

▶He envisions spending lots of money in the future on mechanical equipment with lots of moving parts that can break down.
他打算將來投入大筆資金購置由許多可拆卸的活動部件組成的機械設備。

▶She would be more on her guard in future, however, now that she knew the unpredictable nature of the old lady's malevolence.
由於知道了那個老婦人反覆無常的惡毒本性，她今後就得更小心了。

❶ 零冠詞和冠詞的省略

1. 零冠詞

有些名詞或相當於名詞的結構前是不用加冠詞的，這種用法稱為零冠詞，一般在書寫及口語上不會出現，但也可標記為ø。

(1)用在複數名詞前，泛指一類人或物，或者是數量不確定的人或物。例如：

▶It is said that ø men always get the long eyelashes.
據說，男人的都有長長的睫毛。

(2)用在不可數名詞前，泛指一類物或者是數量不確定的物

a. 用在物質名詞前，表示一般的概念或數量不確定的物。例如：

▶Loss of ø oxygen to the brain causes fainting, and some kids feel a rush as their heartbeat rapidly speeds up and then slows down.
腦部供氧不足導致眩暈，一些孩子感到心跳一陣急速加快後再減慢。

b. 用在抽象名詞或集體名詞前，表示非特指的概念。例如：

▶ I believe each player wish to be treated with ø fairness and ø honesty.
我相信每個參賽者都希望得到公平和誠信的對待。

注意！

如果抽象名詞指的是特定的內容，那就要加上定冠詞。例如：
• the beauty of the scene 美景
• the growing anger at his son 對兒子發火

▶ ø Sheep need careful tending because they are on the menus of so many predators, including bears, coyotes, mountain lions and wolves.
看護羊群要很小心，因為它們是很多捕食者例如熊、郊狼、美洲獅和狼眼中的美味。

(3)用在表示身份、職位或稱號的名詞前

a. 用在表示身份或職位的名詞前，而名詞一般充當句子的表語、補語或者同位語。例如：

▶ They were expelled by ø headmaster Stuart Turner after bombarding PE teacher Stephen with 40 calls threatening to kill him.
他們打了40個恐嚇電話給體育老師斯蒂芬，揚言要殺死他，最後校長斯圖爾特・特納把他們開除了。

▶ John Smith, ø Professor of linguistics at London University.
約翰・史密斯，倫敦大學語言學教授

b. 用在頭銜/稱號＋姓名前，頭銜/稱號通常大寫。例如：ø Dr. Lee，ø Prof. Black，ø Captain Gale等。

c. 頭銜、職位之類的名詞在動詞turn後面作補語時，一般採取零冠詞的用法。例如：turn ø linguist，turn ø principal等。

▶ Her boss turned ø psychologist, when he was 39.
她的老闆在39歲的時候成了心理學家。

注意！

在類似的句子中，動詞換成become 時，名詞前要加冠詞，表示某種職業而非特指。例如：
▶ He studied at Yale and became a lawyer, but preferred teaching.
雖然他畢業于耶魯後來又做了律師，但他還是鍾情於教書。

d. as後面有表示獨一無二的身份或職位的詞時，使用零冠詞，表示作為擁有某種身份或職位的人，如as ø principal，as ø president。例如：

▶ As ø president, she's helped women from across the world relocate here.
作為總統，她曾幫助來自世界各地的婦女在此重新安置。

(4) 用於表示稱呼的名詞前，稱呼一般要大寫。例如：ø Mr. Steven史蒂文先生，ø Ms. Joan瓊女士，ø Uncle Tom湯姆叔叔，ø Waiter 服務員，ø Doctor 醫生。

(5) 用於表示感歎的名詞片語前。例如：

▶ You ø silly fool!
你這笨蛋！

▶ You ø poor thing!
你這可憐的傢伙！

(6) 用在表示地點或機構的名詞前

表示地點或機構的名詞有時充當介係詞的補語，表達一種特定的意思，而非表示地點。例如：go to ø bed 就寢，be in ø hospital住院，go to school上學，at college讀大學，be in prison 服刑。

當這些名詞表示地點和方位的意思時，名詞前通常要用冠詞。例如：go to the bed 走到床那裡，work in a school 在某所學校裡工作。常用的這類表達如下表：

be in bed	go home	come home	leave home
feel at home	be (at) home	go to college	go to class
be in class	go to church	be in church	out of prison
put sb. in prison	send to prison	release sb. from prison	escape from prison
be in jail	put sb. in jail	release sb. from jail	escape from jail
go to jail	throw sb. in jail	go to sea	be in hospital
appear in court	go to court	come to court	throw (a case) out of court
settle (a case) out of court	bring (a case) to court	take sb. to court	go to market

(7) 用於某些介係詞片語中

a. 在by+名詞的介係詞片語中，名詞通常是表示交通或通訊工具的名詞，常用零冠詞。如下表所示：

by bicycle	by bus	by car	by boat	by sea

by ship	by plane	by train	by telephone	by mail
by post	by e-mail	by letter	by fax	by wire
by telegraph	by subway			

b. 在at/by/after/before+表示晝夜時間段的名詞構成的介係詞片語中，通常用零冠詞。如下表所示：

at daybreak	at dawn	at daylight	at dusk	at midnight
at night	at sunrise	at sunset	at noon	at twilight
after nightfall	after dark	after midnight	before dawn	before midnight
before morning came	by dusk	by night	(by) day and night	

注意！

night，daytime，dusk等詞前如果是其他介係詞，有時要加the。例如：in the dust，in the daytime，all through the night，during the night。當表示晝夜時間段的名詞前後有修飾語時，如果特指要加the，如果泛指「某一個」用a/an。例如：the night before=the previous night，a chilly December morning。

其他表示晝夜時間段的名詞前要加定冠詞的情況，可參照P054〈定冠詞〉。

(8)用於專有名詞前

a. 姓名：ø John，ø Smith，ø Zhou Enlai，姓名前面也可用the 或a/an，請參照前面不定冠詞和定冠詞的有關章節

b. 國家、地區、政府機構、自然景觀。參照定冠詞一節

c. 雜誌、月份、星期、節日：ø January，ø February，ø March，ø November，ø December，ø Sunday，ø Wednesday，ø Christmas Eve，ø Easter，ø Halloween，ø Valentine's Day，ø Women's Day。當這些詞前面有修飾語的時候，如果特指要加the，如果泛指「某一個」用a/an

d. 星球、星座：ø Mars，ø Venus，ø Jupiter，ø Taurus，ø Scorpio

(9)用於表示學科的名詞前

在表示學科的名詞前一般使用零冠詞。例如：ø chemistry，ø math，major in ø accounting，be interested in ø literature/history等。如果特指某段歷史而非學科，可用定冠詞the。例如：the history of Ming Dynasty。

(10)用於一些平行結構中

a. 名詞＋and＋名詞結構。例如：day and night，hand and foot，sun and moon，rich and poor，heart and soul。

b. 名詞＋介係詞＋名詞結構。例如：hand in hand，arm in arm，day after day，step by step，year after year，face to face，little by little。

c. from＋名詞＋to＋名詞結構。例如：from top to down，from hand to mouth，from morning to night，from bad to worse，from day to day。

(11) 用於表示體育運動的名詞前

在一些表示體育運動項目的名詞前一般使用零冠詞，與動詞play搭配，構成動詞片語。例如：play ø badminton，play ø basketball，play ø billiards，play ø cards等。

(12) 用於kind of等表示種類的片語中

在a/the/this/that kind of +單數／複數名詞片語中，或者these/those kinds of +複數名詞中，一般採用零冠詞。例如：a/the/this/that kind of bag(s)，these/those kinds of bags。

在有些片語中，還可以用what/this/that kind of a bag。表示兩種以上時，可以用all/these kinds of +複數名詞或複數名詞+ of all kinds。例如：all kinds of bags，bags of all kinds。

表示「某種」時，可以用certain/some + kind(s) of +單數/複數名詞，或者用單數/複數名詞+ of its/that/this kind。例如：certain/some kind(s) of bag(s)，bags of its/that/this kind。type，sort等詞具有與kind相似的用法。

▶ So nothing was done to indicate that **this kind of** ø conduct might be condoned.
所以，沒有跡象說明這樣的行為是能被赦免的。

(13) 用於一些固定片語中。例如：give birth to，make compensation, make contact with，make progress in，make room for，put emphasis upon，put ... to bed，take advantage of，take charge of。

2. 冠詞的省略

冠詞的省略和零冠詞在形式上是一樣的，但是區別在於，冠詞的省略是把結構中原來要使用的定冠詞或不定冠詞省去，零冠詞是結構中原本就不需要定冠詞或不定冠詞。冠詞在以下用法中常常省略：

(1) 新聞標題。例如：

▶ Leaders of Africa Support Arms Embargo
非洲領導人支持武器禁運

▶ World Leaders Highlight Need for Reform
全球領導人強調改革的緊迫性

(2)廣告。例如：

▶ Great drama from the BBC
　BBC出品的精品戲劇

(3)通知。例如：

▶ Attention, you are now under a mandatory evacuation order!
　注意，現在你們必須執行強制撤離的命令！

(4)電報。例如：

▶ Don't worry, firemen pumping water out of house.
　不用擔心，消防員正抽走房裡的水。

其他中位限定詞

❶ 指示限定詞

1. 定義

指示限定詞（Demonstrative Determiners）有this，that，these，those。它們的用處與定冠詞the的特指作用非常接近，但指示限定詞除了用於對人或事物起到特指作用的情況下，還表明所指人或物的數量及其與説話人的時間或空間的遠近距離。

this/these所修飾的名詞或名詞片語，指的是離説話者或作者距離較近的人或物，that/those所修飾的名詞或名詞片語，指的是離説話者或作者距離較遠的人或物。

很多時候指示限定詞的使用取決於心理距離和主觀意願，感覺比較疏遠的、遙遠的、久遠的用that，those，而感覺比較親近的、就近的、近期的多用this，these。

指示限定詞起到的是一種近似形容詞的作用，它們一般放在名詞或名詞片語的前面，起修飾和限定作用，所以又被稱為指示形容詞，但事實上，它們並不屬於形容詞。他們也可以作為指示代名詞（Demonstrative Pronouns），指代人或物。

this/that後面可接單數可數名詞、不可數名詞和單數代名詞one。these/those後面接複數名詞和複數代名詞ones。

2. 作用

(1)空間所指

this/these後面接表示人或物的名詞或名詞片語時，表示的是離説話人時空距離較近的人或物。例如：

▶ **These** storms are dramatically different than those observed 20 years ago.
　這些暴風雨和20年前觀察到的有巨大的差別。

在口語中here和this/these會出現在同一個句子中。例如：

▶ You come **here** and **this** country gives you everything.
　來這個國家，你會得到一切。

that/those後面接表示人或物的名詞或名詞片語時，表示的是離說話人時空距離較遠的人或物。例如：

▶ This facility is more secure than that in the downtown area.
　　這裡的設備比在市中心的更安全。

　　在口語中there和that/those也會出現在同一句子中。例如：

▶ You see that man's still up there?
　　你看那個人還在那兒嗎？

(2)時間所指

　　this/these後面接表示時間的名詞或名詞片語時，表示現在或將來。例如：this morning今天早晨，these days現在。

　　that/those後面接表示時間的名詞或名詞片語時，表示過去的時間。例如：those days那時，that summer那個夏天（不是今年夏天），at that point在那時。

(3)回指

　　this，that，these，those與名詞連用時，表示上文提到過的人或物。例如：

▶ He has been writing a new book. That novel too is a historical novel, written about the time of Tolstoy's grandparents.
　　他一直在寫一本新書，那又是本歷史小說，寫的是托爾斯泰的祖父母那個時代。

(4)後指

　　that/those與名詞連用，可後指句子中將要出現的人或物。that/those與名詞連用，後面接關係子句，確切指明是哪些人或物，可以看作是一種更正式的表達方式。例如：

▶ Andrew showed at his best at this time: he shed those ways that I disliked.
　　安德魯這次真是棒極了，我不喜歡的地方他都改了。

(5)在代名詞one/ones前，起修飾作用

　　this one，that one指的是單數，these ones，those ones指的是複數，此時one/ones可以省略。在one/ones前還可以有其他形容詞，例如this big one，these red ones，此時one/ones不可以省略。

(6)與某些前位或後位限定詞連用修飾名詞。

　　指示限定詞屬於中位限定詞，位置一般處於前位限定詞後面，或後位限定詞前面。

與前位限定詞連用：all that money，all those years，both these books，half this cake。

與後位限定詞數詞連用：these two guys，those three men。

this/that有時也可以和one共同修飾名詞。例如：that one year。

❷ 所有格

1. 定義

所有格（Possessive Determiners）放在名詞或名詞片語前面，說明人或事物歸屬某人或與某人有關。

英語中的人稱代名詞有七個，所有格和所有格代名詞一一對應。

人稱	所有格		所有格代名詞	
	單數	複數	單數	複數
第一人稱	my	our	mine	ours
第二人稱	your	your	yours	yours
第三人稱	his, her, its	their	his/hers	theirs

my將名詞片語與說話者或作者聯繫起來；our將名詞片語與說話者或作者以及聽話者或讀者聯繫起來；your將名詞片語與聽話者或讀者聯繫起來；his，her，its 和their將名詞片語與其他非參與對話者（非說話者也非聽話者）聯繫起來。

代名詞的所有格形式不受名詞片語的單複數、可數和不可數性質的影響。例如：my dress，my work，my children等。

2. 作用

(1)表示人與物的所屬關係

所有格置於名詞前面，表明物體為某個人或某群人所有：my bicycle，your car，his dog，our rooms。例如：

▶I was impressed by his determination, by the fact that he seriously wanted to be with me.
我被他的堅定所震撼，他是如此誠心地想和我在一起。

(2)表示物與物的所屬關係

所有格置於名詞前面，表明物體為某個物或某群物所有，一般是指有生命的動物：their tails (the tails of the monkeys)，its nose (the nose of a dog)。

無生命的事物，一般不用所有格，比如人們常用the window of the room，很少用its window。

(3)表示人體部位的所屬關係

所有格置於表示人體部位的名詞前，將人體部位和人聯繫起來，表示所屬的關係，例如：your feet，my teeth，his arm，their eyes等。

▶Adam put **his head** in **his hands** in mock despair.
亞當雙手抱頭，裝出一副絕望的樣子。

注意！

在「動詞＋sb.＋介係詞＋the＋身體部位」結構中，人體部位前用定冠詞the。例如：hit sb. on the head，hit sb. in the face，take sb. by the arm 等。
結構中不用指示限定詞是因為身體部位與sb.的所屬關係已經明確，為了避免重複，所以用定冠詞。如果表示某人對自己實施動作，則一般用指示限定詞。例如：brush my teeth，grit his teeth 等。

▶I brushed **my** teeth thoroughly with my electric toothbrush.
我用電動牙刷認真地刷了牙。

(4)表示人與人之間的關係

所有格可以表明人與人的關係。例如：my mother，your boss，his doctor等。

▶**My sister** and our friends take their babies out to late movies and fancy restaurants.
我姐姐和我們的朋友不管去看晚場電影還是去高檔餐廳都會帶著自己的寶寶。

(5)表示動作與實施者之間的所屬關係

所有格置於表示動作的名詞前面，說明動作的實施者。例如：our actions，your arrival，his departure等。

▶You do not generally tip bar staff if you want to show **your appreciation**, offer to buy them a drink.
如果你想謝謝酒吧工作人員，通常不用給小費，請他們喝一杯就成。

(6)表示動作與承受者之間的所屬關係

所有格置於表示動作的名詞前面，說明動作的承受者。例如：his promotion，their defeat by Rockets，her dismissal等。

▶To give Tyson his due, he took **his punishment** bravely, never once seeking a way out in dishonor as some predicted he might.
說句公道話，泰森還是勇敢地接受了懲罰，從未像有些人預測的那樣可能採取不光彩的手段為自己開脫。

(7)在所有格後面加own起強調作用。例如：

► She worked for a real estate developer, then for an advertising company, before deciding last year to set up **her own** business.
她曾經在一家房地產開發公司任職，後來又去了一家廣告公司，去年她決心要開創自己的事業。

如果要進一步強調，可在own前加very。例如：

► This was his room, **his very own** private bedroom.
這間房間就是專屬於他的臥室。

❸ 名詞所有格

1. 定義和構成

名詞所有格起到了與代名詞所有格相似的作用，表明兩者之間的歸屬關係，形式是在名詞後面加上-'s，起到了類似形容詞的修飾作用，但不是形容詞，在這裡我們把它歸為限定詞。

(1)單數名詞的所有格

單數名詞後面一般直接加-'s。例如：the lady's hat，the kid's toys，Joan's friend。

以-s結尾的單數名詞後面也可以直接加-'s。例如：the boss's son，the waitress's dress。

(2)複數名詞的所有格

複數名詞後面加「'」。例如：the boys' bicycles，parents' claim。

有些特殊的複數名詞後加-'s。例如：children's performance，women's clothing。

(3)複合名詞和名詞片語的所有格

複合名詞和名詞片語後面加-'s。例如：my mother-in-law's house，his wife Joan's essay。

如果涉及兩人共有，則在第二個人後加-'s。例如：John and Joan's parents表示John 和Joan的父母。

如果表示兩個人分別擁有，則在兩個人後面都加-'s。例如：John's and Joan's parents表示John 和Joan雙方的父母。

2. 名詞所有格的限定作用

名詞所有格中的名詞一般是指有生命的人或者物，因此名詞所有格與代名詞所有格的用法相似，都表示所屬的關係，一般有以下幾種用法：

(1)表示人的名詞所有格。例如：the lady's hat，Joan's parents

(2)表示動物的名詞所有格。例如：the dog's nose，the horse's tail

(3)集合名詞的所有格。例如：the government's policy，the company's staff

(4)表示人格化的事物的名詞所有格。例如：China's future，the hotel's lobby，the university's history

(5)與人類活動有關的名詞所有格。例如：the book's importance，a word's function，love's spirit，in freedom's name

(6)表示時間的名詞所有格。例如：a year's statistics，a month's sales，today's report

3. 名詞所有格的所屬關係

名詞所有格與代名詞所有格的作用相似，表示兩者之間的所屬關係。

(1)表示一般的所屬關係。例如：John's car，the lady's dog，the family's house，the dog's bark

(2)表示人與人之間的所屬關係。例如：my wife's family

(3)表示動作與實施者的所屬關係。例如：the parents' arrival，the boy's claim

(4)表示動作與承受者之間的所屬關係。例如：his father's promotion，the prisoner's release

(5)描述事物性質。例如：a girls' school，a doctor's degree

(6)表示時間。例如：five minutes' break，ten years' war，tomorrow's meeting

❹ 疑問限定詞

1. 定義

疑問限定詞（Wh-word Determiners）是以wh開頭的詞，如which，what，whose，whichever，whatever等，所以也被稱為wh-詞限定詞，一般可以修飾可數、不可數、單數和複數名詞，充當類似形容詞的作用，但仍屬於限定詞。例如：which book，what information，whose parents，whatever problems等。

2. 作用

(1)whose可以用在疑問句、名詞性子句和定語子句中，限定人或物之間的所屬關係，起類似代名詞所有格的作用

a. 在疑問句中。例如：

▶ Whose fault is it that the radio doesn't work?
誰把收音機弄壞了？

▶ I wonder whose Christmas you'll spoil next year, Ed?
我在想，明年你又會去擾亂誰的耶誕節呢，埃德？

b. 在名詞性子句中。例如：

▶Workers hired for the wedding said they didn't know **whose** wedding it was until they arrived at the site.
被雇傭的工人們說，直到來到婚禮現場，他們才知道新人是誰。

c. 在定語子句中。例如：

▶A Canadian **whose** first book was published in 1968, Munro is routinely called one of the finest living writers.
加拿大人芒羅的處女作於1968年問世。她通常被認為是在世的最優秀的作家之一。

(2)what可以用在疑問句和名詞性子句中

a. 在疑問句中

　　what與所修飾的名詞或名詞片語在疑問句中充當提問的焦點，詢問有關某事物的訊息。例如：

▶**What** movie would you like to provide commentary for on a DVD release, and why?
如果要為一部電影的DVD版本寫評論，你會選擇什麼電影，為什麼？

▶She asked **what** my girlfriend thought of my being a trainer, which I thought was strange.
她問我，我女朋友對我當訓練員怎麼看，我覺得她問這個問題有點奇怪。

b. 在名詞性子句中。例如：

▶This place taught me how to be a man; it showed me **what** struggle was.
在這裡，我學會了怎樣做一個男人，也知道了什麼是奮鬥。

(3)which可以用在疑問句、名詞性子句和定語子句中，討論的是一組人或事物中特定的一個或一些。

a. 在疑問句中。例如：

▶**Which** airline is the best?
哪條航線最好？

▶**Which** letter of the English language is the one we use most?
英語中哪個字母我們用得最多？

▶She wonders **which** designers he's been talking to lately.
她想知道最近他都找哪些設計師討論過。

b. 在名詞性子句中。例如：

▶ I am a student and want to know **which** car is the cheapest to run (in terms of petrol, insurance and so on).
我還是個學生，所以想（從汽油、保險等角度綜合考慮）找到最便宜的汽車。

c. 在定語子句中。例如：

▶ It was instinct **which** made her say no.
她本能地拒絕了。

▶ Ruby had said she would be at the office again next morning **by which time** she expected Rain to have found something more profitable for her.
魯比說過明早她會再去辦公室，希望到時雷恩能給她找到利潤更豐厚的東西。

注意！

① in which case 是一個常用片語，表示一種假設。例如：

▶ She may refuse to speak to me, in which case Terry and I will leave immediately.
如果她拒絕和我說話，我和特里就馬上離開。

② which和what的區別在於，which是在限定的一組人或事物中選擇，what 則沒有限定範圍。

(4) whichever/whatever 用於名詞性子句中

whichever在名詞性子句中表示其中任一個或任一些。例如：

▶ Either Thursday or Friday — choose **whichever** day is best for you.
星期四或星期五都行──選一個你最方便的日子。

whatever可以表示任何或所有。例如：

▶ We'll make **whatever** efforts it takes to help these people.
我們會盡一切力量去幫助這些人。

❺ 不定限定詞

1. 定義

不定限定詞（Indefinite Determiners）是沒有明確指出限定物件的限定詞。例如：every/each/some/any/no/either/neither/enough。

不定限定詞修飾名詞或名詞片語，和其他限定詞一樣，有形容詞的作用，所以又有人稱它們為形容詞性不定代名詞。除了every之外，其他的不定限定詞都能充當代名詞。（參見P089〈代名詞〉）

2. 作用

以下我們將一些意義和用法比較相近的詞放在一起說明。

(1) every，each

　　every和each都表示「每個」，修飾單數可數名詞或代名詞one。everyone 和each one 也可作不定代名詞。

a. every指的是由三個或三個以上的人或物組成的團體，強調的是團體中所有成員都包含在內，所以更突出「整體」的概念。例如：

▶ Remember that **every** program you download and install clutters your hard drive, and **every** program that runs in the background slows Windows and increases the likelihood of conflicts.
記住，你下載並安裝的每個程式都會佔用你的硬碟空間，每個在後臺運行的程式都會減慢Windows系統的運行速度，從而增加各種程式相互衝突的可能性。

　　every後面加single起強調作用。例如：

▶ Seeing her struggle to take **every single** breath was heartbreaking.
她每次呼吸都那麼艱難，讓人看著都心碎。

b. every＋minute/day/week/month/year，表示每個時間點都……，意為「每分鐘／每天／每週／每月／每年」。例如：

▶ Approximately 2.5 million people **every year** use a gun successfully to defend themselves from violent crime in America.
在美國，每年都有大約250萬人使用槍枝保護自己免受暴力犯罪的侵害。

c. every+序數詞/ 數詞+表示時間的詞，表示每隔一段時間……。例如：

▶ She gets her hair colored **every three weeks**, watches her diet—sticking to chicken, fish and vegetables—and drinks lots of water, while trying not to drink alcohol.
她每三週染髮一次，非常注意飲食搭配，只吃雞肉、魚和蔬菜，喝大量水，並盡可能不喝酒。

▶ He had his hair cut **every second week** at the barber's near the market square.
每兩週他都去市場廣場附近的理髮店理髮。

d. each指的是由兩個或兩個以上的人或物組成的團體，強調每個成員。相對every而言，each突出「個體」、「各自」的概念。

▶ On average, **each** person in Japan consumes around 100 grams of fish every day, in forms such as sushi, tempura and sashimi.
平均每個日本人每天都會透過吃壽司、天婦羅、生魚片消費掉100克左右的魚。

e. each+minute/day/week/month/year，表示每個時間點都……，意為「每分鐘／每天／每週／每月／每年」。但是，each不能和數詞連用。every other week不能説成each other week；every two weeks不能説成each two weeks。

　　包含every 和each的名詞片語作主詞時，後面的動詞通常用單數形式。

▶ Every parent expects their child to be perfect; parents should accept their children's actual levels and abilities.
每位父母都望子成龍，但他們應該接受孩子實際的水準和能力。

▶ Each passenger is limited to one carry-on bag and one personal item such as a purse or laptop.
每位乘客只允許帶一件手提行李和一件個人物品如錢包或筆記型電腦。

　　回指包含every 和each的名詞片語時，如果指人，則用第三人稱單數，如him/his/her/hers；如果指物，則用it或its。如果性別不明或者説話者（作者）持反對性別歧視的態度，可用第三人稱複數如their/them/they/theirs。

▶ Every woman has feelings of insecurity about her body, stomach, breasts, and thighs.
女人們各個都會對自己的體形、腹部、胸部和大腿不自信。

▶ Every child is different in his or her own way.
每個孩子都有自己的特色。

(2)some，any，no

a. some表示不確定的數量，有「一些」的意思，不確指。some後面可以接複數可數名詞或不可數名詞。例如：

▶ For some industries, the biggest worry is that the weather is becoming more unpredictable.
天氣越來越難以預料，這成了一些行業最頭痛的事。

▶ Playground closed because some equipment did not meet European safety standards and the equipment has not been replaced.
由於一些設施沒有達到歐洲安全標準，而且至今沒有更換，所以運動場被關閉了。

b. some還可以表示某個未知或不重要的人或物，一般和單數可數名詞連用。例如：

▶ Every time you see some woman giving birth on television she's screaming and yelling and there's blood everywhere.
每次你在電視上看見婦女生孩子，都會聽見撕心裂肺的叫喊，看見到處是血跡。

c. some還可以表示對某事物讚美的意思。例如：

▶ It's going to be some party. 這將會是個非常棒的聚會。

d. some＋days/weeks/months/years，指一段時間。例如：

▶ My mother died last year and I was unable for some months even to recollect her face.
去年媽媽去世了，好幾個月裡我甚至不敢回憶她的樣子。

e. some一般用於肯定句中，較少用於疑問句。當用於疑問句時，表示提問者希望得到肯定的回答。例如：

▶ Shall I make some coffee? 要不我去煮點咖啡？

f. any通常用於疑問句和否定句，表示「任何」的意思，後面跟單數、複數可數名詞和不可數名詞，用來談論某事物，但不確定它的具體數量或不確定它是否發生。例如：

▶ Did you send any messages that day?
那天你發過消息嗎？

▶ I'm not making any conditions, I've already changed my will, but I'd like you to do one thing for me.
我不是在談條件，我已修改過遺囑了，但是我希望你為我做件事。

g. any也可以用於肯定句中，這時它表示在一個群體中的任何一個人或事物。例如：

▶ Any person who is convicted of a violation can be fined or imprisoned depending on the number of convictions.
任何人如被判違法，會根據違法次數接受罰款或判刑。

────── 注意！ ──────

包含any的名詞片語作主詞時，後面的動詞用單數形式。例如：

▶ Any person in a senior position within our government during this time bears some element of responsibility for our government's actions.
這段時期在政府任要職的任何人都應該對政府的行為負責。

h. no通常表示人或事物的不存在，可修飾單數、複數可數名詞和不可數名詞。例如：

▶ There is probably no music festival in the world that generates such open-hearted emotion.
也許世界上沒有哪個音樂節能像它一樣讓人如此敞開心扉。

no與not any意義比較接近，但是語氣更強。而且當包含no的片語出現在句首時，不能用not any代替no。比如：no 可以用在告示中，表示「禁止」。

▶NO SMOKING　禁止吸菸

▶NO PARKING　禁止停車

(3)either，neither

a. either和any的意思相似，表示「兩者都……」或「兩者中的任何一個都……」，後面都可以接單數可數名詞。包含either/neither的名詞片語作主詞時，後面的動詞為單數形式。例如：

▶The village in the north-west of the island is only 15 minutes from either town.
村莊坐落在島的西北部，距兩個鎮都只有15分鐘路程。

b. either還有和each相似的意思，表示兩者都有可能性，但應分別考慮。例如：

▶I think either option is inherently unfair.
我覺得兩個選擇本質上都是不公平的。

c. either可以用在否定句中，表示兩者都不，與neither意思相近，但語氣較弱。例如：

▶I've also read the ones that try to make a hero of him, and I don't believe either side.
我也讀過一些文章，把他歌頌成英雄，但兩種觀點我都不認可。

d. neither通常表示「兩者都不」，後面接單數可數名詞，是either的否定形式，即：neither=not either。

▶For many years, neither party made much impact on British politics.
多年來，無論哪個政黨對英國的政治都沒什麼大的影響。

包含neither 的名詞或名詞片語，位於句子的起始部分和主詞前時，主詞和動詞需要倒裝。例如：

▶In neither study did we see increased death rates from bladder cancer among women who used permanent hair dye, not even long-term use of permanent hair dye.
我們在任何研究中都沒有發現曾使用或長期使用持久染髮劑會增加女性的膀胱癌死亡率。

(4) enough

　　enough一般表示足夠的量，可接複數可數名詞和不可數名詞。例如：

▶ The American Red Cross shipped **enough** food this Sunday to feed 1,000 families for a month. 美國紅十字會本周日運送了食物，足夠1,000 個家庭維持一個月。

前位限定詞 ▷

　　前位限定詞主要有以下幾種：

　　1. 量詞：all, both, half。

　　2. 倍數詞：double, twice, three times等。

　　3. 分數詞：one-third, two-fifths等。

　　4. 其他表示限定意思的詞：such, what和quite等。

　　前位限定詞可以放在某些中位限定詞的前面，如冠詞（a/an/the）、所有格限定詞（my/your/his/her）、指示限定詞、名詞所有格等前面。例如：all the people，half a bottle，such a thing，both Helen's parents等。

　　由於前位限定詞本身就含有數量的概念，所以不能放在同樣有數量概念的不定限定詞如every/either/neither/some/any等前面。

　　前位限定詞是互相排斥的，即不能同時使用。例如：可以說all the boys，half the boys，但不能說all half the boys。

◎ all，both，half

❶ all

　　all表示所有或全部，可以作限定詞，也可以作代名詞。

　　1. all可以指事物的全部、整體

(1) 接單數可數名詞或者集體名詞，表示整體，這樣的名詞有way，world，family，crew 等。例如：

▶ The bitter winter had **all** the country in its grip.
整個國家都被寒冬籠罩著。

(2) 接表示時間的詞，指某個時段的全部，一般不使用定冠詞。例如：all day，all afternoon，all night，all week，all month，all year，all spring，all one's life。

▶ They rested most of the day and then walked **all** night.
他們的白天幾乎都用來休息，然後晚上繼續前進。

　　但是也有例外。例如：all the time表示一直或整個時段，定冠詞不能省略。

(3)接不可數名詞，表示全部的數量。例如：

▶ Some places had **all** the rain they would normally expect during the whole of November in just 72 hours.
僅僅在72個小時內，有些地方的雨量就達到了整個11月的正常預期量。

(4)接地區、國家等名詞，表示在各區域裡的全體人員。例如：all China，all Paris等。

▶ And we have a nine-year-old boy on the program tonight who is said to be one of the best violin players in **all** America.
今晚將有一個9歲的男孩上節目，他被譽為全美最棒的小提琴手之一。

注意！

當all表示全體的時候，它與形容詞whole的意思非常相似，通常與表示時間的名詞連用。例如：all day = the whole day。
all與單數可數名詞或者集體名詞連用。例如：all the family = the whole family，all the cake = the whole cake。
如果所修飾的名詞是抽象名詞，一般用the whole而不用all the。例如：the whole truth。

2. all用來概括一個整體中所有成員

all後面接複數可數名詞或不可數名詞，概括每一個可能的人或物，如使用特指限定詞，指一個特定整體中所有成員。例如：

▶ By 2006, **all** teachers must be highly qualified in the subject and grade level they teach.
到2006年，所有教師必須完全達到所教課程和所在年級水準的要求。

▶ Not **all** the stories are equally successful.
不是所有故事都一樣成功。

3. all表示極度的意思

all與介係詞in/with連用，後面接抽象名詞，可以表示極度的意思。例如：in all honesty，with all speed， with all sincerity，with all certainty，in all seriousness。

▶ But in **all** honesty we have all learned a lot from him.
但是，說實話，我們大家從他身上學到了不少。

4. all表示任何的意思

all與any的意思相似，都可以表示任何的意思。all接可數名詞。例如：beyond all expectations，at all costs，at all events，at all hours，at all points，at all risks等。

▶ Langer again paid tribute to his team, who performed beyond all expectations.
出乎所有人的意料，球隊發揮出色，蘭格再一次感謝了他們。

5. all表示唯一的意思

all還可以表示唯一的意思，與only相似。例如：

▶ All the indications that we have confirm the hope of a release of three hostages soon.
從我們得到的所有消息來看，三位人質有希望很快被釋放。

❷ both

both 表示兩個人或物的全部，兩者都包含在內。一般接複數可數名詞，含有both 的名詞片語作主詞，動詞為複數形式。both 可作限定詞，也可作代名詞。例如：

▶ But he figures both houses are worth keeping because they help diversify his investments.
但他認為這兩幢房子能使自己的投資多樣化，挺值的。

❸ half

half表示數量的一半，可接單數、複數可數名詞和不可數名詞。因為是前位限定詞，後面可以跟一些中位限定詞，如不定冠詞a，定冠詞the，例如：half a pound/mile/pint/hour。

half有時還可以作後位限定詞，出現在「a half +名詞」的結構中，例如：a half hour/mile/day。

▶ She has two half day classes.
她有兩個半天的課。

◎ 倍數詞

倍數詞（Multiplicatives）與名詞連用，表示數量和大小，可接單數、複數可數名詞和不可數名詞。倍數詞、分數詞、基數詞和序數詞都可以作為限定詞或代名詞使用，表示明確的數量。（參見P089〈代名詞〉）

倍數詞的構成非常簡單，除了兩倍是twice，其他均由「數詞＋times」組成，例如：three times，four times。由於倍數詞是前位限定詞，所以它後面可以跟一些中位限定詞，如不定冠詞a/an、定冠詞the、所有格限定詞等。

1. 表示時間的倍數。例如：twice a day/week/year。

▶ I have a good friend who goes backpacking about **twice a year** in the Grand Canyon.
  我的一位好朋友每年兩次背著背包徒步去大峽谷旅行。

2 表示數量的倍數。例如：twice the size/number/rate/amount。

▶ Their house is **twice the size** of ours.
  他們的房子是我們的兩倍大。

分數詞

分數詞（Fractional Numerals）與名詞連用表示數量，常指事物或人的團體的一部分，可接各類名詞。分數詞可作名詞、代名詞等。

分數詞由兩部分構成，分子是基數詞（one，two，three等）或a，分母是序數詞（third，fourth，fifth等）或quarter。如果分子大於1，序數詞要用複數。例如：

- 1/3：one/a third
- 2/5：two fifths
- 3/4：three quarters或three fourths

當分數詞作為前位限定詞修飾名詞時，表示分子和分母的詞中間也可以加上連字號。例如：one/a-third pound，two-fifths gallon。

如果是修飾特指事物，分數詞後面還應加the。例如：

▶ three-quarters **the** length
  長度的四分之三

▶ The Pacific Ocean is about one-third **the** circumference of the globe.
  太平洋占了地球面積的約三分之一。

後位限定詞 ▽

後位限定詞位於前位限定詞和中位限定詞後，主要包括基數詞、序數詞和量詞。

基數詞

基數詞指用來表述一個群體中的部分成員的數量，即多少個。如下表所示：

1~10	11~19	20~99	100~1,000,000,000,000
1 one	11 eleven	20 twenty	100 a/one hundred
2 two	12 twelve	21 twenty-one	1,000 a/one thousand
3 three	13 thirteen	22 twenty-two	10,000 ten thousand
4 four	14 fourteen	30 thirty	100,000 a/one hundred thousand
5 five	15 fifteen	31 thirty-one	1,000,000 a/one million
6 six	16 sixteen	40 forty	10,000,000 ten million
7 seven	17 seventeen	50 fifty	100,000,000 a/one hundred million
8 eight	18 eighteen	60 sixty	1,000,000,000 a/one billion
9 nine	19 nineteen	70 seventy	1,000,000,000,000 a/one trillion
10 ten		80 eighty	
		90 ninety	
		99 ninety-nine	

101以上的百位元數字，在百位元和十位間加and，美式英語通常會省略。例如：101為one hundred (and) one。

1001以上的數字，從個位向前，每三位元數為一個單位，用「,」分開。第一個「,」前為thousand，第二個「,」前為 million，第三個「,」前為billion。在讀的時候，這些單位後面不加and，以每三位元數為一個單位朗讀。

- 1,001：a /one thousand, (and) one
- 2,188：two thousand, one hundred (and) eighty-eight
- 423,368：four hundred (and) twenty-three thousand, three hundred (and) sixty-eight
- 21,233,988：twenty-one million, two hundred (and) thirty-three thousand, nine hundred (and) eighty-eight

hundred，thousand 和million在這些表達中要用單數形式。hundred，thousand和million等前面的第一位數是1時，可以用a，也可以用one，可參見上表。一般來說，one比a更具有強調作用。但如果數字1出現在中間，要用one。

基數詞充當限定詞，指明所修飾的名詞的數量，屬於後位限定詞，所以和其他限定詞連用的時候，一般位於其他限定詞之後。它的前面可以用定冠詞、代名詞所有格等特指限定詞，也可以用any，every，one等泛指限定詞。例如：the two sides of a coin，her three naughty kids，any three students等。

▶ She walks up to the village shop **every three days** or so for supplies.
大概每三天她都要步行到村裡的商店買點生活用品。

▶Now the two women were inseparable, although they were quite different in nature, and complemented one another like the two sides of a coin.

儘管她們的性格迥異，但現在這兩個女人已形影不離，像一枚硬幣的正反兩面那樣相伴相隨。

序數詞

❶ 序數詞

序數詞表示某個人或物在一個群體中的順序，即第幾個。如下表所示：

1~10	11~19	20~99
1 first	11 eleventh	20 twentieth
2 second	12 twelfth	21 twenty-first
3 third	13 thirteenth	22 twenty-second
4 fourth	14 fourteenth	30 thirtieth
5 fifth	15 fifteenth	40 fortieth
6 sixth	16 sixteenth	50 fiftieth
7 seventh	17 seventeenth	60 sixtieth
8 eighth	18 eighteenth	70 seventieth
9 ninth	19 nineteenth	80 eightieth
10 tenth		90 ninetieth
		99 ninety-ninth
		100 hundredth

序數詞的構成一般是在基數詞字尾加-th，例如：fourth，sixth，seventh，eleventh等。但是也有特殊寫法，例如：first第一，second 第二，third第三， fifth第五，eighth第八，twelfth第十二等。

對於字尾是以e結尾的情況，去e加-th，例如：ninth第九。對於字尾是以ty結尾的情況，去y加-ieth，例如：thirtieth第三十。

序數詞書寫成數字，在阿拉伯數字後加上相應序數詞的最後兩個字母：1st第一，2nd第二，3rd第三，30th第三十，100th第一百等。

由於序數詞表示具體的順序，有特指的意思，所以一般前面要加定冠詞the或代名詞所有格等特指限定詞。例如：the first reason，the second candidate等。

▶He worked hard right from his first job, as an indentured apprentice in his brother James' Boston printing shop.

他的第一份工作是在哥哥詹姆斯開在波士頓的印刷廠裡做契約學徒，那時的他就勤勤懇懇。

▶I was heavily into the first season of Friends, and then lost interest in it completely at some point.

《六人行》第一季的劇情讓我沉迷其中，但後來某個時候我卻對它完全沒了興趣。

但是也有例外。序數詞前面可以加不定冠詞a，表示「還有」、「再一個」、「又一次」。例如：

▶ Laughing, Maggie kissed her mother a second time, and then kissed her dad.
　瑪姬笑著又親了媽媽一下，接著親了一下爸爸。

當序數詞與基數詞連用時，一般序數詞在前。例如：the first two chapters，the last three persons等。

❷ 一般序數詞

還有幾個比較特殊的序數詞：last，next，other，another。由於這些詞能幫助確定順序，所以也將其歸為序數詞，但為了與其他序數詞區別，稱之為「一般序數詞」，也有學者把它們歸為不定限定詞。

1. last，next

last和next後面可以接單數和複數名詞，也可以和定冠詞或代名詞所有格等特指限定詞連用。如果與基數詞連用，位於基數詞前面。例如：the last two months，the next two pages，his last book等。

▶ The new contract, reached last week, was a rare and relative victory for Europe's unionized workers, who have suffered a series of significant setbacks since June.
　歐洲工會的工人從6月開始遭受了一連串的重大打擊，而上周達成的新協定相對而言算是一個難得的勝利了。

▶ A Spanish bullfight is planned for next month in a specially constructed ring in the Shanghai Sports Stadium.
　下個月，一場西班牙鬥牛表演將在上海體育館專門修建的鬥牛場進行。

但是在一些時間運算式中，通常不用定冠詞。例如：next week，next time，last year。

2. other，another

other可作代名詞、副詞和限定詞。作限定詞時表示「另外的，其他的」，後面可接單數和複數名詞。

如果要特指，前面要加定冠詞the。例如：the other people，any other question，some other friends等。

▶ Archaeologists and other experts recently finished examining the bones, and have solved some of the mysteries surrounding them.
　考古學家和其他專家近期已結束了對骨骼的檢查，並且解開了關於這些骨骼的一些秘密。

another可作代名詞和限定詞。作限定詞時表示「再一個，另一個」，後面可接單數和複數名詞。例如：another girl，another reason，another three years等。

▶ There is **another** possibility that they haven't mentioned.
還有另外一種可能性他們沒有提到。

◎ 量詞

量詞（Quantifiers）是表示人或事物數量的詞，可以作代名詞，也可以作限定詞。前面章節所介紹的all，both，half，any，some，enough和no也屬於量詞，只是位置不同。本節我們討論量詞作為後位限定詞的作用，其代名詞作用請參見代名詞的相關章節。

量詞可分為封閉類量詞（Closed-system Quantifiers）和開放類量詞（Opensystem Quantifiers）。

❶ 封閉類量詞

封閉類量詞可分為只與複數名詞連用和只與不可數名詞連用兩類。

只與複數名詞連用。例如：many，(a) few和several等。

▶ Police, who have seen too **many** accidents in the past couple days, will have a warning for Christmas day drivers.
過去的幾天事故多發，所以在耶誕節期間，員警會對駕駛員提出警告。

只與不可數名詞連用。例如：much，(a) little等。

▶ There's been so **much** expectation on him but I like the way he handles himself.
他身上承載了太多的期望，但是我很欣賞他掌控自己的方式。

1. many

many一般修飾複數可數名詞，前面可加the和代名詞所有格這類的特指限定詞，表示「非常多」，如the many people，the many things等。例如：

▶ One of **the many** things I loved about the movie was that all of the characters behaved in character, yet the choices they made were surprising as well as believable.
我喜歡這部電影的一點就是，所有劇中人物的行為符合他們的個性，他們的選擇雖然是意料之外，但又是情理之中。

many＋不定冠詞a/an，表示很多，是一種很正式的用法。如果作主詞，後面的動詞用單數形式。例如：many a thing（許多事情），many a time（經常）。

▶The growth of home-schooling drives many a public school educator to despair.
　在家上學這一現象的蔓延讓許多公立學校的教育家感到絕望。

　　many和much在比較兩種數目相同的事物時，前後加as：as many/much +名詞+ as。例如：

▶She believes there will be about as many women officials as there are of such Englishmen.
　她相信英國女性官員的人數將和男性一樣多。

2. much

　　much 一般用於否定句或含否定意味的句子和疑問句中，表示「許多」。例如：

▶We haven't got much time, so you had better speak quickly with your comments and questions.
　時間有限，你最好將評論和問題說得快一些。

▶Is there too much violence on TV?
　電視上有過多暴力鏡頭嗎？

3. more，most

　　many和much還有相應的比較級和最高級，即more 和most，它們可與複數可數名詞和不可數名詞連用。more 表示所修飾的名詞的數量比一般還要多。例如：

▶If they paid more attention to the test, I think they'd do better.
　如果他們能對考試多加重視的話，我覺得他們會做得更好。

　　most表示一個特定團體中的大多數人或物，或者某物幾乎所有的部分。例如：

▶But most drivers are not prepared to give up their cars — 80 percent say they could not live without them.
　但是大多數司機不願意不開車，甚至80％的人說，沒了車就沒法生活。

4. few，a few

　　few和a few與複數可數名詞連用。few是小數目的否定意義，表示「幾乎沒有」或「非常少」。例如：

▶With regard to money, few enterprise search vendors can match Google's financial position.
　從資金來看，幾乎沒有其他搜索公司能和谷歌的經濟實力相抗衡。

a few沒有否定意思，表示「一些」，但是數量也很少。例如：

▶ A **few** years ago, I met John Thaw, who died six months ago.
約翰·陶半年前去世了，幾年前我認識了他。

但是a few加上quite，good，not或some還可以表示數目比較大。例如：quite a few，a good few，not a few，some few。其中some few表示的數目比其他幾個結構表示的數目要少，但多於a few。例如：

▶ There are **quite a few** countries that have got kings and queens but they've paid their way.
現在相當多的國家還保留君主，但他們自己養活自己。

▶ If we go to a club in London, there will be **a good few** people in there who will have heard of Westlife.
如果去倫敦的某個俱樂部，那裡還是會有相當多的人知道西城男孩的。

▶ I could understand **some few** syllables that she said to me, by placing my ear close to her lips.
我把耳朵湊近她的嘴唇，還是能聽懂她對我說的幾個音節。

如要特指數量較少的事物或人，可在few前面加the，表示「為數不多」。例如：

▶ These are among **the few** new neighborhoods offering homes for less than $300,000.
這裡是為數不多幾個提供低於30萬美金房子的新社區之一。

few還可與時間單位連用。例如：the last/next few minutes，every few minutes。

▶ He has learned an awful lot from his father in **the last few months**.
在過去的幾個月裡，他從父親身上學到了很多東西。

▶ This safety check will be repeated **every few hours** during the trip.
在旅途中，每隔幾個小時就會重複這樣的安全檢查。

5. fewer，fewest

fewer和fewest分別是few的比較級和最高級，可接複數可數名詞。fewer表示數目更小，如果要比較兩組事物或人中哪組數量更少，可用比較結構「fewer＋名詞＋than……」。例如：

▶ The U.S. labor force has about 5.6 million **fewer workers** now **than** when the recession began in 2001.
與2001年經濟蕭條爆發時相比，美國現在的勞動力少了約560萬。

用最高級fewest表示數量的最小。例如：

▶ Last week, U.S. workers filed the **fewest** applications for unemployment benefits since early September, a sign that the U.S. job picture continues to brighten.
上週，美國申領失業救濟金的人數達到了9月初以來的最低，這說明美國的就業形勢在持續好轉。

6. little，a little

little和a little與不可數名詞連用。little是小數目的否定意義，表示「幾乎沒有」或「非常少」。例如：

▶ Given **little** food, water, or rest, they worked from dawn to dusk gathering, breaking, loading, and moving rocks.
他們從黎明工作到了黃昏，不斷採集、粉碎、裝運岩石，但幾乎得不到食物、水和休息。

a little沒有否定意思，表示「一些」，但是數量也很少。例如：

▶ This sort of drill is also a way for police to warn protesters and perhaps put **a little** fear into anyone who wants to break the law.
這種演練也是員警警告示威者的一種手段，或許能對企圖違法的人產生一些威懾力。

如要特指數量較少的事物，可在little前面加the，表示「少量」。例如：

▶ I can tell you **the little** discussion back and forth between Audrey and Diane worries me. 聽我說，奧德莉和戴安娜之間的小爭辯令我擔心。

如果要強調「僅有一點」，可在little前面加what，構成what little片語，強調量很少。例如：

▶ With **what little** money I had I would try to wear unusual suits or hats, learning a combination of subtlety and the unexpected in order to gain attention. 儘管囊中羞澀，我仍然儘量穿戴得與眾不同，學著在巧妙精細和出人意料上下工夫，以便引起別人的注意。

7. less，least

less和least是little的比較級和最高級，可接不可數名詞。

(1)less表示某事物數目更小，如果要比較兩個事物中哪個數量更少，可用比較結構「less＋名詞＋than……」。例如：

▶ Teachers maybe have known the fact that a large number of children at present leave school at sixteen knowing **less** mathematics **than** when they entered at eleven.
老師們或許已經注意到，現在很多孩子在16歲畢業時所掌握的數學知識比他們11歲入學時還要少。

(2)no less 一般表示「不少於」，還可以強調數量之大或某人某事的重要性。例如：

▶ He has sold **no less than** five cars, each one at a tidy profit.
　他已經賣了不止五輛車了，每賣一輛車他都賺了可觀的一筆。

▶ This brilliant idea had come from **no less a person than** the famous Sylvia Grey— who could sing, dance and play the piano.
　著名的西爾維婭‧格雷不僅能歌善舞還會彈鋼琴，這個偉大的創意只有她才會想得出來。

(3)表示數量的最少，用最高級least。例如：

▶ You have the **least** experience in the golf industry of all the candidates.
　在所有人選中，你在高爾夫行業方面擁有的經驗最少。

❷ 開放類量詞

　　與封閉類量詞相對應的是數量很大的開放類片語量詞，一般由一個數量名詞＋of 組成，前面還會有不定冠詞。

　　一些開放類量詞只能修飾不可數名詞，例如：a great/good deal of，a large/small quantity/amount of。

　　有些只能修飾可數名詞，例如：a great/large/good number of。例如：

▶ During the month, southern Canada saw **a great deal of** unsettled weather.
　在那個月中，加拿大南部的天氣變幻莫測。

▶ If the idea of longer working lives looks like bad news for many employees, **a large number of** employers are less than happy about it either.
　如果對於很多上班族來說，延長工作年限並不是一個好消息，那麼對很多老闆而言，這也不是一件令人開心的事。

　　當「開放類量詞＋不可數名詞」作主詞時，謂語動詞採用第三人稱單數形式；當「開放類量詞＋可數名詞」作主詞時，謂語動詞採用複數形式。

　　還有一些開放類量詞既可修飾複數可數名詞，又可以修飾不可數名詞，例如：plenty of，lots of，a lot of。

▶ I have **plenty of** married friends who aren't all that happy.
　我有很多結了婚的朋友，並非都那麼幸福。

小結 ▽

　　本章介紹了英語中非常重要的一類詞——限定詞。限定詞按照其位置順序可以分為前位、中位和後位限定詞。除了冠詞，限定詞中很多詞可以充當代名詞，也可以扮演副詞的角色。冠詞是限定詞中使用最頻繁的一類詞，而且有很多約定俗成的用法。

代名詞

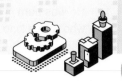

代名詞概說 ▷

　　按照英語字面上的意思，代名詞就是名詞的替身，即起替代名詞的作用。有了代名詞，既能避免名詞在句子中不必要的重複，又能顯現出句子成分如主詞和受詞之間的關係。

代名詞的分類 ▷

　　代名詞大致分為人稱代名詞、代名詞所有格、反身代名詞、相互代名詞、指示代名詞、不定代名詞、疑問代名詞和關係代名詞。

◎ 人稱代名詞

　　人稱代名詞（Personal Pronouns）用於指稱發話者或自己的一方（如I，we）、受話方（如you）、被提及的一方（如he，she，they，it）。

　　1. 第一人稱（First Person）單數「我」，英語用I表示，它總是大寫。複數「我們」，用we表示。例如：

▶I took a modern dance course and learned to make silver jewelry last year.
　去年，我參加了現代舞學習班，還學習了製作銀飾。

▶We took over a building that was vacant for years. 我們接管一棟閒置了好幾年的大樓。

▶I can tell the wholesaler that we didn't make that product.
　我可以告訴那個批發商，那個產品不是我們製造的。

　　2. 第二人稱（Second Person）單數「你」，英語用you表示。複數「你們」，也用相同的形式you表示。例如：

▶Ken, did you see that program last night where they had women dressing up as men and men dressing as women?
　肯，你看了昨天晚上那個將女人打扮成男人、男人打扮成女人的節目嗎？

▶Leith has just been telling me that you both work for the same firm.
　利思正向我說起你們倆在同一個公司工作的事呢。

▶What do you three know about detective work? 有關偵探工作，你們三人知道些什麼？

3. 第三人稱（Third Person）單數「他」、「她」、「它」，分別表示男性、女性和人以外的事物，英語分別用he和she表示。第三人稱的複數全部用they指稱。例如：

▶ **He** was born in the Caribbean, of a woman who probably was a prostitute and the father who was a kind of derelict.
他生於加勒比海，其母可能是妓女，其父是個類似無家可歸的人。

▶ Does **she** resent people thinking that child stars must be in line for a meltdown?
她對人們認為童星註定要失敗這種想法不滿嗎？

▶ As **it** eats and grows, the caterpillar sheds its skin five times over two weeks, then attaches itself to the underside of the leaf and forms a chrysalis.
毛毛蟲邊吃邊長，兩週內脫去5次殼，然後貼附在葉片的背面結成蛹。

▶ But sometimes because **they** are female **they're** more suitable for interviewing men susceptible to so-called feminine charm.
但因為是女性，她們有時更適合與那些容易被所謂的女性魅力所打動的男人面談。

▶ **He** and his England teammates must show **they** are men and not boys at Bristol today. Can **they** do that?
他和他的英格蘭隊友們今天在布里斯托必須證明他們是男子漢，而不是小孩。他們能做到嗎？

▶ **They** are large herbivores, each possessing four legs, a tail and an udder. Where do they live?
它們是巨大的食草動物，長著四條腿、一條尾巴和一隻乳房。它們在何處生活？

4. 泛指人稱one作單數人稱代名詞用，有「一般人」、「每人」的意思。一般用於較正式的場合。例如：

▶ **One** should bear in mind that the media and intellectual elites generally have their particular agendas.
人人都應該記住，媒體和知識份子的精英們通常有他們自己特別的日程表。

▶ **One** should feel sympathy, even grief, for the miserable death of this outstanding writer.
對於這位文壇泰斗的不幸逝世，人人都應該感到同情，甚至是悲痛。

▶ What does **one** call that type of person in polite society?
上流社會中的這類人該稱作什麼？

◎ 所有格代名詞

所有格代名詞（Possessive Pronouns）用於表示事物對人稱代名詞的所屬關係。英語中的第一人稱、第二人稱和第三人稱單數的所有格代名詞分別是mine，yours，his，hers，複數的所有格代名詞分別是ours，yours，theirs。

it沒有所有格代名詞形式。所有格代名詞在句中起相當於名詞片語的作用，充當主詞、主詞補語、受詞、介係詞補語和同位語等功能。例如：

▶ "The trains still aren't on time. **Mine** has just been delayed by another 12 minutes, so I think every day should be a free day at this rate," said one commuter.

一名乘客說：「火車還是誤點。我坐的車次又遲了12分鐘，所以我想，照這樣的速度，每天都應該免費。」

▶ That means that if a hog is on your property, it's considered **yours**.

那就意味著，如果一頭豬在你的院子裡，那它就是你的了。

▶ I've heard of this writer but I've not read anything of **his**.

我聽說過這個作家，但還沒有讀過他的任何作品。

▶ Their equipment is more sophisticated than **ours**.

他們的設備比我們的還要先進。

▶ Robert Altman has well-known political ideas. And **mine** aren't exactly a secret. **Yours** aren't hidden either.

羅伯特·奧爾特曼有許多有名的政治觀點。而且嚴格地講，我的觀點不是秘密，你的也不是。

▶ My view of the future is much different than **theirs**, and it's based on much more detailed information.

關於未來，我的看法與他們的大不相同，我的觀點是建立在更為細節的資訊上的。

所有格代名詞可與of 片語搭配，構成雙重所有格關係。例如：

▶ **A friend of mine** was told she had six months to live, and lived for another four years.

我的一個朋友曾被告知只能活6個月，但她卻又活了4年。

▶ Berger, in his dark suit with **that ravaged face of his**, was a chilling presence as he nodded formally and clicked his heels.

伯傑穿著一套深色的西裝，滿臉創傷，一本正經地點著頭，哧嗒一聲併攏腳跟，他的出現讓人毛骨悚然。

▶ Was **a typical letter of yours** clear, short and to the point, Helen?

海倫，你以前寫信都清楚、簡潔、切題，對嗎？

▶ I'd like to have all three of you if **that mom of yours** goes and spends the rest of her life repenting.

如果你們那個母親天天嘮叨後悔，我就收養你們三人。

▶ I am much more interested in just how much you can do with **those amazing eyes of yours**.

我更感興趣的是你用你那雙令人讚歎的眼睛到底能做些什麼。

🎯 反身代名詞

當句子中的動作實施者與動作對象為同一人稱時，動作對象用反身代名詞（Reflexive Pronouns）表示。英語中的第一人稱、第二人稱和第三人稱單數的反身代名詞分別為myself，yourself，himself，herself，itself，複數的反身代名詞分別為ourselves，yourselves，themselves。

在使用反身代名詞時要注意，第二人稱單複數的反身代名詞的形式是不同的，單數是yourself，複數是yourselves。例如：

▶ I decided to treat **myself** to one of my favourite small indulgences today—dark chocolate wafer cookies.
今天，我決定用一種最喜歡的小東西好好犒勞一下自己——嘗嘗那黑巧克力薄脆餅。

▶ If you've come back in order to prove to **yourself** that Jerry still loves you, I'd think that was a mistake.
如果你回來的目的是要證明傑瑞仍然愛你，我想那你就錯了。

▶ Later he locked **himself** in a hotel room for a month, sobbing and unable to sleep.
後來的一個月裡，他把自己關在飯店的房間裡，整天在哭，無法安眠。

▶ Greek basketball team gave **themselves** a good chance to qualify after holding impressive Spain to a draw.
希臘籃球隊與球技熟練的西班牙隊打了個平局，這給了希臘隊一個取得參賽資格的好機會。

▶ Folly's enthusiasm took over and she found **herself** pouring out the whole story.
愚蠢的狂熱佔據了上風，她不知不覺地把所有的事和盤托出。

▶ The country is under pressure to relieve **itself** of the financial burden of caring for so many refugees.
該國要擺脫因照顧這麼多的難民所帶來的財政負擔，壓力很大。

注意！

反身代名詞一般不與人們作用於自身的動作連用，如給自己穿衣、刮鬍子或洗刷等動作時，就不會使用反身代名詞。但有時為了表達某些讓人驚訝的事情，或為了強調某種情況，就可以使用反身代名詞。例如：

▶ Five years later, Smith can't feed or dress **herself**.
五年之後，史密斯就無法自己吃飯或穿衣了。

在一個句子中，如果主詞和介係詞受詞是同一人稱，句子又沒有直接的受詞，這時介係詞受詞可用反身代名詞表示。但是，如果句子有其直接受詞，這時介係詞後面只能帶人稱代名詞的受格。例如：

▶ The fact is that by nature I am a very reserved person and like to keep my private life to **myself**.
我天生就是一個很矜持的人，喜歡給自己留點個人生活空間，這是個事實。

▶ There can hardly be a man in the Western world who does not know the rules: treat female colleagues with respect, give them equal pay and keep your hands to **yourself**.
在西方世界裡，這些規則幾乎無人不曉：尊重女性同事，同工同酬，行為檢點。

▶The legislation would have allowed principals to remove students from schools if they committed a crime and posed a threat to **themselves** and classmates.

假如學生觸犯了法律、對自己和同學構成了威脅，本法規就允許校長將他們開除。

▶When we're at my in-laws' beach house, my husband and I sometimes leave our kids with their grandparents so we can have some time to **ourselves**.

住在婆家的海濱別墅時，丈夫和我有時讓孩子們和爺爺奶奶待在一起，這樣我們就能有點自己的時間。

▶Purple calls attention to **itself** without being too aggressive.

紫色能引人注意，但又不會顯得過於放肆。

▶He was totally at ease with **himself**, confident about whom he was.

他十分從容自若，對自己充滿信心。

在口語中，人們為了強調和對比，常在介係詞或動詞後面使用反身代名詞而不用人稱代名詞的主格形式。例如：

▶Leighton has told staff that if the company makes profits of 400 million pounds for the year ending in March 2005, all staff, with the exception of **himself**, will receive the bonus.

萊頓告訴職員，如果到2005年3月底公司能賺4億英鎊的年利潤，除了他自己，所有的職員將得到獎勵。

▶It can be wise to cut **yourself** free from a relationship gone sour, whether it's fictional or otherwise.

讓自己擺脫不和諧的關係是明智的，不管它是否真的存在。

▶It might be wise to set **yourself** a maximum target for the number of drinks you are going to have—the fewer better.

先給自己規定最多喝幾杯酒——越少越好，這或許是明智的。

反身代名詞還可以放在同一指稱的人稱代名詞後面，起強調作用。有時，反身代名詞還可以與同一指稱的代名詞相隔一些詞語放在句子末尾。例如：

▶Blanche **herself** was to return home in September, six weeks before the wedding date, with her mother to prepare for the occasion.

布蘭奇本人打算在9月份，即舉行婚禮的6週前回家，以便和母親一起準備婚事。

▶I **myself** spend an hour or two a day in the garden hut with my father-in-law, dismantling the baby's cot and highchair.

在花園的棚屋裡，我自己和岳父一起，一天花上一兩個小時，把嬰兒床、兒童椅一一拆開。

▶Judy believes that London **itself** is depressing.

裘蒂認為倫敦這個地方很壓抑。

▶If you have to pay for something **yourself**, you use it more cautiously.

如果你必須自己為某件東西付錢，你就會更小心地使用它。

▶He designed an attractive plush toy **himself** and brought it to market in 1994.

他自己設計了一種很好看的長毛絨玩具，並於1994年在市場上銷售。

某人在沒有他人的幫助或不受他人打擾的情況下做了某事，對這種情況作陳述時，可用反身代名詞，並通常將其置於句尾。例如：

▶ They're good men—they're pulling their sledges **themselves**.
　　他們是好樣的——他們自己拉著雪橇。

🎯 相互代名詞

　　相互代名詞（Reciprocal Pronouns）用於指稱人們做相同的事、有相同的感覺或相同的關係，相互代名詞主要有each other，one another。相互代名詞只能作動詞的受詞或介係詞的受詞。例如：

▶ When students share their stories, they begin to understand **each other** regardless of what languages they speak.
　　當同學們分享各自的故事時，無論他們講哪種語言都開始相互瞭解。

▶ The twins are 26, live more than a thousand miles apart and enjoy successful careers independent of **each other**.
　　雙胞胎兄弟26歲，各自生活在相隔一千多英哩的地方，彼此獨立，事業有成。

▶ Everybody was in the same boat and everybody helped **one another**.
　　大家處境相同，相互幫助。

▶ Lately the committee's six members e-mail **one another** to discuss indicators such as industrial production, employment, and real income.
　　最近，委員會的6個成員相互之間發送電子郵件，討論諸如工業生產、就業和實際收入等指標。

▶ They were jealous of **each other**, both trying to get the trade, and I understand they really did have some fights.
　　他們相互妒忌，雙方都想得到這筆生意，據我瞭解他們還真的打過幾次架。

注意！

相互代名詞each other 和one another幾乎沒有什麼區別，它們都可用於指稱兩個或兩個以上的人或事物。不過，有的人喜歡用each other指稱只有兩個人或事物的情況，而超出兩個就用one another。

　　相互代名詞each other可以拆開使用。這時each可作主詞，other可作受詞，但other之前需加定冠詞the，而且the other可以有複數的形式。另外，相互代名詞還可以加-'s，表示其所有格形式。例如：

▶ Each one can learn from **the other**.
　　每個人都可以向別人學習。

▶ **Each**, clearly, was trying to persuade the others to go back home.
　　顯然，人人都想勸別人回家。

▶ We gained better friendships and new insight into each other's creativity.
我們建立了更深厚的友誼，對各自的創造力有了新的深刻見解。

▶ These countries are brought up to respect one another's culture, politics and, above all, to regard one another as equals in every sense.
這些國家能相互尊重各自的文化、政治，尤其是能在各個方面相互平等對待。

🎯 指示代名詞

指示代名詞（Demonstrative Pronouns）通常用於指稱事物，可在句子中作為主詞和受詞。當作受詞時，它們不像人稱代名詞那樣作間接受詞，而是作直接受詞。常用的指示代名詞有：this，that，these，those等。例如：

▶ This is a new generation, with new ideas and a new way of thinking.
這是具有新觀念、新思維的一代新人。

▶ That was probably the worst thing that ever happened.
那可能是發生過的最糟糕的事情。

▶ These are good places to go if you want to meet up with friends who might want different types of treatments.
如果你想和一些朋友見面，滿足他們不同的需要，這都是些可去的好地方。

▶ Those are legitimate public health strategies that we can employ.
那些是我們可以利用的合法的公共衛生策略。

儘管指示代名詞通常用於指稱事物，但當需要辨別某人時，可用this和that指稱單個人。同樣，these和those可用於指稱複數人稱。例如：

▶ This is an individual the President describes as a friend.
這就是總統描述為朋友的人。

▶ That is right my hairdresser.
那就是我的美髮師。

▶ These are people who don't have discretionary income.
這些就是沒有可隨意支配收入的人。

▶ Those are mostly people of moderate incomes who either cannot afford private health insurance, their employers don't provide it, or who cannot obtain private insurance because of chronic or severe health problems.
那些人大多數收入一般，他們要不是付不起個人健康保險——他們的雇主沒有提供這一保險，就是得不到個人保險，因為他們患有慢性或嚴重的疾病。

🎯 不定代名詞

　　人們在談論人或事，但又不針對某個具體的人或事時，可用不定代名詞（Indefinite Pronouns）。例如：anybody，everybody，nobody，somebody，anyone，everyone，no one，someone，anything，everything，nothing，something等。

　　以上不定代名詞中，除no one外，其他代名詞都以一個合成詞的形式出現，它們作主詞時，其謂語動詞均為單數；以-thing結尾的不定代名詞用於指稱事物、觀念、情景或活動；以-one和-body結尾的不定代名詞用於指稱人。例如：

▶ **Anybody** has a right to get up there and say whatever they want to say.
　　人人都有權上去，想說什麼就說什麼。

▶ **Nothing** sounded all that special to Moore, but two things impressed him.
　　對於穆爾，別的沒有什麼特別的事，但是有兩件事令他印象深刻。

▶ Did **anything** happen over Christmas in your house that you know would interest or amuse them?
　　你知道耶誕節在你家發生的事中，有什麼讓他們感興趣或高興的嗎？

▶ Did **somebody** ask for Miss Telford's opinion?
　　有人徵求過特爾福德小姐的意見嗎？

▶ The rules were simple: No one left the table until **everyone**'s homework was done.
　　規則很簡單：每個人把家庭作業做完，不然誰也不得離開桌子。

　　不定代名詞在句中作主詞時，謂語動詞的現在時必須是單數的形式。但是，如果用人稱代名詞與它互指，人稱代名詞要用複數的形式。這時，人稱代名詞的格有they，them，their，themselves四種形式。例如：

▶ Somebody's going to get a surprise when **they** hear the result.
　　聽到結果時，有的人會大吃一驚。

▶ If anybody said this to him, Keith would hit **them**.
　　如果有人向基斯提起這事，他不會饒過他們。

▶ Everyone is worried about **their** money and what's going to happen next to their investment.
　　人人都在擔心自己的資金，擔心他們的投資下一步會怎樣。

▶ Anyone who is foolish enough to declare **themselves** the Messiah is either misinformed, demonic or mentally challenged.
　　凡是愚蠢得宣佈自己是救世主的人，要麼是聽了錯誤的資訊，要麼是著了魔，要麼是精神上受到了刺激。

在比較正式的文體中，有的人喜歡用he，him，his，himself 與不定代名詞構成互指關係。例如：

▶ Anyone who's willing to dye **his** hair like that has to be very committed.
　凡是願意把頭髮染成這種樣子的人，必定是豁出去了。

▶ If anyone tries to escape this vicious cycle **he** is quickly punished.
　如果有人企圖逃避這種怪圈，那他就將很快受到懲罰。

▶ Anyone can call **himself** a financial planner.
　人人都可以稱自己是個理財師。

有些不定代名詞後面可以加-'s，表示所屬關係。例如：

▶ The houses were damaged by a storm and it is not **anyone's** fault.
　這些房子被暴風雨毀壞了，這不是某個人的過失。

▶ However, **everyone's** problem quickly becomes nobody's problem.
　然而，每個人的問題很快就會變成不是任何人的問題。

以-thing結尾的不定代名詞通常不能通過加-'s的方式表示所屬關係。例如：the beauty of something是正確的，但something's beauty是錯誤的說法。

不定代名詞可以被不同的成分修飾，但修飾語只能置於其後，通常的修飾語有介係詞片語、定語子句、形容詞以及else等。例如：

▶ Manhattan became unbearable to **anyone** with a sensitive soul.
　曼哈頓曾讓所有神經敏感的人受不了。

▶ We have to give the teachers **something** that they can do to make a difference.
　我們要給教師們一些東西，使他們能發揮影響。

▶ Madrid being linked with big soccer players is **nothing** new.
　馬德里跟大牌足球隊員聯繫在一起，這已不是新鮮事了。

▶ Her children mattered to her more than **anyone or anything else**.
　孩子對於她的重要性超過任何別的人或事。

不定代名詞在句子中具有與名詞相同的文法功能。例如：

★主詞

▶ **Anybody** entering the kitchen from the garden door would spot her immediately.
　凡是從花園門進入廚房的人都會馬上發現她。

★間接受詞

▶ Did you give **someone** your email address then?
那麼，你把你的電子郵件地址給別人了嗎？

★介係詞受詞

▶ He was evidently drunk, and was speaking of **something** that had happened at his school.
顯然，他喝醉了。他在嘮嘮叨叨地說著自己的學校曾經發生過的事。

以some-和every-開頭的不定代名詞大多數情況下用於肯定句，有時也可用於否定句，但不能在否定句中作受詞，除非它之後有介係詞片語或定語子句的修飾。例如：

▶ **Something** needs to be done before this situation gets worse.
得採取點措施，不然，局勢會變得更糟。

▶ She would make **everyone** feel comfortable, respected, and more than that, truly loved.
她要讓每個人感到舒服、受到尊重，而且真正感受到愛。

▶ It's not fair that **somebody** who has been here for so many years, respected the law and tried to adjust his immigration status for so long is treated this way.
有的人在這裡居住了這麼多年，遵守法律，為改變其移民地位而作了長期的努力，他們遭受這樣的對待是不公正的。

帶any-的不定代名詞可在疑問句和否定句中作受詞和介係詞受詞，或在肯定疑問句和否定疑問句中作主詞，但不能在否定句中作主詞。例如：

★受詞

▶ I haven't spoken to **anyone** all day.
我一整天都沒跟任何人說過話。

★介係詞受詞

▶ Does the interview with the Admiral make any difference to **anything**?
與那個海軍上將見面能帶來什麼不同嗎？

★肯定疑問句

▶ Does **anybody** have a suggestion for wording?
對於措辭誰有建議嗎？

★否定疑問句

▶Doesn't anything ever cross your mind when you plan for the future?
當你憧憬未來時，難道沒有什麼想法嗎？

注意！

在肯定句中，anyone和anybody意指「任何人」、「凡是……的人」，而不只是指稱某個人。例如：

▶Anybody buying or selling on eBay needs to be aware of what their tax responsibilities are.
任何在eBay做買賣的人都需要明白他們的稅務責任是什麼。

▶Anyone who's ever been on a ski holiday knows that there's just one thing between you and ski heaven: snow.
凡是曾經滑雪度假的人都知道，你和滑雪的天堂之間只有一樣東西：雪。

帶no-的不定代名詞若和動詞的肯定形式連用，句子帶否定意義。例如：

▶Nobody was looking at Japan but maybe now they'll pay a bit more attention.
以前，沒人注視著日本，但是，現在他們或許應該對它多加留意了。

▶Has no one told him about acid rain or the carcinogens in coal waste?
難道沒人和他講過有關酸雨或煤渣中的致癌物質？

▶The room was small and very quiet and Sophie did nothing to break the silence.
這個房間又狹小又寧靜，索菲不想做任何事去打破寂靜。

疑問代名詞

疑問代名詞（Interrogative Pronouns）用於疑問句。常用的疑問代名詞有：who，whose，whom，what，which。它們可作句子的主詞和受詞，也可作介係詞的受詞。

whose和which還可作限定詞。例如：

▶Who says globalization isn't working?
誰說全球化不起作用？

▶Whose heavy footsteps were shuffling above?
上面誰的腳步拖得那麼響？

▶Whom do people contact if they have a problem with a medication?
如果人們對藥品有疑問，那麼和誰聯繫呢？

▶Which is the drug that suppresses your appetite, Simon?
西蒙，哪種藥品抑制你的食欲？

▶What makes your parents so frightened of meeting strangers?
是什麼讓你的父母這麼害怕見陌生人？

疑問代名詞意指所詢問的資訊，who，whose，whom用於答案為人的問句，what，which用於指稱事物。疑問代名詞可以用於轉述問句。例如：

▶ What makes these people say things like that?
是什麼讓這些人說這樣的事？

▶ Which is your favorite song?
哪首歌你最喜歡？

▶ Who made us so morbid and hysterical and weak?
誰讓我們這麼憂鬱、脆弱和情緒異常？

▶ Whose approach is more effective?
誰的方法更為有效？

▶ Whom should we declare war against?
我們將向誰宣戰？

▶ If her parents asked what she planned to do next, she wouldn't have an answer.
如果父母問她下一步打算做什麼，她就無法回答。

▶ I can't help but wonder who will benefit the most from the $16 million to be spent on mind-body research next year.
我不禁猜想，明年花在身心研究上的1600萬美元中，誰將得益最大。

關係代名詞

　　英語中的關係代名詞（Relative Pronouns）多數與疑問代名詞形式相同，常用的關係代名詞有：who，whom，whose，which，that。

　　關係代名詞有兩種句法功能，即指稱已經提及過的人或事，同時起連接作用，引導出定語子句，使主子句能連接在一起。

　　關係代名詞中，who與whom始終用於指人，which始終用於指事物，that既可指人也可指事物，whose不能單獨出現，必須置於名詞之前表示某事物的歸屬關係。例如：

▶ Actors are usually people who love to be the center of attention.
演員通常是那些喜歡成為關注中心的人。

▶ I feel awful for the family of the person who died to save George.
他為了救喬治而獻身，我為他的家人感到難過。

▶ There are women in my life whom I care deeply about.
我的生活中，有我十分關切的女性。

▶ Many Southeast Asian nations also have large ethnic Chinese and Indian populations, for whom technology is a popular vocation.
許多東南亞國家的人口中也有大量的華人和印度人，他們大多從事技術行業。

▶ Food packaging—20 percent of **which** is made of plastic—is a \$105 billion industry in the United States, and growing.

食品包裝——20%是由塑膠製成的——是一個給美國帶來1050億美元的產業，而且這個數字還在增長。

▶ That bar on Milton Street, **which** by the way is very nice and quite cheap, is owned by Trevor's brother.

密爾頓街上的那家酒吧，順便提一下，服務很好，價格相當便宜，是由特雷弗的兄弟開的。

▶ Today the company's operating costs, **which** are mostly labor, take up just 17% of revenue, compared with 22% at archrival Target.

目前，該公司的運營成本，大部分是勞動力成本，僅占了收入的17%，而其最大的競爭對手塔吉特公司的成本是22%。

▶ I grew up in a family **that** loved politics, but it was for the men, not the women.

我是在一個熱愛政治的家庭長大的，但政治適合男人，不適合女人。

▶ Schools **that** failed to meet standards in 2000 would be on the warning list if they fail this year.

那些在2000年不符合標準的學校，如果今年還不合格，就會被列在受警告的名單上。

▶ William Lange, **whose** friend died in the bombing, walked through the victims' memorial chairs.

威廉·蘭格走過紀念受害者的椅子，他的一位朋友就在那次爆炸中死亡。

代名詞的格

「格」用來區分詞語之間的句法關係。英語的格靠以下三種方式來實現：

(1)加上's，如teacher → teacher's。

(2)置於介係詞之後，如with a man。

(3)詞序變化，如John kissed Jane, and Jane kicked John。

現代英語代名詞有三種格：主格、受格和所有格。在通常的情況下，人稱代名詞在句子中作主詞時用主格，作受詞時用受格，所有格則表示「所有」關係。

代名詞的主格

代名詞的主格是代名詞作為主詞或主詞補語時的一種形式。人稱代名詞的主格有第一、第二、第三人稱以及人稱的單複數之區別（參見P089〈人稱代名詞〉）。例如：

▶ I'm allowed to have dinner with someone, aren't I?

我被允許和別人一起吃飯，對嗎？

▶ Shall **we** terminate our conference for the night?

今晚的會就開到這裡，好嗎？

▶ **You** never know what will happen.

誰也不知將會發生什麼。

🎯 代名詞的受格

代名詞作動詞或介係詞的受詞時用受格形式。作主詞補語時代名詞也可以用受格形式。人稱代名詞有一套受格形式，如me，us，you，him，her，it，them。例如：

▶ Fortunately, the seller, who could have charged me a lot more, was a real gentleman.
那個賣主本來可以收我更多的錢，但幸運的是，他是個真正的紳士。

▶ "I think the gaffer has probably protected us too much in the past," he said.
他說：「我想那老頭子過去或許太保護我們了。」

▶ If Annie betrayed you one day, I wouldn't be surprised.
假如安妮有一天背叛了你，我不會感到驚訝。

▶ Latham then recanted his statement, claiming police had coerced him into making a false confession.
後來萊瑟姆收回了自己的聲明，聲稱是員警逼他做了假的口供。

▶ Such wrangling taught her valuable political lessons.
這樣的爭論給她上了幾堂很有價值的政治課。

▶ At the last moment before the waiter left them, Marcus grabbed the menu and chose a plate of lobster pasta.
就在服務生要離開的最後時刻，馬庫斯一把抓住菜單，點了一盤龍蝦義大利面。

▶ Whom have you turned to for help?
你向誰尋求幫助了？

▶ "I want to help anyone who makes it easier to reintegrate inmates back into society," he said.
他說：「我想幫助每一個能讓更生人更容易重返社會的人。」

🎯 代名詞的所有格

代名詞的所有格可分為名詞性所有格代名詞（Nominal Genitive Pronouns）和限定性所有格代名詞（Determinative Genitive Pronouns）。名詞性所有格代名詞也稱為所有格代名詞（參見P090〈所有格代名詞〉）。

限定性所有格代名詞有：my，your，his，her，its，our，their。例如：

▶ I knew that my destiny was in my hands, and that I needed to ensure that my skills were always up to date.
我知道命運掌握在自己的手中，也知道要讓自己的技術不斷跟著時代進步，才能掌握命運。

▶ If you keep to your promise—to behave yourself in future when I have guests— then I shall try to keep to my promise.
如果你能守信——將來我有客人時你要守規矩——那麼，我也將儘量堅守諾言。

▶ One miserable night, after quitting his job as a short-order cook, getting beaten up, and having his last paycheck stolen, he gave up and bought a plane ticket back to Ohio.
那是個悲傷的夜晚；他辭去速食廚師的工作之後，被人打了一頓，又被人偷了最後一張工資支票。他只好放棄一切，買了張返回俄亥俄的機票。

▶ Despite getting a little help from her parents she left college with student debts totaling more than £12,000.
儘管她的父母給了她一點資助，但她離開大學時還共欠下超過12,000英鎊的學生貸款。

▶ In the wild, the insect lays its eggs in banana leaves and coconut shells, which collect a little water.
在野外，昆蟲在香蕉葉和椰子殼上產卵，因為上面能積蓄少量的水。

▶ This test is going to give you and your teachers a lot of information about how you're doing before the end of the year.
這項測試將為你們和你們的老師提供大量有關你們在年底之前學習狀況的資訊。

▶ Earlier in the summer, during the interval at the opera, a friend overheard two fellow enthusiasts discussing their holiday plans.
初夏一場歌劇的劇間休息時，一個朋友無意中聽到兩個歌迷在談論他們假日的計畫。

代名詞的用法 ▷

🎯 be動詞之後的代名詞用法

代名詞在be動詞之後有主格或受格兩種形式。人們一般認為，在正式語體中要用主格，而在非正式語體中可用受格。例如：

▶ Personally, if I were he, I would have just stayed retired.
在我看來，如果我是他，我就寧願退休。

▶ It was him that ran across the road and nearly got killed!
穿越馬路，差點喪命的是他！

🎯 as和than之後的代名詞用法

在非正式語體中，as和than被當作介係詞，而在正式文體中它們被當作連接詞。因此，它們之後的代名詞可用代名詞的主格或受格。例如：

▶ Her boyfriend had spent the night as sleeplessly as her.
她的男友和她一樣徹夜未眠。

▶ There would not be a man at his table that night who did not eat more and drink deeper than he. 那天晚上，餐桌上的人誰都比他吃得更多，喝得更過癮。

▶ They were shivering worse than me. 他們比我抖得還嚴重。

▶ Most applicants were a lot younger than I. 大多數申請人比我年輕得多。

🎯 代名詞one的用法

代名詞one可以用作替代名詞、類指代名詞和數詞。one用作數詞時具有指示功能（Demonstrative Function）和中心詞功能。

作類指代名詞時，one有其主格、所有格和反身代名詞的形式。作替代名詞時，它有單複數形式。

1. 替代名詞one

替代名詞one有複數形式ones，用於替代某個可數名詞或某個意義相當的名詞性運算式。one的前面可用限定詞修飾，如those ones，the old one，但不直接跟在不定冠詞之後。例如：

▶ In another scene, the prince tries to persuade his father to give him a car by saying: "Mom would give me one."
在另一個場景，王子企圖說服父親給他一輛車，他說：「媽媽就會給我一輛。」

▶ Improve skills, learn new ones or draw attention to what you already do so well.
要改進技術、學習新技術，或把注意力集中在你已經很拿手的事情上。

▶ I have no problem with the conditions, especially those ones which really encourage us to be more disciplined, because that way we're going to be successful.
這些條件，尤其那些真正鼓勵我們更加遵守紀律的條件，對我來說沒有什麼問題，因為只有這樣，我們才會成功。

▶ I don't know if your son told you, but we had two papers here in Dallas and now we just have the one.
不知你的兒子是否告訴過你，但是在達拉斯這裡，我們本來有兩份文件，現在只有這一份了。

2. 類指代名詞one

類指代名詞one用於泛指「人們」，常常包括說話人在內。英語中可用於泛指「人們」的代名詞有one，you，we，they等。

它們之間的區別在於說話者說話的角度和話語的語體正式性。one可作主格和受格，其所有格形式為one's，反身形式為oneself。

one用於正式語體，但為了避免重複，常以he/his取代。例如：

▶ One should always distrust fancy motives.
我們永遠不要相信不切實際的動機。

▶ One should always convert one's hobbies into a career whenever possible.
無論何時，只要可能，大家始終要把自己的愛好轉為職業。

▶ It is a time to really immerse oneself in the joys of nature.
該是把自己真正投入到大自然的懷抱享受一番的時候了。

▶To give someone knowledge of **oneself** is to give someone power.

讓某人瞭解自己就是給某人以力量。

3. 數詞one

數詞one的用法與其他基數詞相同，可用作限定詞，也可用作名詞片語的中心詞。另外，它還可與the other或another對應，用於關聯結構中。例如：

▶He needed to renew his friendship with David and he had to make him remember that all those years ago, he was the **one** boy in his class that stood up for him.

他需要和大衛重溫友情，要讓大衛回憶起多年前的往事：他就是班級裡挺身而出支持大衛的人。

▶Kelly was born in Tullamore, Ireland, **one** of seven children of a company secretary and a housewife.

凱莉出生於愛爾蘭的塔拉莫爾，是公司秘書和家庭主婦七個孩子中的一個。

▶I was in **one** place for two years and **another** place for a year.

我在一個地方住了兩年，在另一個地方住了一年。

▶Should a hospital risk **one** life to save **the other**?

為了救活一條命，醫院就應該拿另一條命去冒險嗎？

小結 ▷

本章討論了代名詞的形態、意義和句法功能。從形態上看，代名詞隨著文法範疇的變化而發生形態上的變化。這些範疇包括人稱、格、性和數等概念。在意義上，代名詞不僅可以替代名詞，而且可以替代一個名詞性片語或同一類事物。在句法上，代名詞有名詞的功能，也有名詞性片語的功能。

Part **4**

動詞

動詞概說 ▷

在句子結構中，動詞是一個不可缺少的重要成分。

根據動詞變化的方式，動詞可以分為規則動詞和不規則動詞、限定和非限定形式；根據動詞的及物特性，可以分為及物和不及物動詞；根據動詞在句子中的作用，還可以分為主動詞、助動詞和情態動詞。

動詞可以單字動詞的形式獨立構成謂語成分，也可以多字動詞或動詞片語的形式來完成謂語的功能。在本章，我們就動詞的分類、功能和意義，以及動詞在句子中所起的作用對動詞進行概括性描述。

動詞的基本類型 ▷

動詞總體可以分為三種基本類型：實義動詞、助動詞和情態動詞（Modal Verbs）。實義動詞屬於開放性詞彙，能夠作句子的主動詞；而基本助動詞be，do，have既能作主動詞，又能作助動詞；情態動詞如will，shall等，有時可以劃分到助動詞的範圍，因此也稱為情態助動詞（Modal Auxiliary Verbs）。

動詞的分類如下表所示：

動詞		限定動詞		非限定動詞		
		動詞原形	過去式	不定詞	現在分詞	過去分詞
實義動詞	及物動詞	make	made	(to) make	making	made
	不及物動詞	sleep	slept	(to) sleep	sleeping	slept
	連綴動詞	is, am, are / appear	was, were /appeared	(to) be / (to) appear	being / appearing	been / appeared
助動詞	be	is, am, are	was, were	(to) be	being	been
	have	have	had			
	do	do	did			

動詞		限定動詞		非限定動詞		
		動詞原形	過去式	不定詞	現在分詞	過去分詞
情態動詞	中心情態動詞	will, shall, can, may, must	would, should, could, might			
	邊緣情態動詞	need, used to, dare, ought to				

🎯 實義動詞

實義動詞也稱為完全動詞（Full Verbs），屬於開放性詞彙，具有實際意義，如動詞 leave，eat，run 等，在句子中作主動詞，是謂語的主要成分。

❶ 實義動詞的結構形式

從詞彙的構成形式上看，動詞分為規則動詞（Regular Verbs）和不規則動詞（Irregular Verbs）。另也分成-s形式（主詞為第三人稱單數時使用）、過去式、現在分詞、過去分詞等形式。

1. 規則動詞。規則動詞的構成形式以動詞call為例：

原形	-s 形式	過去式	現在分詞	過去分詞
call	calls	called	calling	called

(1) 動詞的-s形式用於現在簡單式的句子中，主詞為第三人稱單數名詞。例如：

▶ She calls him every day.
她每天給他打電話。

(2) 動詞的過去式常用於發生在過去的句子中。例如：

▶ She called him yesterday.
她昨天打電話給他了。

(3) 現在分詞可以用於進行中的句子，表示事情正在發生。例如：

▶ She is calling him now.
她正在打電話給他。

(4) 過去分詞可以用於完成式句子中。例如：

▶ She has called him twice today.
她今天打了兩次電話給他。

2. 不規則動詞

不規則動詞的構成形式是不定的。動詞speak、cut及基本動詞be的構成形式如下：

原形	-s 形式	過去式	現在分詞	過去分詞
speak	speaks	spoke	speaking	spoken
cut	cuts	cut	cutting	cut
be	is	was/were	being	been

（參見附錄常用不規則動詞）

❷ 實義動詞的及物性

實義動詞在句子中常常作主動詞，分為及物動詞（Transitive Verbs）和不及物動詞（Intransitive Verbs）。

1. 及物動詞

及物動詞後須接受詞。例如：

▶ Excessive speed played a role in seven of the accidents.
超速行駛是造成其中七起交通事故的原因。

有些及物動詞可以接雙受詞，即直接受詞和間接受詞。例如：

▶ I gave him some advice and told him we backed him completely.
我給了他一些忠告，並且告訴他我們完全支持他。

▶ I spent 20 years doing my work and nobody paid me any attention.
我用了20年的時間來做這項工作，但是沒有人關注過我。

還有的及物動詞後接受詞和受詞補語。例如：

▶ My job is to sweep the shop and keep it clean.
我的工作是打掃商店，保持店裡的清潔。

▶ After being shocked with all these changes, I found myself exhausted and bored.
所有這些變化讓我吃驚，我感到疲憊而無趣。

2. 不及物動詞。不及物動詞後不接受詞。例如：

▶ He got off the bed and walked to the window.
他從床上起來，走向窗邊。

▶ She turned towards the door, but stopped as the telephone rang and Joanna picked it up.
喬安娜轉身走向門口，這時電話鈴響了，她停住腳步，拿起了聽筒。

在一定的上下文中，有些不及物動詞後接狀語，使動詞所表達的意思更完整。例如：

▶ I've **lived in Texas** most of my life.
我大部分時間住在德克薩斯州。

▶ In past years, he **worked in Kazakhstan and Nigeria** on a rotational basis.
過去幾年裡，他在哈薩克和奈及利亞之間輪換工作。

3. 兼作及物和不及物動詞

英語中，大多數動詞既可以作及物動詞，也可以作不及物動詞，動詞的意思基本不變。例如：

▶ But the law has not **stopped some mothers** from abandoning their babies and putting them at risk.
但法律沒能阻止有些母親遺棄嬰兒或將他們置於危險之中。

▶ Every time I **stopped** at a traffic light I felt conscious of all the eyes peering in.
每當我在紅綠燈前停下車時，就感覺到所有的眼睛都在向車內窺視。

常見的這類動詞如下表所示：

borrow	change	clean	cook	draw
drink	dust	eat	film	help
iron	learn	lend	marry	paint
park	point	read	ride	save
sing	smoke	spend	steal	study
type	wash	wave	write	

有些動詞有兩個或更多的意思，表示其中一個意思時為及物動詞，表示另一個意思時為不及物動詞。例如：

▶ He **ran a gas station** down in St. Louis for two years.
他在聖路易斯經營一家加油站已經兩年了。

▶ He **ran** away into the mist.
他跑走了，隱入迷霧中。

▶ **Mind the dog**.
當心有狗。

▶ If you don't **mind**, I'd like to offer a short comment.
假如你不介意，我想簡單談點我的看法。

常見的這類動詞見下表：

add	aim	beat	blow	call	change	cheat
count	draw	dress	drive	escape	exercise	fit
fly	follow	head	hold	hurt	lead	lose
manage	meet	mind	miss	move	pass	play
press	propose	reflect	run	shoot	show	sink
spread	stand	stretch	strike	study	tend	touch
turn	win					

還有一些動詞在兼作及物動詞和不及物動詞時，作及物動詞的受詞和作不及物動詞的主詞可以相互轉換。例如：

▶ Bill Ture, who with his wife, Ruth, opened a contemporary art center known as Western Bridge earlier this year.
今年年初，比爾·圖雷與他的妻子露絲開了一個被外界稱為「西橋」的當代藝術中心。

▶ The 100-acre zoo near the banks of the river opened in 1967.
位於河畔附近的面積為100英畝的動物園於1967年開園。

常見的這類動詞可見下表：

age	bake	begin	bend	boil	break
burn	burst	change	close	continue	cook
crack	darken	decrease	diminish	disperse	double
drown	dry	empty	end	fade	finish
fly	grow	improve	increase	meet	open
park	run	sail	shake	show	shut
slow	sound	spread	stand	start	stop
tear	turn	widen			

❸ 實義動詞的分類

實義動詞分為兩類。一類是單字動詞（Single-word Verbs），如come，take等。另一類是多字動詞（Multi-word Verbs），也稱片語動詞（Phrasal Verbs），如come across，take care of等。

1. 單字動詞

單字動詞是指一個獨立的實義動詞，通常在句子中作主動詞，起謂語作用。

根據單字動詞的意義可以分為表達行為、動作、思維、情感、關係和存在等意義的動詞；根據其文法功能，還可以分為靜態動詞和動態動詞。

(1)單字動詞的語義分類

　　從語義範疇的角度來看，單字動詞可以分為七種：行為動詞（Activity Verbs）、交際動詞（Communication Verbs）、心智動詞（Mental Verbs）、成因動詞（Causation Verbs）、發生動詞（Verbs of Occurrence）、表示存在和關係的動詞（Verbs of Existence or Relationship）、體動詞（Aspectual Verbs)。

　　這種分類是基於動詞的核心意義，也就是說話人首先想到的意義。

a. 行為動詞

　　行為動詞主要表示行為舉止和事件，如buy，carry，come，give，leave，move，open，take，work，bring等。行為動詞以主詞為動作的發出者或施動者。例如：

▶Wholesalers will **buy** fish from the processors and then deliver it by truck to their customers.
批發商從加工者那裡買魚，然後用卡車運給客戶。

▶The storm **is carrying** 100-mph winds but is expected to strengthen before landfall.
暴風以每小時100英里的速度推進，預計在暴風雨登陸前會進一步增強。

▶In fact, Jane was very reluctant to **bring** me down here to meet her sister and brother-in-law at all.
事實上，簡非常不情願帶我來見她的姐姐和姐夫。

　　行為動詞可以是及物動詞，後接直接受詞，也可以是不及物動詞，不接受詞。例如：

▶He **gave** money to schools, libraries and international relief agencies.
他曾向學校、圖書館和國際救援機構捐款。

▶She was born in Indonesia and **went** to high school in Amreica.
她在印尼出生，在美國讀的高中。

b. 交際動詞

　　交際動詞是一種特殊行為的動詞，主要涉及說與寫等語言交流活動。常用的交際動詞有：ask，announce，call，discuss，explain，say，shout，speak，state，suggest，talk，tell，write等。例如：

▶Carol yesterday **spoke** of the enormous relief she felt after her mother survived a cancer scare.
昨天卡蘿爾談及她感到無比寬慰，因為母親經受住了一場癌症的驚嚇。

▶Northwest airlines **announced** it would buy a 14% share of continental airlines for $511 million in cash and stock.
西北航空公司宣佈將以5.11億美元的現款和股票買下大陸航空公司14%的股份。

▶She **asked** the tennis player if it was exhausting travelling around the world to play matches.

她問網球運動員環球旅行打比賽是否很辛苦。

c. 心智動詞

　　心智動詞表達了人們所經歷的心理活動和狀態。在語義上，心智動詞包含：認知活動的動詞，如think，know等；表達不同態度和願望的情感動詞，如love，want等；表示感知動作的動詞，如see，taste等；表達語言交流方式的動詞，如read，hear等。例如：

▶She **knew** that 80 percent of ultraviolet radiation is accumulated in the human body by age 18, meaning that melanoma is "seeded" while we are children.

她知道人類到18歲時體內就聚集了80%的紫外線，這意味著黑色瘤在兒童時期就已經播下了「種子」。

▶I just **wanted** to keep Kenny from getting hurt.

我只是不想讓肯尼受傷。

　　心智動詞所表達的心理活動有時在意義上是動態的，如calculate，consider，discover，learn，solve，study等。例如：

▶In her first year on her job, she often worked from eight in the morning until eleven at night because she hadn't yet **discovered** how to take shortcuts.

剛開始工作的那一年，她經常從早上8點工作到晚上11點，因為她還不懂得如何走捷徑。

　　有些心智動詞所表達的心理活動在意義上是靜態的，如表示認知狀態的動詞believe，doubt，know，remember，understand等和表示情感和態度的動詞enjoy，fear，feel，hate，like，love，prefer，suspect，want等。例如：

▶The more he flew, the more he **believed** that piloting was about learning your limitations and staying within them—but constantly expanding your limitations.

飛行得越多，他就越發相信飛行就是了解個人的極限並維持極限，但又要不斷地拓展這種極限。

▶He **remembered** nights in jail sleeping on a bed with no mattress and being fed putrid food.

他想起在監獄的那些夜晚，睡在沒有床墊的床上，吃的是腐爛的食物。

▶Local art collectors seemed to **prefer** traditional landscapes over these more challenging pieces.

當地的藝術品收藏家似乎更喜歡傳統的風景畫而不是這些更有挑戰性的作品。

d. 成因動詞

　　成因動詞是指由於人類或客觀世界而引起或促成某個事態的形成的動詞。常見的動詞有allow，cause，enable，force，help，let，require，permit等， 通常後接名詞化片語作直接受詞或受詞補語來表示所引發的動作。

　　■成因動詞後接名詞化片語作直接受詞。例如：

▶Unfortunately, the tropical storm **caused massive flooding** and loss of life in that island country.
不幸的是，熱帶風暴引發了大面積洪水，造成了這個島國內的人員傷亡。

▶Does the Constitution **permit imposing the death penalty** on someone who is 16 or 17 years old?
憲法是否允許對16歲或17歲的人實施死刑？

　　■成因動詞後接受詞補語。例如：

▶He was the man who created the situation that **enabled** us **to become the majority party** in the Congress and the majority party in the nation.
正是他創造了局面，使我們黨成為國會的多數黨乃至國家的多數黨。

▶In Iraq, Nicole's job **required** her **to assess** which communities needed the most help.
在伊拉克，妮可的工作是評估哪些社區最需要援助。

e. 發生動詞

　　發生動詞是指表示客觀活動發生的動詞，常用的有：become，change，happen，develop，grow，increase，occur等。例如：

▶Times have **changed**.
時代變了。

▶Apparently, much has **changed** since my last visit to the city.
顯然，自從我上次訪問後，這個城市發生了很大的變化。

▶This month, California **became** the latest state to recognize that some youngsters need to remain in foster care until age 21.
這個月，加利福尼亞成為最新一個認同某些少年需要留在寄養家庭到21歲的州。

f. 表示存在和關係的動詞

　　表示存在和關係的動詞表達了存在於客體之間的一種狀態，這種動詞大多是連綴動詞（Copular Verbs），如be，seem，appear 等，在主詞和謂語之間起連接作用，使謂語表達主詞的特徵。例如：

▶The culture is very much customer orientation, teaming and continuous learning.
這種文化非常看重以顧客為導向，追求合作與堅持不懈的學習。

▶She didn't seem quite as sympathetic as Trish thought she should be.
她並不像崔西認為的那樣富有同情心。

　　還有一些動詞表示一種存在狀態（如exist，live，stay等）或表示客體之間的關係（如contain，include，involve，represent 等）。

　　■表示存在。例如：

▶We stayed with some relatives for a while and then we went to Sea World and Disneyland.
我們在親戚家待了一會兒，然後去了海洋世界和迪士尼樂園。

▶How can a person exist without his soul?
一個人怎能活在世上而沒有靈魂？

　　■表示關係。例如：

▶VOA News Now includes a complete news update at the top and bottom of every hour.
美國之音現時新聞播報在每小時開始和結束時播報完整的即時新聞。

▶My comments represent my views as a middle school principal and former mathematics teacher. 我的評論代表我這個中學校長和前數學教師的觀點。

g. 體動詞

　　體動詞是指表示事件和活動進程中不同階段的特徵的動詞，如begin，continue，finish，keep，start，stop等。例如：

▶I can't stop hoping that I will meet my dad one day, but I know that will not come true.
我忍不住地期望著有一天能與我的父親相見，但是我知道這個願望難以實現。

▶House prices have stopped rising in London for the first time in two years.
兩年來倫敦的房價第一次停止增長了。

　　這種動詞後通常接受詞補語。例如：

▶U.S. economic flexibility has kept the economy expanding.
美國經濟的彈性使其經濟保持發展。

(2) 實義動詞作連綴動詞

　　除了動詞be以外，實義動詞也可以作連綴動詞。如表中所示：

appear	be	become	fall	feel	get
go	grow	keep	look	prove	remain
rest	run	seem	smell	sound	stay
taste	turn				

a. 連綴動詞：仍然動詞

　　主要表示持續存在的狀態。常見的有：be，remain，appear，keep，seem，stay等。例如：

▶ For a moment she remained silent, confused, frightened.
　她沉默了片刻，迷茫又恐懼。

▶ Life went on, and everything seemed pretty distant.
　生活還在繼續，一切似乎都已遠去。

b. 連綴動詞：起來動詞

　　表示感覺和感應的狀態。常見的：look，feel，sound，smell，taste等，表示「看起來」、「聽起來」、「聞起來」等。例如：

▶ When the first two or three girls approached David and held out flowers for him, he smiled and looked genuinely flattered.
　當前面的兩三位女孩走近大衛把花獻給他時，他微笑著，看起來格外高興。

▶ He felt weak, dazed, and almost delirious.
　他感到虛弱、恍惚，幾乎神志不清。

▶ Jay sounds most excited about working in a foreign company.
　對於到外國公司工作，傑伊表現得很激動。

b. 連綴動詞：變得動詞

　　表示一種狀態是由過程發生變化所導致的結果。常見的有：become，get，go，grow，prove，come，turn 等。例如：

▶ When Saddam came to power in 1979, times became tougher for the Kurds.
　當薩達姆1979年當權後，形勢對庫德族來說變得更加嚴峻。

▶ Her eyes grew accustomed to the dark and she pushed back her heavy plaits of hair, rubbing her eyes tiredly.
　她的眼睛漸漸適應了黑暗，她把粗大的辮子推到腦後，疲倦地揉了揉雙眼。

①還有一些片語動詞也具有類似功能，如turn out，end up，wind up 等。例如：

▶ Progress **turned out** to be frustratingly slow.
進展如此之慢，令人沮喪。

▶ Tests for the disease **turned out** negative.
病理化驗的結果是陰性。

② 動詞如go，grow，come等既可以用作連綴動詞，也可以在不同上下文中用作主動詞。例如：

★連綴動詞

▶ The whole of Europe **went** crazy for coffee bars in the 1950s and 60s.
在50年代與60年代期間，整個歐洲都為咖啡吧而瘋狂。

★主動詞

▶ I **went** to the window and looked out at the rain and the clouds.
我走到窗子旁邊，觀看外面的雨勢和雲團。

2. 多字動詞

多字動詞或片語動詞是由兩個或兩個以上的單字構成，實義動詞是動詞片語中的中心詞，可以與介係詞或介副詞搭配，形成一種固定結構，通常表達特定的意義。

(1)動詞＋介係詞

「動詞＋介係詞」後可以接受詞。例如：

▶ TV shopping **accounted for** seven per cent of the market with 25-34 year-olds making up most of the customers.
電視購物占7%的市場份額，由年齡在25到34歲之間的人構成顧客群的主體。

▶ One day, they **came across** 42 sick and starving Vietnamese.
他們遇到了42個病痛與饑餓交加的越南人。

▶ His bodyguards will **deal with** strangers who may be hostile.
由他的保鑣來對付那些有敵意的陌生人。

常見的這類動詞見下表：

account for	allow for	ask for	break into	burst into
call for	call on	care for	come across	come by
count on	cut across	deal with	fall into	get over

go about	go for	head for	hit on	laugh at
look after	look into	look for	run across	run into
see to	set about	stand for	take after	wait on
watch for				

(2)動詞＋介副詞。例如：

▶A transatlantic air fares war broke out yesterday when British Airways slashed prices on 1.5 million seats.

昨天英國航空公司大幅度削減了150萬個座位的價格，因而引發了飛越大西洋航班的機票價格大戰。

▶Life went on—but in a warped way.

生活仍然在繼續——但以一種扭曲的方式延續。

這類片語動詞後也可以接受詞。例如：

▶My Mum brought up five children in a flat far worse than what these immigrants complain about.

我的媽媽在一間公寓房裡養大了五個孩子，那裡的條件比移民們所抱怨的住所差多了。

▶It's really a surprise to me that they brought up some false issues regarding my training and the issue of safety.

讓我感到驚訝的是，他們就我的訓練和安全問題提出了一些錯誤的問題。

受詞也可以放在副詞前。例如：

▶We put this article under that column because yesterday when Alice brought it up, everyone seemed to agree with it

我們把這篇文章放在那個欄目裡，因為昨天愛麗絲提議這樣做時，大家好像一致同意。

▶He gave the orders and we carried them out.

他下達命令，而我們執行命令。

(3)動詞＋介副詞＋介係詞

由「動詞＋介副詞＋介係詞」構成的片語動詞後可以接受詞。例如：

▶Finally, I came up with a plan which, while perhaps not exactly as my boss had requested, was the best.

終於，我想出了一個方案，可能不完全是我的老闆所要求的那樣，但已經是最好的了。

▶These are idol-like figures and both Joe and Bob look up to them as role models and surround their lives with these friends.

這是一些類似偶像的人物，喬與鮑勃都把他們當成楷模來崇拜，生活中總是離不開這些朋友。

這類組合只能看作是「成語」，即片語不能拆開，這與某些「動詞＋受詞＋副詞＋介係詞」的組合有所不同。例如：

▶ These workers will put up with low wages and dangerous conditions that most American workers won't tolerate.
這些工人將忍受低工資待遇與危險的工作條件，而這是大多數美國工人所不能忍受的。

▶ I put ideas up for programs every year but for the last nine years they've said no.
每年我為項目籌劃點子，但是在過去的九年裡都遭到他們拒絕。

　　以上三種動詞的組合都是一些固定搭配，相當於一個及物或不及物的單字動詞，因而也稱為「片語動詞」（Phrasal Verbs）。這些片語動詞與某些非固定搭配片語是不同的。例如：

a. 固定搭配（有特定涵義）

▶ I have not come across a perfume advertisement anything like this at all.
我還從沒有遇到過像這樣的香水廣告。

▶ He was a genuinely upbeat kid, got along with everybody and expressed a desire to do well in school.
他真的是一個積極上進的孩子，與人和睦相處，渴望取得好成績。

b. 非固定搭配

▶ I happened to be walking around the M.I.T. campus this past weekend and came across a hallway filled with photographs of famous alumni.
上週末，我正好在麻省理工學院散步，穿過一個掛滿了照片的走廊，都是一些有名氣的校友們的照片。

▶ Our institution got the new study results along with recent statistics showing declining death rates from prostate cancer.
我們機構所取得的新研究成果及近期的統計資料表明，前列腺癌症的死亡率在下降。

(4) 動詞＋名詞＋介係詞

　　這類片語動詞也屬於固定搭配，也可以歸於「片語動詞」一類。例如：

▶ This summer, he took advantage of this film, which has raked in more than a half billion dollars worldwide.
這個夏季，他利用這部電影在世界範圍內發了大財，賺了五億多美元。

▶ When I learned a little bit of English, they made fun of my accent.
我剛開始學英語時，他們總是取笑我的口音。

3. 複合動詞

複合動詞（Compound Verbs）也稱合成動詞，是由兩個片語合而成，比如：名詞＋動詞、副詞＋動詞、形容詞＋動詞。

(1)名詞＋動詞

名詞與動詞組合生成複合動詞，如mass-produce，roller-skate，proofread，waterski等。

▶Now Japanese factories mass-produce the instruments.
現在日本的工廠批量生產這種儀器。

(2)副詞＋動詞

副詞與動詞組合構成複合動詞，如overthrow，overcome，overestimate，underestimate，undergo，outdo等。

▶I'm not trying to overthrow the government.
我並不想推翻現政府。

(3)形容詞＋動詞

形容詞與動詞組合構成複合動詞，如cross-examine，backtrack，blackmail，safeguard，whitewash等。

▶We have to safeguard our players.
我們要保護我們的隊員。

助動詞

助動詞包含三個：be，do，have，也稱為基本助動詞（Primary Auxiliary Verbs）。助動詞的文法功能是協助主動詞表達不同的意義，如陳述、發問、否定。助動詞與時態變化結合，表示某一動作正在進行或已經完成。

助動詞be還可以跟主動詞的過去分詞結合構成被動式。

1. 在一般陳述句中。例如：

★被動式

▶If they refuse to do what those gangsters order, they are beaten, often with rods or chairs.
如果他們拒絕匪徒的命令，通常會被人用木棒或椅子毒打。

★現在進行式

▶The new government **is searching** for ways to smooth the transition and stem the violence.
新政府正在尋求平穩過渡和阻止暴力的方法。

2. 在一般疑問句中。例如：

▶**Is** Jack **talking** about the same war that the rest of us are talking about?
傑克所談論的戰爭是我們大家正在談論的戰爭嗎？

3. 在否定句中。例如：

▶Jeep **hasn't been** the most innovative automaker in recent years.
近幾年裡，吉普並不是最具創新精神的汽車製造商。

▶She **hasn't seen** her father, a gambler, for more than 20 years.
她有二十多年沒有見過她的賭徒父親了。

❶ 助動詞的功能

　　動詞be，do，have既可以作主動詞，也可以作助動詞。助動詞與情態動詞不同，不像情態動詞能表達更廣泛的意義，如意願、可能性、義務等。

　　1. 作主動詞。例如：

▶He **is** not afraid to lead and make tough decisions.
他不害怕帶頭作出艱難的決定。

▶Local police **did** a pretty comprehensive investigation in this case.
當地警方對案件作了相當全面的調查。

▶They **had** a younger sister named Chasity.
他們有一個妹妹，名字叫查茜蒂。

　　2. 作助動詞。例如：

▶Many people **are** buying more traditional toys because they don't just want plastic, battery-operated replicas of television characters.
許多人買更傳統的玩具，因為他們不滿足於只要那種塑膠的、電池啟動的電視人物複製品。

▶This is an issue that I **have** thought a lot about for the last several years, and an issue that I**'ve** talked a lot.
這是我近幾年來一直在考慮的問題，也是我談論最多的問題。

▶**Did** you pay that freelancer cash?
你付給那位自由職業者現金了嗎？

3. 作連綴動詞，表示主詞的性質和特徵。例如：

▶ Blue **is** my lucky color.
藍色是我的幸運色。

▶ She **was** downstairs in less than an hour, bathed and perfumed and wearing a yellow dress with a low neckline.
不到一小時她就在樓下了，已經沐浴過並噴上了香水，穿著一件低開領的黃色裙裝。

▶ He **was** in front of her, blocking her path.
他在她面前，擋住她的去路。

▶ Another popular way to escape **is** to enter a type of dream or fantasy state.
另外一種常用的逃避方式是進入一種夢幻世界或遐想狀態。

▶ The No. 1 thing you are confused about **is** what a boyfriend is.
最令你困惑的問題是什麼才是男朋友。

🎯 情態動詞

由於情態動詞具有助動詞的功能，也被稱為情態助動詞，可以劃分到助動詞的範圍。

情態動詞分為中心情態動詞（Central Modals）和邊緣情態動詞（Marginal Modals）。邊緣情態動詞也稱為半情態動詞（Semi-modal Verbs）。

中心情態動詞包括九個：can，could，may，might，will，would，shall，should，must。邊緣情態動詞包括四個：dare，need，ought to，used to。

❶ 情態動詞的意義

情態動詞表示情態意義，如表示能力的can，could，表示可能的may，might，can，could， 表示許可的may，can，could，might， 表示義務的should，ought to，must，表示必然的should，ought to，must，表示預見和推測的will，shall，must，would，should，ought to。情態動詞大多一詞多義，在意義和用法上有重疊之處。

1. 表示能力。例如：

▶ She **can** do drama, comedy, she's very good at acting with her eyes, and she's grown so much.
她可以演戲劇、喜劇，特別擅長用眼睛表達，她成長很快。

2. 表示可能性。例如：

▶ The new medicine **may** be comparatively cheap, but not for a country where annual government spending on health is only $50 for each citizen
新藥也許相對便宜一些，但是對於一個政府醫療支出人均每年僅50美元的國家是不適合的。

3. 表示許可。例如：

▶ You **may** not promise employment or any other benefit for political activity.
你不能以政治活動的名義承諾就業保障和其他福利。

▶ You **may** not use your official title or your official authority or influence in connection with convention activities.
凡是涉及大會活動時，你不能使用你的官方頭銜、官方威信或影響。

4. 表示義務或必然性。例如：

▶ Nobody **should** pick out an innocent man as a scapegoat.
任何人都不應該讓一個無辜的人做替罪羊。

▶ They **should** determine whether they want to buy or lease the machines.
他們應該決定到底是想購買機器還是租借機器。

5.表示預見和推測。例如：

▶ He **must** be in love or something, or he wouldn't be so happy.
他肯定是在熱戀之類的，要不怎麼會這麼快樂。

6.表達意願。例如：

▶ If Miss Gradgrind will permit me, I **will** offer to make it for you, as I have often done.
如果葛蕾英小姐同意的話，我願意一如既往地為你製作那個東西。

❷ 情態動詞片語

情態動詞片語在功能上介乎主動詞和助動詞之間，是本身具有意義的動詞片語。常用的情態動詞片語如下：

be going to	be about to	be able to	be bound to
be due to	be to	be sure to	be apt to
be certain to	be likely to	be supposed to	be willing to
have to	have got to	be obliged to	had better
would rather			

例如：

▶ The plane **was due to** leave at 6:48 p.m. from Austin to Dallas Airport.
飛機預定在下午6點48分從奧斯丁起飛，飛往達拉斯機場。

▶ Is this columnist **likely to be** available to make daily comments on the event?
這位專欄作家能否到場對事件作每日評論？

▶ If you have good cash flow, you should be able to sell bonds.
如果你的現金周轉狀況良好，你應該可以出售債券。

▶ We are supposed to have done four drama lessons and so far we've only done one and a half.
我們本應該完成四節戲劇課程，而現在才完成了一節半。

▶ We have had to wait to get the right timing because he has been so busy.
他太忙了，我們得等候恰當的時機。

（有關情態動詞的詳細用法可參見P124〈助動詞和情態動詞〉）

小結 ▷

本章對動詞作了總體概述，從文法、功能和意義等不同角度對動詞進行分類描述。

從動詞的構成形態上看，動詞分為單字動詞和多字動詞、規則動詞和不規則動詞。從功能角度來看，動詞有主動詞、助動詞和情態動詞之分。在語義範疇裡，詞彙動詞的實際意義可以分為：行為動詞、交際動詞、心智動詞、成因動詞、發生動詞、表示存在和關係的動詞，以及體動詞。

當然這種分類也不是絕對的，在英語中許多動詞具有多重意義，在不同的上下文中動詞的意義有變化，不再是其核心意義。

片語動詞由「動詞＋介係詞」、「動詞＋副詞」和「動詞＋副詞＋介係詞」等形式構成，這種構成是固定形式。

本章還就表示延續狀態的連綴動詞及其用法作了介紹。因為助動詞和情態動詞在下一章中將會重點描述，這裡只作簡要介紹。

Part 5

助動詞和情態動詞

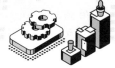

概說

　　英語中的動詞按照功能可分為主動詞（Main Verbs）、助動詞和情態動詞三種基本類別。助動詞包括be，have，do三個基本助動詞，但也有學者將情態動詞歸為助動詞，如will，shall等。

　　情態動詞可分為中心情態動詞和邊緣情態動詞（亦稱半情態動詞）。基本助動詞不能獨立使用，它們輔助主要動詞，構成各種時態、語氣、否定、疑問等結構；情態動詞主要表示看法、意願、可能性等含義。

　　另外，還有處於主動詞和情態動詞之間的半助動詞，主要是一些由基本助動詞be和have引導的情態動詞片語構成。

助動詞

　　助動詞be，have和do既可作主動詞，也可作基本助動詞。作為助動詞，它們本身沒有含義，但能表示時態（過去式、現在式、完成式、進行式）、主動與被動、語氣（陳述、祈使、假設）、否定、疑問等結構。

　　基本助動詞有時態的變化，如下表所示：

原形	現在式		過去式		現在分詞	過去分詞
be	I	am	I		being	been
	we	are	he	was		
	you		she			
	they		it			
	he	is	we	were		
	she		you			
	it		they			

原形	現在式		過去式		現在分詞	過去分詞
have	I	have	I	had	having	had
	we		we			
	you		you			
	they		they			
	he	has	he			
	she		she			
	it		it			
do	I	do	I	did	無	無
	we		we			
	you		you			
	they		they			
	he	does	he			
	she		she			
	it		it			

be

基本助動詞be的用法主要有以下幾種：

1. 與現在分詞構成進行式，「be的各種時態＋現在分詞」構成各種進行式。例如：

★現在進行式

▶The boat **is** doing nearly 10 knots and steaming through the waves.
該船正以近10節的速度乘風破浪向前進。

★過去進行式

▶A few dozen cancer patients **were** taking an obscure new drug with surprising success.
幾十個癌症患者過去一直在嘗試一種療效未知的新藥，獲得了意想不到的成功。

★未來進行式

▶Alan **will be** making the tough decisions.
艾倫將作出艱難的決定。

★現在完成進行式

▶He **has been** working as a waiter in Glasgow.
他一直在格拉斯哥當服務生。

★過去完成進行式

► He, on the other hand, had been gambling because he was short of cash.
　　另一方面，因為那時手頭緊，他一直在賭博。

2. 與過去分詞構成被動式。例如：

► Almost everything in bilingual Canada is written in both English and French.
　　在使用英語和法語的加拿大，幾乎所有東西都會用雙語寫出。

3. 與帶to不定詞連用

(1)計畫、安排以及將來要發生的事情。例如：

► The government is to regulate the pharmaceutical industry.
　　政府將規範製藥行業。

(2)應該做某事或命令某人做某事。例如：

► The first duty of a soldier is to obey.
　　軍人的首要職責就是服從命令。

(3)在條件句中表示假設的情況，一般用were形式。例如：

► Were we to measure the importance of news by its net effect on human happiness, the destruction of Zimbabwe would be regularly on our front pages.
　　如果要根據新聞對人類幸福感造成的最終結果去衡量新聞的重要性，那遭到破壞的辛巴威將經常會被放在首頁。

(4)表示要做而未做的事情。例如：

► He was to have joined me this week, but his train met with an accident, so he's been detained for a few days with an injured ankle.
　　這個禮拜他原本要和我會合，但是由於他乘坐的火車出了事故，導致他的腳踝受了傷，所以推遲了幾天。

4.「have been to＋地點」表示去過某處，而現已不在那裡。例如：

► I have been to France loads of times.
　　我去法國好多次了。

be還可以作主動詞。

①作連綴動詞，類似「是」。例如：

▶He is a trim, balding man with light blue eyes and a subdued sense of humor.
他是個愛整潔、有些禿頭的男人，有著一雙淡藍色的眼睛和些許幽默感。

② be+副詞（或介係詞片語），表示「在」。例如：

▶Gina was downstairs, pretending to write.
吉娜在樓下假裝寫著什麼。

③ there be 句型，表示「存在」或「發生」。例如：

▶There were a few small brown birds in the trees, but no other sign of life.
除了停在樹上的幾隻褐色小鳥，就再沒什麼生機了。

have

基本助動詞have的用法主要有以下幾種：

1. 與過去分詞構成現在完成式與過去完成式。例如：

▶I have participated in many sports in my 46 years, have always given 100% and usually come up short.
46年來我參加了很多運動，全身心投入，但是成效甚少。

▶Tina had worked as a senior graphic designer for a national apparel company before leaving to enter the corporate arena as a senior marketing coordinator in banking.
蒂娜曾經是國內一家服裝公司的高級平面設計師，後來她又進入商界，擔任銀行領域的高級行銷協調員。

2. 與「been＋現在分詞」構成完成進行式。例如：

▶He has been working as a waiter in Glasgow.
他一直在格拉斯哥當服務員。

have還可以作主動詞。

①作靜態的主動詞，表示特點、擁有、疾病、關係。在口語中常用have got 結構代替have。例如：

▶ He **has got** a heart of gold.
他有顆金子般的心。

▶ She **has got** the great personal friendship of the President, so nobody wants to cross her.
她和總統有很好的私人關係，所以沒人想跟她作對。

▶ When you **have** a stomachache, they give you Coca-Cola with lemon.
當你肚子痛的時候，他們會給你加檸檬的可樂。

▶ I **have** a brother who spent two years in Bolivia.
我哥哥在玻利維亞待了兩年。

②作動態的主動詞，表示經歷、吃喝等行為。例如：

▶ I hope you **have** a wonderful holiday.
願你有個愉快的假期。

▶ Do you want to **have** a cup of coffee?
要來杯咖啡嗎？

do

基本助動詞do的用法主要有以下幾種：

1. 用於疑問句、否定句或附加疑問句中。例如：

▶ **Do** you find the problem is better now than it was during the civil rights movement?
你覺得現在這個問題與民權運動期間相比有所好轉了嗎？

▶ I **don't** expect spectacular changes in a short period of time.
我並不期待在短期內會有巨大的轉機。

▶ You own a lot of financial stocks, **don't** you?
你有很多股票，不是嗎？

2.代替前面已經提到的動作。例如：

▶ I used to earn five times as much as I **do** now, but I still have to pay the same maintenance, school fees and commission to agents as I did before.
雖然我現在的收入只有過去的五分之一，但生活費用、學費和付給代理的傭金還是和過去一樣多。

3. 放在實義主動詞前，起強調作用。例如：

▶ Well, don't be discouraged, but **do** be determined.
別氣餒，要堅定。

4. 用於倒裝句

當否定副詞或其他副詞如only，so等位於句首時會引起助動詞與主詞倒裝。例如：

▶ Never **did** I endure so long, so miserable a night as that.
我從來就沒經歷過如此糟糕的漫漫長夜。

▶ Only half a century later **did** the playwright learn the full circumstances of his Jewish background.
劇作家花了半世紀才對他的猶太身世有了充分的瞭解。

▶ So much **did** Brunel value Bob's skills and steady temperament that he made him one of his assistants.
正是由於布魯內爾欣賞鮑勃的技術和平和的性情，才雇他做自己的助手。

注意！

do 還可以作主動詞，主要有以下幾種用法：

①表示「做」某事。例如：

▶ He **did** his best not to disappoint them.
他盡了自己最大的努力不讓他們失望。

▶ Mrs. Green had gone out to **do** some shopping.
格林夫人出去買東西了。

②表示對某人或某事產生作用。例如：

▶ The doctor, however good he might be, could **do** nothing for Katherine now.
儘管醫生技術可能很好，但現在他對凱薩琳也無能為力了。

③表示工作。例如：

▶ Some of you may have plans for what you want to **do** in the future.
或許你們中的某些人已經對將來的工作有了計畫。

④表示「可以接受，足以」。例如：

▶ It will **do** only if we match political support now with economic, social and cultural support in the future.
我們只有將政治、經濟、社會和文化支援相結合，才能有將來的發展。

情態動詞 ▷

情態動詞主要表示説話人的態度、打算、願望或意願等，提出的建議或要求甚至命令，以及表示禮貌、請求等。

在情態動詞中，shall，should 和will，would是比較特殊的詞，它們起情態動詞的作用，表示説話人的意願、建議或打算等，但也能用來表示時態，起助動詞的作用。嚴格地講，它們是介於基本助動詞和情態動詞之間的詞。我們將它們放在情態動詞一節講。

情態動詞的特徵

除了擁有助動詞的特徵之外，情態動詞還有自己的特徵。

1. 接不帶to的動詞不定詞

情態動詞後接不帶to的動詞不定詞，即動詞原形。例如：

▶ He may die if we don't help.
如果我們不救他，他可能有生命危險。

▶ People ought to feel completely at ease, whichever choice they make.
無論做什麼選擇，人們都應覺得澈底地放鬆。

2. 不能同時使用

情態動詞位於主動詞前面，不能同時使用兩個或兩個以上的情態動詞。

情態動詞的分類

情態動詞可以分為中心情態動詞和邊緣情態動詞（或半情態動詞）兩種。情態動詞還可以構成片語，其功能介於主動詞與情態動詞之間。

中心情態動詞共九個：can，could，may，might，will，would，shall，should，must。

邊緣情態動詞又稱為半情態動詞，它們具有情態動詞的作用，可以表示看法、意願、要求等意義，但又不符合情態動詞的所有特徵，是介於情態動詞和主動詞之間的助動詞，共四個：dare，need，ought to，used to。

情態動詞還可以構成片語，表達一般動詞片語的意義，或表達情態動詞的意義。例如：be able to，be obliged to，be willing to，be sure to，be supposed to，be going to，would rather，had better，have to，have got to等。

1. 中心情態動詞can，could

(1)can，could的基本意義

a. 表示能力

can表示現在或將來具備的能力。例如：

▶You're looking for a kid who **can** dance and sing and act but also for a kid with attitude.
你要找的孩子不僅能歌善舞、會表演，而且還要有自己的想法。

could表示過去具備的能力。例如：

▶He **could** make a small one-man plane when he was young.
在他年輕的時候，他就能製造小型的單人駕駛飛機。

b. 表示學到的技術或知識。例如：

▶He **could** not speak and gesture at the same time. 他說話的時候無法同時做手勢。

c. 表示可能性

can和could均可表示做某事的可能性，但語氣上could比can弱。例如：

▶They **can** close us down if they find anything they believe to be in violation of the protocols which they have approved.
只要發現我們有任何違反他們達成的協議的地方，他們都很有可能讓我們關門。

▶He **could** face the death penalty. 他也許會被判死刑。

表示過去的可能，可以用can/could have done來表示。can一般用於否定句和疑問句，could不受限制。例如：

▶I **could have** been allergic or something. 我當時可能是過敏什麼的。

could have done可以表示過去能做某事但沒有做到。例如：

▶The decision **could have** cost us dearly, but luckily it didn't.
這個決定本來可以讓我們付出沉重的代價，但萬幸它沒有。

d. 表示許可

can表示某人被允許做某事。例如：

▶**Can** we ask you some questions while we're waiting?
能趁我們等的時間問你一些問題嗎？

could表示某人在過去被允許做某事，多用於間接引語。例如：

▶ The teacher said we **could** all go home.
老師說我們都可以回家了。

e. 表示請求

can表示直接提出請求，could是更禮貌的用法，語氣比較婉轉。例如：

▶ **Can** I have a chocolate?
我能吃塊巧克力嗎？

▶ **Could** you ask him to phone me?
你能讓他打電話給我嗎？

f. 表示懷疑真實性

用於疑問句或否定句中，could比can顯得更謙遜。例如：

▶ **Can** this be a breakthrough?
這會成為一個突破嗎？

(2) can，could的特殊意義

a. can表示困惑。例如：

▶ Where **can** we be heading?
我們還能去哪裡？

b. could表示提出建議

用於陳述句或疑問句中，主詞常是we，you。例如：

▶ You **could** just hop around the world learning new languages.
你可以邊周遊世界邊學習新的語言。

c. could用於假設語氣句

表示對現在或過去情況的假設。例如：

▶ If he did not want that job, he **could** just say so publicly, and that would be the end of the rumor that he does.
如果他不想要那份工作，他可以明說。這樣，有關於他要任職的傳言就會不攻自破了。

▶ If I had been killed, I **could** have been buried on the farm, next to my father.
如果那次我被殺死了，我就會被葬在農場，緊挨著我父親。

(3) can，could的習慣性用法

a. sb. can't/couldn't help doing sth. 表示情不自禁或不由自主地做某事。例如：

▶ I **couldn't help laughing** to myself at the thought that whether or not I succeeded in making peace in the Middle East, Bosnia, or Northern Ireland, at least I had saved some Aegean sheep.
不管我能否實現中東、波士尼亞和北愛爾蘭的和平，至少我救了愛琴海的羊，一想到這，我就止不住想笑。

b. couldn't be better/worse起強調的作用。例如：

▶ "The timing of the report couldn't be better," he said.
「報告的時間選得太好了。」他說道。

2. 中心情態動詞may，might

(1) may，might的基本意義

a. 表示可能性

表示某事的可能性，但語氣上might比may更不確定。例如：

▶ She **might** have had a heart of gold but she was also a thief and a tart.
儘管她可能心腸很好，但她卻是個小偷和妓女。

表示過去的可能可以用may/might have done來表示。例如：

▶ I mean somebody **might have opened** the envelope and left it somewhere.
我是說有人可能打開了信封，然後把它放在什麼地方了。

b. 表示允許

表示允許某人做某事，might多用於間接引語。例如：

▶ And children under 16 **may** not be tattooed or pierced without a doctor's permission.
16歲以下的孩子未經醫生允許，是不能紋身或打耳洞的。

▶ She said I **might** go for a drink.
她說我可以去喝一杯。

如果用在疑問句中，則是一種請求，表示希望得到允許，這時might的語氣比may更委婉。例如：

▶ **May** I have your autograph? 您能給我簽個名嗎？

▶ **Might** I borrow your pen? 我能借用一下你的筆嗎？

c. 表示讓步

　　may，might可以表示讓步的意思，類似although引導的子句所表達的讓步意義，常與but連用。例如：

▶You **might** need to keep some messages for future reference, **but** they don't need to languish in your inbox.
　或許你需要留幾封信好為將來作個參考，但是也不要讓它們在你的收件箱裡發霉了。

(2) may，might的特殊意義

a. may表示願望。例如：

▶**May** you all have a good Christmas and a healthy and prosperous New Year.
　願你們聖誕快樂，在新的一年裡身體健康、事業興旺！

b. might常在肯定句中表示責備。例如：

▶Now we sit and wonder how the slaughter of 3,000 innocent Americans on 9/11 **might** have been prevented.
　現在我們坐下來反思當初應該如何做才能讓911事件中3,000個無辜的美國人免遭殺戮。

c. might用於假設語氣中。例如：

▶At a time when the miracle **might** have happened, it never happened.
　在一個奇蹟可能會發生的時候，它卻沒有發生。

▶A child's life **might** have been saved if caregivers had not been too terrified to intervene because of threats and violence from her parents.
　如果不是因為孩子的父母的威脅和暴力使得護理員不敢插手，孩子的生命有可能得以挽救。

(3)may，might的習慣性用法

a. may/might as well表示「最好，為好，不妨，不如」。例如：

▶If you want a half-hearted approach I **may as well** not start in the first place.
　如果你要的是個敷衍的方法，那我還不如不要開始。

b. may well表示「理所應當，很有可能」。例如：

▶The delays of rescue **may well** be costing lives.
　救援的延緩會貽誤生機。

3. 中心情態動詞shall，should

(1)情態動詞shall

作為情態動詞，should不是shall的過去式，這是兩個在意義上有著很大區別的詞。

a. 表示徵詢意見

shall 用於疑問句中，主詞通常為第一、第三人稱，表示詢問對方的意見。例如：

▶ **Shall** we watch all night together and see the sun rise?
不然我們通宵來看，正好再一起看日出？

b. 表示決心

we/I shall表示說話人的決心和意志。例如：

▶ **We shall** live openly and speak truth to each other, and create happiness for each other. 我們要坦誠相待，為彼此創造幸福。

c. 表示許諾

主詞常為第二、三人稱。例如：

▶ "You **shall** see my new car tomorrow, father," said Tom.
湯姆說：「爸爸，明天你一定能看到我的新車。」

d. 用於法律或正式的公文中陳述命令、規定。例如：

▶ "He **shall** conduct the European Union's common foreign and security policy," the treaty declares. 條約中聲明：「他應該執行歐盟統一的外交、安全政策。」

▶ All names **shall** be removed to protect the innocent.
為了保護無辜者，所有的名字都要隱去。

(2)情態動詞should

a. 表示「應該……」，類似ought to。例如：

▶ We **should** ask ourselves who we are grateful for and who provides a really good service, and those who do **should** be thanked in whatever ways we feel best.
我們應該自問，我們要感謝誰，是誰為我們提供了優質的服務，對於他們，我們應該用我們認為最好的方式予以感謝。

should have done表示應該做但沒有做的事情。例如：

▶ We **should have done** better in Europe but we haven't.
我們在歐洲原本應該做得更好，但我們卻沒有。

b. 表示提供或徵求建議。例如：

▶ **Should** I call the police?
我要報警嗎？

c. 表示猜想或推測。例如：

▶ His report **should** be ready when I get back.
等我回來的時候，他的報告應該準備好了。

d. 用於that引導的子句中，強調感情、命令、建議等這樣的結構主要有：

It＋be＋名詞＋that子句：

名詞多為表示對事物態度的詞，如：marvel，misfortune，pity，wonder 等。例如：

▶ **It is a pity that** he **should** have so much trouble for nothing.
他遇到這麼多麻煩但是到頭來什麼都沒得到，真是遺憾。

should用於名詞之後的that-子句中，表示命令、建議、決定等。常用的名詞有：advice，decision，demand，instruction，order，desire，request，requirement等。例如：

▶ The president withdrew **his demand that** all ambassadors **should** leave their residences.
總統收回了要求所有大使離開住所的命令。

It＋be ＋形容詞＋that子句：

形容詞多為表達感情色彩的詞，如：advisable，desirable，essential，important，impossible，likely，necessary，possible，proper等。例如：

▶ **It is important that** parents **should** continue to set aside the time to read with their children and encourage them to let their imaginations grow.
父母應該繼續留些時間陪孩子讀書，培養他們的想像力，這非常重要。

It＋be＋過去分詞＋that子句：

常用的過去分詞有：agreed，arranged，decided，demanded，desired，settled，ordered，suggested等。例如：

▶ **It was decided that** Julia **should** go to see Minnie and escort her to Carrie's house.
決定是這樣的：朱麗亞去看明妮，並負責把她送到卡麗家。

should用於動詞之後的that子句中，表示命令、建議、決定等。常用的動詞有：advise，agree，ask，decide，demand，insist，order，prefer，recommend，regret，request，require，suggest等。例如：

▶ Three times doctors gently **suggested** that her parents **should** sanction the switching off of her life support.
醫生曾三次委婉建議她父母同意停止她的生命維持系統。

> **注意！**
>
> should 在美式英語中常省略。

e. 用於假設語氣的條件句中，主詞常為we，I。例如：

▶ If I were you, I **should** not think of the expense.
如果我是你，我就不會去想費用問題。

f. 用於so that，for fear，in case，lest引導的目的副詞子句中，表示「因此」、「唯恐」、「以免」。例如：

▶ Jefferson Craig married Kitty **so that** the child **should** have the name of Craig.
傑斐遜‧克雷格娶了姬蒂，因此孩子跟他姓克雷格。

▶ He could not seem to sleep or rest **for fear** that some danger **should** come from which he would have to flee.
他輾轉難眠，唯恐遇上危險。

g. 用於疑問句How/Why/Who/What＋should ...?，表達驚訝。例如：

▶ **Why should** I be the only one that suffers?
為什麼我要獨自承受？

▶ **How should** I know?
那我怎麼知道？

▶ **What should** I see?
我應該看到什麼？

who和what引導的疑問句還可以是Who/What should ... but ...?結構。例如：

▶ **Who should** come on Tuesday **but** Sir James Martin?
週二除了詹姆斯‧馬丁爵士外，還會有誰來？

▶ **What should** we do but gather in the doorways to the shops, or sit in cars, or seek refuge—and a drink—inside a bar?
要嘛聚集在商店門口，要嘛坐在車裡，或者躲到酒吧喝酒，除此以外，我們還能幹嘛？

4. 中心情態動詞will，would

(1)助動詞will，would

	縮寫形式	否定形式	否定縮寫形式
will	'll	will not	won't
would	'd	would not	wouldn't

a. will 表示未來時間

　　will 適用於各種人稱的主詞，而且shall 在越來越多的情況下被will 代替。例如：

▶ They will celebrate their 60th wedding anniversary next year.
明年他們將慶祝結婚60周年。

b. would表示過去未來時間

　　would是will的過去式，適用於各種人稱作主詞。例如：

▶ McNulty said that teacher quality and accountability would be his first priority as commissioner.
麥克納爾蒂說，提高師資品質和激發教師的責任感將是他作為專員的第一要務。

(2)情態動詞will

a. 表示願意或準備做某事。例如：

▶ "I will help them and give advice because I have more experience," he said, "but you always have to remember the only way forward is to make your own career work for you."
「我比他們經驗豐富，我願意幫助他們，給他們忠告，」他說，「但是你得始終記著，只有讓工作為你服務，你才能獲得進步。」

b. 表示請求

　　常用於第二人稱主詞，構成疑問句或附加問句。例如：

▶ "Will you please open your eyes, and see what you've done to Bert's life?" said Miss Peach tautly.
「睜開眼睛看看吧，你對伯特的人生都做了什麼？」皮奇小姐激動地說。

▶ You won't tell anyone, will you?
你別告訴別人，可以嗎？

c. 表示命令或規定。例如：

▶ Every new teacher **will** take a test starting Sept. 1.
從9月1號開始，每位新來的老師都必須參加考試。

d. 表示一般性的事實。例如：

▶ The sun **will** still shine, we **will** still be going about our daily lives — and wondering what all the fuss was about.
太陽依舊照常升起，我們仍將與往常一樣地生活，弄不明白有什麼可大驚小怪的。

e. 表示現在的習慣。例如：

▶ She **will** teach the youngster basic Spanish at home to prepare him for school there in the New Year.
她在家輔導那個青少年基礎西班牙語，為他新年的學期作準備。

f. 表示推測。例如：

▶ "That **will** be his daughter, Felicity, I was about to tell you about her, don't keep interrupting," said Aunt Lou sternly.
盧阿姨嚴厲地說：「那應該是他女兒，費莉西蒂，我正要和你說她的事情，你別打斷我。」

g. 表示建議或邀請。例如：

▶ **Will** you have a drink before you leave?
在你走之前你願意喝一杯嗎？

(3)情態動詞would

a. 用於假設條件句中，可以表示對現在情況的假設。例如：

▶ If everybody had a little faith, the stock market **would** recover quite quickly.
如果大家都有點信心，那麼股票市場很快就會復甦。

還可以表示對過去情況的假設。例如：

▶ If an air strike had happened last weekend, it **would** have cost another $1 billion.
倘若上週末發生空襲，那就將再損失10億美元。

b. 表示請求

　　用於第二人稱作主詞的句子中，構成疑問句或附加問句，這時would比will顯得更有禮貌。例如：

▶Keep quiet, and sit still, would you?
　安靜點，坐著別動，可以嗎？

c. 表示過去的習慣。例如：

▶He would come down for the weekend before and see to the final arrangements of various things.
　過去他每週末都來，確保大事小事都最終安排妥當。

d. 提出建議或邀請

　　would通常比will顯得更有禮貌。例如：

▶Would you like some coffee?
　願意喝點咖啡嗎？

▶Would you come and sit here?
　請你來這兒坐著好嗎？

e. 在I would think/imagine/say的句子中，表達不確定的意見。例如：

▶I would say we have made progress in terms of women recognizing the signs and symptoms of ovarian cancer.
　我認為在促進女性識別卵巢癌的各種跡象和症狀方面，我們已經取得了進步。

f. 與like等詞連用，表示某人喜歡的做法

　　這種用法的其他動詞有：love，hate，prefer，be glad，be happy等。例如：

▶We would like to have this type of equipment on the astronauts as they go forward with space voyages, monitoring them remotely and providing them assistance.
　我們非常希望能將這種設備裝到太空人身上，伴隨他們一起進行宇宙航行，不但對他們進行遠端監控，也能給他們提供幫助。

g. 與rather構成情態動詞片語，表示更喜歡的做法。例如：

▶We would rather improve the house than stick our money in a pension fund.
　我們寧願改善住房條件也不願意把我們的錢都扔到養老基金裡。

5. 中心情態動詞must

	否定形式	否定縮寫形式
must	must not	mustn't

a. 表示必要。例如：

▶ Everyone must decide for himself.
每個人都必須為自己拿主意。

▶ All children must be given an opportunity for a basic education.
所有的孩子都必須享有接受基礎教育的機會。

▶ When force is used it must be concentrated, overwhelming and, above all, effective.
動用武力時，一定要聚積力量，全力出擊，最重要的是，要起到效果。

注意！

①表示過去的必要，要用had to。例如：

▶ When Aaron applied to study at drama school in New York, he had to answer the question" Why do you wish to become an actor?" on a form designed to weed out candidates before they got to audition.
當亞倫申請紐約的戲劇學院時，他必須回答表格上「為什麼你希望成為一個演員」這一問題，這是特地設計的表格，用來篩選參加試演的候選者。

②對於must引導的疑問句的回答，肯定回答用must，否定回答用needn't，don't have to，don't need to。例如：

▶ —Must I tell the whole truth?
我一定要都說嗎？

—Yes, you must.
是的。

▶ —Must I spell the word out?
我一定要拼出這個詞嗎？

—No, you needn't.
不用。

b. 在否定句中表示禁止。例如：

mustn't在句中的語氣比較強硬。

▶ We mustn't allow this tragedy to continue for one more day.
我們絕對不能讓這個悲劇再多延續一天了。

c. 表示判斷。例如：

▶ She said he **must** be the only nine-year-old boy in the whole of Yorkshire who had a proper bedroom all to himself.
她説，他一定是整個約克郡唯一一個擁有自己真正臥室的9歲男孩。

表示對過去事情的判斷，用must have p.p.。例如：

▶ She had pretty hair and **must have been** nice-looking when she was young.
她有著一頭秀髮，年輕的時候她一定很美。

d. 表示建議做某事

常用於口語，建議別人做某事，特別是説話人認為有趣的事情。例如：

▶ These flowers reminded me of you and our nice dinner together. We **must** do it again some time.
這些花讓我想起了你以及我們共進的那頓美好晚餐。我們什麼時候再聚聚吧。

6. 邊緣情態動詞dare

dare 既可作情態動詞，又可作主動詞。作情態動詞時，後面接不帶to的不定詞。主要用於否定句和疑問句中，或者是與hardly，never，only，no one 等表示否定意義的詞連用。

dare 作主動詞時，後面接帶to的不定詞，而且有時態、人稱的變化，主要用於否定句和疑問句中，或與否定詞連用。

(1)情態動詞dare

情態動詞dare表示「敢……」，既可指現在，也可指過去。

a. 用於否定句或帶否定詞的句中。例如：

▶ We won't open any of the windows now and we **daren't** let Louis out of our sight.
現在我們連一扇窗都不開，我們不敢讓路易士離開我們的視線。

▶ He **daren't** go to the hospital in case they asked for his Identity Card.
因為怕要身份證，他連醫院都不敢去。

▶ Smithson would never **dare** say the bad news to head office.
史密森永遠都不敢把那個壞消息告訴總部。

b. 用於疑問句。例如：

▶ How **dare** you come in my room without saying?
你怎麼敢不説一聲就進我的房間？

c. 用於含有I dare say的句子中

dare作為情態動詞一般不用於陳述句，但I dare say例外，表示猜測、可能。例如：

▶ I dare say your daughter was very much attached to him.
我敢說，你女兒很喜歡他。

(2)主動詞dare

dare作主動詞時通常表示「敢」、「敢於」的意思。例如：

▶ Did he dare to strike me when I was down?
我摔倒的時候，他敢不敢打我？

▶ Her parents didn't dare to challenge me.
她的父母不敢向我挑戰。

> 注意！
>
> dare作為情態
> 動詞，主要用於
> 英式英語的口語
> 中。

表示挑唆某人做某事或發起挑戰，常用dare somebody to do something的結構。例如：

▶ The boys dared each other to look at the corpse when it came out and speculated on whether there'd be maggots.
男孩們慫恿彼此去看屍體，並且猜想那裡是否會有蛆。

7. 邊緣情態動詞need

need與dare用法相似，既可作情態動詞，也可作主動詞。作情態動詞時，後面接不帶to的不定詞，主要用於否定句和疑問句中，或者是與hardly，never，scarcely，no one 等否定詞連用。

need作主動詞時，有時態、人稱變化，後接受詞或帶to的不定詞，可以用於各種句式。

(1)情態動詞need

a. 表示必要，用於否定句或疑問句

need用於否定句或帶否定詞的句子。例如：

▶ Job stress needn't boil over into anger or actual violence.
工作的壓力沒必要轉化成憤怒或是暴力。

▶ You needn't trouble yourself to fret about me.
你不用費神為我操心。

▶ Many cats never need a formal bath.
許多貓從不需要正正經經地洗澡。

▶ The Germans, it seems, never need an excuse for a beer.
德國人喝啤酒好像從來都不需要藉口。

need用於疑問句。例如：

▶ **Need** I tell you where my sister went?
我一定得告訴你我姐姐去哪裡了嗎？

▶ **Need** I go into details?
我得說得再詳細點嗎？

b. needn't have p.p.表示曾經做過實際上沒有必要做的事。例如：

▶ I **needn't have worried** for everyone made me feel welcome.
大家好像都很歡迎我，我都沒必要擔心。

▶ But she **needn't have kept** Caroline locked up.
但她原本沒必要把卡洛琳鎖起來。

(2)主動詞need

a. 表示需要。例如：

▶ She thinks that every child in Iraq **needs** a psychologist.
她認為每個伊拉克的孩子都需要一個心理醫生。

▶ Critics say history doesn't **need** governor's help.
批評家認為歷史不需要統治者去推動。

b. 表示義務。例如：

▶ He **needs** to try to adapt to the conditions better.
他需要努力去更好地適應環境。

8. 邊緣情態動詞used to

	否定形式	否定縮寫形式
used to	used not to / did not use to	didn't use to

　　used to一般表示過去習慣的動作，或者表示以前存在而現在已經不存在的事物，在否定句和疑問句中常與did連用。例如：

▶ We **used to** play table tennis for hours and hours and did everything together.
過去我們經常一起打好幾個小時的乒乓球或是一起做其他的事情。

▶ "There **used to** be a beautiful 19th-century village down there," he said.
他說：「那裡曾經是一個美麗的19世紀的小村莊。」

▶ You **used not to** get so much aggression.
從前你不是這麼咄咄逼人的。

注意！

表示過去習慣的動作時，還可以用would代替used to。例如：

▶We **would** play table tennis for hours and hours and did everything together.
我們以前會一起玩桌球好幾個小時，而且做什麼都在一起。

9.邊緣情態動詞ought to

	否定形式	否定縮寫形式
ought to	ought not to	oughtn't to

a. 表示責任或義務。例如：

▶I feel that capital punishment **ought to** be mandatory under certain crimes.
我認為對於有些罪行，判處死刑是必要的。

注意！

ought to 用於疑問句時，ought通常置於句首。例如：

▶**Ought** I **to** cancel all the plans?
我該取消所有的計畫嗎？

▶**Ought** I **to** be fearful for my life?
我該為我的性命擔憂嗎？

b. ought to have p.p.通常表示過去應該做而未做的事情。例如：

▶"She **ought to have seen** he only wanted her money, and refused him," said Retty.
「她應該看到他只想要她的錢，她真該拒絕他。」蕾蒂說。

c. 表示勸告或建議。例如：

▶You **ought to** be thoroughly ashamed of yourselves.
你們該對自己的行為感到非常羞愧。

▶You **ought to** move back home with your parents.
你該搬回家和父母一起住。

d. 表示推測。例如：

▶Maria felt that she **ought to** have grown by several inches, because she was being pulled so many ways by so many people.
瑪麗亞感到她都該長幾英寸了，因為有這麼多人用不同方式拉扯她。

🎯 情態動詞片語

情態動詞片語由基本助動詞be和have引導。常用的情態動詞片語如下表所示：

be able to	be about to	be apt to	be bound to
be certain to	be due to	be going to	be liable to
be (un)likely to	be obliged to	be supposed to	be sure to
be (un)willing to	be to	have to	have got to

1. be going to

be going to由基本助動詞be引導，主要用於現在式或過去式。

a. 表示打算做某事。例如：

▶ They **are going to** go in depth into his years in school, a period of this great writer's life that does not get a lot of attention elsewhere.
他們打算深入研究這位偉大作家的學生生涯，這段時期還不曾受到別人很多關注。

b. 表示即將發生或可能發生的事情。例如：

▶ It **is going to** take a lot longer than you think to get those doctors out there.
如果要讓那些醫生走出去，花的時間將遠比你想的長。

▶ She'd told my parents she **was going to** do homework in a friend's house, but went to meet Justin instead.
她告訴我父母她要去一個朋友家做功課，但實際上她卻去見了札斯廷。

be about to也表示即將發生的意思。例如：

▶ Now 36 years later, John Glenn **is about to** make history again.
36年後的今天，約翰‧葛蘭將再一次創造歷史。

▶ He **was about to** depart for a year in Australia.
他將離開這裡去澳大利亞待上一年。

2. have to

have to由基本助動詞have和介係詞構成，在使用中會體現have的各種時態，在構成否定句和疑問句時要使用助動詞do。

a. 通常表示義務或有必要做的事。例如：

▶ Did he **have to** be so deliberately rude?
  他就一定要這麼粗魯嗎？

▶ In those days, a drug company didn't **have to** prove a product's safety through animal studies before selling it to the public.
  在過去，藥廠的產品在投入市場前是不用通過動物實驗來證明其安全性的。

b. 表示勸告或建議。例如：

▶ You **have to** distinguish famous paintings from a child's doodles.
  你得分辨得出什麼是名畫，什麼是孩子的塗鴉。

▶ You **have to** do some sort of risk assessment, before you invest.
  在投資前，你得作個風險評估。

c. 表示推測某事發生的可能性或真實性。例如：

▶ This **has to** be one of the smallest mobiles ever made.
  這一定是迄今為止最小的汽車之一。

▶ This **has to** be more than a coincidence.
  這絕不是一個巧合。

小結 ▷

　　本章重點介紹了助動詞和情態動詞。助動詞包括be，have，do三個基本助動詞。基本助動詞除了能充當助動詞，還能擔任主動詞的作用。情態動詞又分為九個中心情態動詞和四個邊緣情態動詞。

Part 6 動詞的時態變化

概說

英語句子中時間的概念通過動詞的結構變化，或者運用助動詞、副詞等方式來表達。在本章裡，我們主要對動詞的時態變化進行系統的描述。

動詞的時態

英語中不同時間發生的動作要用不同的形式表示，稱為「時態變化」。在文法層面上，英語動詞的時態變化有兩種基本形式：現在簡單式（Present Tenses）和過去簡單式（Past Tenses）。另外還有未來式，是由「will/shall＋不帶to的不定詞」構成。

不同的時態，動詞有對應的變化，現在簡單式用動詞原形，但如果主詞是第三人稱單數，則動詞一般要加-s 字尾。例如：

▶ He **plays** the piano and the violin like a professional.
他演奏起鋼琴和小提琴就像專業人士。

現在簡單式主詞為第三人稱單數時，謂語動詞通常直接的變化加-s，例如：

• make → makes   • sit → sits   • play → plays

但在加-s 時要注意以下兩點：

1. 在以ch，sh，s，x或o結尾的詞後要加-es。例如：

• teach → teaches   • publish → publishes

• mix → mixes   • do → does

2. 以「子音＋y」結尾的動詞，先變y為 i 再加-es。例如：

• try → tries   • fly → flies   • study → studies

過去簡單式用動詞的過去形式，除be動詞外（was，were），不分人稱，全用一種形式。規則動詞以加-ed字尾的方式構成過去式。例如：

• ask → asked   • look → looked   • mix → mixed

但加-ed時要注意以下幾點：

1. 若以字母e結尾，過去式只需加-d。例如：

• dance → danced
• hope → hoped
• examine → examined

2. 「子音＋y」結尾：過去式先變y為i，再加-ed。例如：

• study → studied
• try → tried
• fry → fried

3. 母音字母＋一個子音字母結尾，該音節又是重音者，末尾子音字母要雙寫，再加-ed。常見的末尾字母要雙寫的動詞見下表：

allot	ban	bar	bat	beg	chat
chop	commit	compel	confer	control	cram
crop	dam	defer	deter	dip	dot
drag	drop	drum	embed	emit	enrol
equip	excel	expel	fan	fit	grip
handicap	hug	jam	jog	jot	knit
knot	lag	log	man	mob	mop
mug	net	nod	occur	omit	pad
pat	pin	pop	prop	refer	regret
repel	rob	rot	rub	scan	scrub
ship	shop	shrug	shun	sin	sip
skid	skim	skip	slam	slip	slot
snap	sob	spot	stab	star	stem
step	stir	stop	strip	stun	submit
tag	tan	tap	transfer	transmit	throb
tip	top	trap	trip	vet	

在過去式中，不規則動詞變化如下：

• go → went
• buy → bought
• teach → taught
• sit → sat

（參見附錄常用不規則動詞）

149

現在簡單式

現在簡單式主要用來表示現在的情況或狀態、經常發生或反覆發生的動作，還表示不受時間限制的客觀存在。

❶ 表示現時狀態和現在的瞬間動作

現在簡單式表示現在的狀態時通常用靜態動詞。常見的靜態動詞有：

admire	adore	appear	assume	astonish
be	believe	belong	consist	desire
despise	doubt	envy	exist	fear
feel	fit	forget	hate	have
hear	hope	impress	include	involve
keep	know	lack	last	like
love	mean	mind	need	owe
please	possess	prefer	prove	realize
recognize	remember	require	regret	satisfy
seat	see	smell	sound	suppose
suspect	think	understand	want	wish

現在簡單式的狀態可能是短暫的，也可能會延續一段時間。

1. 短暫狀態。例如：

▶ The flight is delayed because of the storm.
由於風暴的關係，航班延誤了。

2. 延續狀態。例如：

▶ As a longer winter is expected this year, the ground still remains frozen.
今年的冬天特別漫長，地面仍然是冰凍的。

現在簡單式可與表示短暫動作的動態動詞連用，常指瞬間發生或完成的動作。例如：

close	hit	jump	kick	knock
open	put	shut	stop	

或與表示改變或移動的動詞連用。例如：

arrive	become	change	come	get
go	grow	leave	reach	turn

現在簡單式表示現時動作時，還有以下幾種用法：

1. 體育運動的實況解説。例如：

▶ "She **takes** the ball, shoots," said the commentator.
「她搶到球，投籃。」評論員説道。

2. 演示説明。例如：

▶ After slicing the ingredients, the chef **puts** them into the pot to boil for about 15 minutes.
廚師把食材切成片，然後放進鍋裡煮15分鐘左右。

3. 動作描述。例如：

▶ He **takes** a bus to town and **shops** for grocery at the supermarket.
他坐公車進城，然後在超市購物。

4. 劇情介紹。例如：

▶ In this movie, the main character **is** a young girl who **has** the ability to predict the future.
該影片中，主人公是一位能夠預測未來的年輕姑娘。

5. 圖片説明。例如：

▶ This painting **shows** the artist's opinions on global warming.
這幅畫表達了畫家對全球暖化的看法。

❷ 表示現在的習慣動作

現在簡單式用來表示現在某種動作經常或反覆發生，已形成了習慣。

1. 經常發生的動作。例如：

▶ He **helps** out at the orphanage every Sunday.
他每個週日到孤兒院幫忙。

2. 反覆發生的動作。例如：

▶ He usually **visits** his grandparents in the weekend.
他經常在週末看望祖父母。

現在簡單式的這種用法通常與頻率副詞連用。常見的頻率副詞有：

always	usually	often	frequently	sometimes
occasionally	seldom	rarely	hardly	never

還可以與其他表示頻率的詞或片語連用：

nowadays	at present	currently	presently	now
recently	once in a while	now and then	time and again	once so often
weekly	monthly	yearly	as usual	as a rule
once every week/month/year				

❸ 表示不受時限的客觀存在

不受時間限制的客觀存在包括客觀真理、格言、科學事實以及其他不受時間限制的事實。句子中可以不用時間狀語來表達具體的時間概念。

1. 真理。例如：

▶ Clouds **are** made of very tiny droplets of water or ice crystals.
雲是由非常微小的水滴或冰晶構成的。

2. 格言。例如：

▶ As the saying goes, you **reap** what you **sow**.
常言道：種瓜得瓜，種豆得豆。

3. 科學事實。例如：

▶ It is scientifically proven that hot air **rises** and cold air **sinks**.
科學實驗證明：熱氣上升，冷氣下降。

4. 其他不受時間限制的事實。例如：

▶ The sun **rises** in the East and **sets** in the West.
太陽從東邊升起，從西邊落下。

❹ 表示未來時間

現在簡單式可以用來表示將要發生的事情。

1. 按計畫或安排。例如：

▶ As planned, the trekking team **sets** off to the summit tomorrow.
按計畫，登山隊明天向山頂進發。

▶ Plans already under review **are expected** to be carried out as planned.
正在審查的計畫將會按原定方案執行。

2. 按規定。例如：

▶According to the law, an author always **needs** to take "reasonable care" that the statements he or she is making are not false.
根據法律，作者應始終對自己的言論的真實性持「合理的謹慎態度」。

▶One **pays** a fine of $5,000 for driving without a license.
無照駕駛按規定罰款5000美元。

3. 按時間表。例如：

▶The postman **comes** every Tuesday at about 3 pm.
郵差每週二下午3點左右到。

4. 與某些動詞連用

現在簡單式經常與hope，bet等動詞連用。例如：

▶I **hope** (that) the parcel from America **arrives** tomorrow.
我希望從美國寄來的包裹明天能到。

▶I **bet** (that) the blue team **wins** the soccer tournament today.
我打賭今天的足球比賽藍隊會贏。

5. 用於某些特殊結構中

現在簡單式還用於某些文法結構中，如條件句與時間副詞子句。例如：

▶"I will go to the party only **if Sharon goes too**," said Felicia.
「只要莎倫參加晚會，我也會去。」費莉西亞說。

▶I reminded Jeremy to bring my CDs **when he drops by** at my office tomorrow.
我提醒傑瑞米明天來我的辦公室時，要把CD給我。

❺ 表示過去時間

在特定情形下現在簡單式還可以表示過去發生的事件。

1. 敘述文體中

在敘述文體中，使用現在簡單式可以使描述更為生動，宛如事情是在敘述時發生，歷歷在目。例如：

▶On a rainy spring afternoon Sam **sits** in a recliner in the living room of his and Donna's small ranch house on Hopkins Street, a block from where he was raised. He **tells** his grandson many interesting anecdotes of the ancestors.
在一個春雨綿綿的下午，山姆坐在小農舍客廳的躺椅上，向他的孫子講述著許多關於祖先們有趣的逸事。小農舍為他與唐娜共有，位於霍普金斯大街上，離他長大的住所僅僅一個街區之遙。

2. 口語中

在口頭交際時，為了便於表達，也可用現在簡單式表示「告訴（tell）、說（say）、講（speak）、聽說（hear）、瞭解（learn）」等意思。例如：

▶ The ten o'clock news says that there's going to be a bad storm.
十點的新聞報告將會有一場嚴重的暴風雨。

🎯 過去簡單式

過去簡單式表示過去發生的事情，由動詞的過去式來實現。

❶ 表示過去時間

1. 表示過去的動作和狀態

過去簡單式主要用來表示在特定的過去時間裡一次完成的動作或一度存在的狀態。例如：

▶ He jumped in joy when he received an acceptance letter from the university.
當接到大學的錄取通知書時，他高興地跳了起來。

▶ This place was a popular hangout for teenager in the 1980s.
這是80年代青少年喜歡光顧的場所。

2. 表示過去的習慣動作。例如：

▶ When he was in secondary school, he played basketball with his friends every Saturday.
上中學時，他每週六和朋友打籃球。

3. 表示已不復存在

過去簡單式所表示的過去時間都與現在時間不發生關係。因此，用過去簡單式表示的動作或狀態都已成為過去，現在已不復存在。例如：

▶ The United Nations was formed in 1945.
聯合國成立於1945年。

▶ This necklace was given to me by my late grandmother.
這項鍊是已經過世的祖母送給我的。

▶ She used to be a very shy girl. However, after attending drama class, she became more sociable and outspoken.
她曾經是一個非常害羞的女孩，可參加了戲劇班後，她變得更開朗，更會交際了。

過去簡單式句子中有明顯的過去時間概念，因此經常與表示過去的時間狀語連用：

last year/ month/ week/ summer	a year/ month/ week ago
two minutes / a while ago	in 1950 / in (the) 1980's
at that time/ moment	during the time / those years
yesterday	when...

還可以與頻率副詞連用談論過去的情況：

always	usually	often	sometimes	seldom	never

當上下文中過去時間明確時，可以不用時間狀語。例如：

▶ My late grandmother **enjoyed** gardening and sewing.
我過世的祖母喜歡園藝和縫紉。

❷ 表示現在和未來

過去簡單式還可用在特定句型中，表示現在時間和將來時間的動作，比如過去簡單式與某些動詞連用表示委婉的口氣。例如：

▶ I will be able to attend the company lunch if **it were tomorrow**.
如果公司的午宴是在明天的話，那我可以去。

雖然可以用現在簡單式表示願望，但口氣不如用過去簡單式婉轉。這一用法限於少數動詞，如want，like，hope，wonder等。例如：

▶ I **wanted** to ask if you would be free to help me with my assignment later.
我想知道你稍後是否有空輔導我做作業。

▶ I **hoped** that you would be able to come for my piano recital this evening.
我期待您今晚能夠光臨我的鋼琴演奏會。

▶ I **wondered** if you could lend me the book for a week.
你能否把這本書借給我一週？

動詞的完成式與進行式 ▶

完成式表述在一段時間內所發生的事件或存在的狀態延續到某個具體的時間。

進行式（Progressive Aspect）表述的是在上下文中所表明的時刻正在進行或延續的事件或狀態。

在結構上，完成式由「助動詞have＋過去分詞」構成；進行式由「助動詞be ＋現在分詞」構成。二者均可與現在式或過去式搭配。

- 現在進行式（Present Progressive Aspect）：is/are + 動詞-ing
- 過去進行式（Past Progressive Aspect）：was/were + 動詞-ing
- 現在完成式（Present Perfective Aspect）：have + 動詞-ed
- 現在完成進行式（Present Perfective Progressive Aspect）：have + been + 動詞-ing
- 過去完成式（Past Perfective Aspect）：had + 動詞-ed
- 過去完成進行式（Past Perfective Progressive Aspect）：had + been +動詞-ing

規則動詞的過去分詞由「動詞原形＋-ed」的方式構成，與動詞的過去形式構成一樣。而現在分詞則由「動詞原形＋-ing」的方式構成。

原形	過去式	過去分詞	現在分詞
ask	asked	asked	asking
look	looked	looked	looking
mix	mixed	mixed	mixing

但加-ed字尾構成過去式及過去分詞，和加-ing字尾構成現在分詞時要注意以下幾點：

1. 以字母e結尾：過去式及過去分詞只需加-d，現在分詞先去掉字母e，再加-ing。例如：

原形	過去式	過去分詞	現在分詞
dance	danced	danced	dancing
hope	hoped	hoped	hoping
examine	examined	examined	examining

2. 以「子音＋y」結尾：過去式及過去分詞先變y為i，再加-ed；現在分詞只需直接加-ing。例如：

原形	過去式	過去分詞	現在分詞
study	studied	studied	studying
try	tried	tried	trying
fry	fried	fried	frying

3. 以母音字母+一個子音字母結尾，該音節又是重音者，末尾子音字母要雙寫，再加-ed或-ing。例如：

原形	過去式	過去分詞	現在分詞
plan	planned	planned	planning
admit	admitted	admitted	admitting
prefer	preferred	preferred	preferring

常見的需要雙寫的動詞表參見P149。在其他情況下，直接加-ed。例如：

原形	過去式	過去分詞	現在分詞
play	played	played	playing
open	opened	opened	opening

不規則動詞的過去分詞變化如下：

原形	過去式	過去分詞
go	went	gone
buy	bought	bought
teach	taught	taught
forget	forgot	forgotten

（參見附錄常用不規則動詞）

現在進行式

現在進行式表示某個時間正在進行的動作，主要有三個層面上的意義：

①事件在一段時間內發生並延續

②事件在某個有限定的時間內發生並延續

③已發生的事件並不一定完成了

1. 表示說話時正在進行的動作

用於進行式的動詞一般是表示持續動作的動態動詞。現在進行式與現在簡單式的區別在於現在簡單式往往具有長久的含義，而現在進行式則表示暫時的含義。請比較：

★現在簡單式

▶My cousin lives in an apartment at the heart of town.
我的表哥住在市中心的一棟公寓裡。

▶The wonderful memories of my late grandfather live on in my mind.
過世的祖父留給我的美好記憶永遠珍藏在我的心裡。

★現在進行式

▶For convenience, the company visitors are living in the hotel just next to our office.
方便起見，公司的來訪者暫住在辦公室旁邊的旅館裡。

▶"It is drizzling now but I think it appears to be stopping soon," said Jenna, looking out of the window.
「正在下小雨，但我想似乎一會兒就要停了。」詹娜一邊看著窗外一邊說。

2. 表示現階段一直在進行的動作

現在進行式也可以表示現階段一直在進行的動作，這裡有一個現在時間段（Duration）的表示。例如：

▶Laurie is taking vitamin supplements after learning of the potential health benefits.
當勞理瞭解到維生素添加劑對健康的潛在好處後，他就在服用了。

注意！

現在簡單式表示長期動作；而現在進行式則表示現階段正在做的事，是暫時性動作。例如：

▶My sister works as a researcher in the laboratory.
我姐姐在實驗室做研究員。

▶The professor is working intently in his laboratory now.
教授正在實驗室裡專注地工作。

3. 表示按計畫安排近期內即將發生的動作

現在進行式還可以用來表示將來時間裡要發生的事情，通常都是按照現在的計畫和安排在近期內即將發生的事。例如：

▶As scheduled, the preliminary round of the tennis competition is starting tomorrow.
根據安排，網球預賽將在明天開始。

以上用法都有一個表示未來（一般指不久的將來）的狀語。例如：

▶Next week, my family is going on a one-week trip to Spain.
下星期，我們全家將到西班牙旅遊一週。

常用於現在進行式上述用法的動詞如下：

arrive	come	do	get	go
have	leave	meet	return	see
spend	start	stay	wear	

4. 現在進行式的其他用法

現在進行式還可以用於以下幾種情況：

(1) 表示剛剛過去的動作

注意！

現在進行式表示剛剛過去的動作時只適用於口語中某些表示說話的動詞，如tell，talk，say等。例如：

▶ He **is saying** that the test was very difficult.
他是在說測試很難。

▶ John **is telling** me not to be affected by the negative reviews of my performance.
約翰告誡我不要受那些對我的表演的負面評價的影響。

▶ Ned **is talking** about the movie they just watched.
內德在談論剛才看過的那場電影。

(2) 表示婉轉的口氣

注意！

現在進行式的這一用法只限於hope，wonder等少數動詞。I'm hoping，I'm wondering 的說法要比I hope，I wonder 的口氣婉轉一些。例如：

▶ I **am hoping** to be selected to represent the faculty in the Olympiad.
我希望能被選拔代表學院參加奧林匹亞競賽。

▶ I **am wondering** if I could borrow your calculator for a while.
我能否借你的計算機用一用？

(3) 表示反覆發生的動作

用於現在進行式的動詞通常是表示持續動作的動詞，如work，study，live等。表示短暫動作的動詞如hit，jump，nod，knock，kick等，用於進行式時表示在一段時間裡反覆發生的動作。例如：

▶ The naughty child **is hitting** the cat with a stick.
淘氣的小孩用棍子不斷地擊打那只貓。

▶ The dog **is jumping** excitedly to get treats from his owner.
那只狗興奮地跳著，想從主人手裡得到美味的食物。

▶ He **is nodding** his head to the loud thumping of the music.
他的頭隨著音樂的強烈節奏不停地擺動。

▶ The carpenter **is knocking** several nails into the wood to secure the legs of the table.
木工把幾枚釘子敲進木板來固定桌子腿。

▶ The boy is kicking at the legs of the table to show that he is bored.
小男孩用腳不停地踢著桌子腿，表示他感到很無聊。

注意！

現在進行式一般不與靜態動詞如own，like，love，understand，realize，know，be連用。但是，當作主動詞用的靜態動詞be用於現在進行式時，句子表達了某種特殊的含義。例如：The neighbours are being friendly. 我的鄰居今天特別友好。（表示鄰居的這種友好是裝出來的，並不一定是誠懇的。）

(4)表示動作的轉換

現在進行式表示由動作引起了一個轉換過程，動作持續一段時間後，從一種狀態逐漸演變成為另一種狀態。比如：

▶ The taxi driver is stopping his car at the filling station.
計程車司機在加油站停車。
▶ Nancy is arriving.
南西就要來了。
▶ The Boeing 747 is taking off.
波音747就要起飛了。
▶ The old man is dying.
老人就快死了。

在現在進行式中，用表示短暫性動作的動詞或片語如stop，arrive，take off，die等表示持續性的意義。

過去進行式

過去進行式表示在過去某個時間某件事情正在進行。過去進行式的用法與現在進行式的許多用法相似，相當於現在時間向過去推移。

1. 表示過去某時正在進行的動作

過去進行式的這一用法通常用時間狀語來表示，或者通過上下文將時間表示出來。例如：

▶ For the past two hours, they were talking about having children together.
兩個小時裡，兩人一直在討論生孩子的事情。
▶ For the past two weeks, Fred was rehearsing for his performance.
在過去的兩週裡，弗雷德一直在為演出排練。

▶ The twins were in good spirits and were laughing and joking with their friends **when they were wheeled out from the radiology department**.
當孿生兄弟從放射室推出來時，兩人情緒很高，不斷地笑著並和朋友們開著玩笑。

▶ My uncle was working at an electronics company **until he retired last year**.
我叔父在去年退休前一直在一家電子公司上班。

2. 表示過去某種習慣動作

過去進行式表示過去時間裡的習慣性動作時，通常指過去某一階段暫時性的習慣。例如：

▶ Before we bought the treadmill, my father **was exercising** at the park every evening.
在買跑步機之前，我父親每天晚上在公園裡鍛煉身體。

過去進行式與副詞always，forever等連用，表示過去反覆發生的動作，帶有一定的感情色彩。例如：

▶ He **was always coming** in late for work and was an irresponsible worker.
他是一個沒有責任心的人，總是上班遲到。

3. 表示過去曾為未來做準備的動作

過去進行式可用於描述在過去的時間中，為尚未發生的事進行準備。例如：

▶ The company **were preparing** for the large-scale seminar scheduled this afternoon.
公司上下都在為定於今天下午召開的大型研討會作準備。

4. 表示現在時間和未來時間的動作

現在進行式用來表示現在時間或未來時間的動作，口氣比較婉轉，與動詞hope，want，wonder連用，表示禮貌的請求。例如：

▶ I **was hoping** that you would agree with my suggestion.
期望您能同意我提出的建議。

5. 過去進行式與過去簡單式用法比較

(1)表示過去時間裡已經完成的動作用過去簡單式，表示正在進行尚未完成的動作用現在進行式。例如：

▶ He **paid** £40,000 for the two-bedroom home while he **was working** as an electrical engineer.
在他當電機工程師期間，他用4萬英鎊買下了有兩個臥室的住房。

(2)過去簡單式通常只說明過去某時發生的事，過去進行式則側重動作持續的時間，而不僅是說明事實。例如：

▶ They **reached** the airport early and **were patiently waiting** for the arrival of their guests. 他們早早就趕到機場，正在耐心地等待客人的到來。

(3)當過去簡單式與過去進行式同時出現在句中時，通常是表示較短的動作用過去簡單式，表示較長的動作用過去進行式。例如：

▶ Jenny **was watching** the television when the postman **came**.
珍妮正在看電視，這時郵差來了。

(4)在口語和記敘文中，首先用過去進行式表示某種正在進行的動作，並以此作為背景，引出用過去簡單式表示的新的事態或情節。例如：

▶ My family **were shopping** at the mall when the fire alarm **rang**.
我們全家正在購物中心買東西，這時火警鈴響起來了。

現在完成式

現在完成式表示動作或狀態已經完成，由「助動詞have+過去分詞」構成。

1. 現在完成式的用法

現在完成式有兩個主要用法：「已完成」用法和「尚未完成」用法。

(1)表示已完成

「已完成」用法指動作發生在說話之前某個沒有明確說出的過去時間，現在已經完成了，並與現在的情況有聯繫。例如：

▶ She **has searched** hard for an apartment and finally found one that she liked.
她費力搜尋，終於找到了自己滿意的公寓。

(2)表示尚未完成

「尚未完成」用法指動作或狀態從過去某時開始，持續到現在，可能持續下去，也可能剛剛結束。例如：

▶ He **has volunteered** at the hospital for ten years.
十年來，他一直在醫院做義工。

2. 搭配的狀語

在日常口語中，使用現在完成式時可以不用時間狀語，但在不少情況下也可以使用狀語。最常見的有以下幾類：

(1)表示頻率的狀語

表示頻率的副詞或片語常見的有：often，ever，frequently，always，never，from time to time，seldom等。例如：

▶ My mom, who now runs a bakery, has always enjoyed baking since her childhood.
我媽媽自小就一直喜歡烘烤點心，現在開了一家麵包房。

▶ Yasmine has baked cookies for her friends from time to time.
亞絲明有時會為朋友做小點心。

▶ We have seldom met each other apart from the occasional class gatherings.
除了偶爾班級聚會，我們很少碰面。

(2)表示由過去到現在這段時間的狀語

常用的副詞和片語有：today，up till now，the past two years，for the last few years，before now，so far 等。例如：

▶ She has maintained regular contact with her pen-pal in Japan up till now.
她到現在還一直與日本的筆友經常保持聯繫。

▶ For the last few years, Vera has saved up half of her monthly salary to buy a car.
在過去的幾年裡，薇拉把每月工資的一半攢下來準備買汽車。

▶ So far, Dan has ran five marathons and participated in two biathlons.
截至現在，丹已經跑了五場馬拉松比賽，還參加了兩次冬季兩項比賽。

(3)表示動作已完成、剛剛完成和有待於完成的狀語

常用的副詞有：already，just，yet等。例如：

▶ Hannah has already tried on several dresses but could not find one that she likes.
漢娜已經試穿了好幾件裙裝，但是沒有一件是她喜歡的。

▶ "Mr. Dexter has just gone for a meeting and will be back in an hour, could I take a message for him?" said the secretary.
「德克斯特先生剛去開會，一小時後回來，您可以留言。」秘書説。

▶ Beatrice has not written a single word for her assignment yet.
碧翠絲到現在作業還沒有寫一個字。

(4)表示事情剛剛發生不久的狀語

常用的副詞有：just，recently，yet等。

▶ He has recently been promoted to Assistant Manager.
他最近被提拔到經理助理的職位。

(5)表示一段時間的狀語

　　由for，since引起狀語，由how long引起疑問句。例如：

▶ Sandy has worked in this company for twenty years.
桑迪在這家公司已經工作了20年了。

▶ Since ten years ago, the number of tourists to this island resort has increased at least fivefold.
自10年前算起，這個島上的遊客至少增加到5倍。

▶ For about how long has Benjamin worked on this project?
班傑明的這個項目大概做了多久了？

　　3. 現在完成式與過去簡單式用法比較

　　現在完成式和過去簡單式都表示過去發生的事情，但說話的目的不同。現在完成式往往說明現在的情況、過去與現在的關係，表示動作或狀態在說話時已經完成而且延續到說話時刻並可能繼續下去。而過去式只是談論動作或狀態本身。例如：

▶ Mandy has secretly left for the harbor while we were asleep.
曼迪趁我們熟睡的時候已經悄悄地去了港口。

　　過去式有明確的過去時間狀語。例如：

yesterday	last year	in 1987	a year ago
the other day	earlier this week	at that time	in the morning

　　含有與過去所發生的事件有明確關聯的具體地點時，常用過去式，一般不用現在完成式。例如：

▶ She has forgotten about what happened to them a year ago in Paris.
她已經忘記了一年前他們在巴黎遇到的事情了。

　　但是有一些時間狀語既可以用於現在完成式，也可以用於過去式。例如：

today	this morning	recently	once	this year

　　這些時間概念如果包括現在，就用現在完成式；如果不包括現在，就用過去式。

◎ 過去完成式

　　過去完成式表示在過去某個時間之前一個動作或狀態已經結束，即過去的過去。它的主要用法與現在完成式相似，不同的是，過去完成式把時間推移到過去某個時間之前，與現在不發生聯繫。

過去完成式由「had＋過去分詞」構成。

1. 過去完成式的用法

(1)過去完成式與現在完成式一樣也有兩個主要用法，即「已完成」用法和「未完成」用法。

a. 表示已完成

「已完成」用法表示在過去某時已完成的動作或狀態。例如：

▶In 1999, I had known this builder for 16 years.
到1999年，我已經認識這位建築商16年了。

▶The alligator has been returned to the park after being found in a drain in Sydney, where it had lived for the past 20 years.
當鱷魚在雪梨的排水溝被發現時，它已經在那裡生活了20年，現已經被送回公園。

b. 表示未完成

「未完成」用法表示一個動作或狀態在過去某時之前已經開始，一直延續到這一過去時間，而且尚未結束，仍有可能繼續下去。例如：

▶She had lived in New York before 1990 and did not intend to move to another place.
她在1990年之前就住在紐約，並沒有打算換地方。

(2)過去完成式用於子句及固定搭配中

a. 用於間接引語或受詞子句。例如：

▶Henry mentioned that he had finished reading the book.
亨利提到過他已經讀完那本書了。

▶Neil believed that a pickpocket had stolen his wallet at the carnival.
尼爾認為小偷在狂歡節上偷走了他的錢包。

▶We found that he had embezzled about $10,000 of company funds.
我們發現他挪用了公司約10,000美元。

▶I thought that Joel had gone to work but he was still sleeping.
我以為喬爾已經去工作了，其實他還在睡覺。

▶Wendy was sorry that she had wrongly accused Johnny of lying to her.
溫蒂很抱歉她曾錯怪強尼對她撒謊。

b. 用於副詞子句。例如：

▶I didn't go for the dinner gathering because I had already bought tickets to a concert on the same day.
我沒去參加聚餐是因為我先前已經買好了同一天的音樂會的票。

c. 用於形容詞子句。例如：

▶My niece gave me a birthday card she had drawn.
我的侄女送給我她親手畫的生日賀卡。

d. 與expect，hope，want，think等詞連用

過去完成式與某些心智動詞連用表示「比⋯⋯更⋯⋯」。例如：

▶The assignment was much more challenging than I had thought.
這次作業比我想像的更具有挑戰性。

▶Due to the traffic jams, the journey took longer than I had expected.
由於交通堵塞，路上花費的時間比我預計的還長。

e. 與time連用

過去完成式與time連用表示第幾次。例如：

▶It was the second time I had noticed him in the library.
這是我在圖書館裡第二次注意到他。

(3)與過去完成式經常連用的過去時間狀語有以下幾種：

a. by+表時間的單字或片語

常見的有：by the time，by two o'clock，by Friday，by June，by 2002等。還可以用表示同樣意義的副詞或片語，如：before，before that等。例如：

▶By the time he reached the railway station, the train had already left.
當他趕到車站時，火車早已離去。

b. 由when，before，after，until 等引導的副詞子句。例如：

▶Tammy had seen the pyramids when she travelled to Egypt last month.
泰咪上個月去埃及旅行時見到了金字塔。

▶Jimmy had waited for her at the café until it was 10 pm, but she never turned up.
吉米在咖啡店一直等她到晚上10點，但是她卻沒有出現。

注意！

由於連接詞before 和after本身已經表示動作的先後順序，因此before 和after 引導的子句有時也可以用過去簡單式。

c. 上下文

在許多情況下，過去時間由上下文表示出來，不需要用表示過去時間的狀語。例如：

▶ The country was experiencing a drought. It **had not rained** for months.
這個國家正在遭受旱災，因為好幾個月都沒有下雨了。

現在完成進行式

1. 現在完成進行式是由完成式與進行式結合而構成：表示由過去某時起一直延續到現在的動作，動作可能剛剛停止，也可能正在進行。

現在完成進行式由「have/has＋been＋現在分詞」構成。

(1)現在完成進行式與現在完成式的「未完成」用法相似，結合了目標和過程兩個階段。例如：

▶ Jenny **has been packing** her room since early morning.
珍妮從一大早開始就在整理自己的屋子。

(2)表示在持續的一段時間中動作不斷重複，也包含了暫時性概念。例如：

▶ He **has been revising** for his exams in the room all night long.
他一整夜都在自己的房間裡複習功課準備考試。

2. 與現在完成進行式經常連用的時間狀語有：

(1)表示一段時間

常用的時間狀語如下：

all day	all night long	all along	all the time
for three years	recently	the whole week	since he was eight

例如：

▶ They have been working **all night long** to complete the project on time.
為了按時完成專案，他們工作了一個晚上。

(2)用how long構成疑問句

這種結構主要為了強調動作持續的時間長度。例如：

▶ **For how long have** you **been taking** aerobic classes?
你參加有氧健身運動有多長時間了？

有些靜態動詞如know，own，last只能用於現在完成式而不能用於現在完成進行體。例如：

▶ They **have known** each other for almost twenty years.
他們相互認識差不多20年了。

▶ My family **has owned** this biscuit factory since 1950.
自1950年以來，我家就擁有這家餅乾廠了。

過去完成進行式

過去完成進行式表示持續到過去某時的動作，由「had been＋現在分詞」構成。它的主要用法與現在完成進行式用法相似，只是時間推移到過去。例如：

▶ In preparation for the beauty pageant last year, Diana **had been watching** her diet carefully.
去年為了準備參加選美比賽，戴安娜小心地控制著飲食。

過去完成進行式中的過去時間可以用以下方式表示：

1. 表示一段時間的片語。例如：

▶ My sister had been saving up to buy an apartment **for two years**.
我的姐姐為了買套公寓已經存了兩年錢了。

2. 由when，before，until等連接詞引導的子句。例如：

▶ The children had been napping **when the burglary took place**.
孩子們正在睡午覺時發生了入室竊盜事件。

▶ The students had been busy revising **before the start of the examinations**.
考試前學生們都在緊張地複習功課。

▶ The troops had been marching **until they reached their next destination**.
軍隊一直在行進，直到抵達下一個目的地。

3. 如果在上下文中明確是談過去的事情，也可以不加時間狀語。

注意！

與現在完成進行式一樣，有些靜態動詞不能用於現在進行式，只可以用於過去完成式。例如：

▶ "**I had known** Aaron since we were kids," said Desmond.
德斯蒙德說：「還是孩子時我就認識了亞倫。」

▶ He **had loved** the magic and mystery of Stonehenge since early childhood.
自小他就對巨石陣的魔力和神祕很迷戀。

▶ She **had owned** this house for almost fifty years.
她擁有這所房子幾乎50年了。

未來式 ▷

　　表示將來要發生的事可以用未來式。未來式一般通過助動詞、情態動詞片語、現在簡單式和現在進行式來實現。

🎯 will/shall + 不帶 to 的不定詞

　　「will/shall＋不帶to的不定詞」常用來表示將來時間。will一般用於第二、三人稱主詞，shall用於第一人稱主詞。例如：

▶ **I shall sign up** for the French language classes starting next month.
我要去報名參加下月開始的法語培訓班。

▶ You **will take over** the family business when you reach twenty-one years of age.
你21歲時就可以接管家族企業。

▶ She **will be migrating** to New Zealand with her family in December.
她和家人將在12月移居紐西蘭。

　　will也可以用於第一人稱，表示「意願」或「意圖」。例如：

▶ "**I will collect** the medicine for you when I go to the pharmacy tomorrow," promised Janice.
「明天我去藥店時幫你把藥取回來。」珍妮絲答應道。

　　「will/shall＋不帶to的進行式不定詞」結構表示自然要發生的含義，不含說話人的主觀意願。例如：

▶ He's co-written a book about his life that **will be coming out** next year.
他與人合著了一本關於他本人生平經歷的書，將在明年出版。

如果要表示將來某一時刻之前已完成的動作便可以用「will/shall＋不帶to的完成式不定詞」。例如：

▶ I am writing the conclusion to the report and shall have done in 5 minutes.
我正在寫報告的結尾，再有5分鐘就好了。

如果要表示一個已經開始的動作到將來某一時間仍在進行，便可以用「will/shall＋不帶to的完成進行式不定詞」。例如：

▶ Most of us will have been doing something or other until late on the Saturday night when warnings of the impending hurricane came.
我們大多數人週六晚上不是做這就是做那直到深夜，這時已經發佈了颶風即將到來的警報。

⊙ be going to + 不帶 to 的不定詞

「be going to＋不帶to的不定詞」這一結構表達的主要意義是「意圖」，即打算在將來某時做某事。例如：

▶ My father is going to call up the hospital to enquire about the bill.
我父親準備給醫院打電話詢問帳單的事。

這一結構的另一個意義表示「預見」，即現在已有的跡象表明將要發生某種情況。例如：

▶ "The stock market is going to reach a new peak today," predicted the business analyst.
「股票交易市場今天將創新高。」業務分析員預測說。

注意！

1. 在含有go和come的句子中，可以直接用go和come的進行式，而不用be going to 結構。例如：

▶ "Are you going to Nick's birthday celebration tonight?" asked Andrea.
「你今晚去參加尼克的生日慶祝會嗎？」安德莉亞問道。

2. 「be going to＋不帶to的不定詞」和「will/shall＋不帶to的不定詞」在許多情況下可以互換。但在表示某事預計要發生而且不可避免要發生時，大多用be going to + 不帶to 的不定詞結構。例如：

▶ It has been raining for many days and the river is going to flood.
雨下了好多天了，河水要氾濫了。

然而表示想要做某事時，則多用「will/shall＋不帶to 的不定詞」結構。例如：

▶ Let me know if you have problems with your homework and I will help you.
　如果做作業時有什麼問題，請告訴我，我會幫助你。

⊚ be＋現在分詞

「be＋現在分詞」這一結構的主要意義是表示按計畫、安排即將發生的動作，常用於表示位置移動的動詞，如：go，come，leave，start，arrive等。例如：

▶ The play is starting in 5 minutes but the theatre is only half-full.
　再5分鐘演出就要開始了，可是劇院還有一半是空的。

⊚ be to＋不帶to的不定詞

1. 「be to＋不帶to的不定詞」這一結構主要用於按計畫、安排即將發生的動作。例如：

▶ The students are to submit their assignment by 12 noon today.
　同學們應該在今天中午12點前交作業。

這種用法還經常見於媒體，用於宣佈官方的計畫或決定，常用於正式語體。例如：

▶ The company is to make a public apology in the national newspapers tomorrow for giving false product information.
　公司因發佈虛假產品資訊，將在明天的國內報紙上公開道歉。

2. 用來表示命令、禁止等。例如：

▶ "Everyone is to assemble at the hall when the alarm rings!" shouted the commander.
　「聽到警報，每個人都到大廳集合！」指揮官喊道。

▶ "No one is to talk during the test," instructed the teacher.
　老師告誡大家：「任何人考試時都不許說話。」

⊚ 現在簡單式

現在簡單式表示將來時間，常用於條件句和副詞子句中。參見P152〈表示未來時間〉。

⊚ 未來式的其他表示形式

1. be about to ＋不帶 to 的不定詞

「be about to＋不帶 to 的不定詞」通常表示即刻發生的事情。例如：

▶The race is about to start, but one runner is missing.
比賽就要開始了，可是有一名選手還沒到。

2. be due to＋不帶 to 的不定詞

「be due to＋不帶to的不定詞」表示按時間表將要發生的事情。例如：

▶The sitcom is due to air on television next month.
這部情境喜劇下個月將在電視上播出。

此外，情態動詞片語如be sure to，be bound to和動詞hope，intend等也可以用來表示未來時間。

過去的未來式 ▽

如果站在過去的觀點，表示過去某時打算做的事情或估計要發生的情況，要將未來式與過去式結合使用。

◎ would＋不帶 to 的不定詞

1. 不管用於什麼人稱主詞，都用「would＋不帶to的不定詞」結構表示過去的未來式，多用於子句中，特別是受詞子句中。例如：

▶Sherry would represent the class in the scrabble competition.
雪莉將代表班級參加拼字比賽。

▶Leslie promised he would come home for Christmas this year.
萊斯利答應今年回家過耶誕節。

2. 如果表示在過去將來某一時刻正在進行的動作，可用「would＋不帶to的進行式不定詞」。例如：

▶"If I remained a journalist, I would be doing a lot more travelling," said Henry.
「如果我還是一個記者，我會更常去旅行。」亨利說。

3. 如果要表示在過去的某時以前已發生的事態，可用「would＋不帶to的完成式不定詞」。例如：

▶According to the schedule, he would have done his field surveys by Tuesday.
根據計畫，他將在週二前完成實地調查。

🎯 was/were going to＋不帶 to 的不定詞

「was/were going to＋不帶 to 的不定詞」表示過去的未來式，通常指按過去的計畫、安排將在某個過去將來時間發生的事態。例如：

▶ Danny **was going to do** his homework for submission the next day, when he realized he left his textbook in school.
丹尼正準備做作業以便第二天上交，這時他才發現他把課本落在學校了。

🎯 was/were to＋不帶 to 的不定詞

「was/were to＋不帶to的不定詞」表示過去的未來式，通常指按過去的計畫、安排將在某個過去將來時間發生的事態。例如：

▶ The accused **was to appear** in court for his role in the robbery case.
被告因參與搶劫案件而要出庭受審。

🎯 was/were about ＋不帶 to 的不定詞

「was/were about to＋不帶to的不定詞」表示過去的未來式。例如：

▶ The fireworks display **was about to start** and all the spectators were very excited.
煙火表演即將開始，觀眾們非常激動。

在一定語境中還可以表示未曾實現的意圖。例如：

▶ The wedding dinner **was about to commence** when the blackout occurred.
婚宴剛要開始，突然停電了。

🎯 現在進行式和過去簡單式

現在進行式和過去簡單式均可以用來表示過去假定會實現的未來。現在進行式通常用於表示移動的動詞，如：go，leave，come等。例如：

▶ We **were going to** the meeting to discuss the project proposals in the upcoming year.
我們正準備開會討論下一年的項目方案。

▶ The backpacker **was leaving to** continue with his journey when he realized his shoes were stolen
背包旅行者正準備繼續行程時發現他的鞋子被人偷了。

▶ The delegates **were coming to** the conference when their bus broke down.
在去開會的路上，代表團乘坐的汽車拋錨了。

過去簡單式表示假定會實現，但沒有實現的未來，通常用於某些條件句和時間副詞子句中。例如：

▶ If I had money, I would study architecture.
如果我有錢，我會選修建築學。

▶ If he had a girlfriend, he would probably spoil her rotten.
假如他有女朋友，他可能會寵壞她。

▶ We were supposed to receive a letter from the landlord last week, but it never came.
我們本應該上周收到房東的來信，但是信現在還沒有到。

小結 ▷

　　英語中，不同時間發生的動作或存在的狀態用不同的時態來表達。英語分成三種主要時態：過去式、現在式、未來式。除此之外可以再細分出進行式及完成式。

　　二者搭配構成現在進行式、過去進行式、現在完成式、過去完成式、現在完成進行式和過去完成進行式。

　　未來式表示形式也有兩種基本形式：未來和假定的未來。除了基本的「will/shall＋不帶to的不定詞」、「would＋不帶to的不定詞」外，還有許多其他形式，如：be going to＋不帶to的不定詞、be about to＋不帶to的不定詞、現在簡單式和現在進行式等。

　　這些時態都可以與相應的時間狀語連用，或是用於有確定時間概念的語境中，同時也用於某些文法結構中，如條件句等。

Part **7**

動詞的被動式

概說 ▷

英語中的動詞有兩種型態：主動式（Active Voice）與被動式（Passive Voice）。主動式表示句子的主詞是動作的發出者和執行者。而被動式則表示句子的主詞是動作的承受者。例如：

★主動式

▶ They can **solve** the problem.
他們能解決這個問題。

★被動式

▶ The problem can **be solved**.
這個問題能解決。

被動式的動詞構成形式主要是：be＋動詞過去分詞。例如：

▶ A businesswoman **was robbed** of her BMW car at gunpoint as she parked it in her drive.
一名女商人在專車道上停泊寶馬車時，被歹徒用槍要脅劫走了車子。

最常見的用於被動式的動詞有：

be asked	be based	be born	be brought	be called
be carried	be concerned	be considered	be described	be determined
be done	be drawn	be expected	be forced	be found
be given	be held	be involved	be kept	be known
be left	be lost	be made	be needed	be paid
be prepared	be put	be reported	be required	be said
be seen	be sent	be set	be shown	be taken
be thought	be told	be treated	be understood	be used

被動式中有時用by片語，有時不用。一般情況下，當動作的發出者或執行者不明確、不重要或者難以説出時，不用by片語。例如：

▶Li **was born** in China and came to the United States in 1982.
　李在中國出生，1982年來到美國。

但有時為了強調動作的執行者，或者由於結構上的需要就必須用by片語。例如：

▶The modifications were done **by teams** of 40 engineers working two eight-hour shifts a day. 這些改造任務是由幾個小組承擔的，每組40個工程師，他們每天兩班輪流，每班工作8小時。

被動式也有不同的時態表現形式。以下是被動式的不同時態：

1. 現在簡單式。例如：

▶Mr. Saversky says he **is forced** to work part time as a real estate agent to keep the private group's work going.
　薩弗斯基先生説為了維持這家私營合作單位的運行，他被迫兼職做房產代理。

2. 過去簡單式。例如：

▶He **was lost** in a generalized astonishment and excitement.
　他沉浸在驚訝和興奮中。

3. 現在進行式。例如：

▶I believe the advising committee **is being examined** and can do a self-evaluation.
　我相信顧問委員會正在接受調查，而後，它可以作一個自我評價。

4. 過去進行式。例如：

▶All their school work **was being faxed** to them so she could homeschool them.
　所有的作業都用傳真發給他們，這樣她就可以在家裡給他們授課。

5. 現在完成式。例如：

▶All she requires, I **have been told** by more than one doctor, is rest, quiet and peace of mind, and these I am determined she shall receive.
　不只一個醫生告訴我，她所需要的是休息、安靜和心靈平靜。這些都是我下決心要讓她得到的。

6. 過去完成式。例如：

▶Louis was told that his grandfather **had been kidnapped and beaten** by gypsies.
　路易斯得知他的祖父已經被吉卜賽人綁架並毆打了。

7. 表示將來時間的「will/shall＋不帶to的不定詞」、「be going to＋不帶to的不定詞」、「be to＋不帶to的不定詞」也有被動式。例如：

▶The new product **will be priced** at $225.
這個新產品將會定價為225美元。

▶Application fees for this college **are going to be increased** by fifteen percent.
這所大學的申請費將增加15%。

8. 情態動詞也能用於被動式。例如：

▶All these side effects **can be dealt with** intelligently by physicians when they are aware of the symptoms and stop the drug at the first appearance.
只要醫生知道這些症狀並在症狀一出現時就停止用藥，所有這些副作用都可得到巧妙的處理。

▶It is argued that no-one **should be chosen** because of their gender; it should simply be the best person for the job.
有人主張不能根據性別來確定人選，而應該只選最適合這項工作的人。

「get＋及物動詞過去分詞」表示的被動式

有時被動式通過「get＋及物動詞過去分詞」來表達，這種被動式大多用於口語等非正式場合，強調動作的結果。這種情況下，一般不用by片語來表示動作的執行者。例如：

▶Alice **got involved** in her family's businesses, establishing and running an investment brokerage operation at Arvest.
愛麗絲通過在阿爾維斯特開設和經營投資經紀人業務來參與家族生意。

即使在口語中，也只有某些動詞可以與get連用。最常見的用於get被動式動詞有：

get hit　　　get involved　　　get left　　　get married　　　get stuck

例如：

▶I went downstairs and they told me they had just **got married**.
當我走下樓梯時，他們告訴我他們剛剛結婚。

大多數與get被動式連用的動詞具有否定的含義，或表示動作有難度，或表示對主詞不利。例如：

▶Now somebody said they **got involved** in endless quarrels.
現在有人説他們已經捲入無休止的爭吵中。

▶The bus **got stuck** in traffic for three hours.
這輛公共汽車在交通堵塞中被困了三個小時。

主動式與被動式的轉換規則 ▷

只有能帶受詞的及物動詞才能有被動式。英語有七個基本句型：

- 主詞＋動詞（SV）
- 主詞＋動詞＋主詞補語（SVSC）
- 主詞＋動詞＋受詞（SVO）
- 主詞＋動詞＋副詞（SVA）
- 主詞＋動詞＋間接受詞＋直接受詞（SVO$_I$O$_D$）
- 主詞＋動詞＋受詞＋受詞補語（SVOC）
- 主詞＋動詞＋受詞＋狀語（SVOA）

在這七個基本句型中，有四個是有及物動詞的，這四個句型有被動式。

1. 主詞＋動詞＋受詞（SVO）

▶ The public loves her performance. 公眾喜愛她的演出。

▶ Her performance is loved (by the public).
她的演出受到（公眾的）喜愛。

2. 主詞＋動詞＋間接受詞＋直接受詞（SVO$_I$O$_D$）

▶ The university has never offered me a staff job.
這所大學從沒有給我提供過在校工作的機會。

▶ I was never offered a staff job by the university.
我從來沒有得過在這所大學工作的機會。

▶ A staff job was never offered to me (by the university).
（這所大學）從來沒有把在校工作的機會給過我。

3. 主詞＋動詞＋受詞＋受詞補語（SVOC）

▶ Richardson considered him a trusted advisor and loyal ally.
理查森認為他是值得信賴的顧問和忠誠的同盟。

▶ He was considered a trusted advisor and loyal ally.
人們認為他是值得信賴的顧問和忠誠的同盟。

4. 主詞＋動詞＋受詞＋狀語（SVOA）

▶ The old woman put the money in the bank. 老婦人把錢存進銀行。

▶ The money was put in the bank (by the old woman).
錢被（老婦人）存進銀行。

通過上述例句可以看出，SVO$_I$O$_D$句型有兩個受詞，因而有兩種被動結構。比較常見的一種是間接受詞用作被動句的主詞，保留直接受詞。例如：

▶ He **was promised** immunity for his testimony.
他得到許諾，如果做污點證人就免於對他的起訴。

另一種是把直接受詞用作主詞，保留間接受詞，這時間接受詞前通常要加介係詞to或for。例如：

▶ Immunity for his testimony **was promised** to him.
有人向他許諾，如果做污點證人就免於對他的起訴。

這種用法中常見的動詞有：

give   lend   offer   pay   promise   send   show   tell

在SVOC句型轉變成被動式時，原句的受詞補語已經轉換成主詞補語。請比較：

★受詞補語

▶ He **named** the boy **Tom**. 他給這個男孩取名為湯姆。

★主詞補語

▶ The boy **was named** Tom. 這個男孩被取名為湯姆。

當句子的受詞為that引導的子句時，用that-子句作主詞就可以構成被動句。但通常用it作先行詞。例如：

▶ The actor believed **that such innovative medical procedures would allow him and millions of others with spinal cord injuries to someday walk again.**
這個演員認為，這些創新的療程能讓他和其他數百萬脊髓受傷者有朝一日重新走路。

▶ **That such innovative medical procedures would allow him and millions of others with spinal cord injuries to someday walk again** was believed by the actor.
這些創新的療程會使他和其他數百萬脊髓受傷者有朝一日重新走路，這個演員是這樣認為的。

▶ **It** is believed by the actor **that such innovative medical procedures would allow him and millions of others with spinal cord injuries to someday walk again.**
這些創新的療程會使他和其他數百萬脊髓受傷者有朝一日重新走路，這個演員是這樣認為的。

以上句子還可以通過動詞的不定詞來表達。例如：

▶ Such innovative medical procedures were believed **to allow the actor and millions of others with spinal cord injuries to someday walk again.**
人們相信，這些創新的療程會使這個演員和其他數百萬脊髓受傷者有朝一日重新走路。

這種有兩種被動式形式的例子還有很多，不定詞中的動詞形式要根據原來子句中的不同時態作相應的變化。

▶ It is expected that the new owner will change the yacht's name.
預期遊艇的新主人會改變其名稱。

▶ The owner is expected to change the yacht's name.
人們預計遊艇的新主人會改變其名稱。

▶ It is said that forty-one people was seriously hurt.
據說，有41人嚴重受傷。

▶ Forty-one people are said to have been seriously hurt.
有41人被認為是嚴重受傷。

　　以下是常用於這類結構的動詞，這些動詞主要表示「估計」、「相信」等意思：

allege	assume	believe	claim	consider	estimate
expect	fear	feel	find	know	presume
report	say	think	understand		

主動式與被動式的互換限制性 ▷

　　不及物動詞因為不帶受詞，所以沒有被動式。但是，有些及物動詞也不用於被動式，這樣的動詞多數是靜態動詞。例如：

▶ The suit fits me. 這套衣服很適合我。

不能說成：I am fitted by my suit.

▶ They have a big house. 他們有棟豪宅。

不能說成：A big house is had by them.

　　以下是一些很少用於被動式的及物動詞：

climb	dare	exclaim	guess	have	hesitate
joke	lack	let	mind	pretend	quit
reply	resemble	survive	swear	thank	try
undergo	want	wonder	yell		

當主詞和受詞互為指代，或者作為受詞的名詞片語是所有格代名詞時，不能用被動式。例如：

▶ Mary could see herself in the mirror.
　瑪麗能在鏡中看到自己。

不能説成：Herself could be seen in the mirror.

▶ Henry wiped his mouth with his handkerchief.
　亨利用手帕擦嘴。

不能説成：His mouth was wiped by Henry.

片語動詞的被動式 ▷

片語動詞包括：動詞＋副詞、動詞＋介係詞、動詞＋副詞＋介係詞、動詞＋名詞＋介係詞。當這些結構在意義上相當於及物動詞時，可以構成被動式。

1. 動詞＋副詞。例如：

▶ The latest research **has been carried** out by a team of scientists working for the European Commission.
這項最新的研究已由為歐盟委員會工作的一個科學家團隊來執行。

▶ In high school he **was put off** by the dogmatism he encountered.
他在中學時期對所遇到的教條主義觀點就有反感。

2. 動詞＋介係詞。例如：

▶ A remedy **was arrived at** with a lot of hard work by my colleagues.
同事們經過許多艱苦努力，終於得到一種新的療法。

▶ Plans for modernization **have been talked about** for years.
現代化的計畫已經談論了好幾年了。

不是所有「動詞＋介係詞」的結構都能用於被動式，以下這些「動詞＋介係詞」就不常用於被動式。

agree to/with	apologize to/for	belong to	bet on	come across
compete with	cope with	correspond to	glance at	laugh at
listen to	live with	look at/like	participate in	smile at
stay with	wait for			

3. 動詞＋副詞＋介係詞。例如：

▶ Over the years some penalties have been done away with and others have been introduced.
幾年來，一些處罰條例被廢除了，另一些新條例則被採用了。

▶ Our investment was broken down into 10 separate units of £800.
我們的投資資金被分為10份，每份800英鎊。

上述三種片語動詞在轉換成被動式時應該看成一個整體，動詞後面的副詞或介係詞不能與動詞拆開。

4. 動詞＋名詞＋介係詞

這種結構轉換成被動式時有兩種形式。第一種與上面的三種結構一樣，把它看作一個整體。例如：

▶ About one-third of the time, she is taken care of by a nurse paid for by her father.
在三分之一的時間裡，她由她父親出錢雇傭的護士看護。

▶ Everybody wants to be sure that their problems are paid attention to.
大家希望確信他們的問題有人關注。

第二種是把結構中的名詞看作句子的受詞，這樣，受詞提前成為被動式的主詞。例如：

▶ No care was taken of the poor girls in this village. 這個村裡的貧困女孩無人照顧。

▶ Attention must be paid to this tremendous writer. 必須注意這位了不起的作家。

被動式的各種形式 ▷

被動式有限定動詞的被動式和非限定動詞的被動式。限定動詞的被動式包括靜態動詞和動態動詞的形式。

靜態動詞被動式主要指的是動作的狀態。例如：

▶ Before the baby was born, Stokes was beautiful, bubbly and outgoing.
在孩子出生前，斯托克斯漂亮、活潑、外向。

而動態動詞的被動式主要強調動作。例如：

▶ Most courses were taught by teaching assistants and part-time faculty.
大部分的課程由助教和兼職教員教授。

兩種結構都可以充當動詞受詞。但是，有些動詞通常與帶to的不定詞結構搭配，有些動詞通常與現在分詞的結構搭配，還有些動詞可以與兩種結構搭配。例如：

▶ They wanted **to be respected**.
　　他們想得到別人的尊重。

▶ Leith's apprentice has enjoyed **being allowed** to make his own bread and tarts.
　　利思的學徒因獲得允許自己做麵包和果餡餅而感到開心。

▶ No one likes **to be fired**, especially after less than a year on the job.
　　誰都不喜歡被解雇，特別是工作還不到一年。

▶ Nobody likes **being injured**.
　　誰都不喜歡受傷。

　　如果非限定動詞的被動結構用作介係詞的受詞，那只能用現在分詞形式的被動結構。例如：

▶ The minute Gary saw her that night, he insisted on **being introduced to her**.
　　那個晚上，加里一看到她，就執意讓別人把自己介紹給她。

　　能夠帶不定詞被動結構的動詞主要有：

allow	ask	encourage	expect	help	intend
permit	want	wish			

　　能夠帶現在分詞被動結構的動詞主要有：

agree to	anticipate	enjoy	insist on	think about

　　既能帶不定詞又能帶現在分詞被動結構的動詞主要有：

forget	hate	like	love	remember

　　在以上例句中，被動結構的邏輯主詞就是主句的主詞，因而在被動結構中不用表示出來。但有時被動結構中的邏輯主詞不是主句的主詞，這時就要把它表示出來。例如：

▶ I wanted **Terry** to be sentenced to death.
　　我希望特裡被判處死刑。

▶ He insists on **the car** being stocked with bottles of still water and Diet Coke.
　　他堅持要在小車裡存放幾瓶純淨水和健怡可樂。

與不帶to 的不定詞連用的動詞如make，see，hear 在被動句中要用帶to 的不定詞。例如：

★主動

▶They made me feel guilty.
他們使我感到內疚。

★被動

▶I was made to feel guilty.
我被弄得感到內疚。

被動句的用法和功能

被動式經常出現在學術文體和新聞報導中。主要用於以下幾種情況：

1. 動作的執行者不明確。例如：

▶King Fahd, 80, is reported to be incapacitated from ill health.
據報導，現年80歲的法赫德國王因為疾病纏身而不能自理。

2. 句子的重點為動作承受者

講話人對動作的承受者更感興趣，而不是動作的執行者。如在學術文體中，作者對客觀事物及其過程的描述更重視。例如：

▶The money was used to improve safety, but often, it wasn't used specifically to prepare for terrorist-related events.
這些錢是用於改善安全環境的，但往往是，它沒有作為專款用在與防恐相關的事宜上。

3. 緩和語氣

講話人為了使語氣委婉，避免提到動作的執行者。例如：

▶The last thing I want is to be taken for an ugly American so I have always been delighted to oblige. 我最不願意的是被當成一個醜陋的美國人，所以我總是高興地去幫忙。

4. 使語句連貫

為了使句子結構緊湊、語句連貫、兩句保持同一主詞而使用被動式。例如：

▶What did she think of his lecture? 她認為他的講座怎麼樣？

▶She was utterly confused. 她完全給弄糊塗了。

5. 構成資訊焦點

被動式在語篇中具有將新資訊變成句子焦點的功能。選用主動結構或者被動結構取決於句子所表達的「已知資訊」和「新資訊」。人們往往把「新資訊」放在句子的末尾，以突出句子的重點。例如：

▶ The play was written **by Shakespeare**.

這個劇本是莎士比亞寫的。

在這個例句中，戲是誰寫的是「新資訊」，通過使用被動式來改變句子的語序，使「新資訊」處於句子末尾重點的位置（End-weight）。

6. 平衡句子結構

人們往往通過使用被動式把較長的和分量較重的詞語放在句子的後部，使句子的結構平衡，不至於出現頭重腳輕的現象。例如：

▶ I was annoyed by **Mary's wanting everybody to do what she likes**.

瑪麗想讓每個人做她喜歡的事，這真讓我惱火。

表示被動意義的結構 ▷

英語句子中常用主動結構表示被動的意義。用於這種語句的動詞通常既可以作及物動詞，又可以作不及物動詞。

當作不及物動詞用時，它們表達的是主詞的內在屬性。這種情況下，主詞通常是表示物體的詞；謂語動詞以現在簡單式為主，也可以與can't，won't，don't/doesn't連用；句中修飾謂語動詞的副詞可以是well，easily，badly，poorly，nicely等。此外，這種句式還可以與一些表示否定意義的詞如not，hardly，scarcely等連用。例如：

▶ His prose **reads like poetry**, and he was also a gifted artist—all the illustrations in The Little Prince are his.

他的散文讀上去像詩歌，同時他也是一個有天賦的藝術家——《小王子》中所有的插圖都是他畫的。

▶ If the book **sells well**, Mr. White stands to become a millionaire.

如果這本書賣得好，懷特先生很可能會成為一個百萬富翁。

▶ The radio **won't work** if you put it into the bathroom.

假如你把收音機帶進浴室，它就不響了。

▶ I thought we are out of gas. But the car **drives**!

我以為我們沒有汽油了。但是車還可以開！

常用於這類特殊句式的動詞有：

act	add up	clean	compare	cook	count	draw
fill	iron	keep	let	lock	make up	open
photograph	peel	read	sell	smoke	spoil	wash
wear

表示感官的連綴動詞，如look，sound，smell，taste，feel也可以在句子中表示被動的意義。例如：

▶ That explanation sounds very reasonable.
那個解釋聽起來很合情合理。

▶ The coffee tastes bitter.
這咖啡味道苦。

某些動詞如need，want，require 加動詞的現在分詞形式也可以表達被動的意義。

例如：

▶ Probably every classroom that was built before the last ten years needs renovating.
所有在十年前建的教室或許都需要翻新。

表示非被動意義的結構 ▷

英語中有些過去分詞可以作形容詞用，它們與be動詞連用時，形式上非常像被動式，但是卻表達了非被動的意義。

在這樣的結構中，be是連綴動詞，過去分詞相當於形容詞，在句子中作表語，突出人或事物所處的狀態。請比較：

★被動式

▶ She was much moved by that movie.
那部影片使她深受感動。

▶ One group of journalists were crowded into a minibus.
一群記者被塞進了一輛小型公車。

★非被動式

▶ She was very moved.
她很感動。

▶ The bus was crowded with schoolchildren.
公共汽車上擠滿了學生。

這樣的非被動式結構通常以現在簡單式或者過去簡單式為主。例如：

★被動式

▶ John **has been given** several honors for his excellent performance in his work.
約翰因為工作出色已經獲得了好幾個榮譽。

▶ She **was convinced** the cat was basically evil.
她相信貓從本質上說是邪惡的。

★非被動式

▶ Many people **are frightened** of solitude.
許多人害怕孤獨。

另外，這樣的非被動式結構常常有固定的搭配。例如：

▶ More and more people **are accustomed to** using the Internet.
越來越多的人習慣於使用網際網路。

▶ We **are interested in** and **concentrated on** doing this job.
我們對這項工作感興趣並專注於做這項工作。

小結 ▷

　　本章著重論述了被動式的結構與特徵。被動式可以由「be＋過去分詞」構成，也可以用「get＋過去分詞」來表達。被動式中根據不同的情況可以用by片語，也可以不用by片語。

　　通常只有能帶受詞的及物動詞才能有被動式。在英語的七大基本句型中，有四個是含有及物動詞的結構：SVO，SVO_iO_D，SVOC，SVOA。這些結構可以有被動式。

　　本章還介紹了主動句如何轉換為被動句；當主動句的受詞是that引導的子句時，該句子如何轉換成被動句。本章還指出，不是所有的及物動詞都有被動式形式，有些及物動詞很少用於被動句；動詞片語以及非限定動詞都可以構成被動式。

　　本章還講解了被動句在用法和意義上與主動句的差別，此外，還分析了習慣上稱為主動結構卻表達被動意義的句式以及以被動的形式表達非被動意義的結構。

Part 8

語氣

語氣概說 ▷

語氣反映説話人對所説事物的態度，如確定、不確定、需要、可能、懷疑等。在英語裡，語氣在形式上通過限定動詞表現出來。英語限定動詞有三種語氣：直述語氣（Indicative Mood）、祈使語氣（Imperative Mood）、假設語氣（Subjunctive Mood）。

直述語氣一般用來敘述事實或提出疑問，主要用於陳述句、疑問句和感嘆句。祈使語氣主要用於祈使句，是説話人向對方下達命令、指示，提出建議、要求、警告、勸告等時用的動詞形式。而假設語氣指的是説話人為表示一種主觀的願望和假設虛擬的情況而採取的一種特殊動詞形式。

本章主要討論假設語氣。

直述語氣 ▷

直述語氣是最常見的語氣，它表示説話人認為自己所陳述的事件是真實的。例如：

▶ Since Venice is located by the sea, the city has many floods.
因為威尼斯地處海邊，所以這個城市常遭遇洪水。

▶ The danger lies in not recognizing it, or in attempting to deny it to ourselves.
危險在於沒有發現危險，或者在於我們自己試圖否定它。

祈使語氣 ▷

祈使語氣是表示説話人意志的動詞形式，即不帶to的不定詞（含被動式、進行式、完成式）。祈使語氣多用於提出建議、勸告、要求、警告，以及下達命令、指示等，使用祈使語氣的句子即祈使句。例如：

▶ Please be sensible.
請理智一點。

▶ Come on, let's go and tell Granddad and Mike.
來吧，我們去告訴爺爺和邁克。

▶First, carry your favorite chocolate with you at all times. Second, don't be ashamed to eat it in public.

首先，要始終帶著你最喜歡吃的巧克力。其次，當著眾人吃巧克力時不要不好意思。

▶Don't take pity on me.

不用憐憫我。

祈使句通常無主詞，有時甚至無動詞，被省略的主詞通常是you。例如：

▶Be conscious of your body language.

要注意你的肢體語言。

▶Best wishes for a speedy recovery to your Dad, Cindy.

辛蒂，衷心祝你父親早日康復。

注意！

1. 某些表示心理、情感或狀態的靜態動詞，不能用於祈使語氣。以下動詞通常不用於祈使語氣：

表示心理狀態的動詞：understand, assume, believe, know, mean, need等。

表示情感的動詞：prefer, regret, want, wish, fear, detest, like 等。

表示存在的動詞：exist, contain, consist of, depend on, own, belong 等。

2. 但是有些動詞如feel，smell，taste等既可以作動態動詞也可以作靜態動詞。這些動詞只有用作動態動詞表示動作時才可以用於祈使語氣。例如：

▶Feel the baby's stomach.

摸摸嬰兒的腹部。

▶Smell the flowers.

聞一下這些花吧。

▶Imagine life without hot water.

想像一下沒有熱水的生活吧。

假設語氣 ▷

假設語氣一般表示說話人的主觀願望、可能性和非真實的情況。例如：

▶I wish he was here so that he could protect his little brother.

但願他能在這兒保護他的弟弟。

▶If we had stayed six months longer we might have made another $100,000.

如果我們當時多待六個月，我們可能又能掙十萬美元了。

▶If I were you, I wouldn't trust anybody's advice.

我要是你的話，誰的建議也不會相信。

現代英文文法一般認為假設語氣有兩種形式：be-型假設語氣（Be-subjunctive）和were-型假設語氣（Were-subjunctive）。be-型假設語氣也稱為現在假設語氣（Present Subjunctive），were-型假設語氣也稱為過去假設語氣（Past Subjunctive）。

🎯 be-型假設語氣

be-型假設語氣只有一種動詞形式，即動詞原形。也就是說，在第三人稱單數作主詞時，主詞和謂語之間沒有現在簡單式中的主謂一致性要求，現在式和過去式也沒有區別。

要注意的是，be-型假設語氣是出於結構的需要，並不表示說話人的主觀願望與實際情況不符或者是實現可能性極小等情況。be-型假設語氣主要用於正式文體中，在其他場合，含有「should＋不帶to的不定詞」的that子句，或帶to的不定詞更為常用。例如：

▶ It's necessary that we win in tomorrow's match.
　我們明天要贏得比賽，這很必要。

▶ It is necessary that we should proceed with the plan as agreed.
　我們必須按照大家都同意的計畫進行工作。

▶ It is necessary to review safety control and management.
　重新考量安全控制和管理是很有必要的。

1. be-型假設語氣結構用於表示命令、決定、建議等詞之後的that子句中

表示命令、決定、建議等詞語如suggest之後的that子句中經常使用be-型假設語氣結構。在這些詞語之後的that子句中，謂語動詞需要使用動詞原形這一假設結構。

使用be-型假設語氣結構的that子句主要包括受詞子句、形容詞子句、同位語子句和主詞子句等。

(1)用於表示命令、決定、建議等動詞後的受詞子句中。

因為be-型假設語氣是出於結構的需要，也就是說，主句用了表示命令、決定、建議等動詞，受詞子句就必須用be-型假設語氣。常見的這類動詞見下表：

arrange	ask	advise	beg	command	demand
decide	deserve	desire	determine	insist	intend
maintain	move	order	plead	pray	propose
recommend	require	request	resolve	suggest	urge

例如：

▶ People demanded that this state get tough on crime.
　人們要求州政府嚴厲打擊犯罪。

▶ In a vain attempt to impress my new American girlfriend I decided that she share in my love for Brighton and Hove Albion.

我判斷我新交的美國女友和我一樣喜歡布里奇頓及霍夫足球俱樂部，想以此打動她，結果白費力氣。

▶ Anyway, The New York Times suggested that perhaps his book be nominated for a history Pulitzer.

不管怎麼說，《紐約時報》提議或許他的這本著作應該得到普立茲歷史書籍獎的提名。

▶ Dairyman Crick insisted that all the dairy people milk different cows every day, not just their favorites.

奶牛場主克理克主張所有的擠奶工每天應給不同的奶牛擠奶，而不是只擠他們最喜歡的那幾頭。

▶ A bill required that insurers provide maternity benefits.

法案要求保險人提供產婦津貼。

注意！

如果動詞suggest表示推測，則不用be- 型假設語氣。例如：

▶ Murtha suggested that public indifference makes it easy for Congress to resist changes to its arcane, tradition-bound structures.

默撒曾表明，公眾的冷漠使得國會很容易抵制改變神祕又被傳統制約的結構。

(2)用於這類動詞的名詞形式所帶的形容詞子句和同位語子句中。

常用的這類名詞見下表：

advice	decision	demand	desire	idea
insistence	motion	order	plan	preference
proposal	recommendation	requirement	resolution	suggestion

例如：

▶ His suggestion is that a renewed and married clergy be able to provide the kinds of leadership needed, particularly in immigrant communities.

他的建議是，一個煥發了新貌的已婚牧師應該發揮各種領導才能，移民社區尤其需要這種能力。

▶ Among the report's recommendations are that all Missouri health-care organizations and professionals disclose errors to patients.

報告中提出的幾條建議是，所有密蘇里的醫療保健機構和專業人士應該向病人告知醫療過失。

▶ There is absolute resolution that we go after and take out and punish the ones who were responsible for the loss.

我們下定了決心，要堅決追查、揪出並懲罰那些應對這次損失負責的人。

▶ A motion that balloting be secret was rejected by a 29-24 vote.

投票應祕密舉行的提議以29票對24票遭到否決。

(3)用於表示命令、決定、建議的動詞-ed形式或形容詞構成的It is v-ed/adj + that 子句中。

　　這類結構主要取決於動詞-ed形式及形容詞。以上提到的表示命令、決定、建議等含義的動詞都可以用於這一結構中，that引導的子句可以視為後置的主詞子句。例如：

▶ I did not betray Mr. Kurtz—it was ordered I never betray him—it was written I should be loyal to the nightmare of my choice.
我沒有背叛庫爾茨先生。有人指示我永遠不能背叛他。我要忠於我這個噩夢般的選擇，這是明文規定了的。

▶ It was proposed by the brother and sister that she join in a walk, some morning or other.
兄妹倆提議某個早晨她也一起來散步。

▶ It was recommended that she come to Italy for convalescence.
有人建議她來義大利療養。

▶ It is decided that she go to Moscow tomorrow.
已經決定她明天去莫斯科。

　　除了這類動詞-ed形式以外，常用於be-型假設語氣主詞子句中的形容詞見下表：

appropriate	advisable	essential	important	imperative
insistent	natural	necessary	probable	possible
strange	urgent	vital		

　　例如：

▶ It is important that concerns be shared quickly in the group.
要迅速地讓小組成員一起分憂，這很重要。

▶ It is advisable that he conserve his muscular energy at the very beginning of the race.
他在每次賽跑開始時保存體能是很明智的。

▶ It is vital that we maintain the environment.
保護環境極為重要。

▶ It is essential that all parties work toward a better understanding of and a solution to the problems of education in this city.
所有參與方朝著更進一步理解本市教育問題並找到解決辦法的目標努力是很重要的。

　　2. 用於由if，though等引導的表示條件、對比的子句中

　　在非常正式的語言中，特別是法律文件中，由if，whether，though， whatever，lest等連接詞引導的子句中有時用be-型假設語氣。這種用法在美式英語中很普遍，尤常見於報刊用語中。例如：

▶ If the truth be told, Havana is not one of the world's premier cities for shopaholics.
如果說實話，對購物狂來說哈瓦那還不算是一個世界頂級城市。

▶**Whether** it **be** smiley faces or violent scenes, children draw what they see.
不論是笑臉還是暴力場面，孩子們把看到的都畫下來了。

▶**Though** this **be** madness, yet there is method in it.
儘管這樣有些瘋狂，但是不失為一個辦法。

▶**Whatever** criticism **be** directed at the human outcomes, genetically modified fruit was delicious.
不論對人類的成果有什麼樣的批評，轉基因水果味道很好。

▶The prosperous career woman, or even the respectable stay-at-home mom, is expected to stay in shape, **lest** she **be** seen as lazy and lacking discipline.
無論是前途光明的職業女性還是受人尊敬的全職媽媽，都被預期保持良好的體態，以免被人視為懶惰、缺乏自律。

3. 用於某些公式化語句中

在某些表示祝願、詛咒、禁止等含義的習慣用語中使用be-型假設語氣。要注意的是這些結構都是非常正式的用法。以下幾例為常見的固定表達：

▶"Long **live** the King, long live the Queen, long **live** everybody and everything!" he cried.
他高呼：「國王萬歲，王后萬歲，萬人萬事萬歲！」

▶**Suffice it to say that** the dollar's dive last year did not take economists by surprise.
只要說去年美元暴跌沒有令經濟學家吃驚就夠了，別的不用說了。

▶**God bless** all our soldiers.
上帝保佑我們所有士兵。

▶**Heaven preserve** me!
願上帝保佑我！

4. 用於某些固定片語搭配中

另外，某些固定片語搭配中也常使用be-型假設語氣。常見的in order that，lest，for fear that 等連接詞引導的子句中有時用be-型假設語氣。例如：

▶Someone has to die **in order that** the rest of us **value** life more.
有的人不得不死去，為的是讓活著的人更加珍愛生命。

▶In earlier times, when organized labor was more prominent in public opinion, companies shrank from using the lockout **for fear that** they **be portrayed** as bullying workers. 在歷史上，當有組織的勞動在公眾輿論中顯得更為重要時，公司就不敢停工，唯恐會被說成是欺壓工人。

▶People just moved away from me **lest** they **be soiled** by my conservative philosophy, which they absolutely loathe and hate.
人們對我就是避而遠之，唯恐被我的保守思想所沾染，因為他們對這種思想痛心疾首。

were-型假設語氣

were-型假設語氣是指不管主詞是什麼人稱,動詞一律用were。were-型假設語氣主要用於動詞wish之後的受詞子句中,以及表示條件、對比的副詞子句中(在if only,as if/though,would rather等結構之後)。例如:

▶ They went up and down as if they were on a roller-coaster.
他們上上下下起伏,彷彿坐在雲霄飛車上一般。

▶ I wish I were better at painting.
我要是擅長繪畫該多好啊。

注意!

在If I were you和as it were(= so to speak)這兩個固定片語中,總是用were而不用was。例如:

▶ If I were you, I should not think of the expense.
如果我是你,我就不去想開銷問題。

▶ Dynasties, as it were, are history.
朝代更迭,可以說就是歷史。

1. 用於某些名詞子句中

were-型假設語氣常用在主句動詞wish之後的受詞子句中,表示與現實情況相反的主觀假設。例如:

▶ I'm so depressed and I wish I were dead!
我心灰意冷得想一死了之。

▶ I wish I were a tremendous musician.
但願我是位音樂巨匠。

were-型假設語氣還可用在主句動詞suppose,imagine等之後的受詞子句中,表示與現實情況相反的主觀設想。例如:

▶ I don't suppose you were able to go for a run this morning in this weather.
我認為,今天這樣的天氣狀況下你是沒法去晨跑的。

▶ Imagine you were living in Mexico City, one of the most polluted environments in the world. 想像你住在墨西哥城——世界上環境污染最嚴重的城市之一。

were-型假設語氣也用在It is high/about time (that)...的結構中,意思是「到了該做……的時候了」,表示對某人本應該做了某事但實際上未做的批評或抱怨。例如:

▶ It is high time that the direct contact were established with all alumni from all the graduation years. 該是和以往各屆畢業生建立直接的校友聯繫的時候了。

2. 用於某些表示條件、對比的副詞子句中

were-型假設語氣可用在as if/though，would rather等結構之後的副詞子句中，表示與現實情況相反的情況。例如：

▶ She was a little afraid of him, as if he were not quite human.
她有點怕他，彷彿他不怎麼懂人情事理。

▶ Josie still felt as if she were in a dream, as if her mother was alive and merely away on holiday somewhere, about to return next week.
喬西仍然覺得她彷彿在夢裡一般，彷彿母親依然活著，只是在別處度假，下個星期就要回來。

▶ They would rather the girls were homemakers and the boys had home businesses.
他們寧願女孩子當家庭主婦而男孩子在家創業。

were-型假設語氣也可用在含有if only的感嘆句中，表示與現實情況相反的願望和懊悔的情緒等，這裡的if only相當於I wish 的結構。例如：

▶ If only business taxes were lower in Washington!
要是華盛頓的營業稅能低一點就好了！

假設語氣在條件句中的使用

含有條件子句的句子稱之為條件句。條件句有兩類：一類是真實條件句（Sentences of Real Condition）；另一類是非真實條件句（Sentences of Unreal Condition），即虛擬條件句。如果假設的情況是有可能發生的，就是真實條件句。例如：

▶ If it doesn't rain and rain a lot soon, scores of Texas farmers and ranchers could be pushed into bankruptcy.
如果不下雨，不下一場及時的大雨，德克薩斯州許多農、牧場主可能會被逼到破產的境地。

▶ I promise no harm will come to you, unless you force me to defend myself.
我保證不傷害你，除非你逼得我正當防衛。

這種真實條件句中謂語都用陳述語氣，但如果假設的情況發生的可能性很小，就是非真實條件句，也即假設語氣條件句。例如：

▶ If I were single [he married Stacy last February], I don't know how I'd be able to deal with the stress every day.
如果我單身的話（他去年2月和史黛西結婚了），我不知道能怎麼應對每天所經受的壓力。

▶ If he hadn't been successful in what he does, Elton would have been a teacher.
要不是愛爾頓所從事的事業如此成功的話，他也許早就成為一名教師了。

1. 假設語氣條件句的分類及主要形式

假設語氣在條件句中的使用從時間上看可分三種：

①與現在事實不符

②與過去事實不符

③與將來事實不符

虛擬條件句的主要分類和形式構成請見下表：

時間	子句	主句
與現在事實不符	過去簡單式	would＋動詞原形
與過去事實不符	had＋過去分詞	would have＋過去分詞
與將來事實不符	should / were to	would＋動詞原形

例如：

▶ **If** my mother **didn't like** how I was dressed, she **would** quickly **take** me away from the bus stop.
假如媽媽不喜歡我穿著的樣子，她就會帶著我迅速離開公車站。

▶ **If** she **didn't come** out, the gang members **would burn** her house down.
假如她不出來，這幫黑道份子就會把她家的房子燒掉。

▶ **If** Cameron **had recognized** him she **would have said** hello.
假如卡梅倫當時認出他來，她就會打招呼了。

▶ **If** he **had had** the strength he **would have broken** the flute, but his left hand was too weak to apply the necessary force.
他如果當時有力氣，就會把笛子摔破，但是他的左手虛弱得使不上勁。

▶ "**If** my life **should end** now, I **would** still **be** the happiest man alive," he said.
他說：「即使我的生命到此結束，我仍舊是世上活得最快樂的人。」

▶ **If** she **were to be expecting** her fourth child, stopping smoking **would reduce** a number of possible problems for that fetus.
如果她要生第四胎，那麼戒菸可以減少許多可能出現的胎兒問題。

▶ **If** Liverpool football team **were to lose** Gerrard, they **would lose** all hope.
利物浦足球隊如果失去了傑勒德，他們將失去所有希望。

　　但有時候在虛擬條件句中，主句與子句所指時間不同，這時主句和子句動詞的形式要根據表示的時間來調整使用：這類句子稱為錯綜時間條件句（Conditional Sentences of Mixed Time）。例如：

▶ **If** we **had not won** yesterday, then no one in Canada **would know** our names now.
如果我們昨天沒有贏，現在在加拿大就沒人會知道我們的名字。

▶If I **had saved** enough money by now, I **would buy** a new computer.
如果我現在有足夠存款的話，我就會買台新電腦。

▶If I **didn't obey** orders, I **would have been killed**.
如果我不遵守命令，早就被殺了。

　　在條件句中，可以用「were/was to＋不帶to的不定詞」的結構表示實現可能性很小的未來假設。例如：

▶If he **were to** come up with some hot idea, he could expand his influence.
要是他能提出很好的觀點，他就會擴大自己的影響力了。

▶If he **were to retire** this year he estimates he could earn almost $40,000 a year on his pension.
他估計，如果今年退休，每年他就能領取差不多四萬美元的退休金。

注意！

1. 不用連接詞if的倒裝句用法
在正式文體中，可以不用連接詞if，而把were移到主詞的前面構成倒裝句。例如：

▶**Were** he **to break** a court order, he **could** go to prison.
他若擾亂法庭秩序，就會坐牢。

▶**Were** she **to be rushed** to hospital, he reasoned, he **could not guarantee** her safety.
他尋思，如果這麼急急忙忙地將她送往醫院，他不能保證她的安全。

2. 條件子句中動詞的語氣和主句中的語氣一致
通常在含有條件子句的複雜句中，條件子句中動詞的語氣和主句中的語氣是一致的，要嘛都是陳述式，要嘛都是假設語氣。例如：

▶If he **beats** Mark in his quarter final he **will play** Tim—but **only if** Tim **wins** against Sebastien.
如果他在四分之一決賽裡戰勝馬克，他就會和提姆打，但這得看提姆是否能贏塞巴斯蒂安。

▶If he **had** courage, he **would** simply **step back** and say, I support candidate "A", and I support candidate "B".
如果他有勇氣，他就會只是置身度外，說：「我支持候選人A，我也支持候選人B。」

　　但有時候子句語氣和主句語氣是不一致的，例如當主句用陳述式時，條件子句可用現在假設語氣。這類句子稱之為混合語氣條件句（Conditional Sentences of Mixed Moods）。例如：

▶If these documents **shouldn't meet** his demands, please **inform** us at once.
假如這些文件不能滿足他的要求，請馬上告知我們。

▶ If I play against Arsenal it **would be** a great achievement for me and I **am very excited** about it.
如果我能跟阿森納隊踢球，這對我而言就是一個巨大的成就，這太讓我興奮了。

2. 假設語氣在其他子句中的使用

如上所述，假設語氣在條件句中的使用，從時間上看有三種主要形式。同樣，在as if/though，would rather，if only，動詞wish等結構之後的子句中，也可用過去完成式表達對過去發生的事情的主觀願望，用過去式來表達某事與現實情況不符的主觀願望（參見P194〈were-型假設語氣〉），或用would/could來表達對未來的願望（參見P196〈假設語氣條件句的分類及主要形式〉）。

(1) 在as if/though結構中。例如：

▶ He **talks as if** he **were** born in that country.
他說起話來彷彿他出生在那個國家一樣。

▶ He **looked** terribly thin, **as if** he **had lost** twenty pounds in the few weeks since she had seen him.
他看起來瘦得可憐，自從她上次見到他，他幾週內好像瘦了20磅。

(2) 在would rather結構中。例如：

▶ I **would rather** you **ate** a peach or an apple to stimulate saliva flow and get something in the body.
寧願你吃一個桃子或一個蘋果來刺激唾液，填填肚子。

▶ I **would rather** we **had lost** because the other team was better.
寧可我們輸了，因為那一個隊實力更強。

(3) 在It is high/about time (that)…的結構中。例如：

▶ **It is time that** government **stepped in** to stop the riot.
是政府出手制止暴亂的時候了。

(4) 在含有if only的感嘆句中。例如：

▶ **If only** Rock's performance **lived up to** his high-mindedness!
要是洛克的表演能與他的高格調相符該多好啊！

▶ **If only** I **had been paying** attention!
要是我一直精力集中就好了！

▶ **If only** his father **would go away** to sea!
真希望他的父親會離開此地去海邊！

(5)在動詞wish之後的受詞子句中。例如：

▶ So that's how much I love the game, and I **wish** every person in the world **knew** how to play checkers.
我熱愛西洋跳棋到了如此這般的程度，所以，願世界上每個人都知道怎麼玩這個遊戲！

▶ The boy **wishes** he'd had a camera when he **went round** the world with his father.
這個男孩後悔，當初和父親環游世界時沒帶相機。

▶ I **wish** my friend **would show up** at Stand Down this weekend.
希望我的那個朋友本週末能出現在老兵休整活動上。

小結 ▷

　　本章主要討論了假設語氣的用法，含有兩種假設語氣形式：be-型假設語氣和were-型假設語氣，也討論了假設語氣在條件句及其他一些子句中的使用情況。

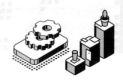

非限定動詞

Part 9

概說

　　非限定動詞也稱非謂語動詞。非限定動詞是不能在句中獨立充當謂語、在文法上不受主詞制約的動詞。英語動詞有三種非限定動詞形式：不定詞、動詞-ing形式（-ing Forms）和動詞-ed形式（-ed Forms）。

　　動詞-ing形式包括我們傳統上說的動名詞和-ing分詞（現在分詞）。非限定動詞保留了動詞的某些特徵，還具有名詞、形容詞和副詞的某些特徵，因而在句中有廣泛的作用。

　　另外，它們還有非謂語性的時態變化形式和用法。三種非限定動詞形式在文法上來說是沒有主詞的，但可以有自己的邏輯主詞。從語言運用上看，非限定動詞在語言中的使用要看非限定動詞各種形式的自身意義和句子結構的需要。

動詞不定詞

不定詞的結構形式

　　動詞不定詞是一種非限定動詞。不定詞的基本形式是「to＋動詞原形」，但具體又分為帶to的不定詞和不帶to的不定詞兩種類型。不定詞沒有過去式，也不受主詞「人稱」和「數」的限制，但可以是簡單式、進行式、完成式和完成進行式。

　　不定詞也有被動態。不定詞的被動態有簡單式被動式和完成式被動式兩種。動詞不定詞的否定式由「not＋動詞不定詞」構成。例如：

▶ She seemed to them **not to have left the world of childhood**, babbling about her American boyfriend.
在他們看來，她好像還沒有離開兒童世界，不停地說她的美國男朋友。

　　動詞不定詞結構通常沒有主詞，但由於表示的是動作，意思上是可以有主詞的。我們稱這個主詞為不定詞結構的邏輯主詞（Logical Subject）。例如：

▶ Russian President Boris Yeltsin's doctors want **him** to stay home.
俄羅斯總統葉利欽的醫生們要求他待在家裡。

動詞不定詞結構的邏輯主詞可以是句子主詞或受詞，也可以是一個由for 引導的片語。例如：

▶ Music is a way **for her** to relax and maintain sanity.
音樂是她放鬆和保持清醒的方式。

1. 不定詞的簡單式、進行式和完成式

	主動	被動
簡單式	to do	to be done
進行式	to be doing	—
完成式	to have done	to have been done
完成進行式	to have been doing	—

(1)不定詞的簡單式

不定詞的簡單式指不定詞動詞所表示的時間動作與謂語動詞所表示的時間動作相一致，或晚於謂語動詞發生。例如：

▶ The young woman could not afford **to buy food** and the hospitals turned her away when she looked for help
這位年輕婦女買不起食物，當她求助時很多家醫院都拒絕了。

不定詞的簡單式有被動態。例如：

▶ How much discussion or attention do you expect **to be paid** in Philadelphia to the idea of mandatory community service?
你估計在費城有多少人關注並且討論義務社區服務？

▶ We are just praying **for her to be returned** to us safely.
我們都在祈禱她能平安回到我們身邊。

(2)不定詞的完成式

不定詞的完成式是指不定詞動詞所表示的動作在謂語所表示的動作發生之前就已經完成。例如：

▶ I am so glad **to have come to a city** where there is such a love of design.
我很高興來到了一個如此熱愛設計的城市。

不定詞的完成式常用在seem，appear之後。例如：

▶ The unlikely allegiance between Apple and IBM **seems to have arisen** out of the principle "The enemy of my enemy is my friend"; in this case, Microsoft and Intel.
蘋果和IBM之間讓人意想不到的忠誠像是印證了「我敵人的敵人就是我的朋友」這一原則。在這個情況裡，微軟和英特爾就是敵人。

▶The ankle problem appeared to have resurfaced during one of the earlier matches, but his later agility belied this.
踝關節的問題看上去在他的前期一場比賽裡重新出現，但是他後來表現的靈敏證實不存在這個問題。

不定詞的完成式也有被動態。例如：

▶Mr. Smith appeared to have been thrown into confusion by the news of his wife's good health.
聽到他妻子身體健康的消息，史密斯先生看上去好像被弄糊塗了。

▶Police says the victim appeared to have been beaten to death.
警方稱受害人看起來是被毆打致死的。

(3)不定詞的進行式
　　如同進行式一樣，不定詞的進行式描述正在進行中的動作。不定詞的進行式強調動作的過程。例如：

▶I just happened to be having a drink the other day with Sir Freddie Roper who is chairman of the board of a well-known chemical company.
我那天恰好在和弗雷迪·羅珀爵士喝酒，他是一家著名化學公司的董事會主席。

　　不定詞的完成進行式表示動作發生的時間早於謂語動詞，且更強調過程。例如：

▶Americans, once hugely enthusiastic about English antiques, do not seem to have been buying seriously since the September 11 attacks.
對英國古董一度極為癡迷的美國人自911事件後好像購買起來沒有那麼熱情了。

　　不定詞的進行式也有被動態，但一般不用。例如：

▶The fear that the aftershocks of the defeat to Manchester United could ruin their confidence seems to be being realized.
輸給曼聯隊後的一系列餘波可能會摧毀他們的信心，這個擔憂看起來現在正變成事實。

　　2. 帶to的不定詞與不帶to的不定詞
　　英語裡絕大多數不定詞片語以to開頭，我們稱之為帶to的不定詞，並用「to＋原形動詞」表示。沒有to的不定詞片語稱作「不帶to的不定詞」。而在有些句子裡，帶to的不定詞和不帶to的不定詞都可以用。
(1)帶to的不定詞
　　英語句子中大多數不定詞屬於帶to的不定詞，用法很廣泛。有時不定詞是否帶to與句子中其他動詞有關。

a. 謂語動詞＋帶to的不定詞。例如：

▶We **try to let the kids have their fun**, and enjoy their time.
我們努力讓孩子們自得其樂，玩得開心。

b. 謂語動詞＋受詞＋帶to的不定詞。例如：

▶He **allowed** foreign doctors **to visit Arafat**, and to airlift him to hospital in Paris.
他允許外國醫生去看望阿拉法特並用飛機將他送到巴黎的醫院。

注意！

動詞不定詞作主詞補語時，既可以帶to也可以不帶to，如果主詞部分有動詞「do」的某種形式，其後通常用不帶to 的不定詞，否則帶to。例如：

▶What we both needed was **to get away** for a couple of days, to go somewhere peaceful, relaxing and free of any association with the past.
我們倆都需要離開一些日子，去一個寧靜、放鬆、與過去沒有聯繫的地方。

▶What she longed to do was **get out** and **walk through the ancient amphitheater**— but, clearly, that was not going to happen.
她一直想出去穿越古老的競技場，但是很明顯這辦不到。

(2)不帶to的不定詞

句子中某些動詞後的不定詞不帶to。

a. 情態動詞＋不帶to的不定詞

在will，would，shall，should，can，could，may，might，must，need，dare等大部分情態動詞之後，動詞不定詞不帶to。例如：

▶**Need I tell you** where my sister went?
我一定得告訴你我姐姐去哪裡了嗎？

▶I should never **dare refuse anything** which he condescended to ask.
他放低姿態要求的任何事情我從來都不敢拒絕。

▶Now more than ever, we **must improve our national security**.
我們必須比以前更努力地提高國家安全。

ought to，have to，used to等情態動詞中的to為情態動詞的組成部分，而非帶to 的不定詞的組成部分。例如：

▶ He **ought to trust me**, and not act as if I was a baby.
他應該信任我，而不是搞得我像是個小孩子似的。

▶ She **used to be a mechanic** before coming to America.
她在來美國之前是機械技師。

b. 固定動詞片語中的不定詞不帶to

在「動詞＋動詞」這類固定的動詞片語中，不定詞不帶to：let go，make believe，make do，let drop，let fall，let fly，let go of，leave go of。例如：

▶ The former Liverpool midfielder **let fly** with his celebrated left foot on four occasions before the interval.
中場休息前，這個利物浦隊前中場隊員用他著名的左腳四次射門。

▶ They **made do** with their father's weekly paycheck from Gillette, where he worked as a maintenance man for 35 years.
他們靠父親每週在吉列的薪水勉強度日，他在那裡當了35年維修工。

▶ I **make believe** that you are at home.
我假裝你在家。

c. 帶情態意義的動詞片語＋不帶to的不定詞

在had better，had best，would/had rather，would sooner，might (just) as well，cannot but等帶情態意義的動詞片語搭配中，動詞不定詞不帶to。例如：

▶ We **had better put an end** to this most mortifying conference.
我們最好結束這個令人不愉快的會議。

▶ One **cannot but regret the loss of lives**, inevitable in war.
人們對戰爭中無法避免的傷亡無不感到遺憾。

▶ "I **would sooner swim** in the pool with the crocodiles than marry you," I had said.
我以前說過：「我寧願在有鱷魚的水塘游泳也不跟你結婚。」

d. help（或help＋受詞）＋不帶to的不定詞

在動詞help（或help +受詞）之後的不定詞可以不帶to。例如：

▶ The easygoing style also **helped keep her** out of trouble.
這種輕鬆的風格也讓她避免陷入麻煩之中。

▶My father helped me understand that we were all put on this Earth for something greater than ourselves, and that's something my mother taught me too.
我父親幫助我懂得我們來到這世上是為了做比自己更偉大的事情，我的母親也教會了我這個道理。

注意！

在help（或help+受詞）後不定詞也可以帶to。

e. why＋不帶to的不定詞

　　「why＋不帶to的不定詞」疑問句結構表示做某事是愚蠢的或毫無意義的；而「why not＋不帶to的不定詞」結構表示建議或勸告等含義。例如：

▶Why operate a business if it can't be profitable on its merits?
如果沒有盈利的話為什麼要做生意呢？

▶Why not leave for a whole day?
為什麼不外出一整天呢？

f. 含but的固定結構＋不帶to的不定詞

　　在can but，cannot but，do nothing but，cannot help but等固定片語結構中，動詞不定詞不帶to。例如：

▶I cannot help but regret that more ambitious reforms were not implemented in practice.
更多宏大的改革沒有付諸實踐，我忍不住感到遺憾。

g. rather than，sooner than等複合連接詞＋不帶to的不定詞

　　當rather than，sooner than 等連接詞置於句首時，其後的動詞不定詞可以不帶to；當出現在句中其他位置時，其後的動詞不定詞有時帶to，有時不帶to。例如：

▶He is in a recovery period, and rather than have him staying in his bed, we'd rather have him up and around in a wheelchair.
他在恢復階段，我們寧願他起床坐在輪椅裡四處轉轉也不願意讓他躺在床上。

▶We prefer to save before we buy rather than repay loans or big credit card bills.
與償還貸款或是大額信用卡帳單相比，我們傾向於存夠錢再買東西。

🎯 不定詞的文法功能

　　不定詞具有動詞、名詞、形容詞、副詞的多種特徵，可以單獨或與其他成分一起構成不定詞片語，在句中具有主詞、受詞、補語、名詞修飾語和狀語等功能，也就是說，它幾乎能充當除了謂語以外的任何句子成分。

1. 不定詞作主詞

　　不定詞作主詞具有明顯的動詞特徵，主要表示個別、具體的意義。而動詞-ing形式作主詞具有更多的名詞特徵，主要表示相對抽象而籠統的意義（參見本章P215〈動詞-ing形式作主詞〉）。例如：

▶ To obey the code that his education and his reason tell him is the right thing to do.
　　正確的做事方式是遵循接受的教育和理智告訴他的規則。

▶ To have a drink with Alvaro is an unforgettable experience.
　　和阿爾瓦羅小酌是次難忘的經歷。

▶ To join them is an amazing challenge and experience which I plan to enjoy.
　　加入他們是驚人的挑戰和經歷，我打算好好享受。

▶ Choosing the best health plan for yourself depends on your health, family status and finances.
　　選擇對你自己而言最好的健康計畫取決於你的健康狀況、家庭狀況和經濟情況。

注意！

當作主詞的不定詞片語太長時，我們往往用it作形式主詞（Preparatory Subject），而將真實主詞（不定詞片語）放在謂語之後。在這種句型裡it 沒有任何意義，它的作用僅僅是填補主詞的位置。這種用法也稱為延遲主詞句型。例如：

▶ It is important to build a good baseball team and it takes time.
　　組建一支好的棒球隊很重要，這需要時間。

2. 不定詞作受詞

　　不定詞能否作受詞取決於謂語動詞，在英語裡不是所有的及物動詞都可以帶不定詞受詞。例如：

▶ We hope to see you right back here at this same time tomorrow night.
　　我們希望明天晚上這個時候能看到你回到這裡。

　　動詞enjoy不能帶不定詞作受詞，而只能帶動詞-ing形式作受詞。例如：

▶ I have really enjoyed hearing your fund raising stories.
　　聽了你籌集基金的故事我真的很喜歡。

　　常用以帶to的不定詞作受詞的動詞有：

afford	agree	aim	appear	apply	arrange
ask	attempt	bear	beg	begin	care
choose	claim	consent	dare	decide	demand

deserve	desire	determine	expect	fail	forget
grow	happen	help	hesitate	hope	intend
learn	like	live	long	manage	mean
need	neglect	offer	opt	pay	plan
prefer	prepare	pretend	promise	prove	reckon
refuse	regret	remember	resolve	start	seek
seem	survive	swear	tend	threaten	trouble
try	undertake	venture	volunteer	vote	wait
want	wish				

例如：

▶He failed to get into West Point last year.
他去年沒能進入西點軍校。

▶He was asked to perform as a clown at a friend's party.
有人要他在一個朋友的聚會上扮演小丑。

注意！

如果作受詞的帶to不定詞有自己的補語，通常用it作形式受詞而將不定詞放在補語之後。例如：

▶Many people found it difficult to understand why he wanted to leave.
許多人難以理解他要離開的原因。

3. 不定詞作複合受詞

不定詞可以跟在某些動詞的受詞之後作複合受詞。在這種「動詞＋受詞＋帶to不定詞」的結構中，受詞通常是不定詞的邏輯主詞。例如：

▶Your father expected you to practice and be a proficient pianist.
你的父親希望你能多多練習，成為技巧高超的鋼琴家。

▶The power company advised customers to prepare for lengthy power outages if Hurricane Ivan hits Northwest Florida.
電力公司提醒顧客如果颶風伊萬襲擊佛羅里達州西北地方，要做好長時間停電的準備。

▶41 percent said Americans should leave immediately and 45 percent said they preferred US forces to leave as soon as a permanent Iraqi government was installed at the end of June.
41%的人認為駐伊美軍應立即撤離，45%的人傾向于美軍在6月底伊拉克永久政府成立後立即撤離。

常用於這種結構的動詞有：

advise	allow	ask	bear	beg	cause
challenge	choose	command	compel	dare	drive
enable	encourage	expect	forbid	force	get help
induce	inspire	instruct	intend	invite	lead
leave	like	mean	move	need	oblige
order	pay	permit	persuade	prefer	press
recommend	request	remind	teach	tell	tempt
tempt	trouble	train	trust	urge	use
want	warn				

注意！

1. 在「動詞＋受詞＋不定詞」結構中，表示「感覺」意義的感觀動詞如feel，hear，listen to，notice，observe，see，watch等，和表示「致使」意義的使役動詞如have，make，let 等之後的動詞不定詞不帶to。例如：

▶He never made me do anything I didn't want to.
他從來沒有讓我做過我不想做的事。

▶He forced a laugh which again made him sound too close to hysteria.
他擠出一聲笑聲，又一次讓他聽起來接近歇斯底里。

2. 這類動詞轉為被動態時，動詞不定詞須帶to（let 除外）。例如：

▶Johnson not only lost his daughter, he was made to pay child support to the kidnapper.
詹森不僅失去了女兒，而且被迫向綁架者支付女兒的撫養費。

▶The contracts are let (to) commence on the first of March nineteen ninety four.
合約從1994年3月1日起生效。

4. 不定詞作主詞補語

不定詞也可作主詞補語，亦稱為表語。例如：

▶His ambition was to travel to Australia and go walk about in the outback.
他志在去澳洲旅行，在內陸地區徒步行走。

▶The car's radical new look is to be unveiled at the Detroit Motor Show next January.
這輛車極為新穎的新款將于明年1月在底特律車展上亮相。

5. 不定詞作狀語

不定詞作狀語能修飾動詞、形容詞、副詞等，表示動作的目的、結果、原因、條件、程度等。

(1)作目的狀語

不定詞作狀語可根據需要放在句首或句尾。例如：

▶ Sometimes one has to make sacrifices **to achieve an objective**.
有時候人們不得不作出犧牲來達到目的。

▶ **To achieve his goal**, Mr. Chase embarked on extensive travels around the world but found that the best place to learn about making potato chips was the most obvious one—the United States.
為了達到目標，蔡斯先生開始環遊世界，但是他發現學習做洋芋片最好的地方顯而易見是美國。

同樣的概念我們也可以用in order to或so as to來表達，尤其是在正式文體中。例如：

▶ We know what has to be done **in order to prevent further spread of H.I.V.** and we have good experience from many countries in the world, from Australia to the Netherlands, from Uganda to Thailand.
我們知道為了防止愛滋病病毒的進一步傳播該做什麼，而且從澳洲到荷蘭，從烏干達到泰國，我們從許多國家獲得了豐富的經驗。

注意！

在否定句中，要用in order not to 或so as not to來表達。不能單獨用不定詞。例如：

▶ She spoke softly **in order not to be overheard**, but her anger was evident.
她說得很輕柔，這樣不會被別人聽到，但是明顯怒氣沖沖。

(2)作結果狀語

▶ He crept downstairs slowly to alert the crew, **only to find them sitting in the armchairs**, drinking champagne from a large black bottle.
他慢慢地悄悄下樓去提醒全體船員注意，卻發現他們坐在扶手椅裡，正從一個大大的黑色瓶子裡倒香檳酒喝。

▶ He turned back to Gloria, **only to find** Hank had taken his place.
他回到格洛麗亞身邊，卻發現漢克取代了他的位置。

1. 我們常常在表示結果的不定詞前加only，even等副詞，以強調意外的結果。另外，有only，even的不定詞常用逗號隔開。例如：

▶ In the past 18 months, there have been 3,000 others like the real Mike Barlow who type their credit cards onto a computer screen, who casually put their purses down while they are trying on sweaters or who fill in their Social Security number on a medical form, only to have their identities stolen.
在過去的18個月裡，有3,000個人像邁克·巴羅一樣發現他們的身份被盜用，而他們僅僅是把信用卡卡號輸入進電腦，或是試穿毛衣時隨手放下錢包，或是在醫療表格上填寫社會保險號。

2. 在「too + 形容詞（或副詞）+不定詞」的結構裡，不定詞一般表示結果。

(3)作原因狀語。例如：

▶ Yesterday Mr. Smith admitted he was overwhelmed to hear how much he had inspired the youngster.
史密斯先生昨天承認，當他聽說自己極大地激勵了年輕人後感到非常激動。

(4)作條件狀語。例如：

▶ To be eligible for the compensation, a family of four must earn less than $33,125 a year.
一個四口之家每年收入低於33,125美元才有資格申請補償金。

(5)作評注性狀語

　　不定詞還可以用來修飾整個句子，表明說話者的態度、看法等。這類不定詞常位於句首。例如：

▶ To be honest, I was completely unprepared for the interview.
說實話，這次面試我完全沒有準備好。

▶ To tell you the truth, my company is forty-nine percent owned by an American company.
實話告訴你，我公司49%的股份由一家美國公司持有。

　　常用的這類不定詞片語有：to be honest，to be sure，to make a long story short，to begin with，to sum up，to tell you the truth等。

這類不定詞的邏輯主詞從內在的意義上看是說話人自己，表示說話人對說話內容所持的態度，因此這裡作評注性狀語處理。

不定詞的文法特徵

如前所示，不定詞在句子中與動詞的關係比較重要，與不同的動詞搭配決定了不定詞是否帶to。此外，不定詞與句子中其他成分的關係也很重要，比如它與名詞、形容詞搭配具有不同的文法作用。

1. 不定詞與名詞的搭配關係

英語中許多名詞都能用不定詞作後置修飾語，「名詞＋帶to的不定詞」主要有以下幾類：

(1)在某些與動詞有關聯的名詞之後

有些名詞如wish，refusal，offer，desire後可以跟動詞不定詞。請比較：

▶I wish to thank John for helpful comments in reviewing this text.
我希望對約翰審閱這篇文章時提出的有益評價表示感謝。

▶He had no wish to see his stepsister.
他不想見他繼母（或繼父）的女兒。

▶He refused to patent his vaccine, giving up a potential fortune so that as many people as possible could be vaccinated.
他不願意給他的疫苗申請專利，放棄了潛在的財富，這樣盡可能多的人都能注射。

▶British Ambassador John Weston said the Security Council absolutely can not accept Iraq's refusal to cooperate fully.
英國大使約翰・韋斯頓說安理會絕對不能接受伊拉克拒絕全面合作的做法。

(2)在time，place，way，reason之類的普通名詞之後。例如：

▶It is time to make some hard decisions.
是做一些艱難決定的時候了。

▶The tourists were asking for a place to stay in.
遊客們在要求一個住的地方。

▶Both of us had reason to feel ashamed.
我們兩人都應感到羞恥。

▶Robert gave him a key to get into the house.
羅伯特給他一把鑰匙進屋子。

▶Experts recommend giving children water or milk to drink.
專家建議給孩子們水或牛奶喝。

▶Patrick was a fine man to work with.
派翠克是位能夠共事的好人。

2. 不定詞與形容詞的搭配關係

許多形容詞之後可以跟動詞不定詞。「形容詞＋動詞不定詞」的結構可以根據所用的形容詞來表達多種意思。

(1)動詞不定詞與某些形容詞搭配表達原因與效果。例如：

▶ He was **privileged and honored to represent the people of New Jersey** for decades, and to be a dedicated advocate for the working people of America.
能幾十年代表新澤西的人民，當美國勞動人民盡職擁護者，他感到光榮和榮幸。

▶ It was **ridiculous to think** that he could help the child.
以為他能幫助這個孩子的想法真是愚蠢。

注意！

在不定詞片語中，當動詞與介係詞連用時，常位於「形容詞＋動詞不定詞」結構的句尾。例如：

▶ Outwardly, cheaters are easy **to get along with**, friendly and very charming.
從表面上看，騙子容易相處，友好又有魅力。

(2)當副詞enough或too修飾「形容詞＋動詞不定詞」時，動詞不定詞表達的是目的或結果。例如：

▶ It was **too** dark **to see his face** but Noreen heard his voice trembling slightly.
天太黑了，看不清他的臉，但是諾琳聽到他的聲音在微微顫抖。

▶ We learned we are not good **enough to compete** unless we are individually committed and focused.
我們瞭解到除非我們每個人都堅定且注意力集中，否則我們實力不夠，無法競爭。

3. 不定詞結構的邏輯主詞

當動詞不定詞意義上的主詞不是謂語動詞的主詞時，它自己的邏輯主詞由「for＋名詞（或代名詞受格）」引出。「for＋名詞（或代名詞受格）＋不定詞」這種結構在句中可作主詞、受詞、主詞補語和狀語等。

(1)作主詞。例如：

▶ Particularly in New York, **for families to save up money** is very difficult.
特別是在紐約，許多家庭很難攢錢。

(2)作受詞。例如：

▶ Do you think **for us to live together possible** after what has happened?
你認為發生這一切以後我們還能住在一起嗎？

(3)作主詞補語。例如：

▶ Another option would be for consumers to use less gas—either by trading in gas guzzling SUVs for more fuel-efficient sedans or electric hybrids, or by simply driving less.

另一種選擇是讓客戶少消耗汽油——要嘛把耗油量大的休旅車換成省油的轎車或複合式電動車，要嘛就是乾脆少開車。

(4)作狀語。例如：

▶ He gestured for her to enter his office and pointed to the chair in front of his desk.

他做手勢讓她進辦公室，指著他桌子面前的椅子讓她坐下。

4. 帶wh-詞的不定詞結構

在帶to不定詞前加wh-詞， 如whom，which，what，when，where，how，whether等，組成一個帶wh-詞的不定詞片語。這樣可使不定詞的含義更加具體。

「wh-詞+不定詞」結構具有名詞性質，在句中主要作受詞、受詞補語、主詞等。例如：

▶ He's deciding whether to lease or buy his premises.

他正在考慮承租還是購買土地。

▶ We don't tell companies how to run their business, but we often have suggestions that may improve their operations.

我們不告訴公司怎麼經營，但是我們通常有些建議可以改善公司的運營。

▶ Where to hold the meeting is under discussion.

在哪兒召開會議正在討論中。

可以與這種不定詞結構共用的動詞通常有：know，ask，tell，explain，show，wonder，consider，find out，understand等。

動詞-ing形式

動詞-ing形式包括現在分詞（Present Participles）和動名詞（Gerunds）。動詞-ing形式作為一種非限定動詞，由動詞原形加-ing構成，有完成式和被動式。

動詞-ing形式的結構形式

動詞-ing形式也是一種非限定動詞。與不定詞一樣，動詞-ing形式也有完成式和被動態。它的基本形式如下表所示：

	主動	被動
一般形式	doing	being done
完成式	having done	having been done

1. 動詞-ing形式的一般形式

動詞-ing形式所表示的時間與謂語動詞所表示的時間相一致，或晚於謂語動詞發生。例如：

▶ Understanding fundamentalism does not mean accepting it or approving of the actions taken in its name.
理解原教旨主義並不意味著接受或贊同以它的名義所進行的一些行為。

▶ His friend told him that predicting the direction of a market as volatile as oil is a fool's game. 他的朋友告訴他，預測像石油這樣起伏不定的市場無疑是傻子的遊戲。

▶ Walking to work is a great way to exercise and save money on gas.
步行去上班是鍛煉和節省汽油開支的絕好辦法。

動詞-ing形式有一般形式被動態。例如：

▶ The loans being offered will have interest rates at the market rate, which is a little above 6.5% for a 30-year mortgage.
提供貸款將按市場利率收取利息，30年按揭的利率約為6.5%多一點。

▶ Last week an international wildlife trade monitoring network, released a report showing the United States is also a major market for illegal ivory, much of it being sold on eBay.
上週國際野生動物貿易監控網路發佈的一篇報告表明美國也是非法象牙買賣的主要市場，主要在eBay上交易。

2. 動詞-ing形式的完成式

指它所表示的動作發生的時間早於主要謂語動詞的時間。例如：

▶ He is also a dedicated movie buff, and boasts of having seen every film in which Tom Cruise has starred. 他也是一個專注的電影迷，吹噓自己看過湯姆·克魯斯主演過的所有影片。

▶ The hardest thing to bear was the feeling of having been rejected.
最難以忍受的事情就是被拒絕的感受。

動詞-ing形式也有完成式被動態。例如：

▶ He qualifies for dual citizenship, having been born in Germany.
他出生在德國，因此有資格獲得雙重公民身份。

▶ There are unconfirmed reports of at least four more people having been killed.
有未經證實的報導稱至少還有四人已遭殺害。

動詞-ing形式的否定式由「not＋動詞-ing形式」構成。例如：

▶**Not having** close family, my friends are everything to me.
沒有親密的家人，我的朋友對我來說最重要。

▶"**Not having** a marriage certificate has affected every aspect of my life now," she says.
她說：「沒有正式結婚現在影響了我生活的各個方面。」

動詞-ing形式的文法功能

動詞-ing形式具有名詞、動詞、形容詞、副詞的多種特徵，可以單獨或與其他成分一起構成-ing片語，在句中作主詞、受詞、補語、名詞修飾語和狀語等各種句子成分。

1. 動詞-ing形式作主詞

作主詞用的動詞-ing形式在一些傳統文法書上被稱為動名詞。作主詞用的動名詞相當於一個名詞，主要表示相對抽象而籠統的意義。例如：

▶**Not having** your license with you while driving is an arrestable offence.
駕駛時沒有帶駕照是可以被逮捕的行為。

▶**Collecting cord blood** takes three to five minutes after a newborn is delivered, and it doesn't hurt the mother or the baby.
在新生兒出生後採集臍帶血要三到五分鐘，這不會傷害產婦和嬰兒。

▶**Spending time** with people who don't share your interests can be disheartening.
與和你興趣不同的人在一起會叫人沮喪。

帶to的不定詞作主詞具有明顯的動詞特徵，主要表示個別、具體的意義（參見本章P206〈不定詞作主詞〉）。但表示抽象而籠統的意義時，不定詞與動詞-ing形式常常交替使用，但後者更常見。例如：

▶**To get rich** through diligence is appropriate.
勤奮致富才是正途。

▶**Fighting** illegal drugs is a priority for President Bush because drugs destroy our neighborhoods, harm our children and ruin lives.
毒品摧毀我們的鄰里社區，毒害我們的孩子，毀掉我們的生活，因此打擊非法販毒是布希總統面臨的首要任務。

注意！

動詞-ing形式片語作主詞時，我們往往用it作形式主詞而將真實主詞（動詞-ing 形式片語）放在謂語之後。例如：

▶It is not worth **spending** much on the car.
不值得在這輛車上花很多錢。

有些結構習慣上要求動詞-ing形式作主詞。常見的有：It is no good... / It is no use... / It is worthwhile... / It is hardly worth...等。例如：

▶ It's no use **struggling** against the inevitable.
與不可避免的事情鬥爭是沒有用的。

2. 動詞-ing形式作主詞補語

動詞-ing形式可用在連綴動詞之後作主詞補語，亦稱為表語。例如：

▶ In evidence, he explains that his first job was **cleaning**.
作證的時候，他解釋他的第一份工作是清潔工作。

▶ I thought Sunday's match against France was **exciting**.
我以為星期天對法國隊的比賽很精彩。

注意！

動詞-ing形式作主詞補語時，通常是說明性的，也相當於一個名詞。但是，還有一類作主詞補語的動詞-ing形式起形容詞的作用，即「現在分詞」。現在分詞已具有形容詞的各種特徵，可以由副詞修飾，也可以有比較級和最高級。它們可以作主詞補語，也可以作名詞修飾語。例如：

▶ With signs in English and Chinese, the museum is **quite interesting** and includes artifacts and displays recording the city's contacts with the West.
這座有中英文標誌的博物館非常有趣，它包括了記錄這座城市與西方交流的手工藝品和展覽品。

▶ For me as a woman it is **very embarrassing** to wear these shoes in the street, but they are the only ones I have.
作為女人對於我來說，在街上穿這雙鞋子很讓人難為情，但是我只有這雙鞋。

此外，也要注意區別作主詞補語的動詞-ing形式和現在分詞。作主詞補語的動詞-ing形式是對主詞的說明，相當於一個名詞或構成名詞片語的成分，也可起形容詞的作用；而現在分詞與助動詞一起構成謂語。例如：

★主詞補語

▶ The hobby I'm most involved with is **collecting** antiquities.
我最熱衷的愛好是收集古器物。

★謂語動詞進行式

▶ She is **collecting** the different colors of stone at the edge of the crater.
她正在火山口的邊緣收集各色石頭。

3. 動詞-ing形式作名詞修飾語

如上所述，起形容詞作用的動詞-ing形式可以作主詞補語，也可以作名詞修飾語。一般而言，單個的動詞-ing形式可以用作前置修飾語，而動詞-ing形式的片語往往用作後置修飾語。例如：

▶ Rats were **disgusting** creatures.
老鼠是叫人噁心的生物。

▶ The girl **sitting** between Cosmo and Hubert looked bewildered.
坐在科斯莫和休伯特中間的女孩看起來很困惑。

注意！

後置修飾語通常是一般形式的主動態或被動態，用作後置修飾語的動詞-ing 形式所起的作用相當於一個定語子句。例如：

▶ The consensus **being sought** may help determine the future of one of today's emerging fields of biotechnology research.
大家正努力達成共識，它可能幫助確定今天新出現的生物科技研究領域的未來。

▶ The aircraft **being sent** to the gulf include electronic warfare planes designed to jam enemy radar and communications.
正在被送往海灣的飛機包括為阻截敵人的雷達和通信手段而設計的電子作戰飛機。

4. 動詞-ing形式作受詞

(1)動詞-ing形式作動詞受詞。例如：

▶ I was near blind in the dazzle of the sun and regretted **not bringing** sunglasses.
我在強烈的陽光下幾乎和失明了一樣，後悔沒有帶墨鏡。

▶ Lorton suggested **going** for a drink, but Dougal refused.
洛頓提議去喝一杯，但杜格爾拒絕了。

在英語裡有些動詞只能帶不定詞（參見本章P206〈不定詞作受詞〉），有些動詞只能帶動詞-ing形式，還有些動詞兩者都可以帶（參見本章P223〈能帶不定詞和動詞-ing形式而意義無區別的動詞〉）。

常見的只能帶動詞-ing形式作受詞的動詞請見下一頁。

常見的只能帶動詞-ing形式作受詞的動詞有：

acknowledge	adore	avoid	admit	anticipate
appreciate	cannot help	celebrate	commence	consider
contemplate	defer	delay	deny	describe
detest	discontinue	dislike	dread	endure
enjoy	escape	excuse	explain	fancy
finish	forgive	imagine	involve	keep
lie	mention	miss	mind	pardon
postpone	practice	prevent	quit	recall
recollect	report	resent	resist	risk
save	sit	stand	stop	suggest
understand	spend			

(2)動詞-ing形式作介係詞受詞

動詞-ing 形式作介係詞受詞大都和固定搭配有關。主要的搭配類型有以下幾種：

a. 動詞＋介係詞＋動詞-ing形式。例如：

▶ Although happy with the practical training, she objected to having to travel to Cardiff three times a week for lectures, as it could take up to four hours to make the round trip.
儘管實際訓練很愉快，她還是拒絕了一週去卡地夫聽三次講座，因為來回要花四個小時。

▶ Have you ever thought of being a full-time mom?
你有沒有想過當全職媽媽？

b. 動詞＋名詞（或名詞片語）＋介係詞＋動詞-ing形式。例如：

▶ It's obviously a mistake on our part to have made a decision without having done the proper background work.
沒有做好合適的幕後工作就作出決定明顯是我們這方面的錯誤。

▶ A breakthrough for sleep-deprived people across the country, researchers will report today that millions of Americans can beat insomnia without sleeping pills by following a few simple rules, such as leaving bed if sleep doesn't come.
研究者今天將報導，數以百萬計的美國人只需遵循一些簡單的規則就可以不吃安眠藥打敗失眠，比如不睏的時候就不要上床躺著。這對全國睡眠不足人群來説是個突破性的研究成果。

c. 名詞＋介係詞＋動詞-ing形式。例如：

▶ Hyundai Motor Chairman said in October he was considering the **possibility of building a U.S. plant**, and Hosford said a committee was formed to study the option.
現代汽車公司董事長在10月時說他正在考慮在美國建立分廠的可能性，而且霍斯福德說已經成立了一個委員會來研究這項提議。

▶ Experts will warn today that sun creams could raise the **risk of getting skin cancer**.
今天專家將發出警告，防曬霜可能增加患皮膚癌的危險。

d. 形容詞＋介係詞＋動詞-ing形式。例如：

▶ He said he was **tired of trying to get by** on his $158—a month's salary as a security guard.
他說他厭倦了當一名靠158美元月薪勉強度日的保安。

▶ She was so **ashamed of cheating** on the test that she went and told the teacher.
她對自己考試時作弊非常羞愧，所以她向老師坦白了自己的行為。

5. 動詞-ing形式作複合受詞

如上所述，動詞不定詞可以作複合受詞，動詞-ing形式也可以用作複合受詞。

在表示「感覺」意義的感觀動詞如feel，hear，listen to，notice，observe，see，watch等詞之後，既可以跟動詞-ing形式結構，也可以跟不帶to的動詞不定詞結構作複合受詞。

但是它們的含義是不同的，雖然動詞-ing形式結構與不帶to的動詞不定詞結構都表示與謂語動詞同時發生的動作，但動詞-ing形式表示動作的進行，強調動作的反覆性和連續性；動詞不定詞則表示動作發生的事實，強調動作的完成過程。例如：

▶ As she rang the bell, she **heard a child crying** somewhere inside the house.
她按門鈴的時候聽見房子裡某個地方傳來了孩子的哭聲。

▶ Emmie thought she had never **heard people laugh** so much or sound so happy.
艾米覺得她從來沒有聽到人們笑得這麼多，聽上去這麼快樂。

▶ He ran upstairs and **saw students running** down the hallway, screaming and crying.
他跑上樓，看到學生們在走廊上奔跑，叫著，喊著。

▶ Allison says he didn't smoke anything in high school and drank only at his senior prom, but Levine says Allison smoked cigarettes and pot regularly and **saw him drink** often at parties.
艾利森說他高中時從不抽菸，只在高中畢業舞會上喝了點酒，但是萊文說艾利森經常抽菸吸大麻，也看到他經常在聚會上喝酒。

在accept，describe，quote，regard，think of等動詞之後，可由as引出作複合受詞的動詞-ing 形式結構。例如：

▶ A Spanish soldier further **described** the attacker **as having a scant beard** and a long face with large, expressive eyes.
一位西班牙士兵進一步描述這位襲擊者留著稀疏的鬍子，長著一張長臉和一雙會說話的大眼睛。

▶ You **regard yourself as having the right to health**, but the governments which runs the country does not have the capacity to give you that right.
你認為自己有權利獲得健康，但是管理國家的政府沒有能力給你提供此權利。

6. 動詞-ing形式作狀語

動詞-ing形式作狀語，表示時間、原因、行為方式及伴隨狀態等。

(1)表示時間

動詞-ing形式相當於一個while/when引導的時間副詞子句，表示分句的動作與謂語動詞之間的時間先後關係。例如：

▶ **Realizing** they needed help, the women spent July and August recruiting a board of directors.
意識到他們需要幫助，這些婦女7月和8月都在招募一批主管。

▶ **Walking** on the coral reef at low tide, we spotted starfish, a vicious-looking moray eel, sea urchins and a mind-boggling variety of shellfish.
低潮時走在珊瑚礁上，我們看到了海星，外表兇惡的海鱔、海膽和種類多得驚人的貝類生物。

為了強調動詞-ing形式的動作與謂語動詞所表示的動作同時發生，往往在動詞-ing形式前加上while，when等連接詞。例如：

▶ **When running for office**, Brown Waite promised to be a workhorse, not a show horse.
布朗‧韋特競選的時候承諾要做個能吃苦的人而不是只會表現的人。

▶ **While looking for work and living out of her truck**, Donnelly says weed work, which pays $6 an hour, is "a great opportunity".
在找工作且居無定所的時候，唐納利說每小時6美元的除草工作是個「極好的機會」。

但是，如果動詞-ing形式的動作發生在謂語動詞表示的動作之前並已完成，應用動詞-ing形式的完成式。例如：

▶**While having published only newsletters in the past**, the foundation is preparing to move the editorial operations of the well-known feminist title into its new offices in hopes of reinvigorating the magazine.

這個基金會過去只出版過報紙，現在準備將這個著名的女性主義雜誌的編輯部搬到新的辦公室裡，希望能夠重振這本雜誌。

▶**Having grown up** in a place where it was taken for granted that nice people did not raise their voices, I was astonished by the directness with which my new friends spoke their minds.

我在一個人們認為有禮貌的人不能大聲說話的地方長大，當我的新朋友直接地說出他們的想法時，我感到很震驚。

(2)表示原因。例如：

▶**Being** a younger person, I had to choose between advancing my accounting career or advancing my political career.

作為年輕人，我得選擇是在會計事業上邁進還是在政治事業上發展。

(3)表示行為方式及伴隨狀態。例如：

▶At night we sat under the stars and chatted, **laughing and telling** each other our life stories.

夜晚我們坐在星空下聊天，笑語不斷，互相說著生活中的故事。

▶I shouted, **slamming** the coffee cup down on its saucer.

我大聲嚷著，使勁把咖啡杯放到杯碟上。

(4) go+動詞-ing形式

在動詞go之後接動詞-ing形式作狀語是一種常見結構，表示「從事某項活動」。例如：

▶In the afternoon, we **went shopping** for sneakers and mobile phones.

我們下午去買了運動鞋和手機。

▶Yesterday we **went swimming** for the first time and it was very encouraging.

我們昨天第一次去游泳，很令人振奮。

常見的搭配有：

go bowling	go camping	go hiking	go jogging	go skating
go sliding	go sailing	go shopping	go swimming	go mountain-climbing

(5)動詞-ing形式的分句作用

動詞-ing形式片語在句中充當某一句子成分時，它與不定詞片語一樣在句中能起分句作用。這種非限定分句與限定分句可以互換使用。例如：

▶ He was really afraid of losing his memory.

= He was really afraid that he might lose his memory.
　他真的很害怕失去記憶。

如上所述，用作後置修飾語的動詞-ing 形式的作用相當於一個關係子句。例如：

▶ The man sitting next to her was like a porcelain Buddha, rotund and self-contained, the skin without a wrinkle despite being fifty or so years old.

= The man who was sitting next to her was like a porcelain Buddha, rotund and self-contained, the skin without a wrinkle despite being fifty or so years old.
　坐在她旁邊的男人像個瓷佛像，矮矮墩墩而泰然自若，儘管五十歲上下，皮膚上一點兒皺紋都沒有。

此外，作狀語的動詞-ing形式也相當於一個副詞子句。

▶ Having fought back from a depressive illness which has affected him for the past two years, he is simply happy to be playing golf again.

= Because he has fought back from a depressive illness which has affected him for the past two years, he is simply happy to be playing golf again.
　憂鬱症影響了他兩年，現在他戰勝了疾病，很高興又能打高爾夫球了。

🎯 動詞-ing形式的邏輯主詞

同動詞不定詞的結構一樣，動詞-ing形式的邏輯主詞有時就是句子謂語動詞的主詞，有時則需從上下文中推斷。

通常可以在動詞-ing形式之前加上名詞、代名詞受格、所有格或者形容詞性的所有格代名詞來表示其邏輯主詞。例如：

▶ This is a flaw which could lead to him making mistakes.
　這是個能使他犯錯誤的毛病。

▶ I am delighted that he has decided to rejoin us at training today and we look forward to him making a vital contribution to the playing side of Liverpool during the 2002-2003 season.
　我很高興他決定今天回到我們中間一起訓練，我們期待他在2002至2003賽季能為利物浦隊作出重大貢獻。

▶ I believe that's the motivation which led to him making the challenge.
　我相信那就是讓他提出挑戰的動機。

🎯 動詞-ing形式的獨立結構

動詞-ing形式的獨立結構也稱為動詞-ing形式的複合結構。一般來説，相當於副詞子句的動詞-ing形式的邏輯主詞就是主句主詞。

但是，有時動詞-ing形式獨立結構帶有自己的邏輯主詞。這個邏輯主詞由名詞通格或代名詞主格表示，位於動詞-ing形式之前。它與動詞-ing形式之間有邏輯上的主謂關係，而與主句沒有句法上的關聯。

動詞-ing形式的獨立結構起副詞子句的作用，可以表示時間、條件、原因、行為方式及伴隨狀態等。例如：

▶**Weather permitting**, he hopes to finish the work next Thursday.
　天氣允許的話，他希望能在下週四結束工作。

▶The Prince had bent and kissed his sons and left, **his eyes staring** blindly ahead like a sleepwalker's.
　王子彎下腰親了親他的幾個兒子後就離開了，他眼神空洞地盯著前方，像個夢遊者一樣。

動詞-ing形式與不定詞結構用法比較

只能帶動詞-ing形式或只能帶不定詞的動詞

如上所述，在英語裡有些動詞只能帶不定詞，有些動詞只能帶動詞-ing形式，還有些動詞兩者都可以帶。

常見的只能帶動詞-ing形式作受詞的動詞參見本章P217〈動詞-ing形式作受詞〉；常見的只能帶動詞-ing形式作複合受詞的動詞參見本章P219〈動詞-ing形式作複合受詞〉。只能帶不定詞作受詞的動詞參見本章P206〈不定詞作受詞〉；只能帶不定詞作複合受詞的動詞參見本章P207〈不定詞作複合受詞〉。

既能帶不定詞又能帶動詞-ing形式的動詞

如上所述，在感觀動詞如feel，hear，listen to，notice，observe，see，watch等之後，既可以跟動詞-ing形式，也可以跟不帶to的動詞不定詞結構作複合受詞，但是它們的含義不同。（參見本章P219〈動詞-ing形式作複合受詞〉）

能帶不定詞和動詞-ing形式而意義無區別的動詞

有些動詞可以帶不定詞或動詞-ing形式作受詞，意義區別不大。常見的這類詞有：

attempt	begin	bother	cease	continue	deserve
fear	hate	like	love	prefer	start

例如：

▶Adam said firmly that he'd **prefer to keep / keeping his secret to himself** for a bit.
　亞當堅定地說他寧願給自己留一點祕密。

▶ She **started to giggle / giggling** and for the first time in many years, she began to feel happy.

她開始咯咯地笑起來，這麼多年來她第一次感到高興。

▶ He had long ago **ceased to compliment / complimenting her** on her appearance but instead frequently made derogatory remarks about a dress not fitting her properly or her hairstyle being old-fashioned.

他已經很久沒有誇獎她的外表了，而是不時地貶損她，說她的哪件衣服如何不合適，她的髮型如何老土。

▶ Tears **began to prick / pricking her eyes**, but she wiped them away.

淚水開始刺痛她的雙眼，但是她擦去了眼淚。

注意！

不定詞表示比較具體的動作，這些動作往往沒發生，而動詞-ing形式表示比較籠統、可能已發生的動作。這種區別的語境依賴性很強。例如：

▶ Simon loves **having** beautiful women paying him attention.
  西蒙喜歡漂亮女子注意他。

▶ He loves **to turn** his friends **into** his slaves.
  他喜歡把朋友當成奴隸一樣使喚。

▶ Apparently Daly prefers **working on** New Year's Eve.
  很明顯戴利更喜歡在除夕夜工作。

▶ As a rule, he prefers not **to comment about** other teams' players, but he makes an exception in Vick.
  通常，他傾向於不評價其他隊的隊員，但卻對維克破了例。

能帶不定詞和動詞-ing形式而意義不同的動詞

　　有少數動詞接不定詞和動詞-ing形式時，意義是完全不同的。常見的這類詞有：forget，remember，regret，stop，go on，try，mean等。

　　1. forget/remember＋不定詞／-ing形式

　　在forget/remember之後使用不定詞表示將來的動作，即不定詞表示的動作晚於謂語動詞的動作。forget to do sth.意為「忘記了要去做某事」，remember to do sth.意為「記住要去做某事」。

　　動詞-ing形式表示已發生的事，即動作先於謂語動詞的動作發生。forget doing sth.意為「忘記做過了某事」，remember doing sth.意為「記得做過了某事」。例如：

▶ I **forgot to tell** everyone that I met the Mayor last night at a restaurant.
我忘了告訴大家我昨晚在餐廳見到了市長。

▶ I shall never **forget waiting** on the dock for the ship to come in, and that moment when he came down the gangway and embraced me, holding me as though he would never let me go.
我永遠忘不了在碼頭等著船開進來，他從跳板上走下來擁抱我，抱著我好像他永遠不想讓我走一樣。

▶ You must **remember to take** enough toilet paper next time.
你下次一定要記得帶足衛生紙。

▶ I don't ever **remember getting** popcorn at the movie until I was a teenager or in my adult life.
直到我十幾歲或成年後，我才記得在看電影時買過爆米花吃。

2. regret＋不定詞／-ing形式

同「forget/remember＋不定詞／-ing形式」的區別一樣，「regret＋不定詞」表示將來的動作，「regret＋-ing形式」表示已發生的動作。例如：

▶ We **regret to announce the death of Laura Sadler**, who died peacefully at 5:30 pm on June 19.
我們很遺憾地宣佈蘿拉·薩德勒已於6月19日下午5:30安詳地去世。

▶ I deeply **regret making that comment** and know that I've let myself and my teammates down.
我很後悔發表那番評論，我知道我讓我和我的隊友都失望了。

3. try＋不定詞／-ing形式

try to do sth. 意為「努力去做某事」，而try doing sth. 意為「嘗試，試驗」。例如：

▶ I met a really nice girl and **tried to grab a slice of happiness**.
我遇見了一個非常好的女孩，努力去得到一絲絲快樂。

▶ To be sure, I haven't **tried visiting Egypt, Syria, Saudi Arabia or Pakistan** since the release of my book.
當然自從我出書以來我一直沒有出訪埃及、敘利亞、沙烏地阿拉伯和巴基斯坦。

4. propose＋不定詞／-ing形式

propose to do sth. 意為「想要或打算做某事」，而propose doing sth. 意為「建議做某事」。例如：

▶ President Bush has **proposed to legalize the status of millions of illegal immigrants from Mexico**.
布希總統打算將從墨西哥來的數百萬非法移民地位合法化。

▶ In early May, after the Bush administration proposed slashing its nuclear research budget from $47 million to $27 million, university administrators were outraged.
5月初，在布希政府提議將核研究的經費從4700萬削減到2700萬後，許多大學管理人員感到十分氣憤。

5. mean＋不定詞／-ing形式

mean to do sth.意為「打算或想要做某事」，mean doing sth.意為「意味著什麼」。例如：

▶ They meant to knock me over the head, kidnap me.
他們想要撞我的頭把我撞倒，再綁架我。

▶ My job means having to give up a lot of things that everyone else takes for granted in their life.
我的工作意味著要放棄生活中許多別人覺得理所當然的事情。

6. stop/go on＋不定詞／-ing形式

stop to do sth.表示停下手頭上在做的事去做另外的事，stop doing sth.表示停止做手頭上在做的事。例如：

▶ He looked happy and relaxed yesterday when he stopped to talk to English journalists.
昨天他停下來和英國記者講話時看起來快樂放鬆。

▶ To be fair to David Beckham, he never stopped working and chasing.
公平地說，大衛·貝克漢從來沒有停止工作和追逐。

go on to do sth.表示繼續去做另外的事。go on doing sth.表示繼續做手頭上在做的事。例如：

▶ She went on to telephone her American friend Lana Marks and express the same worries.
她接著打電話給她的美國朋友拉娜·馬克斯，表達了同樣的擔憂。

▶ Craig went on talking quietly of the bad times past in northern Kenya and how they were changed.
克雷格一直在靜靜地說肯亞北部過去的苦難時光和他們是如何被改變的。

動詞-ed形式 ▷

動詞-ed形式也是一種非限定動詞。不同於動詞-ing形式和不定詞，動詞-ed形式沒有時態的變化。例如：

▶Born in 1926 in New York, Rose and his wife, Zelda, a former biochemist who became a peace activist, have four children who live in Washington State, Massachusetts and North Carolina.

　　羅斯於1926年出生於紐約，他的妻子澤爾達以前是生物化學家，後來成了和平活動家，他們有四個孩子分別住在華盛頓州、麻塞諸塞州和北卡羅來納州。

　　動詞-ed形式也有複合結構。尤其當動詞-ed形式有自己的修飾對象時，常常用複合結構。例如：

▶All my savings gone, I simply can't afford to work for nothing.
　　我所有的積蓄都沒有了，我沒辦法不計報酬地工作了。

動詞-ed形式的文法功能

　　動詞-ed形式主要表示狀態，可以在句子中作狀語、主詞補語、複合受詞和名詞修飾語。

　　1. 動詞-ed形式作狀語

　　動詞-ed形式的邏輯主詞一般是句子的主詞。另外，作狀語用的動詞-ed形式一般都是及物動詞。動詞-ed形式作狀語，表示時間、條件、原因、行為方式及伴隨狀態等。

(1)表示時間。例如：

▶Once caught, the birds are examined for wounds.
　　一旦抓住小鳥，就給它們檢查傷口。

▶Asked why she doesn't talk about it, she said it's not a "big issue" this year.
　　被問及為何不談談這個，她說這還算不上今年的「重大事件」。

(2)表示條件。例如：

▶Given the situation in the world today, he believes he is making the right choice.
　　考慮到當今世界形勢，他相信自己正作出正確的選擇。

▶Treated as handicapped, the child will be handicapped.
　　如果你把一個兒童看成殘疾人的話，那他就是殘疾的了。

(3)表示原因。例如：

▶Weakened by successive storms, this old house was no longer safe.
　　由於受到數次風暴的連續侵襲，這間老屋已經不安全了。

(4)表示行為方式及伴隨狀態。例如：

▶ **Equipped with only a telephone**, he buys money with money, sells money for money.
只配備了一個電話，他就能做匯率交易。

▶ Rita went home late, **utterly exhausted**.
麗塔很晚才回家，此時已疲憊不堪。

2. 動詞-ed形式作主詞補語

動詞-ed形式可用在連綴動詞之後作主詞補語，亦稱作表語。例如：

▶ She was obviously **distressed but convinced of her son's innocence**.
她明顯很沮喪，但是她堅信兒子是無辜的。

注意！

動詞-ed形式作主詞補語時在形式上和被動式很相似。但是作主詞補語的動詞-ed形式一般不帶by結構，而且動詞-ed形式強調狀態，而被動式強調動作。例如：

▶ His left kneecap was **broken**.
他的左膝蓋骨斷了。

▶ The silence was **broken by** Emily.
艾蜜莉打破了寂靜。

3. 動詞-ed形式作複合受詞

動詞-ed形式在句子中可以作複合受詞，補充說明受詞的狀況。例如：

▶ After being bombarded and shocked with all these images and explosions, I found myself **exhausted and bored**.
遭遇所有這些影像和爆炸的轟擊和震撼之後，我感到又疲勞又厭煩。

▶ The law allows insurance companies to set a cap on the amount they will pay for people to have their cars **repaired**.
法律允許保險公司對汽車維修賠償金額設上限。

▶ Now mostly it's middle-class people who want to have their car **repaired**.
如今主要是中產階級想要修理汽車。

注意！

「have＋受詞＋動詞-ed形式」是一種常用結構，表示某事是讓別人做的。上述例子中to have their car **repaired**意為「中產階級想要修理汽車」（請別人修理）。又如：

▶ In the past year, I **have had my hair cut** exactly as it was when I was a teenager.
在過去的一年裡，我把頭髮理得就和我十幾歲時一樣。

這裡要注意區別「have＋sb.＋do」結構，它意為「讓某人做某事」。例如：

▶ His teachers had him write letters in sand, hoping the rough feeling on his fingertips would somehow imprint the swoops and swirls of the alphabet onto his brain.

他的老師們讓他在沙子裡寫字，希望指尖粗糙的觸覺能將字母彎彎繞繞的感覺印到他的大腦裡。

> 注意！
>
> 用作後置修飾語的動詞-ed 形式也相當於一個定語子句。

4. 動詞-ed形式作名詞修飾語

一般而言，單個的動詞-ed形式可以用作前置修飾語，而動詞-ed形式片語往往用作後置修飾語。例如：

▶ A fisherman heard the alert, saw the stolen car and called the police.

一個漁民聽到警報，看到那輛被偷的車，叫了員警。

▶ His mother had stepped in to fill the embarrassed silence.

他的母親走進來打破了僵局。

▶ Craig can't explain the determination made by Wolf, who died in the early 1990s.

克雷格沒法解釋20世紀90年代初去世的沃爾夫所作的決定。

▶ The play put on by the students was successful.

學生們演的那場戲非常成功。

動詞-ing形式與-ed形式的用法比較

動詞-ing形式具有名詞、動詞、形容詞、副詞的多種特徵，可以單獨或與其他成分一起在句中作主詞、受詞、補語、名詞修飾語和狀語。

動詞-ed形式主要表示狀態，可以在句子中作狀語、主詞補語、複合受詞和名詞修飾語。與動詞-ing形式相比，動詞-ed形式一般含有被動意義，而動詞-ing形式則含有主動意義。另外，動詞-ed形式一般有完成的意義，而動詞-ing形式則有進行的意義。例如：

▶ He saw the excited, childish smile on the younger man's face and knew the answer.

他看到這個年輕人臉上興奮又充滿孩子氣的笑容就明白答案是什麼了。

▶ It was an exciting, yet dangerous, life, but one that suited her nature.

這種生活令人激動又充滿危險，但是適合她的性格。

▶ Within the developed countries, health problems associated with pregnancy and delivery are four times as common in low income groups as in the middle classes.

在發達國家，低收入群體與懷孕和分娩相關的健康問題的發生率是中產階級的四倍。

▶ Health advocates cheered last year when George W. Bush announced a five-year, $15 billion plan to fight AIDS in the developing world.

當去年喬治・布希宣佈一項在發展中國家投入150億美元抗擊愛滋病的五年計劃時，衛生保健工作者為之歡呼。

小結 ▷

　　本章討論了英語非限定動詞的三種動詞形式：不定詞、動詞-ing形式和動詞-ed形式。這三種非限定動詞雖然不能作謂語，但由於保留了動詞的某些特徵，在句中有廣泛的句法作用。

　　不定詞在句中具有主詞、受詞、補語、名詞修飾語和狀語等功能，能充當除了謂語以外的任何句子成分。同樣，動詞-ing形式也能在句中作主詞、受詞、補語、名詞修飾語和狀語。動詞-ed形式可以在句子中作狀語、主詞補語、複合受詞和名詞修飾語。

　　另外，本章討論了非限定動詞的變化形式和用法。這三種非限定動詞形式在文法上來說是沒有主詞的，但可以有自己的邏輯主詞。從語言運用上看，非限定動詞在語言中的使用要看非限定動詞各種形式的自身意義和句子結構的需要。

形容詞

形容詞概說 ▷

　　形容詞具有描述、修飾和限定等功能。在形態、文法和語義等方面具有典型特徵。它有動態和靜態之分，又有主動和被動之義。它可以從分詞轉化而來，具有比較級（Comparative Degree）和最高級（Superlative Degree）的形式。根據其在句子中的作用，形容詞可以作名詞的前置修飾語或後置修飾語。

　　在本章裡主要從形容詞的語義、句法和構成等方面來對形容詞作概括性描述。

形容詞的特徵 ▷

◎ 形容詞的典型特徵

　　形容詞的典型特徵可以從下面幾個方面來說明。

　　1. 形態特徵

　　大多數形容詞都有明顯的形態特徵（Morphological Characteristics）。有些形容詞可以有比較級和最高級的形態變化。例如：small，smaller，smallest等。

　　有些形容詞屬於派生形容詞，是由動詞或者名詞加一定形容詞性字尾派生出來的。例如：acceptable，impressive，scientific，chemical等。

　　有些形容詞是由動詞-ing形式或-ed形式構成的。例如：exciting，interesting，surprising，surprised，excited等。

　　有些形容詞屬於複合形容詞，由兩個單字組合而成。例如：kindhearted，man-made等。

　　2. 句法特徵

　　形容詞的主要句法功能是作修飾語（Attributives）和補語。形容詞作修飾語時可以修飾名詞性成分，是名詞片語的組成部分。例如：

▶He's an incredibly interesting person.
　他是個非常有趣的人。

當形容詞作補語的時候，它不是名詞片語的組成部分，而是獨立充當句子的句法成分，即補語。形容詞可以充當主詞補語（表語）或者受詞補語。例如：

★主詞補語（表語）

▶ The material I saw was interesting and somehow down to earth.
我看到的材料非常有趣且比較實際。

★受詞補語

▶ I read two books this year and found them so interesting and closely related, that I decided to use them for my coursework.
今年我讀到兩本書，都非常有趣並且密切關聯，所以我決定把它們用於課堂作業。

3. 語義特徵

形容詞最典型的語義特徵（Semantic Characteristics）是其描述性，用來描述人或事物的性質和狀態。例如：beautiful，kind，heavy，big，shy，serious等。

這些描述性形容詞一般都是可以分等級的（Gradable），表現在它們都可以有比較級和最高級，還可以受程度副詞very，extremely等的修飾。例如：bigger，most beautiful，very kind，extremely serious等。

有些形容詞的作用是對名詞進行限定或分類。例如criminal law, medical student等。這些形容詞都不能分等級（Nongradable），在形式上沒有比較級和最高級，也一般不受程度副詞的修飾。

形容詞的語義分類 ▷

按照形容詞的語義可以從以下幾個角度對形容詞進行分類。

◎ 描述性形容詞和分類性形容詞

形容詞根據其與所修飾的名詞的關係分為描述性形容詞（Descriptors）和分類性形容詞（Classifiers）。

1. 描述性形容詞

描述性形容詞是描述人或事物的顏色、大小、重量、年齡、情緒等特徵的形容詞。這些形容詞大多都是可分等級的。例如：

• 表示顏色或者亮度的形容詞black，dark，grey等
• 表示大小、重量、範圍的形容詞big，deep，heavy，short，large，thin，wide等
• 表示時間、年齡、頻率的形容詞annual，daily，early，new，old等
• 表示評價、判斷的形容詞bad，beautiful，good等

- 表示其他性狀的形容詞cold，private，positive，strange，dead，empty，hot，open，strong，strange，serious 等

▶The dense **grey** sky seemed denser than before, so grey in places that it seemed almost green.
濃灰色的天空似乎愈加發灰了，有幾處幾乎成了綠色。

▶He has experienced a lot in one **short** year, and picked up a lot, but not nearly as much as he is going to pick up in the next two or three years.
在短短的一年裡他經歷了很多，也得到了很多，但是接下來的兩三年裡他會得到更多。

▶Dogs act differently in **strange** environments from how they do at home, no matter how well trained and obedient they normally are.
狗不管在正常情況下訓練得多好，多順從，到了陌生的環境中它們的表現和其在家中的表現都會不同。

2. 分類性形容詞

分類性形容詞的基本功能是限定名詞所表示的人或事物的類別，一般都不能分等級。具體可以細分為下面幾類：

(1) 表示限定的形容詞，主要作用是限定名詞的所指，特別是通過說明與其他名詞所指的關係來限定。常見的有：additional，general，previous，top，various，average，chief，entire，final，following，initial，left，same，latter，inner，outer，upper，elder，utmost，main，only，sole，mere，total 等。例如：

▶She receives **additional** training twice annually.
她每年接受兩次額外的訓練。

▶In **previous** games they have looked indifferent, just doing enough to win and no more.
在先前的比賽中他們表現得漠不關心，所做的僅僅是贏得比賽而已，沒有其他。

▶She was down-to-earth and in the **upper** echelons—a great human being and a great star.
她講求實際，位處上層，是一個偉大的人、偉大的明星。

▶We are on the brink of **total** collapse economically.
我們的經濟已經到了完全崩潰的邊緣。

▶I was an **only** child and was definitely taught the value of cash.
我是家中的獨生子，而且確實接受過有關金錢價值的教育。

這類形容詞一般都只能作名詞修飾語，不能作補語。（參見本章P236〈形容詞的句法功能〉）

(2) 表示所屬關係的形容詞，主要作用是指明所歸屬的國家或者宗教。例如：American，Chinese，Irish，Christian等。

(3)表示主題的形容詞，主要指明所屬的主題領域，一般是由名詞派生出來的。常見的有：commercial，mental，political，social，visual，official，medical，mechanical等。例如：

▶He developed courses in commercial art to meet the needs of studios in west central Scotland.
他開展了商業藝術的課程以滿足蘇格蘭中西部的藝術工作室的需求。

▶Some mental health experts are concerned that drugs are being used for trivial conditions or for unsuitable patients.
一些精神健康方面的專家擔心藥品正在用於一些無關緊要的小病或者不適用的病人。

▶She said that the new train had not exhibited any mechanical problems.
她說新火車還沒有出現任何機械問題。

與描述性形容詞相比，分類性形容詞與所修飾的名詞中心詞關係更密切。因此，如果描述性形容詞和分類性形容詞同時修飾一個名詞中心詞，分類性形容詞緊挨著它所修飾的名詞，二者關係如同一體，一起受描述性形容詞修飾。例如：a delicious Chinese dish。

有些形容詞既屬於描述性形容詞也屬於分類性形容詞。例如criminal既可以作描述性形容詞（criminal activity），又可以作分類性形容詞（criminal law）。

動態形容詞和靜態形容詞

根據形容詞所表示特徵的動態性，可以將形容詞分為動態形容詞和靜態形容詞。靜態形容詞描寫人或物的靜態特徵，這種特徵一般是持久的、穩定的。例如：

▶Suddenly, the door opened and a tall, fat woman came in.
突然門開了，一個又高又胖的女人走了進來。

▶I came to see a beautiful woman whom I missed very much.
我來看一個令我朝思暮想的漂亮女人。

動態形容詞所表示的特徵帶有動作含義。與靜態形容詞相比，動態形容詞所表達的特徵是暫時的、可變化的。常見的有：ambitious，brave，conceited，disagreeable，enthusiastic，faithful，generous，hasty，impudent，jealous，loyal，mischievous，noisy，obstinate，playful，reasonable，suspicious，timid，vicious，wicked等。例如：

▶Annie and Kelly sat drinking sweet tea in a noisy cafe in the center of New York.
安妮和凱莉坐在紐約市中心的一個喧鬧的咖啡館裡喝著甜茶。

▶International terrorism is becoming more impudent, acting more cruelly.
國際恐怖主義活動變得更加倡狂，行徑更為殘暴。

動態形容詞和靜態形容詞在句法上的區別是：

1. 動態形容詞可以與動詞be的進行式搭配，而靜態形容詞通常不可以。例如：

▶I don't think men are capable of being faithful.
我覺得男人不可能忠誠。

▶I was never aware of him being jealous of my success.
我從來沒有覺察出他嫉妒我的成功。

2. 動態形容詞可以用於以動詞be開頭的祈使句，而靜態形容詞通常不可以。例如：

▶Be patient! 耐心些！

▶Be careful! 小心點！

3. 動態形容詞可用於某些不定詞結構，而靜態形容詞通常不可以。例如：

▶We want people to be generous because that's a good human virtue.
我們希望人們都很大方，因為大方是良好的品質。

主動意義的形容詞和被動意義的形容詞

有些形容詞是在動詞的基礎上派生出來的，其意義與原來動詞意義相關。由動詞-ing形式轉化來的形容詞通常具有主動意義，而由及物動詞的-ed形式轉化來的形容詞通常具有被動意義。例如：boiling water，boiled water; a terrifying story，a terrified woman。

▶This terrifying reality obliges us to respond swiftly and skillfully.
恐怖的現實逼迫我們快速並嫻熟地作出反應。

▶He remembered the terrified look on his friend's face as he had spoken.
他還記得他朋友說話時臉上那種驚恐的神情。

除上述形容詞外，其他以-ful，-ous，-some，-able/-ible結尾的形容詞也有類似於主動和被動意義的區別。例如下面的delightful表示主動的意義，而edible則表示被動的意義：

▶We had a wonderful, delightful conversation.
我們進行了一次非常棒的、愉快的談話。

▶Carnivorous birds can spot an edible animal about half a mile away.
食肉鳥類能夠發覺半英里之外的獵物。

形容詞的句法功能 ▷

◎ 形容詞作名詞修飾語

　　形容詞作名詞修飾語（Attributive Adjectives），可以放在所修飾的名詞中心詞前面，也可以放在所修飾的名詞中心詞後面。

　　1. 形容詞作前置名詞修飾語

(1)可以受形容詞修飾的名詞類別

　　形容詞作前置名詞修飾語即在名詞之前，限定詞之後，一般修飾普通名詞。例如：

▶ He thinks the computer is a good servant but a bad master.
　　他認為電腦是一個好奴僕，但卻是一個壞主人。

▶ Americans keep buying the big vehicles they love so dearly.
　　美國人一直在買他們所鍾愛的大型車輛。

▶ I am going to buy a new car.
　　我計畫買一輛新車。

▶ Virtually the same piece of equipment in Japan sells for about $600.
　　幾乎是同樣的機器，在日本賣600美元左右。

　　除了修飾一般名詞之外，形容詞還可以修飾地點名詞。例如：

▶ The art associated with ancient China, dating from before 4,000 BC, influenced all Far Eastern countries, and reached Europe in the late 17th century.
　　中國古代的藝術可以追溯到西元前4000年之前，它不但影響了所有的遠東國家，而且在17世紀末也傳到了歐洲。

▶ He admitted that his Hispanic lineage was a prized political asset in the new America.
　　他承認他的西班牙血統在新時期的美國是一筆寶貴的政治財富。

　　在口語或者文學語言中，形容詞還可以修飾人名。常用的形容詞有：old，elder，young，late等。例如：

▶ "I married a New Jersey girl," the elder Simms once said, "and I venture to say I'm going to live here the rest of my life."
　　大西姆斯曾經說過：「我娶了一個紐澤西州的女孩，我敢說這輩子剩下的時間我就住在這裡了。」

　　有少數形容詞還可以用於感歎句中修飾人稱代名詞。比較常用的有：poor，lucky，silly等。例如：

▶ "Poor you!" said a plump man, noticing I was out of breath.
　　一個胖胖的人看到我氣喘吁吁，對我說：「可憐的人！」

▶ "**Poor me**, I never get enough money," said the Santa.
聖誕老人說：「我真可憐，我從來沒有足夠的錢。」

▶ **Silly me**!
我真傻！

(2)不同類別形容詞作名詞修飾語時的順序

　　如果一個名詞中心詞前面有多個描述性形容詞，常常涉及詞序的問題。一般的順序是：表示說話人評價的形容詞→表示大小、形狀、新舊的形容詞→表示顏色的形容詞→表示國別、來源、材料的形容詞→表示用途或目的的形容詞或分詞、名詞等類別詞→名詞中心詞。例如：

▶ There's plenty to see in town too, from **sturdy medieval buildings** to a whole series of good museums, and just outside the city limits is Edward's **charming old home**.
這個小城裡有很多地方可看，從堅固的中世紀建築到一系列博物館。就在城邊上是愛德華的迷人故居。

▶ Bill's mother was a plump woman with **big red hands** and a kind face.
比爾的媽媽是一個胖胖的女人，有一雙發紅的大手和一張和藹可親的臉。

　　如果一個名詞前面既有描述性形容詞又有分類性形容詞。則描述性形容詞在前，分類性形容詞在後。例如：

▶ Venturi, a **small French sports car** company with a phoenix-like history, has risen from the ashes again with a high-performance, electric two-seater.
文托里是一家小型法國跑車公司，經歷了如鳳凰涅槃的歷史，帶著一款高效電動雙座車浴火重生。

▶ At the heart of this **quaint old English fishing village** is this **quaint old English hotel**.
在這個古雅的英格蘭小漁村中心是這個古雅的英格蘭旅館。

(3)只能作前置名詞修飾語的形容詞

　　有些形容詞只能作前置名詞修飾語而不能作補語，例如分類性形容詞。（參見本章P232〈描述性形容詞和分類性形容詞〉）例如：

▶ "My **main** concern," says Claudio, "was that my son be treated with dignity."
克勞迪奧說：「我最主要的擔心是我的兒子是否能得到有尊嚴的對待方式。」

　　還有一些形容詞，比如the wrong person，指的是「不是要找的人」，而不是「錯的人」。表達這個意思的形容詞wrong就只能作名詞修飾語，不能轉換成補語。又如old friend可以表示年齡大的朋友，還可以表示交往時間長的朋友。表達後一種意思的old也不能作補語。

2. 形容詞作後置名詞修飾語

　　形容詞作修飾語有時候也可以放在名詞中心詞後面。這主要有下面幾種情況：

(1)如果名詞中心詞是some，any，no，every等構成的不定代名詞，其修飾語一定置於
　　其後。例如：

▶ Whether there's anything wrong or not, that's for people to judge.
　　是否有錯誤，那是需要人們去判斷的。

▶ Having grown up with technology, I can't say that anything new surprises me.
　　我伴隨著科技的發展而長大，所以沒有什麼新的事物會讓我驚奇。

▶ I was waiting for somebody better.
　　我在等一個更好的人。

(2)如果形容詞修飾語本身帶有介係詞片語等補足成分，也要後置。例如：

▶ Some students wanted to challenge themselves by learning a language different from
　　that which their parents speak at home.
　　有些學生想通過學習另外一門非母語語言來挑戰自己。

▶ Fires are burning out of control over an area bigger than the state of Delaware.
　　火勢正在失去控制，蔓延範圍已經超過德拉瓦州的面積。

▶ The animals have very humanlike cancers and complex blood similar to that of
　　humans. 動物有類似於人類癌症的病症，並且其血液複雜程度也和人類相似。

　　上面這些例子中也可以將形容詞放在名詞中心詞前面，而將形容詞補足部分放到名
詞中心詞後面。例如：

▶ Some students wanted to challenge themselves by learning a different language from
　　that which their parents speak at home.
　　一些學生想藉由學習家長講的不同語言來挑戰自己。

▶ Fires are burning out of control over a bigger area than the state of Delaware.
　　火勢失控，蔓延範圍比德拉瓦州還要大。

▶ The animals have very humanlike cancers and similar complex blood to that of
　　humans.
　　動物有和人類相像的癌症和與人類相似的複雜血液組成。

(3)有些特定的形容詞作修飾語時一般後置，常見的有：involved，concerned，available，
　　imaginable，possible等。例如：

▶ Most of the information available to Mr. Ross has been supplied by Peter Day, the
　　company secretary.
　　羅斯先生所掌握的絕大多數信息是由公司秘書彼得‧戴提供的。

▶It was a very hard job holding everything together and it required tremendous dedication from **everyone concerned**.
把所有事情整合在一起是一項非常艱苦的工作，這需要每一個相關的人的巨大努力。

▶They talked to three mothers whose babies were saved by the most delicate and advanced **techniques imaginable**.
他們採訪了三位母親，她們的孩子都得到了能想像得到的最精確、最先進的科技的救治。

▶They gave the young man **every chance possible**.
他們給了這個年輕人每個可能的機會。

(4)有時如果有多個形容詞同時修飾一個名詞，為了避免頭重腳輕，也會把一部分形容詞放到名詞後面。例如：

▶He is an impassioned social democrat, **determined and hardworking**.
他是一個充滿激情的社會民主主義者，堅定且勤奮。

　　特別當形容詞成對出現的時候，也習慣放在名詞中心詞後面。例如：

▶It is a European film, **simple and beautiful**.
這是一部歐洲電影，簡單而美麗。

(5)只能作補語的形容詞，如ablaze，afloat，alive等，作修飾語時必須後置。例如：

▶He was a man **ablaze with talent**.
他天賦異稟。

▶Launched in 1817, the ship is now the second oldest ship **afloat**.
這艘船1817年下水，是目前仍在航行的第二古老的船。

形容詞作補語

　　1. 作主詞補語和受詞補語的形容詞

　　形容詞作補語分為兩種情況：主詞補語（表語）和受詞補語。主詞補語在連綴動詞後面，補充說明主詞位置上的名詞性成分。例如：

▶It seems **incredible** that I've gone from being a soldier at weekends to winning an award for bravery.
我因為在週末擔任士兵到拿到一枚勇氣勳章，看起還很不可思議。

▶Mr. and Mrs. Bumble lost their jobs and became **poorer and poorer**, eventually living in poverty in the same workhouse that they had once managed.
本伯夫婦失業後變得愈發貧窮，最後貧困潦倒，住到他們之前經營的一家濟貧院裡去了。

▶ The change in behavior was **significant**, and clearly indicated that the sharks could sense the magnetic field, Meyer said.

邁耶説，鯊魚的行為變化十分明顯，這明確表示鯊魚能夠感受到磁場。

▶ Normal radiation therapy is **impossible**, because it would damage healthy parts of his brain.

正常的放射治療是不可能的，因為這會破壞他大腦中的健康部分。

受詞補語位於直接受詞後面並對其進行補充説明。一般帶受詞補語的動詞有：get，consider，find，make，declare等。例如：

▶ Consumers have said that they find the product **interesting and unique**.

顧客們曾經説過這個產品既有趣又獨特。

▶ Many people consider him **tough and competent**, but also ruthlessly ambitious.

很多人認為他強硬能幹，同時也野心勃勃。

▶ The horrific nature of this crime makes forgiveness **difficult**.

這項罪行令人髮指，難以寬恕。

2. 只能作補語的形容詞

英語中有一部分形容詞只能作補語，不能作名詞修飾語。主要有以下幾種情況：

(1)表示健康狀況的形容詞well，ill。例如：

▶ My father is very **well** at the moment.

目前我父親非常好。

▶ Since I met her during a time when my mother was **ill**, I confided in this woman about my feelings, and she was a great listener.

我認識她的時候我母親正在生病，我找她傾訴，她耐心地傾聽。

注意！

ill 作為定語形容詞時，意思為「壞的，惡劣的」。例如：

▶ ill will 惡毒意願

▶ ill treatment 虐待

▶ Ill news travels apace. 惡事傳千里。

(2)以a-開頭的形容詞：asleep，alone，alike，alive，aloof，aglow，alright，afraid，等。例如：

▶ Sometimes Harriet was **alone** in that great house all day, until Paul came home at about seven to watch the television.

有時哈里特一整天一個人待在那所大房子裡，直到7點鐘左右保羅回家看電視。

▶"If he was **alive**, he would have sent us a letter," his brother Alan said.
　他的兄弟艾倫說：「如果他還活著，他就給我們寫信了。」

(2)帶有介係詞片語的形容詞，例如subject to..., fond of..., tantamount to...等。這種形
　容詞加介係詞片語只能作補語，不能作名詞修飾語。

　　3. 帶補足成分的形容詞作補語
　　作補語的形容詞本身可以是單個形容詞，也可以帶有自己的補足成分，使形容詞表
達的意義更完整。該補足成分可以是介係詞片語、不定詞或that 引導的子句。

(1)介係詞片語作形容詞補足成分。例如：

▶He is **good at selling himself**.
　他善於推銷自己。

▶Murphy is **busy with school and football, Kim with her dream house**.
　墨菲忙著上學和踢足球，金忙著弄她夢想的房子。

▶France remained **faithful to her noblest traditions**.
　法國保持了她高貴的傳統。

▶I think he became **tired of the endless quarrels and disagreements**.
　我想他厭倦了無休止的爭吵和分歧。

(2)不定詞作形容詞補足成分。例如：

▶It is **possible to eat fairly well for a reasonable price in New York**.
　在紐約花合理的價錢吃可口的飯菜是可能的。

▶I was **anxious to avoid too lengthy a conversation with Roger**.
　我極力避免跟羅傑談得太久。

▶He says he is **glad to be alive** after being shot in both legs.
　他說他慶倖自己雙腿都中彈後仍能活著。

(3)that引導的子句作形容詞補足成分。例如：

▶I am **sure that with only a little effort of the imagination you can solve the problem**.
　我確信只要你稍微發揮一下想像力，你就能解決這個問題。

▶I'm **disappointed that Americans don't seem to care about the world outside their borders**.
　我非常失望，美國人似乎對他們國界以外的世界漠不關心。

▶He appeared absolutely **confident that even if the bombs went off, we would survive**.
　他表現出絕對的信心，即使炮彈爆炸我們也能生還。

這種結構中作補語的形容詞及其補足成分為要表達的觀點提供了一個框架，句子的主詞經常用it。例如：

▶ Her husband was an alcoholic and it was soon clear that she would have to support him as well as their daughter and a mentally retarded son.
她丈夫是個酒鬼，很快她顯然不但需要照顧她丈夫而且要照顧他們的女兒和一個智力遲鈍的兒子。

▶ It was difficult to cope with Ray, because he was a big bloke and if he fell on top of you, it was hard to get up.
和雷較量是比較難的，因為他是個大塊頭，如果他壓在你身上，你都站不起來。

🎯 形容詞作其他句法成分

1. 形容詞作名詞片語中心詞

有些形容詞可以作名詞片語的中心詞。例如：

▶ It is quite normal for the poor to hate the rich in that country.
在那個國家窮人憎恨富人再正常不過了。

▶ This is a place where the bold and the beautiful hang out and you can often spot celebrities.
這是一個勇敢者和漂亮人出沒的地方，你經常可以看到各種名人。

但是，這種從形容詞到名詞的轉換並不澈底，因為即使在表示複數意義時，

形容詞也不用複數形式。此外，這類片語可以被副詞very修飾，限定詞一般用the。例如：

▶ Ozone can cause breathing problems in the very young and old, and in people with breathing ailments such as asthma, bronchitis and emphysema.
臭氧可能引起一些人的呼吸問題，包括年齡特別大的老人、年齡比較小的孩子，以及有哮喘，支氣管炎和肺氣腫等呼吸系統疾病的人。

在上述例子中，形容詞作名詞片語的中心詞，表示一類人，謂語動詞用複數。在下面這個例子中，形容詞作名詞片語的中心詞表示抽象事物，謂語動詞用單數。例如：

▶ As James put it elsewhere, "the true is the name of whatever proves itself to be good in the way of belief."
正如詹姆斯在其他場合所說的：「真實就是任何能夠證明其自身價值、可以被相信的東西。」

表示國別和種族的形容詞也可以作名詞中心詞。例如：

▶ The Spanish, who are peculiarly sensitive to changes of heat and light, allow their mealtimes to slide around the day according to what feels most comfortable.
西班牙人對熱和光的變化尤其敏感，他們的吃飯時間往往隨著一天感覺最舒服的時刻滑動。

部分形容詞的最高級也可以作名詞中心詞。例如：

▶ **The latest** is that a hospital spokesman said that yesterday his health condition deteriorated rapidly, and he was put into an intensive care unit so that care could continue.
最新的消息如下：一位醫院發言人說昨天他的健康狀況急轉直下，已經被送進重症監護室觀察治療。

▶ Don't tell me **the best** is in the past, either. 也不要跟我說最好的都在過去。

2. 形容詞起句子銜接作用

形容詞或形容詞片語有時可以起到銜接子句或句子的作用。能有這種用法的形容詞比較少，多數是表示說話者對某件事情的感覺，如好奇、奇怪等。比如curious，funny，odd，strange，surprising等，或者是受more或most修飾的形容詞。例如：

▶ **Still more important**, he says he now feels comfortable with the idea of using his new putter. 更為重要的是，他說現在他感到很舒服，因為想到可以用新的高爾夫推桿了。

▶ **Strange**, smelly boys want to be thought of as sinister and dangerous.
很奇怪，臭氣烘烘的男孩希望別人認為他們兇惡且危險。

3. 形容詞片語修飾句子

形容詞片語修飾整個句子，主要描述和說明主句主詞的性質和狀態。例如：

▶ **Unhappy with the basic cellphone his parents gave him at 11**, he saved to buy a fancy one on which he could download songs for ringer tones. 父母在他11歲時給了他一個簡單的手機，對此他感到不高興，自己存錢買了一款很炫的手機，可以下載歌曲作為手機鈴聲。

▶ **Anxious for a negotiated peace in 1917**, he was forced from office.
1917年他急於透過談判達成和平，因此被迫下野。

▶ **Nervous**, she called police to check out the car.
她非常緊張，打電話叫了員警來檢查這輛車。

4. 形容詞作附加性修飾成分

形容詞作附加性修飾成分可以是一個描述主詞的獨立子句。和上面第三種情況不同的是，附加性子句一般都有一個關係代名詞。例如：

▶ **Whether right or wrong**, Jay said such kind of strange gates were what buyers wanted.
不管正確與否，傑伊說這種奇怪的門正是買家所想要的。

▶ **If possible**, pay with a personal credit card.
如果可能，用個人信用卡付款。

▶ **If necessary**, we would re-mortgage the house to send her to Italy.
如果有必要，我們會再抵押房子送她去義大利。

形容詞作附加性修飾成分還可以描述或說明主句的受詞，說明主句動作發生時受詞所處的狀態。例如：

▶ "Why not eat it fresh?" he wonders.
「為什麼不趁新鮮吃呢？」他想。

▶ Amazon.co.uk launched its Marketplace service two weeks ago, allowing customers to buy and sell new, used and collectable items through a third party person or company on the same page that Amazon sells the item new.
亞馬遜英國網站兩周前開始了一項新的市場舉措，允許顧客通過協力廠商個人或公司在其銷售新產品的同一頁面上買賣新產品、二手物品及收藏品。

▶ In the end, she chose to drink the milk hot.
最後她決定趁熱喝牛奶。

▶ More kids prefer to eat the broccoli raw.
更多孩子喜歡生吃花椰菜。

5. 形容詞起感嘆句作用

形容詞經常可以起感嘆句作用（Adjectives as Exclamations），尤其在對話中或小說的對白中。例如：Great!，Good!，Wonderful!，Amazing!，Sorry!，Excellent!，Terrible!，Marvelous!，Ridiculous!，Terrific!，Alright!，Horrible!，Lucky!，Miraculous!，Oh right! 等。參見下面的例句：

▶ Great! Thank you for coming.
棒極了！謝謝你能來。

▶ Horrible! I thought he was dreaming, but he wasn't.
太可怕了！我以為他在做夢，可是他沒有。

▶ "After that Columbus says that we're going to the Indies by sailing west. Ridiculous! The world is FLAT. We're going to tip over the edge," said the oldman.
這位老人說：「那之後哥倫布說我們可以向西航行到達印度群島。荒謬至極！地球是平的！我們會在邊緣掉下去。」

形容詞的比較級和最高級 ▷

🎯 形容詞比較級和最高級的形式

大部分描述性形容詞都是可以分等級的，有程度強弱的差別，可以受程度副詞的修飾。例如：

▶ Why is it **so difficult** to keep military costs under control?
為什麼控制軍事開支如此困難？

▶ He's **very intense, very persuasive and charming**.
他非常嚴肅、有說服力、有魅力！

這些形容詞可以表達比較級和最高級的概念。有兩種方法表示比較級和最高級：一種是在形容詞原形後加-er和-est；另一種是在形容詞前加more和most。

非等級的分類形容詞一般都沒有比較級和最高級，例如不能説more final，most medical等；也不能受程度副詞very的修飾，例如不能説very final，very medical。

1. 加-er和-est的比較級和最高級形式

一般來説，單音節形容詞的比較級和最高級多直接加-er或-est。以不發音的字母e結尾的形容詞要先去掉e，再加-er或-est。以母音字母加一個子音字母結尾的形容詞要雙寫最後一個字母再加-er或-est。以母音字母加子音字母加y結尾的形容詞要把y變成i再加-er或-est。例如：

形容詞原形	比較級	最高級
cold	colder	coldest
nice	nicer	nicest
safe	safer	safest
big	bigger	biggest
tidy	tidier	tidiest

有少數形容詞的比較級和最高級的變化是不規則形式。例如：

形容詞原形	比較級	最高級
good/well	better	best
bad	worse	worst
few/little	less	least
much	more	most
old	older/elder	oldest/eldest
far	further/farther	furthest/farthest

以非重音的母音y結尾的雙音節形容詞通常都加-er或-est。例如：easy，easier，easiest。其他的單字有：angry，bloody，busy，crazy，dirty，empty，funny，gloomy，happy，healthy，heavy，hungry，lengthy，lucky，nasty，pretty，ready，sexy，silly，tidy，tiny，wealthy等。

以ow結尾的雙音節形容詞一般也加-er或-est，例如narrow，narrower，narrowest。其他的單字有：mellow，shallow，yellow等。以-er，-ere，-ure結尾的雙音節形容詞也可以加-er或-est。例如：

形容詞原形	比較級	最高級
clever	cleverer	cleverest
slender	slenderer	slenderest
severe	severer	severest
secure	securer	securest

2. 加more和most的片語型比較級和最高級形式。

一般三個音節或多於三個音節的形容詞，特別是以-ful，-less，-al，-ive，-ous等結尾的形容詞，以及動詞-ing形式和-ed形式的形容詞，通常都採用在形容詞前加more和most的方式。例如：

形容詞原形	比較級	最高級
instructive	more instructive	most instructive
difficult	more difficult	most difficult
useful	more useful	most useful
effective	more effective	most effective
bored	more bored	most bored
boring	more boring	most boring

另外一些雙音節形容詞，如proper，limpid，rapid，common，也採用加more和most的形式。

有一部分雙音節形容詞的比較級和最高級既可加-er或-est，也可加more和most，例如costly，deadly，lively，lonely，lovely，ugly等。例如：

▶ Such training programs are far more costly, about $150 a day per person.
這樣的培訓項目非常貴，每人每天大約150美元。

▶ With costlier tickets, the city will collect more revenue.
票價比以前貴了，這個城市會得到更多的收入。

▶ I feel more lively, less lethargic and generally so much better for giving up.
我少了一些倦怠，多了一些活力。總的來說感覺放棄更好。

▶ Things get livelier as you move west, with the street crowded by an increasing number of musicians, panhandlers and hard-core hippie burnouts.

越往西走越熱鬧，街上擠著越來越多的街頭音樂家、乞丐及頑固的嬉皮士。

▶ Suddenly, everything seems that little bit starker and more ugly.

忽然，所有事物都似乎更加荒涼和醜陋。

▶ Objects in the mirror may be uglier than they appear.

鏡子中的事物或許比他們實際看起來要更加難看。

3. 本身含有最高級含義的形容詞

有些形容詞本身已經包含了最高級別的含義。例如：dead，empty，full，excellent，perfect，superior，inferior，crucial等。這些形容詞一般都沒有比較級和最高級形式，也不用very修飾。但是在少數情況下為了強調也可以用very修飾或用比較級。例如：

▶ He was very dead, and there was blood all over the floor.

他確實死了，地板上全是血。

▶ My soul has been impaired by the fashionable world, I have a restless fancy, an insatiable heart; whatever I get is not enough; my life becomes more empty day by day; there is only one remedy left for me: to travel.

我的靈魂受到這個時髦社會的侵害，內心躁動不安且貪求無厭。無論我得到什麼都不滿足，生活一天比一天空虛。唯一剩下的解決辦法就是去旅行。

▶ The ad featured a crowd of young people, ostensibly from all corners of the earth, learning to sing the words "Coca-Cola" in perfect harmony while smiling through even more perfect white teeth.

在這個廣告中，一群假裝來自世界各地的年輕人一邊學習用完美的和聲唱「可口可樂」，一邊露出更加完美的潔白牙齒微笑著。

比較級句子結構

當形容詞比較級表達比較概念時，比較的物件一般不會直接明白表示。讀者可以從上下文中推測出比較的物件。例如：

▶ So-called teleworking, telecommuting or e-commuting is becoming more popular with companies and employees as modern technology makes working from home an effective alternative.

所謂的遠端工作、遠端辦公或電子辦公在公司和雇員中間變得越來越流行。現代技術使得在家也能有效工作。

為了明確比較的物件，可能會在形容詞比較級後接比較級片語或子句。例如：

▶ Almost 95 percent of 16 to 19-year-olds drink alcohol and cannabis is more popular than tobacco. 16至19歲的人中幾乎有95%的人喝酒，且大麻比菸草更受歡迎。

1. 比較結構

形容詞比較級句子結構主要有兩種。其中，「as＋形容詞＋as＋片語（或分句）」是同級比較；「形容詞比較級＋than＋片語（或子句）」是比較級，包含了形容詞的比較級形式。例如：

(1) as＋形容詞＋as＋片語（或分句）。例如：

▶ "The non-food market is as big as the food market and so we see a really good opportunity to grow there," he adds.
「這個非食品市場和食品市場一樣大，所以我們在那裡會找到非常好的發展機會。」他說。

▶ Few women manage to look as good as you do in the mornings.
沒有幾個女人能夠和你一樣在早上就讓自己看上去那麼棒。

▶ Maybe you're half as good as you think you are.
或許你只有你自己想像的一半那麼棒。

▶ He's not as brilliant as he was.
他現在沒有以前那麼輝煌。

▶ The aim of education is wisdom, and each must have the chance to become as wise as he can.
教育的目的是智慧，每個人必須有機會獲得最大可能的智慧。

(2)形容詞比較級＋than＋片語（或分句）。例如：

▶ He was tall, taller than Magee's six feet, dressed in faded jeans and baseball boots which made his feet look enormous.
他很高，比6英尺的馬吉還要高，穿著褪色的牛仔褲和讓他的腳看起來巨大無比的棒球靴。

▶ In the U.S, the Democrats in power will be less effective than the Democrats out of power.
在美國，當權民主黨人沒有在野民主黨人那麼有效率。

▶ "I'm more disappointed than anyone else," he said.
他說：「我比其他任何人都更失望。」

▶ The service in this fast-food restaurant was faster than McDonald's and the food a thousand times better.
這個速食店裡的服務比麥當勞要快，並且食物比麥當勞要好上千倍。

2. 比較結構的特殊用法

(1)as＋形容詞＋as結構

　　英語中有大量的慣用語都是採用這種結構。例如：

as brave as a lion	as bright as day	as busy as bees
as cheerful as a lark	as cold as ice	as cunning as a fox
as fat as a pig	as fierce as a tiger	as graceful as a swan
as greedy as a wolf	as innocent as a dove	as light as a feather
as loud as thunder	as obstinate as a mule	as proud as a peacock
as quick as lightning	as quiet as a lamb	as red as a cherry
as sharp as a needle	as silly as a goose	as slippery as an eel
as strong as a horse	as stupid as a donkey	as sweet as honey
as tame as a cat	as timid as a hare	as thin as a rail
as thick skinned as an elephant	as true as a die	as true as steel
as unstable as water	as vain as a peacock	as welcome as flowers in May
as white as a ghost	as white as milk	as white as snow

　　as ... as 結構還可以有另外一種形式是「as＋形容詞＋名詞片語＋as-子句」。例如：

▶ When I do retire I want to leave **as impressive a record as** I possibly can.
當我真的退休時，我希望盡可能留下令人印象深刻的紀錄。

▶ He's **as efficient a scorer as** former Jordan teammate Bernard King.
他是一個和喬丹前隊友伯納德‧金一樣出色的得分手。

　　as ... as結構還可以用來比較一個事物的兩個方面。例如：

▶ This guy was about **as wide as** he was tall with a beard and long hair.
這個傢伙留著落腮鬍和長頭髮，身高和體寬幾乎一樣。

(2) the more ... the more和more and more結構

　　the more ... the more結構表示兩個同時變化的過程，相當於「越……越……」。例如：

▶ **The sooner** she got back on to the track **the better**.
她越早返回跑道越好。

▶ **The more** he read, **the more uneasy** he became.
他越讀越不安。

more and more用在同一件事中，表示「越來越……」的意思。例如：

▶ The cars start off slow and get then faster and faster.
　汽車慢慢啟動，然後越來越快。

▶ Despite the problems, China's drivers are getting better and better as they become more experienced.
　中國的司機們儘管還是有許多問題，但是隨著經驗的增加也在變得越來越好。

▶ It's becoming more and more important for law enforcement officers to get a higher education.
　讓執法者獲得高等教育，這一點正在變得越來越重要。

(3)「good and＋形容詞」和「nice and＋形容詞」結構

　　以good and或者nice and開頭的片語是為了強調後一個形容詞。在文學語言和口語中用得較多。例如：

▶ We won't have a baby until we're good and ready.
　在我們自己完全準備好之前不會要孩子。

▶ By the time you get to the center of the town, the signal is nice and strong.
　等你到城中心的時候，信號剛好非常強勁。

▶ Everything looks nice and burnt!
　一切看上去都焦乎乎的！

　　與此相對的是，類似的順序如果作名詞修飾語就沒有相同的加強效果。例如：

▶ During that time, he says he got to know Dan Rather as a good and dedicated journalist.
　他說那段時間他開始認識到丹‧拉瑟是一位優秀的、具有奉獻精神的新聞工作者。

▶ As you may know, Jacqueline Wilson is a very good and interesting author and Nick is a great illustrator.
　你或許知道賈桂琳‧威爾遜是一位非常好、非常有趣的作家，尼克是一個偉大的插圖畫家。

🎯 形容詞比較級的修飾語

　　形容詞比較級前可以加表示程度的修飾語。常見的有：far，much，a lot，a little，a bit，a good deal等。例如：

▶ Far more important is learning how to have a ski holiday in style.
　瞭解如何讓滑雪節過得有特色更為重要。

▶ This year, they've redesigned it, and the result is much better.
　今年，他們修改了設計，效果好多了。

▶They need to have a much closer working relationship.
他們需要更為密切的工作關係。

▶You have to go a bit quicker if you can.
如果可能，你應該快一點。

形容詞比較級前還可以加by far，rather， somewhat，even，any，no，some，still，all等詞修飾。例如：

▶We need to be somewhat more careful.
我們需要稍微再仔細一點。

▶The job was made all the easier by having the proper tools.
有了合適的工具，工作更容易做了。

形容詞比較級前還可以加表示數量的詞。例如：

▶China is growing at eight percent a year—three times faster than anywhere else in the world.
中國正以每年8%的速度發展——是世界上其他任何地區的三倍。

▶She is six years older than him and obviously cared for him very much.
她比他大6歲，很顯然，她非常喜歡他。

形容詞最高級的用法

如果表示三個或三個以上範圍的人或者事物的對比，則使用形容詞的最高級。所比較的範圍可以用介係詞片語來表達。例如：

▶It was difficult to believe that the most careful farmer in the area would lose all his harvest because of a moment's forgetfulness.
令人難以相信，該地區最認真的農場主因為一時的疏忽喪失了全部的收成。

▶Britons work the longest hours in Europe, and these figures show that much of it is unpaid overtime.
在歐洲英國人的工作時間最長，並且這些資料顯示很大一部分是無酬勞超時工作。

▶Now she faces the greatest challenge of her career.
現在她正面對她職業生涯中最大的挑戰。

比較範圍也可以用子句來表達。例如：

▶That's the best news since I returned to Paris.
這是我回巴黎後最好的消息。

比較範圍還可以是隱含的，但是可以通過上下文推斷出來。例如：

▶ He thinks that film is the least useful art form.
他認為電影是最沒用的藝術形式。

注意！

形容詞最高級前要加定冠詞。例如：

▶ David is the best player in the world in his position.
在這個位置上大衛是全世界最棒的球員。

但是，形容詞最高級前有人稱代名詞的所有格或名詞所有格時不能用定冠詞。例如：

▶ This is her best record so far.
這是她目前最好的紀錄。

形容詞最高級表示「非常」的意思時，不用定冠詞。例如：

▶ Technology issues have been most prominent in this meeting.
技術問題在這次會議上非常突出。

▶ This is a most remarkable occasion.
這是一個極其不尋常的活動。

形容詞的構成

根據構詞法的不同，形容詞可以分為以下幾類：分詞形容詞、派生形容詞和複合形容詞。

分詞形容詞

1. 動詞-ing形式轉化來的形容詞

由動詞-ing形式轉化來的形容詞常常有主動意義。常見的有：

absorbing	amazing	approving	balding	boiling
boring	charming	chilling	convincing	disappointing
disgusting	encouraging	endearing	engaging	exciting
fascinating	fatiguing	frustrating	following	governing
gushing	humbling	humiliating	increasing	interesting
inviting	irritating	killing	laboring	lasting
maddening	moving	neighboring	owing	perishing
persevering	shocking	sparkling	tempting	wearing

2. 由動詞-ed形式轉化來的形容詞

由動詞-ed形式轉化來的形容詞通常有被動意義。常見的有：

advanced	appointed	astonished	blessed	considered
constrained	destroyed	determined	discovered	educated
elected	elevated	exhausted	frightened	frustrated
governed	heated	involved	irritated	jammed
oriented	rejected	terrified	startled	unabashed
unattained	unbalanced	undressed		

派生形容詞

1. 以-al結尾的形容詞。這類派生形容詞最普遍。例如：

additional	central	commercial	critical	final
general	ideal	industrial	international	legal
local	medical	mental	moral	national
natural	normal	official	oral	original
personal	physical	political	practical	professional
real	royal	sexual	social	special
total	typical	usual	vital	

2. 以-ent結尾的形容詞。例如：

absent	adjacent	ancient	apparent	confident
consistent	current	decent	dependent	efficient
excellent	frequent	independent	innocent	intelligent
prominent	recent	silent	subsequent	sufficient

3. 以-ive結尾的形容詞。例如：

active	aggressive	attractive	cognitive	comprehensive
creative	distinctive	effective	excessive	exclusive
expensive	extensive	impressive	negative	positive
relative				

4. 以-ous結尾的形容詞。例如：

anxious	conscious	continuous	curious	dangerous
enormous	famous	nervous	obvious	previous
religious	serious	various		

5. 以-ate結尾的形容詞。例如：

accurate	adequate	appropriate	immediate	intimate
moderate	private	separate		

6. 以-ful結尾的形容詞。例如：

awful	beautiful	careful	cheerful	grateful
helpful	painful	peaceful	powerful	successful
useful	wonderful			

7. 以-less結尾的形容詞。例如：

endless	helpless	homeless	useless

複合形容詞

複合形容詞的構成可以是多種多樣的，可以表達各種複雜的資訊。複合形容詞的形式多種多樣，有很多組合。例如：

1. 副詞＋形容詞。例如：

already-tight	blisteringly-fast	fiercely-competitive
grimly-familiar	highly-sensitive	nearly-equal
politically-independent		

2. 副詞＋動詞-ed形式。例如：

badly-wounded	carefully-honed	comparably-sized
extensively-researched	fiercely-contested	half-built
highly-praised	ill-suited	lavishly-produced
newly-invented	newly-restored	psychologically-disturbed
recently-installed	strongly-worded	well-organized

3. 副詞＋動詞-ing形式。例如：

brightly-shining	constantly-changing	early-maturing
equally-damaging	free-spending	harder-hitting
slowly-sinking	straight-speaking	tightly-fitting

4. 複製形容詞。例如：

curly-whirly	easy-peasy	goody-goody	lovey-dovey	okey-dokey
oldy-worldy	roly-poly	super-duper	wishy-washy	

5. 形容詞＋顏色形容詞。例如：

| dark-blue | gray-white | light-blue | royal-blue | silvery-green |

6. 形容詞+動詞-ed形式。例如：

| clean-shaven | ready-made | soft-textured | strait-laced | white-washed |

7. 形容詞＋動詞-ing形式。例如：

| biggest-selling | double-crossing | free-standing | funny-looking |
| longest-serving | lovely-sounding | sickly-smelling | |

8. 名詞＋形容詞。例如：

| age-old | battle-weary | grease-free | iron-rich | life-long |
| sea-blue | sex-specific | smoke-free | subsidy-free | waist-high |

9. 名詞＋動詞-ed形式。例如：

| church-owned | classroom-based | dome-shaped | family-oriented | germ-ridden |
| health-related | home-baked | poverty-stricken | state-run | world-renowned |

10. 名詞＋動詞-ing形式。例如：

| confidence-boosting | eye-catching | hair-raising | law-abiding |
| life-prolonging | nerve-wracking | peace-keeping | |

11. 形容詞＋名詞。例如：

big-name	cutting-edge	double-digit	free-market	general-purpose
hard-core	inner-city	large-scale	left-hand	long-distance
present-day	single-storey	working-class		

12. 分詞＋副詞小品詞。例如：

| blown-out | boarded-up | left-over | paid-up | sawn-off |

小結

　　本章詳細介紹了形容詞的特點和用法。形容詞的典型特徵是具有描述性，有比較級、最高級的形態變化，可以作修飾語和補語。

　　形容詞作名詞修飾語的時候可以在名詞前面也可以在名詞後面。形容詞既可以作主詞補語也可以作受詞補語。除了作修飾語和補語這兩個主要句法功能以外，形容詞還有其他一些功能，比如起句子銜接作用和修飾整個句子等。規則形容詞的比較級和最高級是其後加-er，-est或其前加more，most。

Part 11

副詞

副詞概說

　　副詞是所有詞類裡面次類最繁多的一類，用法也十分複雜。副詞和形容詞有著密切的關係。很多副詞就是由形容詞加詞綴-ly轉變來的，例如：nicely，beautifully，fondly，slowly等副詞都是由相應的形容詞轉變而來的。

　　和形容詞一樣，大多副詞也有程度的差別，所以可以受另外的程度副詞修飾，可以有比較級和最高級。例如：

▶ All my children could draw and paint really beautifully.
　　我的所有孩子都會畫非常漂亮的畫。

▶ Domesticated dogs read peoples' glances and gestures far more skillfully than chimpanzees, wolves, or wild dogs do.
　　寵物狗遠比大猩猩、狼和野狗更嫻熟地讀懂人們的眼神和手勢。

　　副詞和形容詞都可以作修飾成分，不同的是形容詞用來修飾名詞片語，而副詞主要是用來修飾動詞片語、形容詞片語和其他副詞。例如：

▶ Shane's a careful and calculating driver, very neat and precise in his driving technique.
　　尚恩是一個細心精明的司機，他的駕駛技巧非常精准。

▶ We went carefully along the beach, but there were no boats and no wild men.
　　我們非常細心地沿著海灘走，但是沒有發現任何船隻，也沒有任何野人。

　　上面的形容詞careful修飾名詞片語，相應的副詞carefully修飾動詞片語。有的副詞還可以修飾整個句子。例如：

▶ A hearing on this issue will be held shortly.
　　很快就會召開關於這件事情的聽證會。

▶ Surprisingly, few Americans I met seemed to think of Pakistan as an ally.
　　不可思議的是，我認識的美國人中沒有幾個把巴基斯坦當作是同盟。

副詞的形式

儘管有一部分副詞是通過形容詞加字尾-ly形成的，但是並不是所有的副詞都是這種形式。副詞的構成主要有下面幾種形式：

1. 簡單副詞

簡單副詞是由單個字根構成的副詞。例如：well，too，rather，quite，soon，here等。有些簡單副詞是兼類詞，同時兼有副詞和其他詞性，例如fast和long是副詞同時也是形容詞；down和round是副詞同時也是介係詞。

一些口語中常用的副詞都是簡單副詞。例如：again，always，already，far，here，there，never，soon，now，still，yet，then，very，rather，quite，pretty等。

2. 複合副詞

複合副詞是指由兩個或兩個以上簡單單字構成的副詞。例如：anyway，nowhere，heretofore，sometimes，upstairs，maybe，inside 等。

3. 派生副詞

派生副詞是指由其他詞類加副詞字尾構成的副詞。最常見的副詞字尾是-ly。例如：clearly，possibly，obviously，generally，exactly等。

其他的副詞字尾還有-wise，-ward(s) 等。例如：piecewise，homewards，seawards，onward，afterwards 等。

派生副詞表示方式、態度、精確性等，在正式語體中使用頻繁。例如：obviously，possibly，generally，entirely，particularly，exactly等。

4. 固定副詞片語

有些固定片語也可以作為副詞來用，這種副詞在形式上多種多樣，片語中的每個單字都已經失去了本來的意義，而是整個片語表達副詞的含義。例如：of course，kind of，at last等。

與形容詞同形的副詞、形容詞加-ly形成的副詞

有些副詞與形容詞同形。常見的有：fast，easy，fair，firm，slow，clear，quick，clean，short，close，hard等。例如：

★形容詞

▶ He's a very **fast** learner, very sensitive to people's feelings and very pastoral in his attitude.
他學得很快，注重別人的感受，並且態度非常虔誠。

▶ Predicting weather is by no means an **easy** task.
天氣預報絕不是一件容易的事情。

▶ We consider Senator Jeffords a fair and honorable person.
我們認為參議員傑福茲是一個公平高尚的人。

▶ She had made a firm promise.
她作出一個堅定的承諾。

★副詞

▶ He couldn't write fast enough to pass the exam.
他寫得不夠快，所以考不及格。

▶ Last time we played here two years ago, he beat me easy.
上次兩年前我們也是在這裡比賽，他很輕鬆地贏了我。

▶ The government must now decide whether Microsoft has played fair in its bid to win customers and whether consumers will continue to benefit if competition continues to shrink.
政府現在必須決定微軟在贏得客戶的過程中是否光明磊落，以及如果競爭持續縮水，客戶是否能繼續受益。

▶ We will hold firm to our tough fiscal rules which have helped deliver stability and sustain growth.
我們會堅定地執行我們強硬的財政政策，這有利於經濟穩定和持續增長。

　　上面這些副詞與形容詞同形，而同時這些形容詞又可以通過加-ly字尾的方式形成副詞。通過兩種不同手段形成的兩種副詞，有些含義相同，有些含義差別很大。這些詞的主要用法如下：

　　1. clean（完全地，澈底地），cleanly（乾淨俐落地）。例如：

▶ When the fisherman saw his baby son, all thoughts about the splendor of the sea king's palace went clean out of his head.
當漁夫看到了他的寶貝兒子，所有關於海王輝煌宮殿的想法都拋到九霄雲外去了。

▶ Anyway, I've been so concerned about you, and I clean forgot to feel sorry for myself.
不管怎麼說，我是那麼關心你，以至於我完全忘記了為自己難過。

▶ Did he lack the courage to kill the fish cleanly?
他沒有勇氣乾淨俐落地把魚殺掉嗎？

　　2. clear（清楚地，完全地），clearly（清楚地，顯然地）。例如：

▶ The Savage had seized him by the collar, lifted him clear over the chair and, with a smart box on the ears sent him howling away.
野蠻人抓住他的領子，把他從椅子上整個提起來，摑了他一記響亮的耳光，再將哭嚎著的他扔了出去。

▶ The other patients steer clear of me because they think I can't speak at all.
其他的病人完全避開我，因為他們認為我根本不會講話。

▶Some people cannot see **clearly** because the lenses in their eyes do not focus the light on the retina.

有些人看不清楚，因為他們眼球的水晶體不能將光線聚焦在視網膜上。

在下列結構中用clear和clearly都可。例如：

▶This time, the American people have said loud and **clear** they don't want their president impeached.

這次美國人民的聲音響亮而且清楚，他們不希望他們的總統被彈劾。

▶Winston spoke **clearly** so that everyone could hear.

溫斯頓說得很清楚，以便每個人都能聽見。

3. close（接近地），closely（嚴密地）。例如：

▶Tamara was adopted by a Jewish couple who lived **close** to Central Park in Manhattan.

塔瑪拉被住在曼哈頓中央公園附近的一對猶太夫婦收養了。

▶All life on Earth is **closely** related.

地球上所有的生命形式都是密切相關的。

4. full（極其，非常），fully（完全地）。例如：

▶They knew **full** well he was the main danger.

他們非常清楚地知道他是主要的危險人物。

▶Earlier, the Israeli army claimed to have **fully** withdrawn from Palestinian territories.

早些時候，以色列軍隊聲稱他們已經完全地撤出巴勒斯坦地區。

5. hard（努力地），hardly（幾乎不）。例如：

▶I've worked **hard** since I was 14 and I don't expect to depend on the government to take care of me in my old age.

我從14歲起就努力工作，我不期望老的時候能依靠政府來照顧。

▶I **hardly** recognized his face, but I could recognize his clothes.

我幾乎認不出他的臉，但是能認出他的衣服。

6. high（高高地），highly（非常地，高度地）。例如：

▶He stood up, grinning, and held his glass **high**.

他站起來，咧開嘴笑著，高高地舉起玻璃杯。

▶Neighbors expressed shock and spoke **highly** of the family.

鄰居們都表示震驚，對這家人評價非常高。

7. just（只是，剛好），justly（公平地）。例如：

▶ "When I was just a boy," Dougherty said, "my father spoke very fondly of his days in Boston."
多爾蒂說：「當我還是一個孩子的時候，我的父親總喜歡談起他在波士頓的日子。」

▶ Our role is to do the work properly, justly and fairly.
我們的任務是把工作做得正確、公平、合理。

8. late（遲，晚），lately（最近）。例如：

▶ "I stayed up late last night getting ready for today's class," he said.
他說：「我昨天晚上為了準備今天的課，熬夜到很晚。」

▶ Have you heard from Joyce or Amy lately?
你最近有喬伊絲或者艾咪的消息嗎？

9. most（最，非常），mostly（主要地）。例如：

▶ She considered most carefully whether life was or was not worth living before she killed herself.
自殺前她對到底生活是否值得繼續下去這個問題考慮得非常仔細。

▶ In years past spammers and virus writers were mostly sociopathic creeps.
在過去這些年裡垃圾郵件發送者和病毒製造者大都是反社會的小人。

10. near（靠近地），nearly（幾乎）。例如：

▶ They lived near enough to one another to share a cab home.
他們住得很近，可以共乘一輛計程車回家。

▶ There are 167 million coffee drinkers in the U.S., and they consumed nearly 6.3billion gallons last year alone.
在美國有1.67億人喝咖啡，他們僅去年一年就幾乎消費了63億加侖咖啡。

11. sharp〔（指時刻）……整〕，sharply（敏捷地）。例如：

▶ They are supposed to meet in the pub at eight o'clock sharp, but do not get down to business until 10 past.
他們應該8點整在酒吧見面，但是直到10點都過了才談正經事。

▶ He jumped into the driver's seat and sharply pulled the handbrake.
他跳上了司機的座位，敏捷地拉上了手煞車。

12. short（達不到目標地），shortly（立刻）。例如：

▶ He wanted to be more than he was and fell **short**.
他想提高自己，但是卻沒有成功。

▶ He had been killed in the war **shortly** after Sara was born.
莎拉出生後不久他就在戰爭中死去了。

13. wide（張得或開得大地），widely（廣泛地）。例如：

▶ She opened the door **wide** without another word and stood back to let the two women into her flat.
她沒再說一句話，敞開大門，站在一邊，讓這兩個婦女進了她的公寓。

▶ President Lyndon Johnson—still **widely** popular—was dispatching the first U.S. ground troops to Vietnam.
林登‧詹森總統正把第一批美國地面部隊派遣到越南。當時，他仍然很受民眾歡迎。

副詞的語義分類

🎯 方式副詞

方式副詞（Adverbs of Manner）表達句子所述動作進行的方式。常用的方式副詞有：happily，automatically，quickly，fast，abreast，well，quietly等。例如：

▶ Pagan and I are **happily** married, with babies as well as jobs.
帕甘和我婚姻幸福，有孩子，也有工作。

▶ He had acted **quickly** to help her.
他迅速採取行動去幫她。

▶ The nonprofit group has been **quietly** experimenting with the crop for two years.
這個非營利性組織已經悄悄地拿這種農作物實驗兩年了。

🎯 程度副詞

程度副詞（Adverbs of Degree）描述某種性狀的程度。常用的程度副詞可以分成兩類：表示程度重的副詞和表示程度輕的副詞。表示程度重的副詞中使用頻率最高的是very，so，too。例如：

▶ Elizabeth seems a **very** lovely lady but she has lived in my neighborhood for nine months.
伊莉莎白看上去是一位非常可愛的女士，只是她在這附近才住了九個月。

▶ He was **so** wise and astute in official affairs.
他處理官方事務非常精明敏銳。

▶ "We have to try everything before it's **too** late," he said.
「我們必須趁還來得及時嘗試各種事情。」他說。

其他表示程度重的副詞有：more，really，extremely，almost，thoroughly，completely，totally，awfully，perfectly，bloody，fully，absolutely，damn，entirely，incredibly，terribly，highly，strongly等。例如：

▶ I know many **extremely** intelligent people who are not successful.
我認識很多非常聰明但是卻不成功的人。

▶ Actors I work with either have to be **totally** crazy or **totally** confident.
和我一起工作的演員不是完全瘋狂就是完全自信。

▶ The company designs **highly** complex custom software for biotech businesses.
該公司為生物科技行業設計非常複雜的客戶軟體。

▶ If I hadn't been so **bloody** selfish and gone to a stupid party instead of working with her then none of this would have happened. 如果我當時不是如此自私，參加了一個愚蠢的聚會，而是和她一起工作，那麼現在的一切都不會發生了。

▶ He's done **awfully** well at the university and now he's got a job, an important job as well. 他在大學裡表現非常出色，現在他有了工作，還是非常重要的工作。

▶ This method is **dead** simple to set up and ensures that you always have an up-to-date version of your data. 這個方法操作非常簡單，並且能保證你一直擁有最新的資料。

上面最後兩個例子中的awfully和dead既可以用作方式副詞也可以用作程度副詞。當作程度副詞的時候，便喪失了本來的字面意義，只是表示單純的程度加深。

表示程度輕的副詞最常用的有quite和pretty, 其中quite更多地在英式英語中出現，pretty更多地在美式英語中出現。其他表示程度輕的副詞有：nearly，relatively，fairly，almost，slightly，somewhat，rather等。例如：

▶ Her mother's voice was **slightly** puzzled.
他母親的聲音有些困惑。

▶ The situation is **somewhat** different in Japan.
在日本情況略有不同。

▶ He is **somewhat** embarrassed and proud at the same time.
他有點尷尬，但同時也感到自豪。

還有些程度副詞只是從意義上強調。常見的有：especially，even，just，exactly，only，simply等。例如：

▶ **Even** a policeman wouldn't dare to poke about without a search warrant—and you're not a policeman.
即使是員警沒有搜索令也不敢亂翻——何況你還不是一個員警。

▶ **Just** at that time the manager was the only man supposed to have any right to fire him.
就在那時候，經理是唯一一個有權解雇他的人。

🎯 時間副詞

時間副詞（Adverbs of Time）表達和時間有關的意義。

- 表達確定的時間：yesterday，today，tomorrow，last week，a month ago等。
- 有的表達不確定時間：recently，nowadays，still，immediately，just等。
- 有的表達一種時間關係或序列：already，now，then，before，ago，first，next，later，soon，still，yet，since，just等。
- 有的表達時間頻率：always，often，sometimes，never，constantly，frequently，hardly，ever，rarely，seldom，scarcely，usually等。

▶ I have six goldfish **now**.
我現在有六條金魚。

▶ She **always** brought me wonderful chocolates when she came to visit Grandma when I was living there.
當我住在外婆那裡的時候，每次她去看外婆時都給我非常棒的巧克力。

▶ Family members point out that they have **already** given hundreds of millions of dollars.
家人指出他們已經給過數億美元了。

🎯 地點副詞

地點副詞（Adverbs of Place）表示和地點、方向有關的含義。常見的有：here，away，outside，left，right，straight，west，in，down，above，below，up，downstairs，anywhere，everywhere等。例如：

▶ When my mother passed **away**, she didn't want a funeral or anything.
我母親過世的時候，她不想要葬禮或其他任何儀式。

▶ He took his hand **away** from hers and lit a cigarette with trembling fingers.
他把手從她的手中抽出，用顫抖的手指點上了一支香煙。

▶ As he stepped **down** from the ladder to gulp his breakfast, he asked me to help him.
他從梯子上下來，準備狼吞虎嚥地把早飯吃掉，這時他讓我幫他一個忙。

🎯 連接副詞

連接副詞（Conjunctive Adverbs）主要用來連接句子或者分句，表述句子之間的語義聯繫，使整個篇章更連貫和流暢。連接副詞主要有下面幾種：

1. 表示順序和附加的連接副詞。常見的有：first，secondly，thirdly，additionally，moreover，besides等。例如：

▶ There are three problems. **First**, not all personal digital assistants are created equal.
一共有三個問題：首先，不是所有的個人數位助理都具有同等的重要性。

2. 表示總結的連接副詞。常見的有：altogether，overall，insum，to conclude等。例如：

▶ **Overall**, 14 percent of teachers did not have their credentials.
總的來說，有14%的教師沒有教師證。

3. 表示解說的連接副詞。常見的有：namely，for example，that is，for instance，in other words等。例如：

▶ They all agreed on the absolute essentiality of solidarity among the three countries—**namely**, Japan, South Korea, and the United States.
對於日本、韓國和美國三個國家之間要保持團結的絕對重要性他們取得了一致意見。

4. 表示因果的連接副詞。常見的有：therefore，thus，consequently，so，accordingly，hence等。例如：

▶ I write this journal for myself and, **consequently**, anything that I may toss into it will become, for me, a precious memory.
我的日記為自己而寫，因此我寫進去的任何事情都將會成為我寶貴的記憶。

5. 表示對比的連接副詞。常見的有：though，however，but，nevertheless等。例如：

▶ If he passes the exam, he thinks his chances of finding a job will improve, **though** competition among laid-off blue-collar workers will be brutal.
他覺得如果他能通過考試，他找到工作的機會就會增加，儘管下崗藍領工人之間的競爭會很殘酷。

評注副詞

評注副詞（Stance Adverbs）一般表示說話者對命題內容的確定性、真實性或者來源等的判斷。常見的有：probably，definitely，actually，really，apparently，reportedly，honestly，surely，frankly，clearly，certainly，evidently，possibly，briefly，luckily，fortunately，surprisingly，naturally，typically，inevitably，likely等。例如：

▶ **Apparently** he is lunching with an old business friend at the clubhouse, and then will fly immediately to Paris in his private jet.
很明顯，他在俱樂部和一個老客戶吃午飯，然後他將乘坐私人飛機直接飛往巴黎。

▶ I think he is **probably** getting worried about your brother.
我想他可能在擔心你的弟弟。

► **Actually**, the Red Cross report suggests that somewhere between 70 and 90 percent of those who have been incarcerated since the beginning of the Iraq war are guilty of no crimes, terrorist activities or otherwise.

實際上，紅十字會報告認為，從伊拉克戰爭開始起被監禁的那些人中有70%至90%都沒有犯任何罪行，沒有進行任何恐怖攻擊。

► One 14-year-old boy was **reportedly** hit by a stray bullet and taken to the hospital.

據報導，一名14歲的男孩被流彈打中，並被送進了醫院。

評注副詞也可表示模糊的概念。常見的有：kind of，sort of，roughly，like，approximately，about，nearly，maybe等。例如：

► I think it would be **kind of** nice to actually experience a holiday abroad.

我認為親身體驗一次國外度假應該會不錯。

► We have **roughly** the same employment as we had in May on a seasonally adjusted basis.

經過一次季節性調整，我們現在的雇員數量基本上和5月份差不多。

► The tobacco company donates **approximately** $240,000 each year in student and college scholarships.

菸草公司每年大約捐獻24萬美元用作學生或大學獎學金。

副詞的句法功能

副詞的句法功能分為兩大類，一是作片語修飾成分，修飾動詞、形容詞、副詞和名詞等。二是副詞獨立作句法成分，可以作狀語、補語和介係詞受詞等。

副詞作片語修飾成分

1. 副詞修飾動詞

方式副詞、時間副詞、地點副詞、程度副詞都可以直接用來修飾動詞。例如：

► Emma herself did not much like green tea, but she pretended enthusiasm and sipped **politely**.

艾瑪自己並不太喜歡綠茶，不過她假裝非常感興趣，禮貌地喝著茶。

► She is pretty turbo-charged herself, **cheerfully** working a 10 to 12 hour day.

她像是給自己安裝了一個發動機，每天快樂地工作10到12小時。

► Alex went **upstairs** to her old bedroom to take off her white dress and to put on her pale-blue linen dress.

艾利克斯回到樓上她原來的臥室，脫下白色的裙子，換上了那條淺藍色亞麻裙子。

▶ Mr. Brown has **already** recommended reforms, but some could take years to bring into effect.
布朗先生已經提出了改革建議，但是有些可能需要數年才能見效。

▶ In 1995, the train in this country was **completely** modernized.
1995年這個國家的火車已經完全現代化了。

2. 副詞修飾形容詞

程度副詞常用來修飾形容詞。例如：

▶ "I'm a fiercely independent kind of guy and **rather** proud of it," Frank told the reporter.
法蘭克告訴記者：「我是一個絕對獨立的人，並且以此為榮。」

▶ Decades of this politician's humbuggery had created a **deeply** skeptical public.
這個政客數十年來一直欺騙大家，已經讓公眾對他產生深深的懷疑。

有些程度副詞可以用來修飾形容詞的比較級。例如：

▶ The death rate was **slightly** higher—38 per 100,000—for women who had taken estrogen for at least 10 years but had stopped by the time they enrolled in the study.
這些女人一直服用雌激素，最短的也有十年，直到她們參加這項研究時才停止服用。對這些人來說，十萬分之三十八的死亡率有點兒高。

▶ The economic outlook is now **much** stronger than previously thought.
現在的經濟前景比之前預期的要好很多。

在口語中有一些常用的「副詞＋形容片語組合」。常見的有：pretty good，really good，very good，quite good，very nice，too bad等。例如：

▶ Pets can take care of themselves, especially cats are **pretty good** about being independent.
寵物可以自己照顧自己，特別是貓在自理方面還不錯。

▶ I think everyone out here was **very nice** to me.
我認為這裡的每個人對我都非常好。

上面這些例子中，副詞都在所修飾的形容詞前面。有些副詞修飾形容詞的時候必須位於形容詞後面。常見的有：enough，ago等。例如：

▶ I'm old **enough** to look after myself.
我已經足夠大，可以自己照顧自己。

▶ Their father is a drunk whose wife left him long **ago**; their foul-mouthed grandmother lives with them.
他們的父親是一個酒鬼，妻子早就棄他而去，滿嘴髒話的奶奶和他們住在一起。

3. 副詞修飾其他副詞。例如：

▶ I had to write down his phone number **really** fast.
　我必須快速地寫下他的電話號碼。

▶ Business life consists **almost** entirely of projects, one after the other.
　商業生活幾乎全部是由專案組成，一個接著一個。

　　也有很多常用的「副詞＋副詞」組合。常見的有：right now，pretty much，right here，so much，very much，much more，much better，pretty soon，pretty well，very well，too much，much less，so fast，so well，just now，really well，very often 等。例如：

▶ His daughter is just a little more mature than other kids **right now**.
　他的女兒現在只比其他孩子成熟一點點。

▶ After the heart operation, she is doing **much better**.
　經過心臟手術以後，她現在好多了。

　　有些程度副詞可以修飾副詞的比較級。例如：

▶ He told Rufus to drive **a bit** more slowly.
　他告訴魯弗斯開車再慢一點。

▶ The young mother is working **a lot** harder to just meet basic living expenses.
　這位年輕的媽媽為了支付基本生活開支，工作更加辛苦了。

　　4. 副詞修飾其他成分

　　副詞還可以修飾名詞片語、介係詞片語、數量片語等。能修飾名詞片語的副詞主要有rather，quite，even等少數幾個副詞，用來增強語氣。例如：

▶ There's going to be **quite** a show tomorrow.
　明天將有一場不錯的演出。

▶ His mother was **rather** a stranger to him, so he didn't feel the loss of her so keenly.
　他的母親對他來講是個陌生人，所以對於她的去世，他不覺得有多悲痛。

　　有些時間地點副詞也可以修飾名詞，但是位置在名詞之後。常見的有：here，there，before，yesterday等。例如：

▶ Summer is too hot and winter is too cold, but life **here** is easy and peaceful, and people are friendly even.
　夏天太熱而冬天太冷，不過這裡的生活安逸而平靜，並且這裡的人特別友好。

▶ She had given up her job the week **before**.　她前一個星期已經辭職了。

能修飾介係詞片語的副詞主要有well，right，just，directly 等少數幾個副詞。例如：

▶ Most of them are well over the age of 50.
他們中的大多數超過50歲。

▶ Father took three steps towards me and smacked me on the ear right in front of a roomful of people.
父親朝我走了三步，然後當著一屋子人的面摑了我一個耳光。

能修飾數量片語的副詞有：quite，about，virtually，roughly，more than，approximately等。例如：

▶ Social workers estimate that about 6,000 men, women and children scratch out a living on San Diego streets, a population that tends to climb in winter.
社會工作者估計在聖地牙哥有大約6,000個男人、女人和孩子在大街上流浪為生。冬天這個數字還會增加。

▶ Virtually every hotel in Sweden halves its prices in summer, bringing even the most palatial hotels within reach of most travelers.
瑞典的夏季幾乎每家旅館都降為半價，連最富麗堂皇的旅館也能讓大部分旅客享受得起了。

▶ Last year, police in this state investigated roughly 3,000 cases, including aggravated assaults, shootings, rapes and 94 murders.
去年該州的員警調查了約3,000起案件，包括惡性襲擊、槍擊、強姦和94起謀殺案件。

副詞作狀語

副詞作狀語是副詞單獨充當獨立的句法成分。副詞作狀語主要有三種：狀態性狀語（Circumstance Adverbials）、評注性狀語（Stance Adverbials或Disjuncts）、連線性狀語（Linking Adverbs或Conjuncts）。（參見P320〈狀語〉）

1. 狀態性狀語

狀態性狀語的主要功能是為句子所述的動作提供更加詳細的描述資訊，如動作進行的時間、方式和地點等。例如：

▶ Then he strode out of the shop.
然後他大踏步走出商店。

▶ She went to London and is doing very well now.
她去了倫敦，現在做得非常好。

▶ To her horror he slowly turned the canoe out into the lake instead of into shore.
讓她感到恐怖的是他慢慢地把小舟划向湖裡，而不是岸邊。

2. 評注性狀語

評注性狀語表示說話者對句子所述命題內容的評注，包括對命題內容的確定性、態度等。常見的這類副詞有：maybe，probably，undoubtedly，unfortunately，amazingly，surprisingly，honestly，frankly等。例如：

▶ He was undoubtedly the star of the show, and had a wonderful chemistry with the rest of the cast that brought their onstage friendship to life beautifully.
毫無疑問，他是這場演出的明星，並且他和其他演員合作極好，他們的友誼也從臺上延伸到臺下。

▶ Amazingly, the storms that have often brought rains to quench the region's patched farmlands have wreaked little destruction.
令人驚訝的是，狂風和隨之而來的暴雨澆灌了該地區成片的農田，卻幾乎沒有造成破壞。

▶ I am anxious, frankly, that we are not bringing digital technology into the classroom as fast as I believe we should.
坦白說，我擔心我們沒有像應該做的那樣儘快把數位技術帶進課堂。

3. 連線性狀語

連線性狀語主要是起連接上下文的作用，其中上下文包括片語、句子、段落甚至篇章。例如：

▶ Capitalism is, therefore, inherently unstable, being subject to crises of booms and slumps.
因此，資本主義從本質上來說就是不穩定的，有繁榮也有蕭條。

副詞作主詞補語或受詞補語

與方向有關的地點副詞可以用在連綴動詞後面，作主詞補語（表語）。常見的有：in，down，out，off，behind，round，around，through，along，on，over，back，away，here，downstairs，abroad等。例如：

▶ "All they know is that Daddy is away on a trip," she said.
「他們所知道的是父親去旅行了。」她說。

▶ I'm delighted he will be around to help Jeff and mentor him.
我很高興他會過來幫傑夫並指導他。

▶ He's not here at the moment, but he'll be back by half past three.
他現在不在這裡，不過他三點半之前會回來。

▶ The soft drink industry brings in $54 billion a year, and consumption is up 43% since 1985.
非酒精飲料工業每年帶來540億美元的收入，而且，自1985年以來，非酒精飲料消費增長了43%。

上面某些副詞還可以作受詞補語。例如：

▶ "Let me in," Laura demanded. 「讓我進來。」蘿拉要求道。

▶ His Mom saw Jack out. 他媽媽送傑克離開。

▶ "Their support was fantastic and that helped me through," he said.
「他們的支持非常棒，幫助我渡過了難關。」他說。

副詞作介係詞受詞

有些表示地點、時間的副詞可以用作介係詞受詞。例如：

▶ I speeded up the walking a little to get away from there.
我加快了腳步離開那裡。

▶ If he missed this fast train, there was no other until tomorrow.
如果他錯過了快車，明天之前沒有其他車了。

▶ Mr. and Mrs. McAllister were last seen in town the day before yesterday in a cab on 5th Avenue. 麥卡利斯特夫婦最後一次在鎮上出現是前天在第五大道的一輛計程車裡。

副詞獨立使用

在口語中副詞可以單獨使用。有時把前面句子中的副詞狀語剝離出來，單獨放在下一句中使用，用來強調句子所表述的內容。例如：

▶ A: I found them uninterested in her novel.
B: Yeah. Totally and utterly.
A：我發覺他們對她的小說不感興趣。
B：是的，完全如此。

▶ A: Things are changing, aren't they?
B: Yeah. Slowly but surely.
A：事情在變化，不是嗎？
B：是的，儘管很緩慢但是確實在變。

有時，副詞單獨使用在對話的回應句中，表示回答、贊同或者疑問。常用的有：exactly，surely，definitely，really，seriously，honestly，probably等。例如：

▶ A: Are you gonna drink a lot tonight?
B: Yeah. Definitely.
A: Really?
B: Yeah. I'm not even joking.
A：你今晚要喝很多嗎？
B：是的，絕對是。
A：真的？
B：是的，我沒有開玩笑。

▶A: People can be quite capable or they can be surprisingly bad.

B: **Exactly**.

A：人們既可以十分地聰明能幹，也可以出奇地糟糕。

B：確實如此。

▶A: I think they're the fastest growing religious group in the world too.

B: **Really**?

A: That's what my professor said.

A：我認為他們也是世界上人數增長最快的宗教團體。

B：真的？

A：那是我的教授説的。

▶A: You're just using us as excuses.

B: But I'm sure whatever you have will be fine. **Honestly**.

A：你只是用我們當藉口。

B：但是我確信你們有的一切都會好起來的，真的。

副詞的位置 ▷

　　副詞充當介係詞的受詞和補語時位置都是固定的。本節主要講副詞作片語修飾成分和作狀語時的位置。總體來説副詞的位置非常靈活，可以在句首、句中或句末位置。具體到某一類副詞來説，有的副詞在三種位置都能出現，有的副詞只能出現在其中某兩個位置，有的副詞只能出現在其中某一個位置。副詞在句中的位置又可以區分為位於主詞後、情態動詞或助動詞後、動詞後等不同情況。下面詳細介紹各類副詞的位置。

◎ 時間副詞的位置

　　表示時間或區間的副詞，一般放在句末位置。例如：

▶Somebody wanted to know what we're doing **tomorrow**.

有人想知道我們明天做什麼。

▶A young man set fire to dozens of luxury homes in Charles County **last week**.

上週一個年輕男子縱火燒了查理斯縣的數十座豪華住宅。

　　有時為了強調和對照也可將時間副詞放在句首。例如：

▶**Tomorrow**, we're going to talk about how to make America's teaching force more diverse to match its student body.

明天我們將討論如何讓美國的教學隊伍更多樣化來滿足學生群體的要求。

▶**Last week**, Richard Seed, a Chicago medical researcher, said he had the means to start cloning human beings and could soon open a clinic to do so.

上週理查·錫德，一個芝加哥醫學研究者，説他有複製人類的辦法並且很快就可以開一個診所來實施這件事。

表示時間序列和頻率的副詞，如sometimes，often，soon，finally，presently，once，now等，位置更為靈活，可以置於句首、句中（主詞後、動詞前或助動詞、情態動詞及動詞be後）或句末。如果句中有情態動詞或助動詞，頻率副詞就放在這類動詞後面、主要動詞前面。例如：

▶I can **always** phone my sister to ask for advice.
我總可以打電話給我姐姐尋求建議。

▶He was a little too fond of drink and would **occasionally** get into fights.
他有點太愛喝酒了，有時會和別人打架。

▶Teenagers will **soon** play government-designed computer games featuring mythical heroes from Russian folklore battling evil serpents.
青少年很快就可以玩政府設計的電腦遊戲，這些遊戲是按英雄和惡魔戰鬥的俄羅斯民間故事設計的。

如果句中沒有情態動詞、助動詞，且句子的主要動詞是實義動詞，則頻率副詞通常在實義動詞前面、主詞後面。例如：

▶It is said that divorce **often** takes place on the initiative of the wife.
據說離婚通常是由妻子主動提出。

▶My dog **usually** gets two scoops of dried dog food and one or two biscuits a day.
我的狗通常每天吃兩勺乾的狗食另加一兩塊餅乾。

▶"Mother Nature **sometimes** makes rocks that look like humans made them," he said.
他說：「大自然母親有時會製作一些看起來像是人造的石頭。」

▶They **finally** took the girl to the local Iraqi police station.
他們最終把這個女孩帶到了伊拉克當地警察局。

如果句中有連綴動詞，頻率副詞位於連綴動詞之後。例如：

▶He had taken a teaching job in Florida and **was seldom** home.
他在佛羅里達找到一份教書的工作，很少在家。

▶The loans **were frequently** for six months or less and typically paid interest equal to 20 percent a year.
貸款通常情況下為期6個月甚至更少，並且所付的利息相當於一年20%。

有時為了表示強調，頻率副詞也會偏離上述位置。

1. 在句首位置。例如：

▶**Always** she chose the most deserted routes in her journey.
她總是選擇最荒蕪的路線去旅行。

▶Sometimes your real limits are different from what you think.
有時你真正的底線和你認為的並不一樣。

▶Finally, he brought his family to live with him.
最後，他將家人接來和他一起住。

2. 在情態動詞或助動詞前。例如：

▶He never has used performance-enhancing drugs and never has had a positive drug test.
他從來沒有使用興奮劑，在藥檢中也從來沒有顯示陽性。

▶Drugs called antidepressants sometimes can treat depression in children and teens.
抗憂鬱藥物有時能治療孩子和青少年的憂鬱。

3. 在句末位置。例如：

▶Talk to your child's teacher early and often.
早點和你孩子的老師交流，也要經常交流。

▶I actually encourage my wife to spend money sometimes.
實際上有時我還鼓勵我妻子花錢。

▶Rock music is back, finally.
搖滾樂終於又回來了。

🎯 地點副詞的位置

表示地點的副詞一般在動詞後的位置。例如：

▶Sara went upstairs to the front bedroom, dumped her knapsack on the floor, took off her socks and shorts and sat on one of the beds.
莎拉上樓去到前面的臥室裡，把她的背包裡的東西一股腦兒倒在地板上，脫下襪子和短褲坐到其中一張床上。

▶She stayed here for several days.
她在這裡待了幾天。

▶He pushed the letter under the door and went away.
他把信塞到門底下然後離開了。

但是有時為了上下文連貫或保持句子平衡，地點副詞也可出現在句首位置。這時一般會引起主謂倒裝語序。

有些與介係詞同形的副詞，既可以放在受詞之前，也可放在受詞之後。例如：put on the coat 或put the coat on。但如果受詞是人稱代名詞，只能放置在受詞後面。例如：put it on。其他類似的副詞還有：out，up，down，in，away等。

方式副詞的位置

表示動作方式的副詞多放在動詞片語後面。如果是不及物動詞，直接放在其後面。如果是及物動詞，則方式副詞一般在受詞的後面。例如：

▶ Just three weeks ago it rained **heavily** for the first time in four years.
就在三週前下了四年內的第一場大雨。

▶ It is found that sugars that occur **naturally** in breast milk reduce the number of harmful bugs in a baby's stomach.
人們發現母乳中自然產生的糖分能夠減少嬰兒胃中的有害細菌。

▶ Both Kitty and Jefferson greeted him **warmly** and told him how pleased they were that he had come.
凱蒂和傑弗遜都熱情地接待了他，並告訴他他的到來讓他們感到多麼高興。

▶ If you do it **intentionally**, you can end up in jail.
如果你是有意去做的，你最終會進監獄。

有時為了表示對動作的強調，方式副詞可以放在主詞後面，動詞前面。例如：

▶ He **intentionally** worsened the relationship between the two sides of the negotiation.
他故意讓談判雙方的關係惡化。

▶ The website is informative and forthright, and I **warmly** recommend it.
這個網站不但訊息量大而且直言不諱，因此我熱情推薦它。

▶ She let the tears well into her huge eyes, but she **bravely** wiped them away.
淚水湧進了她大大的眼睛，不過她勇敢地擦乾了淚珠。

如果受詞部分較長，方式副詞還可以放在動詞和受詞之間。例如：

▶ She should think **carefully** about all her options before she makes a decision.
她在作出決定以前應該仔細地考慮所有選擇。

▶ We examine **carefully** any measures which might enhance the nation's security.
我們仔細地研究了所有可能加強國家安全的措施。

連接副詞的位置

連接副詞一般都位於句子或子句的開頭。例如：

▶ Overall, most drinks are less expensive than in the UK and US.
總之，大部分飲料比在英國或美國便宜。

▶ Thus the factory manager is not necessarily crazy for sticking with older, energy inefficient machines.
這樣這個工廠的經理就沒有必要固執地守住那些古老的、浪費能源的機器了。

▶ For instance, he taught me how to use nitrous oxide for its effect in combating physical pain.
例如他教我如何使用氧化亞氮（笑氣）的功效來對抗身體疼痛。

▶ Similarly, another fat-soluble vitamin, namely vitamin D, differs, depending on its form.
同樣地，另外的脂溶性維生素，即維生素D，也因形式不同而不同。

評注副詞的位置

修飾整個句子的評注副詞通常位於句首的位置。例如：

▶ Luckily, X-rays showed Johnny broke no bones.
幸運的是，X光顯示強尼沒有摔斷骨頭。

▶ Evidently, she believed she would find that inner peace in New Zealand.
很明顯，她相信她可以在紐西蘭找到內心的平靜。

▶ Perhaps I've misunderstood my girlfriend.
或許我誤解了我的女友。

有時也可以放在句中或句末位置。

1. 主詞和主要動詞之間。例如：

▶ He evidently wished to say something, but faltered.
他明顯想說些什麼，但是卻支支吾吾。

▶ They certainly respect their grandfather.
他們當然尊敬他們的祖父。

2. 助動詞或情態動詞和主要動詞之間。例如：

▶ Anna's letter had evidently taken some time to reach Brian.
顯然安娜的信需要一段時間才能到布雷恩那裡。

▶ He should certainly be able to check whether or not the feather came from a swan.
他一定能夠檢查這根羽毛是否來自一隻天鵝。

3. 句末。例如：

▶ There's some reason for his resignation, surely.
他辭職了，這其中必有緣由。

▶ There are problems, inevitably.
有問題不可避免。

▶ Not everybody agreed, inevitably.
不是每個人都同意，這是不可避免的。

◎ 程度副詞的位置

程度副詞一般放在所修飾的詞前。例如：

▶ We are so awfully tired.
我們非常累。

▶ His office was in the west wing and fairly well equipped, with a bathroom and a small bedroom.
他的辦公室在西側，裝修不錯，有一個浴室和一個小的臥室。

▶ Although Murphy is very busy, she is not always in the school's lab.
儘管墨菲非常忙，她也不是一直在學校實驗室裡。

有些表示程度重的副詞也可以放在句末位置。例如：

▶ His attitude towards the war changed completely.
他對戰爭的態度完全改變了。

▶ You have to breathe deeply.
你必須深呼吸。

▶ Your decision touched me deeply.
你的決定深深地打動了我。

程度副詞enough 放在所修飾的形容詞、副詞之後。例如：

▶ The park as a whole is large enough to absorb the great numbers of visitors.
這個公園總體來說足夠大，可以容納大量遊客。

▶ He couldn't get away fast enough.
他沒能快速動身離開。

副詞的比較級和最高級 ▷

副詞的比較級和最高級形式

　　副詞比較級和最高級的使用遠不及形容詞頻繁。比較級和最高級形式僅限於部分時間副詞、方式副詞和程度副詞等。

　　單音節及少數雙音節副詞的比較級和最高級形式加-er 和-est構成。大部分雙音節及多音節副詞的比較級和最高級形式加more 和most 構成。例如：

★加-er和-est：

副詞原形	比較級	最高級
hard	harder	hardest
early	earlier	earliest

★加more和most：

副詞原形	比較級	最高級
often	more often	most often
slowly	more slowly	most slowly
carefully	more carefully	most carefully

★少數不規則形式，例如：

副詞原形	比較級	最高級
well	better	best
much	more	most
little	less	least
far	farther (further)	farthest (furthest)
badly	worse	worst

副詞的比較結構

　　和形容詞一樣，副詞也可以用來表示比較。副詞的比較結構主要有下面幾種：

　　1. 副詞比較級＋than＋片語（或子句）。例如：

▶ If government spending grows more quickly than the national income as a whole, the government will be spending a larger share of our income and taxes will have to rise.
如果政府開支增長速度超過國民收入整體增長速度，政府將會花掉我們更多的錢，稅收也將被迫增加。

2. as + 副詞+ as +片語（或子句）。例如：

▶ The more we can use technology as quickly as possible, the better we can manage disease and lower costs.
我們應用科技的速度越快，就越能更好地控制疾病並降低成本。

▶ We're not doing as well as we could.
我們沒有盡全力做到最好。

▶ She couldn't dance as well as Mandy and Diana.
她跳舞沒有曼迪和戴安娜那麼好。

副詞的比較級和最高級的特殊用法

有少數副詞的比較級和最高級有一些習慣用法。

1. 副詞比較級＋and＋副詞比較級（越來越……）。例如：

▶ They met more and more frequently as the months went by.
隨著歲月流逝他們見面越來越頻繁。

▶ "I am just a little ship," Aunt Emily said, "drifting farther and farther out to sea."
「我只是一葉小舟，」艾蜜莉阿姨說，「在大海上越漂越遠。」

2. the＋副詞比較級……，the＋副詞比較級……（越……越……）。例如：

▶ The faster you lead your life and the more isolated you are because you're sitting at your computer all day, the more you would seek a community to counteract that isolation.
你生活節奏越快，你越會孤立，因為你整天都坐在電腦前面，你越感覺到需要一個群體來驅趕孤獨。

▶ The less alone we all feel, the better off we all are.
我們越是不感到孤獨，越是過得好。

3. had better/best（最好）。例如：

▶ We had better tell him nothing.
我們最好什麼也不告訴他。

▶ You had best keep what I said in mind.
你最好把我說的記在腦子裡。

4. know better than to...（知道不應做……）。例如：

▶ You should know better than to ask such a question after all I've tried to teach you.
你應該知道不宜問這樣的問題，畢竟我試圖教過你。

▶ You should know better than to walk out into strange streets alone.
你應該知道不要獨自一個人去陌生的街道。

5. think better of（改變主意）。例如：

▶Rose was about to protest, but thought better of it.
羅斯剛要抗議，不過他又改變了主意。

▶He also ordered French fries, but thought better of it when the restaurant suggested onion rings instead.
他也點了炸薯條，但是當餐廳推薦洋蔥圈的時候他改變了主意。

小結 ▷

　　本章詳細介紹了副詞的特點和用法。有些副詞和形容詞關係密切，由形容詞加-ly派生而來，有些簡單副詞和形容詞同形。

　　副詞按照其語義可以分為方式副詞、程度副詞、時間副詞、地點副詞、連接副詞、評注副詞等。不同類別的副詞不但具有不同的句法功能，可以作修飾語、狀語和補語等，而且其在句子中的位置也各不相同。副詞在句中的位置不但取決於副詞本身的類別，也取決於具體的語境，即說話者想強調什麼內容。規則副詞的比較級和最高級也是加-er，est或more，most。

Part 12

介係詞和介係詞片語

介係詞的種類

介係詞一般位於名詞、動詞-ing形式和代名詞前，表示介係詞前後兩個事物或人所處的地點、方位、時間或歸屬、因果、輔助等關係。介係詞主要可以分為簡單介係詞（Simple Prepositions）、複雜介係詞（Complex Prepositions）和具有介係詞功能的動詞-ing形式組成的邊緣介係詞（Marginal Prepositions）。

簡單介係詞

大多數介係詞為簡單介係詞，即由一個單字組成的單一介係詞。主要有：

about	above	across	after	against	along	amidst
around	as	at	before	behind	below	beside
besides	between	but	by	despite	down	during
except	for	from	in	inside	into	like
near	of	off	on	onto	out	over
past	since	than	through	till	to	toward
under	up	upon	with	within	without	

複雜介係詞

複雜介係詞可以由兩個或三個單字組成。

1. 由兩個片語成。一般前一個為副詞、形容詞或連接詞，後一個為單一介係詞。例如：

ahead of	along with	apart from	as for	as from
as regards	as to	away from	because of	but for
contrary to	due to	except for	inside of	instead of
next to	out of	owing to	prior to	together with
up to				

2. 由三個片語成。一般前後兩個詞為簡單介係詞，中間一個多為名詞或形容詞。例如：

as far as	by means of	by virtue of	for (the) sake of
in accordance with	in case of	in favor of	in front of
in need of	in place of	in process of	in/with regard to
in respect of	in/with respect to	in spite of	in view of
on account of	on behalf of	on grounds of	on top of
with reference to			

邊緣介係詞

一些類似其他詞類的詞充當介係詞時被稱為邊緣介係詞。最常見的是某些動詞-ing形式充當介係詞。例如：considering，excepting，including，regarding等。

介係詞的意義

介係詞主要表達介係詞前後兩個事物或人所處的空間、時間或歸屬、因果、輔助手段等方面的關係。

表示空間關係

1. 表示位置和地點

通常用來表示方位和地點的介係詞有：at，on，in，away from，off，out of等。

(1)at

在「A is at B」這樣的結構中，A被看成B位置上的點，表示「A在B處」。例如：at the airport，at the bus stop，at the cinema，at the corner，at home，at school等。

▶ They had been in the same class **at** school, and although he was very popular she'd never paid any attention to him, nor he to her.
他們曾經是同班同學，雖然那時他很受歡迎，但他們彼此卻從來沒注意過對方。

表示「A不在B處」，可用away from。例如：

▶ She had to get **away from** London, **away from** Toby. 她必須得離開倫敦，離開托比。

(2)on

在「A is on B」這樣的結構中，B可以表示一條線或一個面，A被B支撐或與B接觸。例如：on the desk，on the grass，on the hill，on the road，on one's shoulders，on the table等。

▶ Since Armstrong strode out on to the surface of the moon on July 20, 1969, only 12 men have stood **on** the surface of the moon.
自從1969年7月20日阿姆斯壯踏上月球的那刻起，迄今為止也只有12個人登上過月球。

表示「A不在某個線或面上」，可用 off。例如：

▶ As the kids raced outside screaming, Jim hunched down to hide but lost his balance and toppled **off** the roof.
孩子們尖叫著跑出去時，吉姆彎下腰想躲起來，但沒想到失去了平衡，從屋頂摔了下來。

(3)in

在「A is in B」這樣的結構中，B是一個立體的空間，A處於B這個封閉的空間裡。例如：in China，in the field，in the kitchen，in prison，in the room，in a village，in the world等。

▶ I've never had a parent **in** prison, but I can imagine how hard it would be.
雖然我的父母親沒有坐過牢，但我可以想像那種經歷該有多艱難。

表示「A不在B這個空間內」，可用out of。例如：

▶ She was a heavy, sarcastic little girl and had been kicked **out of** class.
她是個身體笨重、愛諷刺人的小女孩，還被人從課堂上趕出去過。

2. 表示相對位置、垂直或平行

通常用於表示相對位置、相互垂直或平行關係的介係詞有：above，over，under，below，in front of，before，behind，after 等。其中，above，over，under，below常常表示垂直方向的關係；而in front of，before，behind，after表示水平方向的關係。

(1) above，over

above，over作地點介係詞，表示「在……之上」。它們的區別在於：above僅表示在更高的位置，而over 指正好垂直的位置，即正上方，但都沒有產生接觸。例如：

▶ The sunset opened like an orange flower **above** the desert.
落日的餘暉就像盛開在沙漠上空的一朵柑橘花一樣。

▶ When I surfaced, gasping, the sky was intensely blue and I saw the moon, cratered and radiant, high **over** the tower on the distant Mount.
我浮出了水面，大口喘著氣，天是那麼碧藍，表面凹凸不平的月亮散發著光，高高地掛在遠處山上的塔頂上。

over也可以表示接觸，即「覆蓋」。例如：

▶ To make the place more like a classroom, teachers spread scraps of blue carpet **over** the concrete floor and added a computer and a round table that seats 8 to 12 students.
為了讓這個地方更有教室的感覺，老師們在水泥地上鋪上了藍色的小地毯，添置了一台電腦和一張能坐8到12個學生的圓桌。

(2)below，under

below, under表示和above, over相反的意思；below表示在更低的位置，under指正好垂直的關係，正下方。例如：

▶ Her brother lives **below** us in the basement.
她哥哥住在我們下面的地下室裡。

▶ By looking at the colored chromosomes **under** a microscope, the doctor can easily tell whether the embryo is male or female.
通過用顯微鏡觀察染色體，醫生很容易就能分辨胚胎的性別。

under可以表示「被覆蓋」。例如：

▶ She took the key from the front door, walked outside on to the drive and locked it behind her, placing the key **under** the mat.
她從前門拿了鑰匙，出門走向車道，轉身鎖了門，把鑰匙放在墊子下。

(3)in front of，before，behind，after

in front of和before都表示「在……的前面」，它們的細微差別在於：in front of 還可以表示「在……的正面，面對……」，before表示的地點常與先後順序或重要性的大小有關。

另外，before還可以表示時間上的前後順序。behind和after分別是in front of和before的反義詞。例如：

▶ He stood **in front of** his wife in dinner jacket and trousers, black tie dangling.
他穿著晚禮服站在妻子面前，黑色的領帶鬆垮垮地垂著。

▶ You were **before** me in the queue.
你排在我前面。

▶ He crouches down **behind** a chair.
他蜷縮在椅子後面。

▶ Whose name is **after** yours on the list?
名單上誰的名字排在你的後面？

3. 表示在……之間

通常表示「在……之間」方位關係的介係詞有：between，among，amid，in the middle of 等。

(1) between

between通常表示某兩個人或事物之間的方位關係，而這些人或物體是相互分離的。between較少用於兩者以上，即便這樣使用，也是將人、物或地點一對一對來看。例如：

▶ Why didn't you alert me that there was trouble between you and your boss?
為什麼你沒提醒我你和你老闆之間有矛盾？

▶ For nearly 600 years, the land that lies between the villages of Agincourt,Tramecourt and Maisoncelle has been the honored resting place of thousands who fought there on October 25, 1415.
近600年以來，那片位於阿讓庫爾村、特拉姆考特村和邁松西裡村之間的土地是1415年10月25日數千名在此地戰鬥而犧牲了的人榮耀的安息之地。

(2)among

among表示一組人或物之間的方位關係，常用於三者或三者以上，這些人或物是作為一個整體來看待的。例如：

▶ The ancient Chinese were among the first people to develop farming, growing rice along the banks of the Yangtze River.
古代中國人是最先開始耕作的文明之一，他們在長江兩岸種植水稻。

注意！

between和among的區別就在於：between所指的是相互分離的人或物之間的方位關係，among將人或物看成一個整體。

(3)amid

amid也寫成amidst，多用於正式文體如文學作品中，表示「在……中」，與among類似，可指在一組人或事物中。例如：

▶ On July 20, amid a heavy snowstorm, the team finally reached the summit of the mountain.
7月20日，隊伍冒著暴風雪終於登頂。

(4)in the middle of

in the middle of通常表示在兩個地點之間接近中心點的位置。例如：

▶We took him to a remote coral island in the middle of the Indian Ocean, serving as a key strategic location for U.S. and British air strikes against Iraq.
我們把他帶到印度洋中一個偏遠的珊瑚島，那裡是美英聯軍對伊拉克實施空襲的主要戰略基地。

4. 表示在周圍或圍繞

around通常是表示在四周圍繞等空間方位的介係詞。

(1)表示在某個範圍內的各處。例如：

▶The fall of a Hong Kong investment company has shaken financial markets around the world.
一家香港投資公司的失敗震動了世界金融市場。

(2)表示「圍繞……運動」。例如：

▶As a planet moves around a star, its gravity pulls on the star, causing it to wobbles lightly.
當行星環繞恆星的時候，它自身的重力會使得恆星有輕微的搖晃。

(3)表示在某人或某物的附近。例如：

▶District police have been training over the past week in how to spot terrorists masquerading as truckers and large trucks have been banned from an area around the U.S. Capitol.
過去的一周裡，地區員警都在訓練如何辨認假扮成卡車司機的恐怖分子，而在美國國會大廈附近區域，大型卡車已被禁止入內。

(4)表示環繞某個位置。例如：

▶Daniel supported her with an arm around her waist.
丹尼爾用手臂扶住了她的腰。

5. 表示通過

across，through，over，past，by等介係詞常用來表示人或物變動和移動位置的動態空間方位關係，如「通過……」。

(1)across，through，over

這三個詞都表示空間移動，從一邊穿越到另一邊。區別在於：across穿越的是一個

平面；through穿越的是一個立體的空間；over穿越的是狹長的地方，如河流、溝渠、柵欄和馬路等。例如：

▶ They are building a new bridge **across** the river.
他們正在河上修建新橋。

▶ He likes wandering aimlessly **through** the city.
他喜歡在城市裡毫無目的地四處遊蕩。

▶ He jumped **over** the flowerpots in front of the hotel and kept on running to the end of the street.
他躍過擺在酒店前的花盆，跑到了街的盡頭。

(2)past，by

這兩個介係詞通常能夠確切地表示經過某處或某人，兩個詞可以互換，但past更為常用。例如：

▶ I spoke to him but he walked **past** me as though I wasn't there.
我對他說話，但他卻當我不存在一樣從我身邊走過。

▶ I walked **by** the library and decided to go in and ask for a job.
路過圖書館，我決定進去找找工作。

6. 表示運動的方向

通常表示運動方向的介係詞有：to，for，towards，at，on，onto，in，into，away from，out of等。

(1)to，for，towards，at

to，for，towards都表示運動的方向，但to強調了到達點；for強調了目的地，後面常加地名；towards指出了運動的方向，但沒有明確指出是否到達。例如：

▶ Blindly, Alan ran **to** his room, where he beat and punched his bed and cried aloud in a rage like a child.
艾倫摸索著沖進了自己的房間，朝著床又打又捶，像個孩子一樣氣得大哭。

▶ The night before Kate left **for** London, she decided to tell Judy she would never get back. 在凱特去倫敦的前一晚，她決定告訴裘蒂自己再也不會回來了。

▶ Suddenly 12 guys emerged from the SUVs and came **towards** me.
突然有12個人從越野車裡冒了出來，朝我走來。

at表示朝某個方向發出的動作，但結果未明確。例如：

▶ They were afraid of people shooting **at** our bus.
他們怕有人朝我們的汽車開槍射擊。

(2) in，on，onto，into，off，out of

in，on可以表示在某個位置的靜止狀態，也可以表示一種運動的狀態。例如：

▶ If you must use the stove, first put the children **in** a safe place where you can see and hear them.
如果你一定要用爐子，首先要讓孩子們待在一個安全的地方，而且你要看得見、聽得見他們。

▶ She threw herself down **on** the sofa, and slept. 她倒在沙發上，睡著了。

into，onto強調了運動的方向，動詞後面使用into，onto還表示到達運動目標點。例如：

▶ Nancy walked **into** his classroom on a warm summer evening.
一個炎熱夏日的晚上，南茜走進了他的教室。

▶ Spotting the tsunami, he and his wife corralled the children **onto** a motorboat and outran the waves, seconds before their orphanage was crushed by a 30-foot wall of water.
覺察到海嘯即將來臨，他和妻子把孩子們趕上摩托艇，迅速駛離躲避巨浪，幾秒鐘後他們的孤兒院就被30英尺高的巨浪給擊垮了。

off，out of表示朝相反方向運動，即離開。

▶ A low pressure storm moves **off** the Atlantic seaboard.
低氣壓暴雨團離開了大西洋海岸。

▶ He took **out of** a thick envelope a sheet of thick paper.
他從一個厚信封裡掏出一張厚厚的紙。

7. 表示遍及或貫穿

(all) over，throughout等介係詞通常表達遍及或貫穿的意思。

over表示遍及某物或某地的各處或大部分，與all連用時表示全部；throughout同樣強調的是遍佈各處。一般情況下，這兩個介係詞可互換。例如：

▶ Miami is a transit point for illegal immigrants from **all over** the world.
邁阿密是全球非法移民的中轉站。

▶ The pattern of violence is repeated **throughout** the film, as we are forced to view one atrocity after another.
整部影片不斷重複著暴力情節，而我們也被迫看著一個接一個的暴力鏡頭。

表示時間關係

1. 表示時間位置

介係詞at，on，in除了可以表示空間方位外，還可以表示時間位置。

(1) at

a. at較多指的是時間點（如鐘點），或某個時刻（如黎明、黃昏、日出、日落等）。
例如：at 6 o'clock，at dawn，at dusk，at sunrise，at sunset，at the moment，at
present，at that time，at the time (of)等。例如：

▶ I had to be home **at** 10 o'clock every night.
　我必須每晚10點到家。

▶ Moving into Europe has few attractions **at** the moment.
　現在移居歐洲已經不太吸引人了。

b. at也指一段時間（如中午、夜晚、週末、某個節日）。例如：at noon，at night，at
Christmas，at Easter等。例如：

▶ I had trouble sleeping **at night**.
　晚上我很難入睡。

▶ My brother will take care of my son until I can join him **at Easter**.
　我和哥哥在復活節會合，這之前他都會幫我帶兒子。

注意！

1. at Easter指復活節前後的一段時間，而非僅指復活節當天，同樣at Christmas 指
　的也是耶誕節期間。
2. 在美式英語中「在週末」表示為 on the weekend。

c. 指年齡。例如：at the age of 28，at age 18，at my/your age等。

▶ He died at his Los Angeles home yesterday **at the age of** 85.
　昨天他在洛杉磯的家中去世，享年85歲。

(2) on

　　on常指具體的某一天。

a. 星期幾。例如：on Sunday，on Saturday等。

▶ A new movie about his father's life opens **on Friday**.
　一部有關他父親生平的電影將在週五上映。

b. 具體日期。例如：on (the) 23rd of May，on the evening of April the second等。

1. 表示晝夜時間段（morning，noon，evening，daytime）且沒有其他修飾詞時，介係詞用in。例如：in the morning，in the afternoon，in the evening。

2. 如果這些時間段前面有yesterday，tomorrow，next，last，this，that等詞限定，一般不用介係詞。例如：yesterday morning，next morning，this morning。

3. 如果這些時間段有星期幾或日期修飾時，要加介係詞on。例如：

▶ The product is due to go on sale **on** Sunday morning.
這商品預計將在週日上午上市。

c. 具體某日（如作為單日考慮的某個節日、生日等）。例如：on my birthday，on Christmas Eve，on New Year's Day等。

▶ He was born **on** Christmas Eve 1818 in London and worked in Manchester.
他於1818年聖誕前夜生於倫敦，後來在曼徹斯特工作。

(3) in

　　in常與表示時間的名詞片語連用。

a. 表示晝夜時間。例如： in the morning，in the afternoon，in the evening，in the daytime等。

　　night通常與介係詞at搭配。例如：at night。

b. 表示月份、季節、年份、年代、世紀。例如：in April，in summer，in 2002，in 1970's，in the 21st century等。

▶ She also is accused of murdering her young daughters **in** June.
她也被指控在6月謀殺了她年幼的女兒們。

　　2. 表示持續的時間

　　介係詞for，during，over，through，throughout，between...and，from...to，until，up to，by通常用來表示一段持續的時間。

(1) for

　　for 表示某個動作或某種狀態持續時間的長度。例如：

▶ He sat **for** 12 hours looking outside a little slat window.
他在那裡坐了12個小時，不斷向小百葉窗外張望著。

(2)during

during可以表示「在⋯⋯期間，貫穿始終」，常常與一些表示持續動作的動詞如 stay，work等連用，類似throughout的意思。例如：

▶ He died at the age of 21 in the same room his father had slept in during his stay in Italy.
21歲時他死在他父親當年在義大利逗留期間睡過的那個房間。

during也可表示持續時間範圍內的一個特定時間段或時間點，類似in的意思。例如：

▶ Her husband Ambrose had been killed during the war and she had remarried a rich American lawyer, and stayed on, raising and educating her four children as Americans.
她的丈夫安布羅斯死於戰爭，後來她改嫁了，與一個富有的美國律師結了婚，並在美國定居了下來，用美國人的方式來撫養和教育她的四個孩子。

(3) over

over表示在做某事期間發生另一件事，體現兩事的同時性。例如：

▶ The quarrel was not resolved over dinner.
吃晚飯的時候，爭吵還是沒有停息。

▶ Politics, religion and sex are still taboo over dinner at my father's farm.
在爸爸的農莊裡，政治、宗教和性仍是飯桌談話的禁忌。

over還可表示貫穿某個時間段，常與表示節假日的名詞片語搭配。例如：

▶ Many skiers and snowboarders want to travel to Canada over Christmas and the New Year.
許多滑雪者和單板滑雪愛好者想在聖誕和新年時去加拿大旅遊。

(4)through，throughout

這兩個介係詞表達了自始至終的意思，強調時間的連貫性，throughout比through的語氣更強烈。例如：

▶ He lay awake through the night wishing he could go home or into the sitting room and watch a horror movie.
他整晚都睡不著，夢想著能回到家或去客廳看部恐怖片。

▶ The city absorbed four times its population throughout the year.
這個城市在一年中吸收了相當於其人口四倍的外來人。

(5) between...and，from...to

這兩個介係詞片語都指明了一段時間的起點和終點，但區別在於from...to表示動作在這段時間內的持續性，但between...and表示動作會在這段時間內的某個或某些時間點發生。例如：

▶ Alaska's nurse-to-population ratio dropped 19.5 percent between 1996 and 2000.
在阿拉斯加，護士與人口的比率在1996年到2000年間下降了19.5%。

▶ The number of U.S. births rose steadily from 1998 to 2000.
在1998年到2000年間，美國出生的人口數量平穩增長。

(6) till，until，by

這些詞都表示了一段時間的終點，till和until在肯定語氣中一般與表示持續動作的動詞連用，但在否定語氣中既可與表示持續動作的動詞也可與表示瞬間動作的動詞連用；而by通常只與表示瞬間動作的動詞連用。例如：

▶ He waited until (till) she had finished speaking.
他一直等到她講完。

▶ It was not until (till) Friday morning that highway officials announced that tolls on those roads would be suspended.
直到週五早晨高速公路工作人員才宣佈這些路段的收費將暫緩。

▶ They questioned his confident prediction that by next year the UK economy would be back to rapid growth.
他自信地預言，明年英國經濟會重新實現高速增長，對此他們提出了質疑。

3. 表示時間順序

常常用來表示時間順序的介係詞有：before，after，in等。這些介係詞既可以表示空間方位，也可以表示時間順序。例如：the day before yesterday，the day after tomorrow，in a few days/weeks/years等。

其中after，in都表示「在……之後」發生，但in常以現在的時間為起點，所以in常與將來時態連用；after正好相反，涉及的是非現在的一個時間點。例如：

▶ After the war, Japan emerged as a world power.
戰後，日本作為一個世界強國崛起。

▶ After the war, the couple actually returned to Kuwait to resume their careers.
戰後，這對夫妻實際上回到了科威特又重新開始他們的事業。

▶ Your eyes will get used to the dark in a minute.
你的眼睛一會兒就會適應黑暗。

表示原因、目的、目標

because of，on account of，owing to 等介係詞片語常用來表示原因、目的和目標。

1. because of，on account of，owing to，due to

以上介係詞片語都表示原因，一般情況下可以互換。

▶ Some 13,000 lives are saved each year because of seat belts.
　每年安全帶能拯救約13,000條生命。

▶ Due to the traffic jams, the journey took longer than I had expected.
　由於交通堵塞，路上花費的時間比我預計的要長。

▶ A village barbecue was recently cancelled, owing to lack of interest.
　由於大家興致不高，鄉村燒烤活動最近被取消了。

注意！

① on account of 和owing to 更多地用在正式語體中。
② due to 多作表語，而owing to 多作狀語修飾動詞。

2. out of，for

out of，for都表達動機，out of多為心理、情感原因。例如：out of pity/kindness/gratitude/generosity/curiosity/mischief/spite/malice/sympathy 等。

for 可表達心理動機，也可表達其他原因。例如：for joy/fear/love/sorrow等。例如：

▶ People mobbed the brokerage firms, some out of curiosity but others out of necessity.
　人們湧進仲介公司，一些人出於好奇，其他人則是必須這樣做。

▶ Thank you, Geoff, for taking time to talk with us.
　傑夫，謝謝你花時間和我們談話。

3. to，for

如果to和for後面跟表示人或動物的名詞片語，人或動物均代表接受者或目標。區別在於：to表示接受者已經接收到；for表示設定的接受者是否收到不明確，有可能收到，也可能沒有。例如：

▶ It sounds exciting to the children but the reality of leaving their home, their friends, their schools and facing a future in a country they don't know could be different.
　這在孩子們聽起來是讓人激動的事，但事實上，離開家、離開朋友和學校，面對在另一個陌生國家的生活，卻絕不是什麼令人興奮的事情。

▶ Mr. Clare told his son he had been saving the money he would have spent on his university education for him.
　克雷爾先生告訴兒子，自己一直在為他籌上大學的錢。

4. of，from

當表示死亡原因的時候，die of表示自然的原因，如年老或疾病；die from表示非自然的原因，如車禍、勞累等，但現在它們的區別已經慢慢消失。例如：

▶ Her son died **from/of** a gunshot to the back of the head after his store was robbed of $300 in 1985.
1985年她兒子的店鋪被搶劫了300美金，而她兒子在那次搶劫中被子彈擊中後腦而死。

表示工具、行為者、手段

1. with，by

with表示「用……工具」；by表示「被……人」，即施動者，常用於被動語態。例如：

▶ He prefers writing **with** a pen to typing.
他更喜歡用鋼筆寫字而不是打字。

▶ He was taught football **by** his father, Felix Mourinho, an international goalkeeper.
他的足球是父親菲力克斯‧莫里尼奧教的，他父親是個國際守門員。

2. by

by表示交通或通信工具，通常使用零冠詞。常用的片語如下：

by air	by bicycle	by bus	by car	by taxi	by sea
by ship	by boat	by plane	by train	by telephone	by e-mail
by mail	by letter	by fax	by subway	by wire	by telegraph

例如：

▶ Hangzhou can be reached **by** train in a couple of hours from Shanghai.
從上海坐火車幾個小時就能到杭州。

表示贊成或反對

通常用來表示贊成或反對的介係詞有：for，with，against等。

1. for，with

for 和with 都表示支持或相一致，而against 則通常表示反對，但with 還可以表示「與……對立或反對……」。例如：fight/argue/quarrel/compete with。

在這種情況下，against 又與with 的意義相近，但with 後面常常接表示人的名詞，表達的是人與人之間的對抗，如在戰鬥或者比賽中，而against 則沒有這樣的限制。例如：

▶The arguments **for** and **against** the project are not just focusing on land use issues.
對於這個專案的爭論並不僅僅集中在土地使用問題上。

▶They agreed **with** Greenpeace that the best solution to vitamin A deficiency is a diverse diet.
綠色和平組織認為治療維生素A缺乏症最好的方法是均衡飲食，對此他們表示贊同。

▶Wendy, 34, told her husband she would support him in his fight **with** cancer.
34歲的溫蒂告訴丈夫，她將支持他與癌症作鬥爭。

2. against

against表示反對某人或某事，還可表示違反。例如：

▶He also advised the jury **against** reading any newspaper articles concerning the trial or listening to anyone else's views.
他還建議陪審團不要讀任何與案件有關的新聞也不要聽其他任何人對此案發表的意見。

▶In Washington, it's **against** the law to dump large loads of electronic equipment in ordinary landfills.
在華盛頓，往生活垃圾堆中傾倒大量電子設備是違法的。

表示例外、除外

介係詞except，but，except for，with the exception of，excepting，apart from，aside from等常用來表示例外或除外的意思。

1. except，but，excepting，with the exception of

以上介係詞或介係詞片語表達的都是同等事物的例外。例如：

▶The museum is open daily **except** Sunday to guided tours.
博物館只在週日不對旅行團開放。

在上例中，daily和Sunday表達的是同種類的事物，所以這些詞或片語排除的是同種類的事物中的一部分。

except和with the exception of可以互換，excepting用於比較正式的文體。例如：

▶All of the concerts last for around an hour, **with the exception of / except a** performance of Indian classical music which is programmed to go on until dawn.
所有的音樂會持續約一個小時左右，但印度古典音樂演奏例外，它將一直持續到黎明。

▶Faith had left all her jewelry, **excepting** mother's pearl ring, to Dorothea.
除了媽媽的珍珠戒指，費絲把所有的首飾都留給了多羅西婭。

只有當but前面出現all，everyone，anyone，anything，any等詞和否定詞nobody，none，nowhere以及疑問詞who，where時，but才表示例外，才能與except互換。例如：

▶ The bankers I talked to seem to be interested in anything **but/except** lending.
和我交談的銀行家看上去對什麼都感興趣，除了貸款。

2. except for，apart from，aside from

這些介係詞或介係詞片語表達的都是整體中部分的例外。例如：

▶ He won't watch much television **except for** baseball and other sports.
除了棒球和其他運動賽事，他不怎麼看電視。

在上例中，baseball，other sports和television屬於不同的類別，被排除的baseball，other sports是和television這個電視節目總稱有關的具體的節目。

apart from，aside from和except for之間可以互換，aside from多用於美式英語。例如：

▶ The oil baron and entrepreneur, **aside from** his petroleum profits, made a fortune selling an electrical device that claimed to restore graying hair to its original color.
除了石油利潤，這個石油大王及企業家還靠銷售據說能使灰白頭髮恢復本色的電器賺了不少錢。

▶ Her grandmother took no photographs at all, **apart from** her passport.
除了護照上的照片，她奶奶就沒拍過其他照片。

表示附加

besides，in addition to，as well as，apart from，aside from常常用來表示附加的意思。和上一頁表示例外的介係詞或介係詞片語互為反義詞。

besides和 in addition to可以互換。例如：

▶ Most of his songs were written there, **besides** my favorite one.
除了我最喜歡的那首，他的大多數作品也都是在那兒寫的。

▶ The school environment, **in addition to** being crowded, often feels unfamiliar to him.
學校的環境和那擁擠的感覺常常讓他覺得陌生。

當as well as 後面接名詞的時候，也可以和besides，in addition to 互換。例如：

▶ Experience can lead to cynicism **as well as / besides / in addition to** reluctance.
經驗會導致憤世嫉俗和不情願。

▶ Sports car drivers are tough **as well as** quick.
賽車手不僅反應敏捷而且頑強。

apart from，aside from比較特殊，既可表示除外又可表示附加。例如：

▶ **Apart from** being cheap and instant, a romantic text is both intimate and personal, allowing you to tailor your message rather than rely on the sentiments of a mass produced greeting card.
一個浪漫的簡訊不僅花費少、傳遞快，而且親密、個人化，能讓你選擇屬於自己風格的文本而不落入大批量生產的賀卡的俗套。

▶ In effect, **aside from** being a savior, she's also a scapegoat.
實際上，她是個救世主，也是個替罪羊。

表示讓步

in spite of，despite都表示讓步關係。例如：

▶ Her husband refused to have a child **in spite of** all her pleadings.
不管她如何苦苦哀求，丈夫還是拒絕要孩子。

▶ Rose Clare has maintained a sense of humor **despite** her deteriorating health.
儘管健康狀況不斷惡化，羅絲·克雷爾還保持著一份幽默感。

介係詞與動詞的搭配

在英語中，很多詞後面的介係詞搭配是固定的，有時相同的詞搭配不同的介係詞，意義也會產生變化。

1. 不及物動詞＋介係詞

(1) 後面常接against的不及物動詞。例如：

go	offend	insure	militate

(2) 後面常接at的不及物動詞。例如：

aim	gaze	glance	grin	laugh	look
marvel	rejoice	shout	smile	stare	wave

例如：

▶ People laugh **at** what they're too thick to understand.
對於自己弄不懂的東西人們就以嘲笑待之。

與動詞搭配的介係詞發生變化後會影響動詞片語的意義。例如：aim at（瞄準，針對），aim for（力爭），look at（注視），look for（尋找）。但有些介係詞變化對意義影響不大。例如：shout at/to（呼喊），point to/at（指向）。

(3) 後面常接for的不及物動詞。例如：

account	apply	ask	hope	pray
search	sit	wait		

例如：

▶ She called out his name and searched **for** him up and down their street and in a nearby park.
她不斷喊著他的名字，在大街和附近公園四處尋找他。

(4) 後面常接in 的不及物動詞。例如：

engage	consist	differ	indulge	participate
persist	specialize	succeed		

例如：

▶ The inmates engaged **in** violent behavior for about 30 minutes before officers persuaded them to return to their cells.
囚犯們打鬥了近半小時，直到警官把他們勸回各自的牢房。

(5) 後面常接into 的不及物動詞。例如：

burst	change	fall	grow	turn

例如：

▶ Members of the audience burst **into** applause.
觀眾中爆發出了熱烈的掌聲。

(6) 後面常接on/upon的不及物動詞。例如：

call（拜訪）	concentrate	count	depend	live	touch
insist	operate	prevail	reflect	rely	

例如：

▶He insists on the integrity of a story, based very closely on his own recollections.
他堅持故事的完整性，那是密切建立在他回憶的基礎上。

▶My son insists on sleeping in our bed and either my husband or I have to tuck in with him until he falls asleep, and then carry him back to his own bed.
兒子堅持要睡在我們的床上，我或丈夫只能為他蓋好被子，直到他睡著了才抱他回自己的床上。

(7)後面常接to的不及物動詞。例如：

adhere	amount	appeal	attribute	contribute	lead
listen	object	refer	resort	respond	stick
turn（求助）	yield				

例如：

▶The rule of law, property rights, advances in science and technology, and large increases in worker productivity all have contributed to the United States' leading edge in global markets.
美國在全球市場的領先優勢得益於其法治、財產權保障、科技的進步和生產力的巨大增長。

(8)後面常接with的不及物動詞。例如：

argue	associate	bear	begin	compete
cooperate	cope	dispense	fight	meddle
part	play	quarrel	sympathize	unite

例如：

▶I sympathize with the good people of America and share their grief and horror over these despicable terrorist attacks.
我同情善良的美國人民，對他們在卑劣的恐怖襲擊中遭受到的痛苦和恐懼，我感同身受。

2. 及物動詞＋名詞＋介係詞

不同的及物動詞與相同的介係詞搭配表達類似的意思。

(1) 及物動詞＋名詞1＋against＋名詞2，表示預防。例如：

guard	inoculate	insure	protect	safeguard	vaccinate

例如：

▶a cream to protect the skin against sunburn
一種防曬霜

(2) 及物動詞＋名詞1＋as＋名詞2，表示作為、當作。例如：

accept	consider	interpret	label	perceive
regard	respect	think	treat	view
use				

例如：

▶ Leo had **treated** Kate **as** his own daughter and her marriage to James hadn't changed that.
利奧把凱特當成自己的女兒，即使她嫁給了詹姆斯之後，這一切都沒有改變。

(3) 及物動詞＋名詞1＋from＋名詞2，表示去除。例如：

cut	detach	disconnect	drop	eliminate
exclude	exile	extract	vacate	release
remove	separate	take		

例如：

▶ The police **released** him **from** custody last Monday.
上週一員警釋放了他。

(4) 及物動詞＋名詞1＋from＋名詞2，表示保護、隱藏。例如：

conceal	guard	hide	keep	protect
shelter	shield	withhold		

例如：

▶ The company had **concealed** the incident **from** the outside world.
公司對外界隱瞞了這件事。

(5) 及物動詞＋名詞1＋from＋名詞2，表示防止。例如：

ban	discourage	disqualify	dissuade	hinder
prevent	prohibit	save	stop	keep

例如：

▶ The recent warm winters **prevented** the lakes **from** freezing, causing them to continue evaporating year-round.
近年的暖冬讓湖水難以結冰，整年都在不斷蒸發。

(6)及物動詞＋名詞1＋of＋名詞2，表示剝奪。例如：

absolve	cleanse	cure	deprive	dispossess
relieve	rob	strip	divest	

例如：

▶The severe drought hitting the Pacific Northwest will deprive California of a critical source of hydroelectricity.
太平洋沿岸西北部地區遭受的嚴重旱情會使加州失去重要的水力發電能源。

(7) 及物動詞＋名詞1＋into＋名詞2，表示變化。例如：

change	chop	convert	develop	divide
resolve	transform	translate	turn	grow

例如：

▶When we bought our apartment, we converted a bedroom into my bathroom.
我們買了公寓之後，把其中一個臥室變成了我的浴室。

(8) 及物動詞＋名詞1＋with＋名詞2，表示提供。例如：

arm	feed	fill	furnish	impress
provide	present	stuff	supply	invest

例如：

▶Quite frankly, Birmingham has provided me with a breath of fresh air.
老實說，伯明罕讓我呼吸到了新鮮的空氣。

介係詞與形容詞的搭配 ▶

◎ 後面常接about的形容詞。例如：

angry	annoyed	anxious	crazy	worried
passionate	enthusiastic	ignorant		

例如：

▶He drives the car to work and is enthusiastic about showing it to customers.
他開著車去上班，迫不及待地想讓他的客戶看看。

注意！

①有些形容詞後的介係詞變化不影響意義。例如：

▶ angry about = angry at

▶ annoyed about = annoyed at = annoyed by

▶ ignorant about = ignorant of

②有些介係詞的變化會影響整體意義。例如：

▶ annoyed about/at/by sth. 由於……而氣惱

▶ annoyed with someone 對某人感到惱怒

▶ anxious about 擔憂

▶ anxious for 渴望

後面常接at的形容詞。例如：

amazed	angry	annoyed	delighted	disappointed	good
mad	proficient	puzzled	surprised	skilled	

例如：

▶ Older parents are good at exposing their children to positive influences in media and education than younger parents might be.

相對於年輕的父母，年齡大些的父母可能更善於讓孩子受媒體和教育的積極影響。

注意！

①有些形容詞後的介係詞變化不影響意義。例如：

▶ surprised at = surprised with

②有些介係詞的變化會影響整體意義。例如：

▶ mad at 發怒

▶ mad with 著迷

後面常接for的形容詞。例如：

anxious	beneficial	eligible	famous	fit	homesick
marvelous	noted	ready	responsible	sorry	

例如：

▶ She taught Year One pupils and was **responsible for** many extra-curricular activities such as netball and football. 她教一年級的孩子，還負責很多課外活動，例如無擋板籃球和足球。

注意！

有些形容詞後的介係詞變化不影響意義。例如：
▶ beneficial for = beneficial to

🎯 後面常接from的形容詞。例如：

absent	different	exempt	free	remote
separate	inseparable			

例如：

▶ His academic subjects were **different from** mine, but we shared a classical music class taught by Professor Smith.
他和我修的專業課不一樣，但我們一起上史密斯教授的古典音樂課。

🎯 後面常接in 的形容詞。例如：

abundant	affluent	deficient	indulgent	interested
lacking	rich			

例如：

▶ If you are **interested in** developing your traditional drawing and painting skills in a digital direction, this book would be an excellent tutor.
如果你想在數位領域裡發展傳統繪畫的技能，這是本很棒的輔導書。

🎯 後面常接of的形容詞。例如：

afraid	aware	capable	confident	conscious	critical
devoid	envious	frightened	full	guilty	ignorant
independent	proud	sensible	suspicious		

例如：

▶ She was **afraid of** what he would say, and yet wished to hear it.
她既害怕聽到他要說的話，但又希望能聽到。

▶ He certainly didn't look like someone who was **afraid of** the water.
他顯然不像是個怕水的人。

🎯 後面常接on的形容詞。例如：

dependent	keen	intent		

例如：

▶ A government inquiry found that between 6,000 and 8,000 rural jobs were **dependent on** the sport.
政府調查顯示這一體育運動為鄉村地區提供了6000至8000個工作機會。

🎯 後面常接to的形容詞。例如：

agreeable	attentive	awake	averse	beneficial
essential	evident	deaf	dedicated	devoted
equal	fair	faithful	hostile	indifferent
inferior	likely	loyal	nice	obedient
susceptible	open	opposite	partial	related
sensitive	similar	superior		

例如：

▶ It's not **fair to** blame me for everything!
把一切都怪在我頭上，這不公平！

🎯 後面常接with的形容詞。例如：

content	familiar	identical	impatient	sympathetic
patient	popular			

例如：

▶ Many moviegoers may not be **familiar with** his work, but in 1967 he starred in a film alongside Elizabeth Taylor and Marlon Brando.
或許不少電影觀眾對他的作品並不熟悉，但在1967 年他和伊莉莎白・泰勒、馬龍・白蘭度一起合作出演了一部電影。

介係詞與名詞的搭配 ▷

🎯 名詞＋介係詞

1. 後面常接at的名詞。例如：

attempt	attendance	disappointment	glance	skill

例如：

▶The columnist called Holland's attempt at a multicultural society a failure.
這位專欄作家認為荷蘭試圖建立一個多元文化社會的努力是失敗的。

注意！

有些名詞後的介係詞變化不影響意義。例如：
▶disappointment at = disappointment with = disappointment over
▶skill at = skill in

2. 後面常接against的名詞。例如：

aggression	battle	campaign	defense	discrimination
fight	game	insurance	legislation	match
offence	safeguard	war	violence	

例如：

▶The lesson of three decades of war against terrorism in Northern Ireland is that simplistic military solutions alone cannot defeat it.
近三十年北愛爾蘭反恐鬥爭得出的教訓是，單單依靠軍事手段是沒用的。

3. 後面常接for的名詞。例如：

admiration	affection	appreciation	capacity	contempt
desire	dislike	disrespect	enthusiasm	hatred
love	need	passion		

例如：

▶A pop singer renowned for his enthusiasm for fast cars was banned for six months yesterday for speeding at 105mph.
一名以開飛車而著稱的流行歌手由於昨天車輛時速達到105英里而被吊扣駕照6個月。

4. 後面常接of的名詞。例如：

abundance	awareness	envy	ignorance	independence

例如：

▶Our health care system is the envy of the world, because we believe in making sure that the decisions are made by doctors and patients, not by officials in the nation's capital. 我們堅信要確保決定權掌握在醫生和病人手中，而不是國家官員手中，這便是我們的醫療制度讓其他國家羨慕不已的原因。

5. 後面常接in 的名詞。例如：

belief	confidence	decline	decrease	skill
expert	faith	fall	improvement	increase
interest	persistence	pride		

例如：

▶She is a recognized **expert in** international affairs, a distinguished teacher and academic leader, and a public servant with years of White House experience.
她是公認的國際事務專家、著名的教師和學術領導人，而且還是個擁有在白宮多年工作經驗的公務員。

有些名詞後的介係詞變化不影響意義。例如：
▶expert in = expert at

6. 後面常接to的名詞。例如：

attention	contribution	devotion	similarity	solution	objection

例如：

▶He has a strong loyalty and **devotion to** his jobs.
對於自己的工作，他有著強烈的忠誠感和奉獻精神。

7. 後面常接with的名詞。例如：

acquaintance	alliance	discussion	equality	friendship
negotiation	popularity	sympathy		

例如：

▶My **acquaintance with** languages pure and simple also began early—perhaps a key to an enthusiasm and aptitude for learning a foreign tongue.
我開始語言啟蒙教育的時間也很早——或許這就是激發我學外語的熱情、挖掘我在此方面天賦的關鍵。

注意！

同源的詞很多情況下搭配的介係詞也相同。例如：
• acquainted with／acquaintance with ／acquaint...with...
• devoted to ／devotion to／ devote...to...
但也有例外：
• equality with／ equal to

Part
12
介係詞和介係詞片語

介係詞＋名詞

　　有些名詞前面的介係詞是固定的，例如表示時間關係的介係詞：表示時間點、年齡，介係詞常用at；表示具體某天，常用on；表示一段時間，常用in。

　　在表示地點關係的介係詞中，存在於某個封閉空間，介係詞用in等；表示交通工具、媒介等常用by。

　　還有一些固定的搭配，如下表中所示：

by accident	by chance	for good	in general
in surprise	in tears	in practice	in admiration of
in association of	in a sense	on second thoughts	under suspicion
with regret	with the aid of	in haste	with care

　　例如：

▶He got into the film business by accident in the '60s, distributing foreign films and independent releases while still working as an attorney.

在60年代他偶然進入了電影業，在發行外國和獨立製作的電影的同時還兼做律師的工作。

介係詞片語的句法功能

　　介係詞和它後面所接的成分（如名詞、代名詞、動詞-ing形式等）組成介係詞片語。介係詞片語在句中主要有下列一些作用。

介係詞片語作定語

　　介係詞片語能在句中位於名詞後並修飾名詞，充當類似形容詞的作用。有些介係詞的特殊性決定了它所組成的介係詞片語常常充當定語。

1. for

　　for可以表示對某人、某物的感情，常接表示感情的名詞如admiration，affection，love等，具體請參見本章P303〈名詞＋介係詞〉。例如：

▶Even political foes express affection for his forgiving and gentle manner.

即使是政治上的反對者都欣賞他寬大和溫和的態度。

2. in

(1)表示某人的穿戴衣物等。例如：

▶Security forces in Northern Ireland are hunting a woman in black.

保安部隊正在北愛爾蘭地區尋找一個穿黑衣的婦女。

(2)表示人的大概年齡。例如：

▶ He was a man **in** his forties, straight-backed, with thinning brown hair and silver rimmed glasses.

他四十多歲，腰板挺直，有著稀疏的褐色頭髮，戴著鑲銀邊的眼鏡。

3. of

(1)表示某人某物所具有的特點或特性。例如：

▶ President Jacques Chirac visited the hospital late in the morning to offer condolences to Arafat's widow, and praise her husband as "a man **of** courage and conviction".

法國總統雅克・希拉克在上午晚些時候去醫院弔慰了阿拉法特的遺孀，並稱讚阿拉法特是一個充滿勇氣和堅定信念的人。

(2)表示人的年齡。例如：

▶ As a girl **of** 16, she was taken from her home in Russia and shipped to Germany to work in its factories.

那時她才16歲，從故鄉俄羅斯被帶到了德國，並在那裡的工廠工作。

(3)表示與某事有關的資訊或其涉及的內容。例如：

▶ "Urban depopulation leads to depleted services, empty property, a growing sense **of** abandonment, decay and population polarization, with the poorer left behind," the professor of social policy told the BBC.

社會政策學教授告訴BBC（英國廣播公司）：「城市人口的減少導致了一系列問題：服務業衰落、住宅空置、越來越強烈的被遺棄感、城市衰敗、人口兩極分化，以及貧富差距的進一步擴大。」

介係詞片語作表語

介係詞片語放於連綴動詞之後，充當主詞補語（表語），補充說明主詞意義。

1. 表示時間的介係詞片語。例如：

▶ His last patient is **at four o'clock**.

他的最後一位病人約在4點。

2. 表示地點的介係詞片語。例如：

▶ Hector was **behind the door**, as if he'd been hiding there, painfully thin, still unshaven, a stained rag over his eyes.

赫克托在門後，就好像他一直都躲在那裡一樣。他瘦得可憐，鬍子也沒刮，眼睛上蒙著塊滿是污漬的布。

3. against

(1) 表示反對。例如：

▶ They are **against** abortion rights and gay marriage, in favor of the death penalty and the war in Iraq.
他們反對墮胎權和同性結婚，支持死刑和伊拉克戰爭。

(2) 表示違反。例如：

▶ In fact, it's **against** the law in some states to leave children alone in vehicles, even for a few minutes.
實際上，在一些州，把孩子獨自留在車裡，即使是幾分鐘都是犯法的。

4. in

in表示一種狀態。如下表所示：

in anger	in a mess	in a temper	in danger	in disorder	in need
in pain	in order	in tears	in risks	in demand	

例如：

▶ Mum was **in pain** and Dad couldn't help.
媽媽陷入了痛苦，但爸爸卻無能為力。

5. under

(1) 表示受某人或某事的影響。例如：

under arrest	under consideration	under control
under examination	under investigation	under pressure

例如：

▶ The fire was **under control** about half an hour later, but little was left of the house.
半小時後火勢才得到控制，但房子幾乎被燒光了。

(2) 表示數量或年齡低於……。例如：

▶ And children **under 16** may not be tattooed or pierced without a doctor's permission.
沒有醫生的允許，16歲以下的孩子不得紋身或穿耳洞。

介係詞片語作受詞補語

介係詞片語常常與一些及物動詞搭配充當受詞補語，補充説明受詞的成分。含有受詞補語的基本句型為：主詞＋動詞＋受詞＋受詞補語（SVOC）。

1. consider

▶ She considers Darwinian evolution as an atheistic theory.
她把達爾文的進化論看成是無神論的學説。

2. find

▶ In 1996, Oprah Winfrey found herself in legal trouble with Texas cattlemen because of her on-air statements about mad cow disease.
1996年，歐普拉‧溫芙蕾發現自己在電視上發表的有關狂牛症的言論使自己惹上了與德克薩斯養牛人的官司。

3.leave

▶ His neighbors thanked him and left him in peace to comfort his dying horse.
他的鄰居們謝過他之後，就留他一個人安慰他垂死的馬。

4. keep

▶ Since the injury kept her from gymnastics temporarily, she used the time to work on something else—like earning her driver's license.
由於受傷使她暫時無法進行體操訓練，她就把時間花在其他事情上——例如考駕照。

5. put

▶ Doctors put him on psychiatric medications, and he seemed to get better.
醫生對他進行精神藥物治療之後，他看上去好多了。

6. think

▶ And only 34 percent thought the President in touch with ordinary people, down from 42 percent.
原先有42％的人認為總統平易近人，但現在這個比率已經降到了34％。

介係詞片語作狀語

狀語是修飾動詞、形容詞、副詞以及子句的句子成分，介係詞片語充當的狀語主要有修飾性狀語和連線性狀語。

1. 介係詞片語作修飾性狀語

修飾性狀語是我們最常見的一類狀語，也是種類最多的一類狀語，介係詞片語可充當時間狀語、地點狀語、原因狀語、讓步狀語、方式狀語等。

(1)時間狀語

表示時間的介係詞片語可充當時間狀語。例如：

▶ **On Saturday morning**, Joanna jogged along the street, pausing for a rest near the ice-cream shop.

週六的早晨，喬安娜沿著大街慢跑，在冰淇淋店附近休息了一會兒。

(2)地點狀語

表示地點的介係詞片語可充當地點狀語。例如：

▶ Turn left **at the traffic lights**, and you'll see the hospital straight ahead.

在紅綠燈處左轉，往前直行你就看到醫院了。

(3)原因狀語

表示原因的介係詞所引導的片語可充當原因狀語。例如：

because of	for	for fear of	for reasons of	owing to
out of	on account of			

例如：

▶ **Because of** feelings of isolation, many teens succumb to depression, early sexual activity and drug use.

孤獨感導致很多十多歲的少年憂鬱、過早地發生性行為甚至吸毒。

(4)讓步狀語

表示讓步的介係詞所引導的片語可充當讓步狀語，例如in spite of，despite，for all等。

▶ I don't envy her much, **in spite of** her money, for after all, rich people have about as many worries as poor ones.

我並不很嫉妒她，不管她多有錢，畢竟富人擁有的煩惱並不比窮人少。

(5)方式狀語

　　表示方式的介係詞所引導的片語可充當方式狀語，例如in...way，in...manner等。例如：

▶My goal is to teach an important life lesson in a non-preachy, fun way that kids can relate to.
我的目標是用一種非說教的、有趣的、孩子可以理解的方式去教授他們重要的人生道理。

2. 介係詞片語作連線性狀語

　　連線性狀語主要用來連接句子。可充當連線性狀語的介係詞片語如下：

at any rate	at this rate	by any means	by no means
in any case	in that case	on the contrary	under no circumstances

　　例如：

▶Jones, in any case, is far off her best fitness and under a cloud from the drug scandal.
不管怎樣，籠罩在興奮劑醜聞陰影下的瓊斯已經沒有了最好的狀態。

小結

　　本章主要介紹了介係詞類別、語義和在句子中的功能。介係詞主要分為簡單介係詞、複雜介係詞和邊緣介係詞。介係詞主要體現的是空間和時間上的意義，還能表示因果、輔助等關係。

　　介係詞和其他詞類的搭配也是本章的重點之一，英語中很多介係詞和其他詞的搭配有時是固定的，表達的意義也是特定的。介係詞和它後面所接成分組成的介係詞片語，在句子中能充當定語、狀語、表語等。

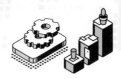

連接詞

連接詞概說 ▷

連接詞屬於封閉性詞類，不能獨立擔任任何句子成分。它具有連接不同的句子成分的功能，可以連接單字、片語、子句或句子，並在它們之間建立起意義之間的關聯。這一章我們就連接詞的分類、功能和意義，以及連接詞在句子中所起的作用對連接詞作整體的描述。

連接詞的種類 ▷

英語中連接詞按照它們在句中的作用主要分為兩類：對等連接詞和從屬連接詞。

◎ 對等連接詞

並列是指分句、片語或單字相互連接的一種方式。如果一個連接詞連接的是兩個分句、片語或單字，這兩個部分的功能相同，這兩個同等重要的部分就構成了並列。

我們把這種起連接作用的連接詞稱之為對等連接詞。對等連接詞連接的句子就是並列句。主要的對等連接詞有：and，or，but，nor 等。and，or，but可連接並列的子句、片語或單字。例如：

▶ Everybody worked 60 hours a week and nobody had a nickel.
每人每週工作60小時，但是沒有人掙到一分錢。

▶ He has now won 14 of his last 15 matches, and nobody can accuse him of not trying in this season.
他在最近的15場比賽裡贏了14場，沒有人能指責他在這個賽季沒有盡力。

▶ Ultraviolet radiation doesn't disappear on cloudy days or in winter.
多雲天氣或冬天並非沒有紫外線。

▶ The results were official but not final.
結果是正式的但不是最終的。

如存在兩項以上的並列時，連接詞用在最後的兩項之間。例如：

▶ Because caffeine can make the heart work harder, doctors recommend that people with heart or circulation problems avoid drinking coffee, coke or tea.
咖啡因會加重心臟的負擔，因此，醫生建議有心臟病和血液循環疾病的人不要喝咖啡、可樂或是茶。

▶ He's not my cousin, he doesn't love me and he's not going to marry me.
他不是我的表哥，他不愛我而且也不打算和我結婚。

相關連接詞（Correlative Conjunction），是指由兩個片語組成，並被一個或多個其他的詞分隔開的連接詞。常用的相關連接詞有both...and，not only...but also，either...or，not...but，neither...nor 等。

相關連接詞與對等連接詞一樣連接語法上同等性質的詞或片語。例如：

▶ Both girls' and boys' voices become deeper during puberty.
男孩和女孩的聲音在青春期都會變得低沉。

▶ Both young and old are embracing the Internet.
老老少少都歡迎網際網路時代的到來。

▶ The children were not only beautiful in their fine clothes but were also very sweet in their behavior.
孩子們不僅穿得漂亮而且舉止十分乖巧。

▶ After years in the West, many returnees bring back not only academic expertise but also a wealth of business experience.
在西方居住多年的歸國人士不僅帶回了學術專長，而且帶回了豐富的從商經驗。

▶ It isn't that Sam doesn't like Tania but Tania and I gang up on him.
不是薩姆不喜歡塔妮婭，而是塔妮婭和我聯合起來對付他。

▶ He bought a CD-RW drive, which doesn't have DVD support but does a great job of reading and writing audio CDs.
他買了個CD燒錄機，這個燒錄機不支持DVD，但是其讀取和寫入CD的功能很好。

從屬連接詞

如果一個連接詞連接一個主要子句和一個從屬子句，起這種連接作用的連接詞被稱為從屬連接詞。這時從屬連接詞連接的子句依附於主句，即構成複合句。從屬連接詞連接的子句主要有名詞性子句和副詞子句。

具體而言，引導名詞性子句的連接詞主要指引導主詞子句、受詞子句、表語子句和同位語子句的連接詞。引導副詞子句的連接詞主要指引導時間副詞子句、原因副詞子句、地點副詞子句、結果副詞子句、條件副詞子句、目的副詞子句、讓步副詞子句、方式副詞子句和比較副詞子句的連接詞。

1. 從屬連接詞連接名詞性子句。例如：

▶ **That** she was a candidate for a job at Shell headquarters is no surprise, if you look at her resume.
如果你看了她的簡歷，就不會因她曾在殼牌總部應聘工作而感到驚奇。

▶ Tony was teaching Maureen to drive and Anne asked **if** he would teach her too.
托尼正在教莫琳開車，安妮問他是否願意也教教她。

▶ He wondered **whether** she had taken a lover during the last five years.
他想知道她在過去的五年裡是否有愛人。

2. 從屬連接詞連接副詞子句。例如：

▶ He ran, **when** everybody ran, to see what happened.
當所有人都跑的時候，他也跟著大家跑了起來，去看發生了什麼。

▶ We don't need to replant that grass **because** we're going to dig it up again soon.
我們不需要重新種植那片草地，因為我們打算不久後再翻耕一下。

▶ It's only fair to give us permanent residence **because** we work hard and don't receive any benefits. 我們工作勤奮，卻沒有享受到任何福利，因此只有我們獲得永久居住權才算公平。

▶ Matilda stays **where** she is and it is up to you to see that she behaves herself.
瑪蒂爾達在原處沒動，你該讓她規矩點。

▶ You can drink this cocktail with William, **as long as** you don't tell him it came from me.
只要你不告訴威廉這雞尾酒是我的，你可以和他喝一杯。

▶ I make sure she has everything, **even if** I don't have anything.
我會保證她應有盡有，即使我一無所有。

▶ I don't want my private life touched, **even if** I'm a public personality.
即使我是個公眾人物，我也不希望我的私生活被打擾。

　　用對等連接詞或從屬連接詞或同時使用對等連接詞和從屬連接詞可以將兩個或更多的子句連成一個句子。並列子句和子句並存構成的新句子叫並列複合句。例如：

▶ I was satisfied to work with these guys **and** they were satisfied **that** I could continue my training. 和這些小夥子一起工作，我感到心滿意足，而且，他們也很高興能繼續接受我的培訓。

　　上述例句裡and是對等連接詞，它將兩個並列句連接起來。that為從屬連接詞，連接後一個並列句中的從屬子句。

　　主要的從屬連接詞有：after，when，before，as，while，since，until，till，although，though，if，even if，unless，lest，because，than，that，whether，so that，as soon as，as long as，in order that，as if，as though，suppose (that)，provided (that)，in case (that)，now that，seeing that，so ... that，such ... that，as...as，so...as等。

連接詞在語篇中的功能 ▷

連接詞的功能在於把句子或語篇中的思想連接在一起。對等連接詞可以表達同等關係、選擇關係和轉折關係。

對等連接詞and表達意義上的連接、增加或列舉。例如：

▶He is the victim here **and** he deserves criminal injuries compensation.
在這裡他是受害者，他應該得到刑事傷害的賠償金。

相關連接詞both...and 連接兩個分句時，強調兩個都是真實的或可能的事實。例如：

▶You know **both** where he'll be **and** what he is going to do.
你知道他要去哪裡，也知道他要做什麼。

▶Charismatic and articulate, Johnson was **both** famous **and** infamous at the dawn of the 20th century. 詹森魅力超群，能說會道，是20世紀初既鼎鼎大名又臭名昭著的人物。

對等連接詞or 則表達意義上的選擇關係，此外還有其強調形式or else。例如：

▶He bought the goods at car boot sales **or** they were gifts from friends.
這些東西要嘛是他在舊貨攤上買的，要嘛是他從朋友那裡得來的禮物。

▶His body language told her nothing, **or else** it was simply a message she couldn't decipher.
他的肢體語言沒有向她傳達任何資訊，又或許他表達了某種資訊，但她未能理解。

相關連接詞either...or 連接的則是兩種選擇。例如：

▶We **either** have to give the proposal to them **or** they have to understand it.
在這件事上，要嘛我們向他們提出建議，要嘛就讓他們自己去理解。

▶They'll **either** get you, **or** they won't.
他們要嘛能理解你，要嘛不能。

對等連接詞but表示轉折關係，引導的是意外的事。例如：

▶Potter is bitter about losing his job, **but** he feels no shame.
丟了工作，波特覺得不滿，但是他並不感到羞愧。

▶Ben's a fine man, **but** he does talk so much.
班是個好人，但是他的話太多了。

相關連接詞not...but強調兩個相關的事實，特別是強調第二個事實。例如：

▶He was **not** exactly reserved, **but** he was uncomfortable being open or emotional.
他並不是完全內向的人，但是當表現出外向或是情緒化的一面時，他會感覺不自在。

▶He was **not** pure evil, **but** he was a nasty character.
他不是個十惡不赦的壞人，但卻是個令人生厭的人。

用相關連接詞neither...nor 連接的則是兩個被否定的部分。例如：

▶**Neither** has she been able to stop writing about the South Africa, **nor** will she do so.
她一直未能停止過關於南非這一話題的創作，以後也不會停止。

從屬連接詞主要引導名詞性子句和副詞子句，引導副詞子句的連接詞可以表示副詞子句的各種含義：時間、原因、地點、結果、條件、目的、讓步、方式和比較等。

從屬連接詞引導名詞性子句

1. 從屬連接詞引導主詞子句。例如：

▶**Whether** those companies were invited to the events is unknown.
那些公司是否曾被邀請出席這些活動尚不得知。

2. 從屬連接詞引導受詞子句。例如：

▶Do you happen to know **if** she left a will?
你知不知道她是否留有遺囑？

▶I don't know **if** she has been in contact with her older sister.
我不知道她是否一直和她姐姐保持聯繫。

3. 從屬連接詞引導形容詞子句。例如：

▶The problem is **that** any doctor can call himself a plastic or cosmetic surgeon.
問題在於任何一名醫生都能管自己叫整形外科醫生或美容外科醫生。

▶The fact is **that** I have little aptitude for reflection.
事實是我一點也不善於思考。

4. 從屬連接詞引導同位語子句。例如：

▶The news **that** they had married caused widespread astonishment in literary circles.
他們結婚的消息使文學界上上下下一片震驚。

從屬連接詞引導副詞子句

1. 從屬連接詞引導時間副詞子句。例如：

▶She smiled at her father **while** they talked.
談話時她一直對父親微笑著。

2. 從屬連接詞引導原因副詞子句。例如：

▶We don't have a stable food tradition, **since** we've had so many different groups.
因為我們一直擁有眾多不同的群體，所以在吃的方面我們沒有固定的習慣。

3. 從屬連接詞引導地點副詞子句。例如：

▶**Wherever** people feel deserted by their governments, they are vulnerable to darker, crankier, more dangerous currents.
無論在哪裡，只要人們覺得被政府拋棄了，便容易受更陰暗、更古怪也更危險的思潮影響。

4. 從屬連接詞引導結果副詞子句。例如：

▶Molly was just **so** determined **that** she wasn't going to accept the fate that had been decreed to her and no institution was going to defeat her.
莫莉是如此意志堅決，她拒絕接受命運的裁決，而且沒有什麼機構會將她打敗。

5. 從屬連接詞引導條件副詞子句。例如：

▶I can't make people believe you **unless** we have some kind of evidence.
除非我們有某些證據，否則我無法讓人們相信你。

6. 從屬連接詞引導目的副詞子句。例如：

▶We must demand investment in training, in education, **in order that** we can provide those quality services for our customers.
我們必須強烈要求在員工培訓和教育方面投入資金，以便能為客戶提供那些品質上乘的服務。

7. 從屬連接詞引導讓步副詞子句。例如：

▶**Although** she has so many male fans, she insists she will never court publicity.
儘管她的男粉絲很多，但她堅稱自己永遠不會刻意追求知名度。

8. 從屬連接詞引導比較副詞子句。例如：

▶ The pounding stopped **as** suddenly **as** it had started.
砰砰的撞擊聲就像剛才突然響起一樣，突然就停了。

注意！

其實，除了連接詞以外，還有很多其他的詞也可以起連接詞的作用，來幫助連接句子的上下文。

某些副詞，比如anyway，anyhow，consequently，therefore，besides，moreover，also，too，still，then，thus，yet，hence，nevertheless等，都有類似的作用。這些起連接作用的副詞稱為連接副詞，也可以稱這些起連接作用的副詞為連線性狀語。如：

▶ Appealing as they sound, **though**, both candidates' plans have drawn criticism.
儘管兩個候選人的計畫聽上去都很吸引人，但也都招來了批評。

▶ We see the meeting as a critical time and potentially a turning point in the oil crisis. **And therefore,** we do think that this is also a very important meeting.
我們將這次會議視為石油危機中的關鍵時刻和潛在轉捩點。因此，我們確信這也是個極為重要的會議。

▶ Some years ago, studies showed that people who used "sun blocks" were more likely to develop malignant melanomas than those who didn't use them but stayed in the sun only for short periods. **Consequently,** the sale of lotions containing SPF30 and over was banned.
幾年前，研究表明，比起沒有塗防曬乳而只在太陽下待一小會的人，塗了防曬霜的人更容易長惡性黑色素瘤。因此SPF值大於等於30的防曬乳已被禁止出售。

▶ These three top managers have demonstrated the same behavior over time and had employee morale issues. **And moreover,** their behaviors are putting the company at risk.
這三個最高級別的經理做事老是千篇一律，使職員幹勁低落。更有甚者，他們的行為正在將公司推進危險的境地。

同樣，有些片語，例如：the result is，that is why，on the other hand，for that reason，in this way等，也有這些功能。例如：

▶ I'm really not wedded to his solution strongly, **but on the other hand,** I'm wondering about the alternative.
我對他的解決方法真的不是很贊同，而另一方面，我一直在想是否還有別的方法。

▶ In China, people are living longer and **the result is** a population that is on average getting older.
在中國，人們越來越長壽，結果是導致平均人口高齡化。

小結 ▷

　　從分類來看，連接詞主要有對等連接詞和從屬連接詞兩類；從功能作用來看，連接詞起連接的作用，連接句子上下文；在連接語篇時，連接詞的意義亦幫助語篇意義的構建。但如上所述，有些文法學家將起連接作用的一些副詞也歸類為連接詞，因為從語篇功能看，它們都起連接上下文的作用，對語篇意義的表達具有相當重要的意義。

狀語

狀語概說 ▷

　　狀語是修飾動詞、形容詞、副詞、介係詞片語以及子句的句子成分,可由副詞、介係詞片語、形容詞、分詞或子句擔任。按照狀語的語義功能,可分為修飾性狀語、評注性狀語和連線性狀語。

修飾性狀語 ▷

　　修飾性狀語對句中的行為或狀態進行描述,常對類似「何時(when)」、「何地(where)」、「多少(how much)」、「為何(why)」等問題進行回答,它起著與句子的其他成分相似的重要作用。修飾性狀語種類較多,一般可分為時間、地點、方式、原因、結果、目的、讓步、條件、程度等狀語。

◎ 時間修飾性狀語

　　時間修飾性狀語可以用介係詞片語或名詞片語來表示,主要表示下列四種語義關係:

　　1. 時間點。例如:

▶ He's scheduled to return to Washington tomorrow morning.
他打算明天一早就回華盛頓。

　　2. 時間持續。例如:

▶ Over the past several years, most of the top underclassmen have left school early to enter the NBA.
在過去的幾年裡,多數拔尖的大學低年級學生為了參加NBA而過早地離開了學校。

　　3. 頻率。例如:

▶ Most of our urban parents work every single day, sometimes one and two and three jobs.
大多數城市裡的家長每天都要工作,有時還要兼職一份甚至兩三份工作。

4. 時間先後關係。

表明兩個事件發生的先後順序，如before，after引導的片語或子句。例如：

▶ He will be staying in the capital only a few days before leaving on a series of visits to neighboring countries.
他僅會在首都待上幾天，之後將會開始對周邊國家的一系列訪問。

地點修飾性狀語

地點修飾性狀語多用介係詞片語、名詞片語等表示，主要表示下列三種語義關係：

1. 距離

表示距離關係的修飾性狀語回答了類似「多遠（how far）」的問題，有兩種表達方式，大概的（General）和確切的（Specific）。例如：

▶ We've come a long way in a very short period of time.
在短短的時間內，我們就走了很長一段路。

▶ Johnny had walked ten miles out to the airport every day for a week to help unload the planes of their cargo of syringes and drugs.
整整一個星期內，強尼每天都要走10英里路到機場，幫助卸載飛機上的注射器和藥物。

2. 方向

表示方向關係的修飾性狀語包括方向（Orientation）、來源（Origin）和目標（Destination）。例如：

▶ After a while he went downstairs and inspected the front door.
過了一會兒，他下樓去檢查了前門。

▶ I only arrived from London a minute ago.
我從倫敦來，一分鐘前才到。

▶ They moved to a house in the same quiet village, and were just as happy.
他們搬進了同一個安靜村莊裡的一幢屋子，和以前一樣快樂。

3. 位置。例如：

▶ As a child, Pern helped his mother in the kitchen.
還是個孩子的時候，佩恩就在廚房幫媽媽的忙了。

① 當時間和地點修飾性狀語同時使用時，地點狀語通常放在時間狀語前。例如：

▶He has been there for seven years, forging a close, amicable and fruitful relationship with the neighbors.

他在那裡已經住了7年，其間和鄰居們建立了親密、友好和卓有成效的鄰里關係。

② 當兩個或兩個以上時間狀語同時使用時，按照從小到大的順序排列。例如：

▶We go to bed at one o'clock in the morning.

我們凌晨一點上床睡覺。

③ 當兩個或兩個以上地點狀語同時使用時，也按照從小到大的順序排列。例如：

▶Taylor, with a tankard of something to drink, was sitting on the high sofa in the billiard-room, and Oscar was talking to Victor by the door in the far corner.

泰勒正拿著一杯喝的坐在撞球室的高沙發上，而奧斯卡正在遠處的角落靠著門，和維克托聊著天。

◎ 方式修飾性狀語

方式修飾性狀語可由副詞、介係詞片語、名詞片語或子句表示，並可細分為下列四種語義關係：

1. 方式

這類狀語說明的是事情完成的方式，可由副詞或片語構成。例如：片語in a/an + adj. + manner/way/style，以及副詞carelessly，obviously，thoroughly 等。例如：

▶French players like to be bossed in a schoolmasterly manner.

法國球員喜歡學校式的管理方式。

▶Do you seek professional help for your child in a timely manner, if needed?

如果有需要，你是否會為自己的孩子及時尋求專業的幫助？

另外，比較狀語（Comparison Adverbials）也被認為是方式修飾性狀語的一類。在此類狀語中，常由as，like引導的介係詞片語組成。例如：

▶She behaved like an obedient child, loud meaning bad, soft meaning playful.

她表現得像一個乖孩子，對她來說，大聲叫喊是不好的，柔聲細語意味著開玩笑。

2. 手段

這類狀語介紹的是完成某個行為所借助的手段，多為介係詞by引導的片語。例如：

▶ He arrived in Florida **by sea** in 1985, his wife three years later.
1985年，他坐船到了佛羅里達，三年後他妻子也去了那裡。

3. 工具

此類狀語多為介係詞with引導的片語。例如：

▶ Celia corrected the mistakes **with a pen**.
西莉亞用筆把錯誤改正了。

4. 施動

在被動語態中出現的動作的實施者多為介係詞by引導的片語。例如：

▶ Monaghan was crushed **by** his father's death.
父親的離世把莫納漢給擊垮了。

原因修飾性狀語

原因修飾性狀語多由because of，on account of，for，for fear of，for reasons of 等引導的介係詞片語或其他子句組成。例如：

▶ Sometimes, I was not able to do so **because of** the deterioration of the security situation.
有時，因為安全局勢日益惡化，我就不能這麼做。

▶ Today's economy is vulnerable **because of** the current-account deficit.
經常帳戶赤字使得現在的經濟脆弱不堪。

▶ I accept the responsibility **because** I am an older player working alongside a lot of youngsters.
在一大群年輕隊員中，我算是年長的，所以我來承擔這個重任。

目的修飾性狀語

目的修飾性狀語多由不定詞片語及for，for the purpose of等引導的介係詞片語或子句組成。例如：

▶ The business development committee exists **for the purpose of** helping to open channels for investment.
企業發展委員會存在的目的是為了幫助開拓投資管道。

▶ They face a continuing battle **to** protect their servers from hackers.
他們面臨著一場持久戰，去保護他們的伺服器不受駭客攻擊。

⊙ 結果修飾性狀語

結果修飾性狀語多由不定詞片語或子句組成。片語有only to...這樣的結構，子句有so...that...這樣的結構。例如：

▶ I came into the office one morning, **only to** find that there had been a burglary.
一天早上，我走進辦公室，卻發現那兒被洗劫了。

▶ Her face has become **so** well-known **that** preventing her being recognized will be a major concern.
她的那張面孔那麼有名，所以如何讓她不被認出來是最主要的。

⊙ 條件修飾性狀語

條件修飾性狀語多由if，unless，provided (that)，but for，so/as long as，on condition that，supposing 等引導的子句組成，表示某種假設條件下可能發生的事情。例如：

▶ "**If** we had just targeted traditional voters, we would have missed an entire generation of voters," he said.
他說道：「如果當初我們只顧那些老選民，那我們早就已經喪失了整整一代的選民。」

▶ Young kids can learn a lot, **provided that** the teachers do not try to teach all children the same topics at the same time but build on individual activities and personal involvement for each child.
教師不是在同一時間向所有孩子傳授相同的內容，而是讓每個孩子都參與適合自己的活動，只有這樣，孩子們才可以學到很多東西。

⊙ 讓步修飾性狀語

讓步修飾性狀語可以由in spite of，despite引導的片語組成，也可以由although，though，as，even if/though，whether...or，no matter + 疑問詞或疑問詞 + -ever等引導的子句組成，表示雖然、儘管、即使等概念。例如：

▶ **Despite** troubles in overseas markets, the revenues in international markets for her company were also much stronger.
雖然海外市場困難重重，但是那裡獲得的收益對她的公司來說還是更可觀。

▶ **Although** I'm a retired person, today I have a beautiful outlook on life.
儘管我已經退休，但現如今我還是對人生抱有美好的憧憬。

▶ "**Whatever** Karen asks me to do, I do it," says Dan Graham.
丹·格雷厄姆說：「無論卡倫讓我做什麼，我都會去做的。」

注意！

① 在由though，as引導的讓步副詞子句中，表語或狀語通常會移至子句的句首構成倒裝。例如：

▶ She wanted to know, painful **though** it was.
即使真相讓人痛苦，她還是想知道。

其中painful though it was = though it was painful.

② although，though不能與but同時使用，但可以和yet，still等詞連用。例如：

▶ **Although** I am retiring from Congress, I **still** look forward to working within our community to make it stronger and an even better place to live and work.
雖然我要從國會退休了，但我還是希望能繼續在社區工作，讓它越來越強大，將它變成大家工作和生活的更理想之地。

程度修飾性狀語

程度修飾性狀語多由副詞very，hardly，enough，slightly等、片語a little bit, very much，to what extent，to some degree/to a certain degree等、子句to such an extent that/to the extent that...等組成，說明主句中動作或行為發生的程度，回答諸如「多少（how much/many）」、「到達什麼程度（to what extent）」等問題。例如：

▶ I think he's **a little bit** envious because I took those meadows back.
我把牧場給拿回來了，我想他還是有些嫉妒的。

▶ **To what extent** do you use the net for shopping?
你對網購的熱衷程度如何？

伴隨修飾性狀語

伴隨修飾性狀語多由片語和獨立主格構成，表示伴隨著主句的動作。例如：

▶ He went out, **gun in hand**.
他拿著槍走了出去。

▶ She was sitting at her desk, **a book on the desk**.
她坐在書桌邊，桌上還放著一本書。

比較修飾性狀語

比較修飾性狀語多由比較副詞子句構成，常用的有than，as...as等結構。例如：

▶ Matt's old, in some ways much older **than** his 34 years.
馬特老了，而且從某種程度上說，他比自己的實際年齡34歲還要老很多。

評注性狀語 ▷

如果說修飾性狀語起著和句子的主詞、賓語等其他成分相似的作用,那評注性狀語和整個句子的關係更緊密,有時甚至有統領全句的作用,表示說話者或作者對陳述內容的看法或評價。它們常由副詞、介係詞片語或子句充當,可位於句首、句中、句末,有時也用逗號與句子其他部分分開。

評注性狀語可細分為內容評注性狀語(Content Disjuncts)、語體評注性狀語(Style Disjuncts)和態度評注性狀語(Attitude Disjuncts)。

◎ 內容評注性狀語

說話者或作者對其所表述的內容的真實性、可靠性和局限性等作出的評判稱為內容評注性狀語。

1. 表示某種程度上的懷疑

常用的副詞或片語如下:

arguably	apparently	conceivably	I guess	likely	maybe
most likely	perhaps	possibly	quite likely	supposedly	very likely

例如:

▶ **Probably** the best book on English translations of the Bible is sadly out of print, but well worth seeking out in libraries and secondhand bookshops.
可惜的是,也許算是最好的聖經英譯本已經停印了,但它還是值得人們去圖書館和二手書店碰碰運氣。

▶ **Maybe** Janice went to a different school.
或許珍妮絲上的是另外一個學校。

2. 表示肯定

常用的副詞如下:

certainly	definitely	incontestably	indeed	no doubt	of course
surely	unarguably	undeniably	undoubtedly	unquestionably	

例如:

▶ I think parents should **definitely** spend more time on the road with their teenage drivers because the kids don't seem to want to adhere to the rules.
我認為,如果十幾歲的孩子開車,父母絕對有必要在路上多陪陪他們,因為這些孩子好像沒有遵守交通規則的意識。

▶ Somehow, **no doubt**, wars will continue to be fought, and furtive cruelties will carry on in darker corners.
毫無疑問,戰爭還將繼續,在更黑暗的角落,殘酷的事件還會悄然發生。

3. 表示真實性

常用的副詞或片語如下：

actually	factually	for a fact	in (actual) fact	really	truly

例如：

▶ Firm management actually motivates creative thinking.
事實上，嚴格的管理才能激發創造性的思維。

▶ In fact, whole milk is only four percent fat and semi-skimmed two percent fat.
實際上，全脂牛奶的含脂量也只有4％，而半脫脂牛奶是2％。

4. 表示資訊的來源

常用的副詞或片語如下：

according to...	clearly	evidently	manifestly	obviously
patently	plainly	reportedly	reputedly	

例如：

▶ According to Standard & Poor's, U.S. companies bought back $178 billion in stock this year through October, 52 percent more than last year.
根據標準普爾的研究，截至今年10月份為止，美國公司從股市中買回1780億美元，比去年增加了52％。

▶ Clearly, luxury means different things to different people.
很明顯，奢華對不同人意味著不同的東西。

5. 表示某種局限性

常用的副詞或片語如下：

generally	in general	in most cases	largely	mainly	typically

例如：

▶ In general, a driver's license would be issued to those citizens and permanent legal residents who could show proof of residency and had a Social Security number.
一般來說，只有那些能夠證明其住所並提供社會保障號碼的市民和合法的永久居民才能獲得駕駛執照。

▶ In most cases, hypertension is chronic, which means you will always need to be checked to make sure it's under control.
大多數情況下，高血壓是慢性的，病人需要經常檢查，以確保病情得到控制。

6. 表示某人的觀點

常用的片語如下：

from one's perspective	in one's opinion	in one's view

例如：

▶ In my opinion, the finest wines are those from France.
我認為，最好的葡萄酒是法國產的。

態度評注性狀語

說話者或作者對其所表述的內容表現出的某種態度或作出的一種評估稱為態度評注性狀語。

1. 表示意料之中或意料之外

常用的副詞或片語如下：

amazingly	as might be expected	astonishingly	inevitably
incredibly	naturally	not surprisingly	predictably
remarkably	to one's (great) surprise	understandably	unexpectedly

例如：

▶ Astonishingly, Sarah—a former girlfriend of Prince Charles—turned to Diana and said: "This could all have been happening to me."
讓人驚訝的是，查理斯王子的前女友莎拉竟然跟戴安娜說：「這一切本來完全可能發生在我身上。」

▶ To my surprise, he invited me to give a poetry reading in Madrid.
讓我驚訝的是，他竟然邀請我去馬德里舉辦詩歌朗誦會。

2. 表示滿意與否

常用的副詞或片語如下：

agreeably	annoyingly	cheerfully	delightfully	disappointingly
disturbingly	irritatingly	pleasingly	regrettably	to one's regret

例如：

▶ Annoyingly, I'm not particularly good at sport.
讓我鬱悶的是，體育不是我的專長。

▶ To his regret, he never mastered the violin.
讓他遺憾的是，他從未精通過小提琴。

3. 表示其他的一些評價

常用的副詞或片語如下：

amusingly	conveniently	even more important	even worse	fortunately
importantly	justly	happily	hopefully	luckily
most important of all	reasonably	rightly	sadly	sensibly
significantly	thankfully	to be sure	unfortunately	unhappily
unluckily	unreasonably	what's more important	wisely	with justice
wrongly				

例如：

▶**Fortunately**, there are ways to make long journeys less of a chore.
萬幸的是，已經有辦法讓漫長的旅途不再那麼乏味。

▶**Hopefully** this story will show other girls how dangerous the sun can be.
這個故事有望讓別的女孩子們知道，太陽是多麼地可怕。

🎯 語體評注性狀語

說話者或作者對其資訊傳達的方式進行的評論稱為語體評注性狀語。常用的副詞或片語如下：

briefly	broadly	confidentially	figuratively	frankly
honestly	generally	in a word	in short	personally
putting it bluntly	seriously	simply	strictly	technically speaking
truly	truthfully			

也常在一些副詞後面加上speaking，最常見的有：frankly speaking，generally speaking，personally speaking等。例如：

▶**Honestly**, I haven't watched Miss America since last year.
坦白說，從去年開始我就不看美國小姐選美了。

▶"**Personally**, I've been fishing longline for 20 years and I've never seen a whale on a hook," he said.
「就我本人而言，我已經釣了20年的延繩釣了，但還從沒見過一條鯨魚上鉤呢。」他說道。

連線性狀語 ▷

連線性狀語體現了說話者或作者對話語之間的關係，起到了連接句子的作用。連線性狀語主要由副詞、介係詞片語構成。（參見P256〈副詞〉和P312〈連接詞〉）

1. 表示列舉

常用的副詞或片語如下：

first(ly)	second(ly)	third(ly)	first of all
for a start	for one thing... for another (thing)	in the first place	in the second place
finally	to begin/start with	last(ly)	on the one hand... on the other hand
next	then		

例如：

▶ Firstly, the machine doesn't detect all cancers and, secondly, when it does detect cancer, it cannot predict how that cancer will behave.
首先，機器無法識別所有的癌症；其次，即使是識別了，它也無法預測癌症將如何發作。

▶ I tried being nice, but that made him target me more. Finally, my friend reminded me that people hate to be ignored.
我嘗試著對他友善，但這讓他變得更加針對我了。最後，我的朋友提醒我說，人們討厭被忽視的感覺。

2. 表示增加

常用的副詞或片語如下：

above all	also	besides	by the same token
correspondingly	equally	further(more)	in addition
in particular	in the same way	likewise	moreover
similarly	then	what's more	

例如：

▶ There are countless organizations in existence, furthermore, to prod our indignation, to bring to our attention some outrage that calls for immediate redress.
另外，還有不計其數的團體，它們會激起我們的憤慨，讓我們去關注那些需要緊急化解的怨恨情緒。

▶ He was a Cambridge man, with a degree, what's more, in Moral Sciences.
他畢業於劍橋，而且學的是道德科學。

3. 表示總結

常用的副詞或片語如下：

altogether	(all) in all	in a word	in conclusion
in sum	overall	then	thus
to conclude	to sum up	to summarize	

例如：

▶ **All in all**, he expects 2003 will be a pretty good year for investors within the context of the aftermath of a bear market.

總之，他希望經歷了熊市（股市行情下跌）之後，2003年將成為投資者的豐收之年。

▶ **In conclusion**, the Russian industry was full of potential, but yet, due to the distribution of wealth, there was not the vital spark to set it off.

總之，俄羅斯工業極富潛力，但是由於財力分配的限制，還沒有足夠的能力去激發這些潛力。

4. 表示同位關係

表示位於狀語後的部分是對前者的解釋或者包含在前者中。常用的副詞或片語如下：

for example(e.g.)	for instance	in other words	namely
specifically	that is(i.e.)	that is to say	

例如：

▶ Mr. Ressam, **for example**, panicked when he was stopped at the US-Canadian border and tried to run away.

拿雷薩姆先生來説，當他在美加邊境被攔住的時候，他害怕極了，還企圖逃走。

▶ What draws him to Internet stocks is their high margins—**that is**, the portion of their revenue that turns into profits.

是網路股巨大的利潤空間吸引了他，也就是那部分能轉化成利潤的收入。

5. 表示結果

常用的副詞或片語如下：

accordingly	as a consequence	as a result	consequently	hence
in consequence	so	therefore	thus	

例如：

▶ Instead, she boosted her immune system with a mixture of nutritional therapy, yoga, meditation, positive thinking and laughter. **Consequently**, she led a full and active life right up to the last couple of weeks when her condition suddenly worsened.

相反，她通過營養調理、瑜伽、沉思、積極的心態和笑聲增強了自己的免疫力。所以，直到她的健康狀況突然惡化的幾周前，她活得還是那麼充實、那麼積極。

▶ Every day at 4 pm, the guards would let the detainees out of their cells, **so** they could hang out in the common room and watch TV.

每天下午4點，警衛都會讓被拘留者走出牢房，這樣他們就可以在休息室四處走走或看看電視。

6. 表示對比

常用的副詞或片語如下：

by comparison	by contrast	conversely	instead
in comparison	in contrast	on the contrary	(on the one hand...) on the other hand

例如：

▶ Charles, **by contrast**, was distraught.
查理斯卻感到心煩意亂了。

▶ CIA, which is not a prosecutorial body, has less restrictive rules than domestic law enforcement for conducting data-gathering activities and sometimes comes across information on US citizens. The FBI, **conversely**, must abide by more stringent standards, such as those related to obtaining search warrants or wiretaps.
中情局不是檢察機關，在收集資料方面，要遵循的規定相比國內執法部門要寬鬆一些，因而有時可以獲取美國公民的資訊。相反，聯邦調查局必須遵守更嚴格的標準，諸如獲得令狀方可搜查或竊聽等。

7. 表示讓步

常用的副詞或片語如下：

after all	all the same	at any rate	anyhow	anyway	however
in any case	in spite of that	nevertheless	still	though	yet

例如：

▶ Jones, **in any case**, is far off her best fitness and under a cloud from the drug scandal.
不管怎樣，籠罩在興奮劑醜聞陰影下的瓊斯已經再沒有了最佳狀態。

▶ Her eyes were moist but twinkling **nevertheless**.
她的雙眸濕潤了，但還是那麼炯炯有神。

8. 表示變換說法

常用的副詞或片語如下：

alternatively	in other words	more accurately	more exactly	more precisely	rather

例如：

▶ Instead of treating a disease called asthma, doctors will individualize drug therapies to produce the greatest good and avoid the worst side effects. Medicine, **in other words**, is getting personal.
醫生將因人治病，以求將藥的療效發揮到最好，同時將副作用減到最低，而不是只限於治哮喘病本身。換句話說，醫師用藥因人而異。

▶An infra-red photograph of your face provides a thermal map of your skin's temperature, or more accurately, shows the heat emitted by your face.
你臉部的紅外線照片呈現了皮膚溫度的熱量圖，更確切地說，它顯示了你臉部發出的熱量高低。

9. 表示改變

(1)話題改變

常用的副詞或片語如下：

by the way	incidentally

例如：

▶**By the way**, I've got that list of addresses you wanted.
順便說一句，我已經拿到你要的那個位址目錄了。

▶**Incidentally**, my upstairs neighbour is a scriptwriter.
附帶提一句，我樓上的鄰居是個編劇。

(2)時間變換

常用的副詞或片語如下：

meantime	meanwhile	in the meantime	in the meanwhile

例如：

▶Boeing is already banned from working on satellite rocket launchers for the Air Force because of a separate ethics scandal, and federal prosecutors are reportedly looking into Boeing's role as the lead contractor on a 100-billion-dollar Army program. **Meantime**, Boeing is facing increased competition for its lucrative government work.
因為道德醜聞，波音公司早就被禁止為空軍提供衛星火箭發射器。而且據報導，聯邦檢察官正在著手調查波音作為1,000億美元的軍隊合同主要承包人的問題。同時，在其有利可圖的政府生意方面，波音公司面臨著越來越激烈的競爭。

小結 ▷

本章著重介紹了狀語的分類。按語義功能，狀語主要分為三類，即修飾性狀語、評注性狀語和連線性狀語。修飾性狀語起到了類似主詞、謂語等其他句子成分的作用；評注性狀語不再拘泥於局部，而是與句子的整體結構密切相關，時常起統領全句的作用，是對整句內容的評價；連線性狀語起到了連接句子與句子的作用。

Part 15

句子的種類

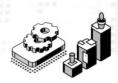

句子的構成 ▷

　　句子是建立在語素、詞和片語之上的文法單位，是具有完整意義並能獨立存在的最高一級文法單位。一個句子通常包含兩個基本部分：主詞部分（Subjects）和謂語部分（Predicates）。

　　主詞部分通常由名詞片語或相當於名詞片語的成分組成；謂語部分通常由動詞或動詞片語組成。從語義學上來說，主詞部分是句子的主題（Topics），例如人、事物或觀念等內容，謂語部分是對主題予以評述（Comments）的部分。例如：

They	shouldn't give up.	他們不應該放棄。
主詞	謂語	
主題	評述	

◎ 完全句和不完全句

　　從結構上劃分，句子有完全句（Full Sentences）和不完全句（Minor Sentences）之分，而完全句又可以分為簡單句（Simple Sentences）、並列句（Compound Sentences）和複合句（Complex Sentences）。

　　由至少一個主詞和謂語結構組成的句子稱為完全句，和補語為謂語的下位成分，定語和狀語為句子的附加成分。主謂結構不完整，即不同時具備主詞和謂語結構兩個部分的句子稱為不完全句。不完全句在祈使句中比較常見，主詞you往往省略。例如：

▶ Come and see if you can make him calmer, please! 你來看看是不是能讓他安靜些！

　　例句省略了主詞you，完全句應為：

▶ You come and see if you can make him calmer, please!

　　在口語中，為了方便，也會省略主詞。例如：

▶ Roger, thank you very much, and good luck in this enormous project you're undertaking.
羅傑，非常謝謝！也祝你正在做的這個大項目進展順利。

　　完全句應為：

▶ Roger, I thank you very much, and I wish you good luck in this enormous project you're undertaking.

另外，根據不同的場景，可使用簡短的表達形式，例如表示禁止的標語：

▶ **No Smoking!** 請勿吸煙！

▶ **No Parking!** 請勿停車！

▶ **No Spitting.** 請勿隨地吐痰。

功能上分類

英語中的句子在功能上能夠分成陳述句、疑問句、祈使句和感嘆句。總的來說，這四種句型寬泛地對應四種基本的言語行為功能：

句型	言語行為功能
陳述句	告知信息
疑問句	引出實情
祈使句	指示命令
感嘆句	表達感情

但是在實際使用時也經常出現不一致的情況。這四種句子的形式和功能都將在下面的章節中進行描述。

陳述句

陳述句的主要功能是給予資訊或者陳述說話人的看法，不期待對方的回答。例如：

▶ Andy went to hospital and had a four-hour wait, and then he took a load of painkillers.
安迪去了醫院並等了四個小時，然後他吃了大量的止痛藥。

▶ He should be more considerate of his neighbors.
他應該多體諒鄰居們。

上面兩句均為肯定陳述句。如果要表達否定的陳述，那麼有兩種情況：一是在be動詞、情態動詞或助動詞do，did後面加否定詞not。例如：

▶ She was **not** afraid, or blinded by glory.
她沒有因榮譽而畏懼，也沒有因榮譽而得意忘形。

▶ I might **not** even know until the rest of the world does, because he wants to keep his privacy.
我可能要等全世界都知道後才能知道，因為他想要保留自己的隱私。

▶ She does **not** like to stray far from home, but on occasion she travels.
她不喜歡離家太遠，但有時她也旅行。

另一種是在句子中運用如no，never，nobody，none，neither 等這些否定詞。例如：

▶ They **never** gave us the opportunity to get the training that we needed to get good jobs.
他們從來沒有給我們機會獲得找好工作所需的培訓。

🎯 疑問句

疑問句主要功能是尋求資訊，得到對方的應答。英語中有四種疑問句：特殊疑問句、一般疑問句、選擇疑問句和附加疑問句。

1. 特殊疑問句

特殊疑問句一般以疑問詞who，whom，whose，which，what，when，where，why，how開頭，一般用倒裝語序，它主要要求對方提供資訊。例如：

▶ **What** did they learn from this experience?
他們從這次經歷中學到了什麼？

如果主詞是疑問代名詞或有疑問代名詞修飾，則用正常語序。例如：

▶ **Who** won the award in the National League that season?
誰獲得了那個賽季的全國聯賽獎？

2. 一般疑問句

一般疑問句以助動詞、情態動詞、be動詞或have開頭，通常要求對方回答yes或no。它的主要功能是讓對方確認命題是否正確。例如：

▶ **Is** she able to bring me those shoes?
她能給我帶來那些鞋子嗎？

▶ **Could** you change your attitude towards Israel?
你能改變對以色列的態度嗎？

▶ **Does** he believe that our country was under threat?
他相信我們國家曾經受到過威脅嗎？

一般疑問句有時可以用否定形式。這時，它的功能是表示驚訝、失望、讚嘆或建議等。例如：

▶ **Wasn't** it wonderful?
難道不奇妙嗎？

▶ **Don't** you think we should learn a lot from our readers?
你不認為我們應該從我們的讀者中學到許多嗎？

在回答否定問句時要注意，如果回答是否定的，要用yes，否則用no。例如：

▶ A: Don't you think I deserve to be told the truth?
　 B: Yes, you do.
　　A：你不認為我應該被告知真相嗎？
　　B：不，你應該被告知真相。

▶ A: Doesn't she ever talk about her personal life?
　 B: No, she doesn't.
　　A：她從來沒有談起過她的私生活嗎？
　　B：是，她沒有談過。

3. 選擇疑問句

選擇疑問句提出兩個選項，看哪一個是正確的。它有兩種結構。一種類似一般疑問句。例如：

▶ Would you like coffee or tea?
　 你要咖啡還是茶？

還有一種類似特殊疑問句，兩個選項間用or連接。例如：

▶ What city has the world's largest black population, New York or San Francisco?
　 世界上哪個城市的黑人人口最多，是紐約還是舊金山？

4. 附加疑問句

附加疑問句是提出看法或情況，看對方同不同意自己的話語，也可以表示是否同意別人的話語。前一部分用陳述句的方式，後一部分是一個附著前一部分的簡短問句。

如果前一部分為肯定形式，後一部分就用否定形式；如果前一部分用否定形式，後一部分就用肯定形式。因此，根據上述規則，附加疑問句有以下幾種形式：

★肯定陳述句＋否定附加疑問

▶ He is a student, isn't he?
　 他是個學生，不是嗎？

★否定陳述句＋肯定附加疑問

▶ He isn't a student, is he?
　 他不是學生，他是嗎？

當陳述部分為肯定式，附加疑問句為否定式時，如果答案是肯定的，要用yes，否則用no。當陳述部分為否定式，附加疑問句為肯定式時，如果答案是否定的，要用yes，否則用no。

附加疑問句還有以下幾種特別的形式：

(1)如果陳述部分包含no，never，scarcely，hardly等詞，這部分就是否定，附加疑問部分的動詞用肯定。例如：

▶He never eats bread and butter like you, does he?
他從來不像你一樣吃麵包和奶油，是嗎？

(2)如果陳述部分的主詞是everybody，somebody，nobody等，附加疑問部分經常用they。例如：

▶Before you attended the meeting somebody handed that to you, didn't they?
在你參加會議前，有人把那個東西交給你，不是嗎？

(3)如果陳述部分是I'm，附加疑問部分一般用 aren't I。例如：

▶I'm allowed to have dinner with someone, aren't I?
我被允許與某人共進晚餐，不是嗎？

(4)如果陳述部分是that引導的受詞子句，附加疑問部分一般與主句的主謂保持一致。例如：

▶He said that he really found enormous difficulty in understanding this book, didn't he?
他說他確實發現要理解這本書相當困難，不是嗎？

但是，當主句部分是I加上心智動詞如think，suppose，believe時，附加疑問部分常常與子句中的主謂保持一致。例如：

▶I think he's a professional footballer, isn't he?
我認為他是一名職業足球運動員，他不是嗎？

◎ 祈使句

祈使句表示請求、命令、叮嚀、號召等，謂語動詞要用原形。祈使句可以分成第二人稱祈使句、第一人稱祈使句和第三人稱祈使句。

不同人稱的祈使句各有不同的使用時機，在運用時要注意，小心別出錯了！

1. 第二人稱祈使句

第二人稱祈使句是最常見的，主詞you通常不表示出來。例如：

▶ Look at her lovely long neck and her beautiful eyelashes.
看看她可愛的長脖子和美麗的眼睫毛。

有時在動詞前加do以強調語氣。例如：

▶ Do try to help one another.
一定要努力互相幫助。

這種句子的否定形式以don't引導，也可用never。例如：

▶ Don't rely on memory.
不要依賴記憶。

▶ Never eat your evening meal less than three hours before bed.
不要在上床睡覺前三小時內吃晚飯。

在第二人稱祈使句後面，可以用附加疑問句will you?或won't you?表示提醒或請求。
例如：

▶ Don't let your mother sell those books, will you?
不要讓你的媽媽賣掉那些書，好嗎？

▶ Try to think him a good man, won't you?
就把他當作好人，好嗎？

但有時為了表示命令、告誡或責備，可以加上主詞you。例如：

▶ You speak confidently. 你，說話要有信心。

2. 第一人稱祈使句

第一人稱祈使句往往表示某人所在的集體應該一起做某事，用Let's＋動詞原形。例
如：

▶ Let's mute the TV for a minute.
讓我們把電視靜音一下。

否定形式用Let's not。例如：

▶ Let's not create unnecessary expense.
我們別造成不必要的開支。

在Let's開頭的祈使句後面，附加疑問部分用shall we?，表示建議做某事。例如：

▶ **Let's** just sit down and be quiet, *shall we*?
讓我們坐下來，安靜一會，好嗎？

3. 第三人稱祈使句

第三人稱祈使句指明向誰發佈命令或指示，主詞一般要表示出來。例如：

▶ **Somebody** videotape the wedding.
要有人幫婚禮錄影。

▶ **Ginny,** look after mummy, won't you?
金妮，照看媽媽，好嗎？

感嘆句

感嘆句表示說話者的情緒，比如驚奇、讚嘆、憤怒等。通常用what或how引導。what修飾名詞，how修飾形容詞、副詞或動詞。例如：

▶ **What** a great dog you've got!
你有一條多棒的狗啊！

▶ **How** lovely the little river is with its dark, changing wavelets!
這條小河翻騰著深色的浪花，細小又多變，多可愛啊！

結構上分類

簡單句

簡單句是一個主謂結構的句子，句子的各個成分都只有單字或片語。主詞及謂語都可以不只一個，但句子的主詞不會變換。例如：

▶ He went to Paris in 1970 as a private individual.
1970年，他以個人的身份去了巴黎。

有時兩個或更多的主詞共用一個謂語，也是簡單句。例如：

▶ He and his friends even made a video of themselves in their new clothes.
他和朋友甚至拍攝了他們自己穿著新衣服時的影片。

有時兩個或更多的謂語共用一個主詞。例如：

▶ She went out eventually and turned the lights off.
她終於走出去並關了燈。

有時可以有兩個主詞和兩個以上的謂語。例如：

▶ She and her parents bought a farmhouse in the north of Mexico and turned it into a carpentry shop.
她和父母在墨西哥北部買了一幢農舍並把它改造成了木工店鋪。

🎯 並列句

並列句是句子包含兩個或更多的主謂結構的子句，子句的主詞不同，不同子句間可以用and，but，or等連接詞連接。例如：

▶ Your baby's been sleeping on your sheets **and** they smell less than fresh.
你的寶寶一直在你的床單上睡覺，床單聞著都有點味道了。

▶ He wants to pack in his job, **but** his boss uses unfair and foul means to try to stop him.
他想辭職，但是他的老闆用不公平和卑鄙的手段企圖阻止他。

有時可以不用連接詞，而用一個逗號或分號分開。例如：

▶ Her husband liked to have power over his family, his mother tried to brainwash him to get what she wanted.
她的丈夫喜歡掌管家庭事務，而他的母親卻想方設法給他洗腦以便得到她所要的。

由兩個以上的子句構成並列句時，只在最後一個項目前用對等連接詞，其他之間用逗號連接。例如：

▶ My brother is working hard, my sisters are all doing great work **and** we're all in different places in our careers.
我哥哥工作努力，我的姐妹們都幹得很好，我們的事業都在不同的領域。

在有些並列句中，其中一個分句是由主子句構成，這種句子稱為並列複雜句。例如：

▶ She might come, **but** I don't think she will.
她也許會來，但我認為她不會的。

在以上並列句中，but 之後的句子由主句I don't think和子句she will組成。

🎯 複合句

複合句包含兩個或更多的主謂結構，它們是主從關係，其中有一個主謂結構充當句子的某一成分，如主詞、表語、受詞、定語、狀語、同位語等。

1. 主詞子句

主詞子句（Subject Clauses）在句子中作主詞，主要由that引導，或由wh-詞引導。

(1) that引導的主詞子句常見於正式的書面文體如新聞、學術文章中。例如：

▶ That she was being merely tiresome was undoubted.
毫無疑問，她表現得只是討人厭而已。

但通常情況下，it可以用作先行詞，作形式主詞，而將that引導的子句後置。例如：

▶ It is evident that you made your attack on him when you were consumed with anger and bitterness
顯然是在你內心充滿憤怒和痛苦時，你攻擊了他。

用it作先行詞的主詞子句有以下幾種形式：

a. It＋be＋形容詞＋that引導的子句

這些形容詞從語義上說主要是表示肯定性的形容詞和表示情感的形容詞，最常見的有：

acceptable	apparent	appropriate	awful	certain
clear	correct	doubtful	evident	false
good	great	interesting	(un)likely	natural
obvious	(im)possible	right	sad	true
unusual	well-known	wonderful		

例如：

▶ It is certain that even more shocking images will emerge in this TV program.
能夠肯定的是，在這個電視節目中會出現更令人震驚的圖像。

語義上表示重要性、必要性的形容詞和表示評論性的形容詞也可以用在這種結構中，但that引導的子句中的動詞要用原形或「should＋動詞原形」。（參見P188〈Part8 語氣〉）這些形容詞主要有：

advisable	amazing	crucial	desirable	essential	imperative
important	necessary	odd	shocking	strange	vital

例如：

▶ It is essential that we take every reasonable step to deter terrorist activities.
我們有必要採取一切合理的措施來阻止恐怖活動。

b. It＋be＋名詞片語＋that引導的子句。例如：

▶It is a fact that minorities are more likely to be victims of violent crime than the majority.
事實是少數族群比大多數人更可能成為暴力犯罪的受害人。

c. It＋be＋過去分詞＋that引導的子句。例如：

▶It is known that Murphy's elder sisters were artists' models.
據瞭解，墨菲的姐姐們是畫家的模特。

d. It＋seem/happen＋that引導的子句。例如：

▶It seems that people are still willing to borrow money to buy things in New York.
在紐約人們似乎依然願意借錢買東西。

(2)主詞子句由疑問代名詞what，which，who，whom，whose，或疑問副詞where，when，how，why引導，從特殊疑問句轉化而來。也可以用whether引導，從一般疑問句轉化而來。例如：

▶Which animals he likes is none of my business.
他喜歡什麼樣的動物不關我事。

▶How the economy affects presidential elections isn't clear.
還不清楚經濟如何影響總統選舉。

　　有時也用於帶有it先行詞的結構中。例如：

▶It is not clear when he'll be able to resume his full duties, and what those duties are.
還不清楚他何時能恢復全職，也不確定他的職責又是什麼。

注意！

if 引導的子句不能作主詞，但是whether引導的子句可以作主詞。例如：

▶Whether the way I do things is good or bad is up to others to decide.
我做事的方法是好是壞由別人裁決。

(3)主詞子句由作關係代名詞的what，whatever，whoever等引導這類句子相當於名詞加上一個關係子句。例如：

▶What the local plan provides for the city is up to 4000 new houses by 2011.
該城市計畫到2011年新建近4000套住宅。

由作關係代名詞的wh-詞引導的子句與疑問代名詞wh-詞引導的子句有時較難區分。但是，前者可以指人或指物，而後者表示間接的問句。試比較下面兩個句子：

★由關係代名詞型wh-詞引導的子句，what相當於the thing which/that：

▶What caused the car accident was a flat tire.
爆胎是引起車禍的原因。

★這是一句由疑問代名詞wh-詞引導的子句

▶What caused the car accident is a mystery.
是什麼引起了車禍還是一個謎。

2. 形容詞子句

形容詞子句（Predicative Clauses）在句子中作表語或成為主詞補語，主要由that引導，也可以由wh- 詞引導。

(1)that引導的形容詞子句有下面幾種形式：

a. 表示被接受的事實、真理等的實際內容，常用來作主詞的詞有：fact，news，truth，advantage，explanation，position，problem等。例如：

▶The fact is that television is such a powerful medium that it seems to me that you have to learn how to use it.
事實是，電視已成為一種強大的媒體，依我看來，你得學習如何使用它。

▶The news is that our rate of reduction of crime is much greater than any metropolitan area in the U.S.
有新聞説，我們減少犯罪的速度比美國任何一座大都市都要快。

b. 表示某人的意見、信念等實際內容，常用來作主詞的詞有：idea，hope，doubt，belief，view等。例如：

▶Our belief is that the consumer is gradually discerning quality because of the great variety of different products on the market now.
我們相信，由於目前市場上不同的產品種類繁多，消費者已逐漸能夠鑑別出產品的品質。

▶His hope is that his book will get people thinking about how to once again change America for the better.
他希望，他的書能夠引導人們思考：如何再次改變美國，使之變得更好。

c. 表示理由、結果或結論的實際內容，常用來作主詞的詞有：conclusion，reason等。
例如：

▶ My **conclusion** is that there was unethical conduct that occurred in the bid process.
投標過程存在不符合職業道德的行為，這就是我的結論。

(2) 由疑問代名詞what，which，who，whom，whose等，或疑問副詞where，when，
how，why，以及whether/if引導的形容詞子句。例如：

▶ The point is **where** we go for 56 tons of oil in a short period of time.
關鍵是我們在短時間內去哪裡弄到56噸油。

(3) 由作關係代名詞的what，whatever，whoever 等引導的形容詞子句。例如：

▶ That is **what** lawyers are supposed to do — look for the best result for their client.
那就是律師應該做的——幫客戶找尋最好的結果。

3. 受詞子句

受詞子句（Object Clauses）在句子中作受詞，主要由that引導，或由wh-詞引導。

(1) that引導的受詞子句用得最多的是作謂語動詞的受詞。這些動詞從語義角度看包括三
類：心智動詞（主要是認知活動的動詞，以及一些情感動詞）、行為動詞和交際動
詞。下面是比較常見的這些動詞：

admit	agree	announce	argue	assume
believe	bet	conclude	decide	doubt
ensure	expect	feel	find	guess
hear	hope	imagine	indicate	insist
know	mean	prove	notice	read
realize	recognize	remember	say	see
show	suggest	suppose	think	understand
wish				

that引導的受詞子句主要有以下幾種形式：

a. 謂語動詞＋that引導的子句。例如：

▶ We **believed that** one day we'd become famous.
我們相信有一天我們會出名的。

b. 謂語動詞＋名詞片語＋that引導的子句。例如：

▶ They no longer have the faith that education is going to lead to something productive and bright future.
他們不再相信教育能夠帶來某種富有成效的東西和光明的前程。

c. 謂語動詞＋to＋名詞片語＋that引導的子句。例如：

▶ The manager spoke to the employee that the company might go bankrupt.
經理告知職工公司可能要破產。

有時用先行詞it作受詞，後跟that引導的子句。例如：

▶ The invitation had made it quite clear that it was a Jewish club and only Jews would be welcome.
請柬上清楚地寫明，這是一個猶太人俱樂部，只接待猶太人。

在交際動詞suggest，propose，require等後，that引導的子句一般用「should＋動詞原形」或be型假設語氣。（參見P188〈Part8語氣〉）例如：

▶ He suggests that parents closely monitor their children's behavior and take note of out-of-control behavior.
他建議家長密切監控孩子的行為並記錄下失控的行為。

當主句謂語動詞為think，imagine，believe等認知活動的動詞時，其後作受詞的子句若帶有否定的意思，通常將否定詞not移到主句中。例如：

▶ I don't think they understand how much creative content we have to come up with all the time.
我們一直以來必須想出多少有創意的東西，我認為對於這點他們並不理解。

(2)由疑問代名詞what，which，who，whom，whose等，疑問副詞where，when，how，why，或由關係代名詞型what等引導的受詞子句

wh-詞引導的子句可以作動詞的受詞，這些動詞從語義上說包括行為動詞、心智動詞（表示認知活動的動詞、表示感知動作的動詞和表達不同態度和願望的情感動詞）和交際動詞。常見的詞有：

argue	ask	believe	confess	consider
confirm	criticize	debate	depend (on)	discuss
explain	express	find (out)	guess	imagine
inquire (about/into)	know	look (at)	notice	observe

perceive	point out	prove	question	realize
remember	report	say	see	show
tell	think (about)	understand	wonder	

wh- 詞引導的受詞子句主要有以下幾種形式：

a. 謂語動詞＋wh-子句。例如：

▶ He **remembered when** the changes had started.
他記得變化是從什麼時候開始的。

b. 謂語動詞＋名詞片語＋wh-子句。例如：

▶ I **ask my boyfriend where** he learnt to speak English.
我問我的男朋友他是在哪裡學說英語的。

在上述結構中，子句的正常語序是「主詞＋謂語」。

wh- 詞引導的子句也可以充當介係詞的受詞，而that引導的子句則不行。例如：

▶ We tried to just think about **who's been loyal and who's been trustworthy**.
我們努力思考誰是忠誠的，誰是可信賴的。

(3)whether/if 引導的受詞子句

一般情況下，受詞子句中的if可以替代whether，whether也可以替代if，而且並不改變句子的意思。if更經常出現在口語文體中，if引導的受詞子句經常出現在以下動詞後面：

ask	care	determine	doubt	find (out)	know
matter	mind	remember	see	wonder	

例如：

▶ Customers don't **mind if we may be a few dollars more** because they know they'll get the value.
顧客不介意我們可能貴幾美元，因為他們知道物有所值。

whether引導的受詞子句經常出現在以下動詞後面：

ask	care	consider	decide	determine	doubt
establish	find (out)	indicate	investigate	judge	know
mind	remember	say	see	tell	wonder

例如：

▶ I don't remember whether we won or lost most of the games, but we sure did have fun. 我不記得我們大多數比賽是贏了還是輸了，但可以肯定的是，我們的確過得很開心。

注意！

在whether後可以跟or not，但if 後不能跟or not。例如：

▶ He didn't know whether or not he would benefit from going to church.
他不知道他是否能從去教堂做禮拜中受益。

(4) be＋形容詞＋that引導的子句中，that引導的子句在概念上接近受詞，通常以人為主詞。這些形容詞從語義上說包括兩類：表示確定程度的形容詞和表示情感心理狀態的形容詞。最常見的這些形容詞有：

afraid	amazed	amused	angry	annoyed	astonished
careful	certain	confident	depressed	disappointed	encouraged
evident	frightened	glad	happy	hopeful	hurt
mad	pleased	right	sad	satisfied	shocked
sorry	sure	surprised	upset	worried	

例如：

▶ I'm sure that the selection process will be fair and open.
我確信遴選過程會是公正和公開的。

▶ I'm afraid that the situation is developing very, very fast and probably everything will be out of control.
恐怕形勢的發展會非常非常快，很有可能一切都會失控。

be＋形容詞＋ wh-詞引導的子句與be＋形容詞＋that引導的子句相似。例如：

▶ Scientists are not certain what causes the disease or how it is transmitted.
科學家不確定是什麼引起了疾病或者疾病是如何傳播的。

4. 同位語子句

同位語子句（Appositive Clauses）在句子中作同位語，主要由that引導，或由wh-詞引導。常以that引導的子句作同位語的名詞有：

answer	belief	conclusion	decision	evidence	fact
hope	idea	news	opinion	possibility	problem
report	rumor	thought	truth	wish	

例如：

▶ **The fact** that this clever puzzle was done by someone so young is astonishing.
這個巧妙的難題被這麼年輕的人解決了，這個事實是令人驚訝的。

由疑問代名詞what，which，who，whom，whose等和疑問副詞where，when，how，why引導的同位語子句。例如：

▶ There is no question *what* the best technology is.
什麼才是最好的技術，這是沒有異議的。

由關係代名詞型what等引導的同位語子句。例如：

▶ There is an e-mail address *where* people can send in any advice they want all along the way.
有一個電子信箱，人們可以一直發送任何他們想要的建議。

5. 關係子句

由關係代名詞或關係副詞所引導的作定語的子句稱為關係子句。關係子句總是跟在它所修飾的先行詞（Antecedent）之後，而這個先行詞往往是名詞片語。

(1)限定性關係子句

限定性關係子句修飾先行詞，是先行詞不可缺少的一個組成部分。如果缺少，意思就不完整。因而限定性的關係子句在口語中沒有停頓，在書面語中沒有逗號。例如：

▶ The three Presidents are releasing a statement today, talking about their common efforts and the proposals *that they've been making* to try to move that process forward.
三位總統今天將發佈聲明，談論他們所作出的共同努力，以及他們為推動那個進程而提出的建議。

(2)非限定性關係子句

非限定性關係子句主要補充說明先行詞，與先行詞的關係比較鬆散。如果缺少，不會影響主要意思。因而非限定性的關係子句在口語中有停頓，在書面語中用逗號與主句分開。例如：

▶ Helen had her own set of principles, *which she changed and updated depending on the situation*.
海倫有自己的一套原則，而且，她會根據不同的形勢改變和更新這些原則。

有時，非限定性關係子句的先行詞不是一個名詞片語，而是前面的整個句子或者前面所敘述的某一事件，這時子句主要是評論主句所說的事。例如：

▶ The western counties had great snowfalls, which was good for winter sports and recreation.
西部的幾個郡降大雪，這對冬季運動和娛樂有好處。

(3)在限定性關係子句中關係代名詞的選擇

在限定性的關係子句中主要的關係代名詞有：

限定性關係子句		
	指人	指物
作主詞	who/that	which/that
作受詞	whom/who/that	which/that
所有格	whose	whose/of which

a. 關係代名詞在子句中作主詞

一般情況下，在指人的限定性關係子句中，who和that用來作主詞，兩個詞可以互換。例如：

▶ People who didn't notice you before will suddenly find you scintillating.
那些以前沒有注意到你的人會突然發現你聰明靈巧的一面。

在指物的限定性關係子句中，可以選擇which和that作主詞，這兩個詞也可以互換。例如：

▶ The restaurant which is next to the pub is really good.
挨著酒館的那家餐廳真的很不錯。

b. 關係代名詞在子句中作受詞

當whom，who和that在子句中作受詞用來指人時，它們也可以互換。例如：

▶ Beside us a sea captain in shorts has offered an ice cream to a young boy whom I noticed playing with a football.
我們旁邊穿短褲的船長給了小男孩一個冰淇淋，我注意到那男孩當時正在玩足球。

在正式英語文體中，whom作受詞更多見。

當which和that作受詞用來指物時，它們也可以互換。例如：

▶ Jackson is also working on a motivational lifestyle scheme which he hopes to launch at the end of the year, and he has already signed a commentary deal with the BBC.
傑克遜也在實施一個激發積極性的生活方式計畫，他希望年底開始這一計畫，而且他已經跟英國廣播公司簽署了解說協議。

c. 關係代名詞的所有格

whose加上名詞在子句中可以作主詞，也可以作受詞。它一般用來指人。例如：

▶ Prices of meat and vegetables have leapt—a boon to farmers whose incomes have long stagnated, but a source of worry that the poorest people are suffering. 肉和蔬菜的價格飛快上漲，這對收入長期停滯不前的農夫是件好事，但也令人擔憂，因為最貧困的人要受苦。

whose加上名詞有時也可以用來指物。例如：

▶ South Korea and Mexico are just two examples of nations whose economies have pursued political reform while reforming their economies and expanding trade.
韓國和墨西哥是兩個例子，在改革經濟和擴大貿易的同時，其經濟推動了政治改革。

但是，我們常常用of which來替代指物或者抽象的概念。例如：

▶ It's a smart 1880s terraced house of which only the exterior walls are original; everything else is new.
這是一座漂亮的19世紀80年代的排屋（多幢相連的雙層或多層房屋），只有外牆是原來固有的，其他所有的都是新的。

注意！

that引導的關係子句與that引導的同位語子句非常相像，但是它們是不同的。關係子句中的that一般是句子中的一個成分（主詞或受詞），它修飾其前面的一個先行詞。而同位語子句中的that不是句子的一個成分，它往往說明它所修飾的詞到底是怎樣的。試比較：

★that引導關係子句，that是子句的主詞

▶ He spread the news that came this morning.
他傳播了今天早上來的新聞。

★that引導同位語子句，that具體說明news

▶ He spread the news that John had been caught.
他傳播了這條新聞，那就是約翰被捕了。

(4)在限定性關係子句中關係代名詞的其他用法

在限定性關係子句中，一般用which/that指物。但在以下情況中通常用that。

a. 當先行詞為不定代名詞all，everything，anything等時。例如：

▶ However, in most cases, we've not been able to give them **all** that they asked for.
然而，在大多數情況下，我們做不到他們要什麼就給他們什麼。

b. 在形容詞最高級修飾的詞後。例如：

▶ $25,000 luxury sedan is **the most expensive vehicle** that Hyundai has ever offered.
價值2.5萬美元的豪華轎車是現代公司有史以來出售的最昂貴的車輛。

c. 在序數詞修飾的詞後面。例如：

▶ We're proud that **the first place** that the sun rises in Russia is here.
這裡是俄羅斯境內太陽最早升起的地方，我們對此感到驕傲。

(5)在非限定性關係子句中關係代名詞的選擇

非限定性關係子句		
	指人	指物
作主詞	who	which
作受詞	whom/who	which
所有格	whose	whose/of which

a. 關係代名詞在子句中作主詞

在非限定性關係子句中，只能用who指人，用which指物，不能用that替代。例如：

▶ Atomic Kitten singer Jenny Frost, **who used to date Beckham**, will be one of five bridesmaids.
曾經跟貝克漢約會過的「原子少女貓」組合的歌手珍妮‧弗羅斯特，將成為五個伴娘中的一個。

▶ This library, **which has no physical home**, keeps its books online.
這個沒有實體館的圖書館，是在網上保存書籍。

b. 關係代名詞在子句中作受詞

在非限定性關係子句中，作受詞用whom和who指人，which指物不能用that。例如：

▶ Although Woods recently split with law student Joanna, 23, **whom he dated for more than two years**, don't bet on his getting involved again soon. 儘管伍茲最近剛跟23歲的法學專業大學生喬安娜分手，他們交往已經兩年多，但他不大可能很快再次陷入一份感情之中。

▶ Most older people trade down to smaller, cheaper properties, **which they can buy outright**. 大多數年長的人降低消費購買更小更便宜的房產，這樣他們就可以一次性付清房款了。

c. 關係代名詞的所有格

在非限定性關係子句中，whose的用法同限定性關係子句。例如：

▶ The chief executive officer, whose brother Gary was among the victims, said he would donate $1 million to a foundation for the families.
首席執行官説他將捐贈100萬美元給受害者家庭基金會，他的兄弟蓋瑞也是受害人之一。

▶ More than 8,000 pieces of artifacts are still missing, of which almost 30 are considered of unique historical and artistic importance.
8000多件手工藝品仍然失蹤，其中有近30件是被視為有獨特歷史與藝術價值的物品。

(6)關係副詞的用法

關係副詞有when，where和why。

when用在表示時間的先行詞time，day，year之後，可以引導限定性關係子句，也可以引導非限定性關係子句。例如：

▶ Hill was unceremoniously dumped by Williams in the year when he won the drivers' world championship back in 1996.
早在1996年贏得駕駛員世界錦標賽的那一年，希爾就被威廉斯像廢物一樣隨意丟棄了。

▶ New Year's Day, meanwhile, is Russia's biggest festival of the year, when gifts are exchanged and livers mercilessly punished.
新年是俄羅斯一年中最盛大的節日，這時大家會互相交換禮物，但這時也是他們的肝臟最遭罪的時候。

where用在表示具體地點的先行詞place，house，road之後，也可以用在表示抽象的地點如situation，case，point之後。可以引導限定性關係子句，也可以引導非限定性關係子句。例如：

▶ We drove to the house where everything had been prepared by Aunt Beatrice to give the newly married couple a suitable welcome home.
我們駕車到那座房子，比阿特麗斯姨媽已經在那裡準備好了一切，要給新婚夫婦一個溫馨的家。

▶ When he was 12, his family moved to a different part of the town, where they attended a church on Sundays.
在他12歲時，他的家搬到鎮裡的另一個地方，在那裡他們星期日都去教堂。

why用在表示原因的先行詞reason之後，只能引導限定性關係子句。例如：

▶ The reason why this marvelous production has swept around the world like a tornado is the drenching sorrow and bigness of its vision.
這部絕妙的電影像旋風一樣席捲全球，其原因是影片浸染著悲傷，極具洞察力。

the time/the day when，the reason why中的when，why 都可以被that 替代。例如：

▶ This was the year that every piece of e-mail became a potential threat, and every website became a potential booby trap.
在這樣的一年裡，每一封電子郵件都成為了一種潛在的威脅，每一個網站成為了一個潛在的陷阱。

▶ A large part of the reason that the economic performance has been strong is because of the increased volume of exports that we're sending abroad.
經濟功績強大的一大部分原因在於我們對外出口商品量的增加。

　　when，where和why都能用介係詞加which替代，介係詞取決於與前面片語的搭配關係。例如：

▶ August 4 marks the 90th anniversary of the day on which Britain declared war on Germany and embarked on four years of war.
8月4日是英國向德國宣戰並開始長達四年之久的戰爭的一天，而今是其90周年的紀念日。

▶ If people ask about the room in which she died, we don't tell them.
如果人們問起她去世時所處的那間屋子，我們不要告訴他們。

▶ This will be the reason for which we don't support your plan.
這是我們不支持你的計畫的理由。

(7)由「介係詞＋關係代名詞」引導的子句結構
　　不管是在限定性還是在非限定性關係子句中，關係代名詞作介係詞受詞時，可以把介係詞前置。在這種情況下，只能用whom指人，用which指物。例如：

▶ Most beginners for whom the book is presumably intended will find this useful, although there are one or two slips.
這本針對初學者而編的書，儘管有一兩處紕漏，但是大多數初學者會發現它是有用的。

▶ She always told me to get a degree with which I can support myself.
她總是告訴我要去拿一個學位來養活自己。

　　也可以把介係詞後置，這時who和that可以充當介係詞的受詞。所以上面兩句也可以寫成：

▶ Most beginners whom/who/that the book is presumably intended for will find this useful, although there are one or two slips.

▶ She always told me to get a degree which/that I can support myself with.

注意！

在以介係詞結尾的動詞片語中，介係詞不能前置。例如：

▶ This disgusting man is the one whom Angel has hoped to hear from.
安潔兒正是希望從這個令人厭惡的人那裡收到信。

(8)關係代名詞的省略問題

　　在非正式文體中，在限定性的關係子句中作受詞的關係代名詞whom，who，which，that常常可以省略。例如：

▶ It saddens me to see a girl I've looked up to have this horrible disease.
讓我感到悲哀的是，我所尊敬的女孩患了這種可怕的疾病。

　　當that用於表示方式、時間、地點的詞語後取代when，where，why和in which時，常常可以省略。例如：

▶ On the day he was shot, according to police, a judge was planning to fine Joice for not following court orders.
據員警說，在喬伊絲被槍殺的那天，一名法官正打算對他罰款，因為他沒有遵守法庭的指令。

　　當主句是there be結構時，如果關係代名詞在子句中作主詞，在一些口語文體中才可以省去。例如：

▶ There were a lot of people (who) went there.
有許多人去那裡。

(9)雙重關係子句

　　雙重關係子句是指同一個先行詞有兩個關係子句，它有兩種情況。第一種情況是兩個關係子句屬於同一層次，用對等連接詞連接。例如：

▶ These are women whom headhunters adore and whose phone calls you want to return. 這些女人就是獵頭會喜歡、你會想回電的類型。

　　後一種情況屬於不同的層次。例如：

▶ You may recall Latrell Spreewell, the player I dislike who assaulted and choked his coach last year.
你可能記得拉特雷爾·斯普雷韋爾，那個我不喜歡的球員，他去年襲擊了他的教練並勒住他的脖子。

注意！

　　雙重關係子句的關係代名詞的選擇和省略，與關係子句的關係代名詞的選擇和省略相似，但當兩個關係子句屬於同一層次時，只能省略第一個關係子句中用作受詞的關係代名詞。例如：

▶ I'm surprised you're interested in the movie you've been watching and which is criticized by the media.
我感到驚訝的是，你對那部你一直在看而且遭到媒體批評的電影感興趣。

(10)嵌入式關係子句

　　嵌入式關係子句是指在同一個句子中出現幾個關係子句，而且有不同的先行詞。例如：

▶I told her about the man that would later become my husband who would definitely make me happy.
我跟她說了那個將來會成為我丈夫的人，那個人肯定會給我幸福的。

6. 副詞子句

　　副詞子句（Adverbial Clauses）指在句中起副詞作用的主謂結構，用從屬連接詞引入可以表示時間、地點、原因、目的、結果、讓步、方式、對照和比較。

(1)時間副詞子句

　　時間副詞子句是用來表示時間關係的子句。主要引導詞有：

after	before	since	ever since	till
until	when	while	as	the moment
the minute	as soon as	once	as long as	directly

　　例如：

▶As soon as the band had left the stage, the crowd began streaming out like meek sheep.
樂隊一離開舞臺，人群便像溫順的綿羊一樣湧了出來。

(2)地點副詞子句

　　地點副詞子句是用來表示空間關係的子句。連接詞主要有where，wherever。例如：

▶I didn't want to stay where I felt unhappy.
我不想待在讓我感到不快樂的地方。

▶He's allowed to go wherever he wants and do whatever he likes.
他可以去任何他想去的地方，做任何他想幹的事。

(3)方式副詞子句

　　方式副詞子句描述動作方式。主要連接詞有as，just as，the way，as if，as though 等。例如：

▶Children are expected to do as they are told and not encouraged to discuss their feelings.
人們期望孩子聽話，而不鼓勵他們談論自己的感情。

用as if 或as though時，如果表示與現在事實相反，子句中的動詞用過去簡單式。如果表示與過去事實相反，則動詞用過去完成式。例如：

▶ I examine the chamber (of the gun), **as if** I didn't know it was loaded.
我檢查了槍膛，好像我不知道它已經裝滿了子彈。

▶ The factory collapsed **as if** a major earthquake had struck, and rescuers used techniques honed in the disaster zones of Turkey, Japan and Afghanistan.
工廠倒塌了，好像遭受了一場大地震，救援者用上了在土耳其、日本和阿富汗災區磨煉出來的技術。

(4)原因副詞子句用來表示原因、理由。主要由以下詞引導：

because	as	since	in that	inasmuch as
now that	seeing that	considering that	not that...but that	

例如：

▶ The militia, **seeing that** they were outnumbered, told the villagers to flee into the bush but some ran to their thatched huts.
發現敵人的數量多於自己，民兵督促村民們逃往灌木叢，但是有些村民們卻逃向他們的茅屋。

(5)結果副詞子句

結果副詞子句用來表示事態發展的結果，通常放在句末。主要連接詞為so that，so...that，such...that，with the result that，非正式語體中可以用so。例如：

▶ We also have an ever-growing harbor complex, **with the result that** over half the city's workforce are dependent on the transportation industry for their livelihood.
我們還有一個不斷發展壯大的海港作業區，其結果是城市裡超過一半的勞動力都依賴運輸業謀生。

(6)目的副詞子句

目的副詞子句表示目的，它隱含著動作執行者的意圖和計畫。目的副詞子句裡一般會有情態動詞。目的副詞子句主要由so that，in order that，lest，for fear that，in case，so 等引導。in order that常用於正式的文體。例如：

▶ I wished to be more at my wife's side **in order that** I can keep an eye on her.
我希望能更多地陪伴在妻子身邊，以便照看她。

(7)條件副詞子句

　　條件副詞子句表示在某種條件或情況下，主句的情況會出現。條件句可以分為真實條件句（Real Conditions）和非真實條件句（Unreal Conditions）。

　　真實條件句一般表示事情將來可能發生，子句用現在簡單式，主句用will/shall加上動詞的不定詞結構。例如：

▶ I'm actually going to The Eagles concert right after dinner if it doesn't rain.
如果不下雨，晚飯後我要去參加老鷹樂隊的音樂會。

　　真實條件句也可以表示討論的事情可能是真實的，或經常發生的，子句和主句用動詞的現在簡單式或現在進行式表示。例如：

▶ A woman can be more frightening if she is superbly turned out, superb looking and immaculately polite.
一個女人如果受過極好的培養，又有出眾的容貌和周全文雅的舉止，那將更可怕。

　　如果用真實條件句談論過去有可能發生的事情的話，子句和主句都要用過去簡單式或過去進行式。例如：

▶ Other prisoners vowed to kill him and his family if he talked to the police.
其他囚犯發誓，如果他向員警報告，他們就把他和他的家人都殺掉。

　　非真實條件子句說明與事實相反的假設條件。它有三種情況：

a. 表示與現在事實相反的設想，子句用過去簡單式或用were，主句用would/should/could/might＋不帶to的不定詞。例如：

▶ If I were you I'd call Security and have them thrown in jail.
如果我是你的話，我會給保全機構打電話，把他們都送進監獄。

b. 表示與過去事實相反的假設時，子句用過去完成式，主句用would/should/could/might＋不帶to的不定詞完成式。例如：

▶ If they had known about the situation in New Zealand they would have taken out a separate policy to cover personal injury.
要是早知道紐西蘭的情況，他們就會對個人意外傷害進行單獨投保了。

c. 表示與將來事實相反的假設或者將來實現的可能性很小的設想時，子句用過去簡單式，或were，或should/could/might＋不帶to的不定詞，或用were＋帶to的不定詞，主句用would/should/could/might＋不帶to的不定詞。例如：

▶ It is believed the American could earn £158,000 if she were to win the women's 100 meters race.
據信那個美國人如果贏了女子百米賽跑，她會獲得15.8 萬英鎊。

> **注意！**
>
> 在非真實條件子句中，如果子句中有should，had，were等，可以用省略if的倒裝結構來表示假設語氣。這種用法一般用在比較正式的文體裡。例如：
>
> ▶ **Had it not been for** (=If it had not been for) Charlie, we might never have heard of this program.
> 要是沒有查理的幫助，我們可能根本不會知道有這個方案。
>
> ▶ **Were it not for immigration** (=If it were not for immigration), some countries wouldn't develop so quickly.
> 如果沒有移民政策，有些國家不會發展得如此迅速。

(8)讓步副詞子句

讓步副詞子句表示在某種相反的條件或情況下，主句的情況仍然出現。引導讓步副詞子句的主要有：

although	though	even if	even though
while	whereas	in spite of the fact that	despite the fact that

例如：

▶ I have insurance on my house, **even though I don't think it's going to burn down**.
即使我覺得房子不會被燒毀，我還是給它投了保。

▶ **While the statewide survey found employment had decreased among the homeless**, it stayed steady in Fargo, with 41 percent of homeless people holding a steady job, and 18 percent employed full time.
雖然遍及全州的調查發現，街友的就業率呈下降趨勢，但是在法戈裡還是保持著平穩的就業率，41%的街友擁有一份固定的工作，18%是全職。

(9)副詞子句的用法

副詞子句可以用來修飾謂語動詞或其他動詞，也可以修飾定語或狀語，有時可以修飾整個句子。例如：

▶ **If I can't get married in Jersey**, I will go wherever I can get married and come back to live here.

如果我不能在澤西結婚，我就去任何我可以結婚的地方，然後再回來居住。

▶ Harry was beginning to do well enough **that his doctor had let him out to spend the day with his family**, but obviously the visit had not gone as smoothly as everyone had hoped.

哈利的病情正在好轉，醫生允許他與家人一起待上一天，但是，這次團聚顯然並不像每個人所希望的那樣一帆風順。

▶ He was always extremely focused **no matter what happened**.

不管發生什麼，他總是特別專注。

(10)when, while, as, before, after, until, since的用法

a. when，while，as

　　when是最常見的表示時間的連接詞，意義也相當廣泛。它一般用來表示在某個時刻發生了、正在發生或即將發生的某件事。例如：

▶ **When he was at home** his mother wouldn't allow him to go out anywhere and do anything.

他在家裡時，他媽媽哪兒也不讓他去，什麼也不讓他做。

　　when還可以表示一個動作緊接著另一個動作發生。例如：

▶ **When Michael went to sleep** Liz redecorated his house with Christmas decorations.

當麥可去睡覺後，莉茲用聖誕的裝飾品重新裝飾了他的房子。

　　when還可以用在句子中表示「正在那時」、「突然」。例如：

▶ Sharron wasn't looking for romance **when she met Tony on a flight back from Australia**.

莎倫並未追求愛情，可就在從澳洲回來的航班上，她與東尼相遇了。

　　表示經常發生的動作時，可以用whenever替代when。例如：

▶ The scenic grandeur of the place took his breath away **whenever he saw it**, and he saw it every time he went to Africa.

每每看到這些，他都會對這裡的美景感慨萬千，所以每次到非洲他都會來這裡觀光。

while表示兩個動作同時發生，持續時間較長。例如：

▶ **While he was sipping hot chocolate**, we were fighting for our lives.
當他在啜飲著熱巧克力時，我們在為我們的生活奮鬥。

as連接兩個同時發生、持續時間較短的動作。例如：

▶ The rain came down heavier **as we both danced about pretending to be prince and princess**.
當我們假裝王子和公主在跳舞時，雨下大了。

as還能表示在同一時期同時發生變化的兩個動作。例如：

▶ So we'll be able to see, **as they get older**, how this stuff is working.
所以，等他們漸漸長大，我們將能看到那個東西是如何運轉的。

b. before，after

before表示一個動作發生在另一個動作之前。例如：

▶ She was ejected from six private schools and quit high school **before she was 15**.
在15歲前，她曾被六所私立學校開除，高中又輟學。

用after表示一個動作發生在另一個動作之後。例如：

▶ In Baghdad, 20 officers were punished **after they were caught accepting bribes**.
在巴格達，20名官員在受賄行徑敗露後受到了懲罰。

c. until

until表示主句的謂語動詞所表示的動作延續到子句的謂語動詞所表示的動作發生為止。例如：

▶ Lily waited **until she heard the girl going downstairs before she let herself grin**.
莉莉一直等到她聽到女孩下樓後才露出笑容。

當主句的謂語動詞不能延續時，要用否定。例如：

▶ She did not want him to exercise his leg **until the infected burn had healed completely**.
她一直等到受感染的燒傷完全癒合後才讓他鍛練腿。

如果把not until放在句首，主句的主詞和謂語要倒裝。例如：

▶ **Not until the door was firmly closed behind them** did Michael speak again.
一直等到他們身後的門緊緊地關閉後，麥可才重新開口。

注意！

> when，as，while，after，before，until引導的副詞子句中，子句用現在式來表示
> 將來時間。例如：
>
> ▶ Brocket also has affairs of the heart to attend to when he returns to Britain
> tomorrow.
> 布羅克特在他明天回英國後也有重要的事件要處理。

d. since

since表示一個動作持續到現在，因而主句用現在完成式，子句用過去簡單式。例
如：

▶ She hasn't led a normal life since she was 16, and I think she's trying to break away
from that.
從16歲起，她就沒有過過正常生活，我想她正努力擺脫那種不正常的生活。

(11) because, for, since, as, now that的用法

a. because，for，since，as

because通常置於主句之後，特別強調原因時也可以置於主句之前。例如：

▶ You might even develop physical problems because you work too much.
你工作過度，你或許會因此而積勞成疾。

▶ Because CT scans are so useful, doctors are using them more and more frequently.
CT電腦斷層掃描用處很大，因此越來越頻繁地被醫生所使用。

because比as，since的語氣要強，因此在回答以why開頭的問句中，只能用
because，不能用as，since。例如：

▶ Why were you late for class? —Because I overslept this morning.
你為什麼遲到了？——因為我早上睡過頭了。

as，since引導的子句通常位於句首，但也有置於主句之後的。一般說來，這兩個
詞表示其原因或理由在說話人看來已經很明顯，或者已經為聽話人所熟悉，不需加以強
調。因此這類句子均強調原因引起的結果，而原因只是附帶說明。since比as稍正式一
些。例如：

▶They had planned on a fall wedding, but since they were pressed for time they decided to push the date back to next January.

他們原打算在秋天舉辦婚禮，但由於時間太緊，他們決定把日子推後到明年一月。

▶If you have had a stressful day your body will be depleted of B-vitamins, as they're used by the nervous system to fight stress.

如果你度過緊張的一天，你體內的維他命B將會被耗盡，因為它們是神經系統用來調節壓力的。

for 表明所說的理由是一個補充說明，不能放在句子的開頭。例如：

▶Force will be used only as necessary, for we are not terrorists and do not intend to strike innocent civilians.

只有在必要時才採用武力，因為我們不是恐怖分子，不打算襲擊無辜的平民。

b. now that

now that一般用在句首，有時間的含義，說明一種新情況，常翻譯成「既然」。例如：

▶Now that they are married, she has a statutory right to take the elected share against the will.

既然他們結婚了，她就有法定權利不遵照遺囑，得到一份遺產。

(12)關於so that與so...that結構

so...that表示主句的動作或狀態達到何種程度所引起的結果，通常放在句末，so 用在形容詞或副詞之前。例如：

▶He's been so influential that an annual, national award was established in his name in 1989 to recognize individuals who improve the quality of life for those with disabilities.

他很有影響力，所以，一個以他的名字命名的一年一度的國家獎項於1989年就設立起來了。本獎項旨在表彰那些為身障者改善生活品質的人。

有時為了強調可以把so 放在句首，這時主謂語的語序要倒裝。例如：

▶So insistent was the noise that he padded downstairs in his nightshirt and picked up the handset.

電話鈴聲持續不斷，於是他便穿著睡衣輕步下樓，拿起了電話聽筒。

如果修飾名詞，就要用such...that。例如：

▶He is such a wonderful man that everyone seems poor in comparison.

他真是棒極了，其他人則相形見絀。

so that一般表示目的，如果主句中的謂語動詞是現在簡單式或者現在完成式，那麼子句中一般用can，may，will，shall。如果主句中的謂語動詞指的是過去，那麼子句中的情態動詞一般用could，might，would，should。例如：

▶Care should be exercised **so that** this translation can be accessible to Spanish speaking students from different origins.
　務必留意，讓出身於不同背景的説西班牙語的學生能得到這個譯本。

▶Together we shouted at the man, and told him we would tell this story all over London **so that** his name would be hated.
　我們一起朝著那人喊叫，告訴他我們要把他的醜聞告訴全倫敦人，讓所有人都憎恨他。

　　so that也可以引導結果副詞子句。它與so that引導的目的副詞子句的不同可以從語義上判斷，也可以子句法上進行分辨。

　　從句法上講，應該從以下幾個方面考慮：

a. 目的副詞子句中多有情態動詞；結果副詞子句一般沒有情態動詞。

　　比較下面兩句：

　　★目的副詞子句

▶He shut the door **so that he could feel warm**.
　為了能感到暖和些，他把門關上了。

　　★結果副詞子句

▶He shut the door **so that he felt warm**.
　他把門關上後就覺得暖和些了。

b. 目的副詞子句可以前置，但結果副詞子句不可以。例如：

▶**So that everybody can take some books away with them when they go**, we'll leave some here as well and put them here in the literature rack.
　為了讓每人走的時候都可以拿一些書，我們將會留一些在這裡，放在文學架上。

c. 結果副詞子句的so不能用in order替代。

(13)關於unless與if...not

　　在真實條件句中，unless的含義相當於if...not。例如：

▶They will not share your data **unless you specifically give them permission to do so**. 他們不會使用你的資料，除非你特別允許他們這麼做。

但是在許多時候，unless不能替代if...not。如果不是因為受限於一定的條件，某件事情就有可能發生，這時可以用unless；但是預測某種情況未出現時將會發生什麼事情，這時不用unless。表示與過去或現在的事實相反的願望和假設也不能用unless。例如下面的句子中都不能用unless替代if...not。

▶ I will be surprised **if he doesn't have an accident**.
　他不出事才怪。

▶ I would go to the party **if I didn't have the cold**.
　如果不是感冒，我會去參加聚會的。

(14)關於though與although

　　though和although這兩個詞同義，可以互相替換，但後者比前者語氣要重。因此，though常用於非正式的口語和書面語，而although經常用於各種文體。例如：

▶ He refuses to visit his sister, **though he knows that it will lead her to depression**.
　他拒絕去拜訪他的姐姐，儘管他知道那會讓她沮喪。

▶ **Although he at times has worn the crown of world's richest person**, Buffett has made his share of mistakes—some of them big
　儘管巴菲特時而榮獲世界首富的桂冠，他也犯過一些錯誤——其中有些是大錯誤。

注意！

although，though引導讓步副詞子句時，主句中不能用but。如果要加強主句的語氣，可用still，nevertheless，just the same。例如：

▶ **Although the ads have gotten shorter over the decades**, they still tend to pack more information—both true and false—into each 30-second spot.
　儘管幾十年來廣告語變得短了，但在30秒的時段裡，它卻容納更多的資訊——有的真，有的假。

---

　　though可以引導特殊的讓步結構，在正式文體中，把子句的狀語或補語放在句首。as也可以用在同樣的句型中。例如：

▶ **Stupid though it might appear**, she went upstairs and spoke to them from an upper window.
　儘管看上去很傻，但她還是爬上樓從樓上的視窗跟他們說話。

▶ **Young as I was**, I sensed his words were more in the nature of an accusation than a supposition.
　儘管我嫩了點，但我還是感覺他的話本質上是指控而不是推測。

在功能上，句子可以分成陳述句、疑問句、祈使句和感嘆句。疑問句又可以分成特殊疑問句、一般疑問句、選擇疑問句和附加疑問句。祈使句根據它的不同用法又有第二人稱祈使句、第一人稱祈使句和第三人稱祈使句。

在結構上，句子可以分為簡單句、並列句和複合句。根據子句在複合句中所起的作用，又可以分成主詞子句、形容詞子句、受詞子句、同位語子句、關係子句和副詞子句。關係子句有限定性關係子句和非限定性關係子句之別。副詞子句包括時間副詞子句、地點副詞子句、方式副詞子句、原因副詞子句、結果副詞子句、目的副詞子句、條件副詞子句和讓步副詞子句。本章還就副詞子句中出現的部分常用連接詞的用法作了介紹和對比。

Part 16

否定

否定概說

從對句子意義否定的範圍來看，否定可分為句子否定、局部否定、謂體否定和部分否定。

句子否定是指通過否定句子的成分對整個句子的意義作出否定；局部否定是指否定片語成分後而達到的局部否定的結果；謂體否定是指否定謂語（不包括第一助動詞）後所得到的否定意義；部分否定是指對諸如all，every等詞的否定而得到的否定意義。

從否定的形式來看，否定可分為一般否定和局部否定，前者指對謂語的否定，後者指對謂語以外成分的否定。在否定的形式和否定的意義範圍之間，並沒有一一對應的十分清晰的界限。例如，She did not stay with her parents在形式上是個一般否定的句子，是對謂語的否定，但是在意義上，句子的重點卻是對句子中with her parents部分的否定，強調的是「她沒有和父母住在一起」。又如，They seem not to be able to deal with the matter properly是局部否定，但意義與一般否定相同，即：They do not seem to be able to deal with the matter properly。

否定形式在口語中出現的頻率比書面語高。英語中主要有兩個詞承擔否定功能，即not和no。除此之外也有很多詞彙表示否定的意思，例如：neither，none，nothing，never，no more，nowhere，nor，nobody，few，little，scarcely，hardly，rarely，seldom，without等。

另外有一些詞綴也表示否定的意義，例如：字首a- (amoral)，de- (deforestation)，dis- (dissatisfaction)，il-(illegally)，im- (immodest)，in- (inhuman)，ir- (irregular)，non-(non-believer)，un- (unhappy) 等。字尾-less也表示否定的含義，例如：harmless，useless等。

not否定

not的位置

否定詞（Negator）not直接跟在助動詞be或者情態動詞的後面，構成否定形式。例如：

▶ Internet users at home are not nearly as safe online as they believe, according to a nationwide inspection by researchers.
根據研究者在全國範圍內的調查，網際網路用戶在家裡上網並沒有他們想像的那麼安全。

▶ You can't make children feel what you want them to feel.
你沒法讓孩子感覺到你想讓他們得到的感覺。

如果句子沒有情態動詞或者助動詞be，需要先插入助動詞do，然後再在其後面加not。例如：

▶ I don't feel guilty about running away because it's what I want.
我並不因為逃走而愧疚，因為這是我想做的。

祈使句的否定形式比較特殊，儘管句子中有be，還需要加上助動詞do，再加not構成否定形式。例如：

▶ Don't be ridiculous. 別傻了。

⊙ have, dare, need等詞的否定形式

如果句子的謂語動詞是have，該句子可以有三種否定形式。第一種形式是前面插入助動詞do，再在其後加入not否定。例如：

▶ He doesn't have problems with his offsprings.
他在子女方面沒有什麼問題。

▶ These children don't have enough money to pay for basic needs like food, clothing, medical care and housing.
這些孩子沒有足夠的錢來支付生活的基本需求，如食物、衣服、醫療和住宿。

第二種形式是直接在have後面加not否定。例如：

▶ People just haven't time to read through the mail.
人們是沒有時間把信從頭看到尾。

▶ Most kids (and adults, for that matter) haven't a clue about the particulars of adoption.
大多數小孩（就此事也包括大人）對於收養的細節問題都不知情。

第三種形式是在have後面加no構成否定。例如：

▶ Personally, I have no regrets about my part in the World Cup and, in fact, I have a huge amount of pride and a real sense of achievement from the way we performed.
就我個人來講，我對於我在世界盃中的表現毫無遺憾。事實上，我對我們的表現極為驕傲並感覺到真正的成就感。

▶ I have no intention of giving up. 我並不打算放棄。

包含dare，need等詞的句子有兩種否定形式。第一種形式是前面插入助動詞do，再在其後加not。在這種否定形式中dare和need被看作普通動詞。美式英語中經常採用這種否定形式。例如：

▶I **don't dare** to argue in case they stop me going to your house.
　我不敢爭論，怕萬一他們不讓我進你的房子。

▶I always believed in the movie I was making, but you **don't dare** to hope for such an incredible scenario.
　我一直相信我製作的電影，卻不敢奢望有如此精彩的劇情。

▶I don't want to say I'm going to be No.1. I **don't need** to justify myself.
　我不想說我將是第一名。我不需要證明自己。

▶He **doesn't need** to tell me that they'll be back next year because I know they will be.
　他不需要告訴我他們明年回來，因為我知道他們會的。

　　第二種形式是直接在這些詞後面加not否定。在這種否定形式中，dare和need被看作情態動詞，其後的動詞之前不加to。這種否定形式一般都是現在式。例如：

▶I **dare not** think too far into the future on the risk that I'll miss the present.
　我不敢冒著錯過現在的危險對未來想得太遠。

▶The future **need not** be all doom and gloom.
　將來未必全是絕望的。

◎ not的縮寫形式

　　not在句中出現有三種形式。

　　一種是完全形式。例如：are not，is not，can not，do not，will not，shall not等。這種形式比較正式，一般用於學術文體等正式文體中。例如：

▶Unlike mosquitoes, bedbugs **are not** known to transmit disease to human prey.
　臭蟲和蚊子不一樣，它不會向被咬的人傳播疾病。

　　第二種是縮寫形式，not和之前的助動詞或情態動詞縮寫在一起。例如：aren't，isn't，can't，don't，won't，shan't等。縮寫形式通常在口語和新聞語體中較多出現。例如：

▶There **aren't** many shops in the city that are open until 2:00 or 3:00 in the morning.
　在這個城市裡沒有多少商店到凌晨2、3點還開門。

在否定疑問句中，如果主詞是第一人稱單數，否定謂語形式可以是am I not。但在實際的語言應用中更多的是用aren't。例如：

▶ I am right, **am I not**?
我是對的，不是嗎？

▶ Why **am I** not allowed to touch the map?
為什麼不允許我碰這個地圖？

▶ I'm going to get into trouble, **aren't I**?
我要有麻煩了，是嗎？

▶ **Aren't I** entitled to be worried about my brother?
我難道沒有權利擔心我的兄弟嗎？

情態動詞may和might後面加not，一般都用完全形式，沒有縮寫形式。例如：

▶ He himself **might not** be able to afford to send her the money, especially as he has a young family.
他自己可能沒有能力給她寄錢，特別是他還有一個建立不久的家庭。

not在句中出現的第三種形式是： 主詞和am，is，are，have，has，had，will，would等助動詞或情態動詞縮寫在一起，not單獨出現。如果主詞是人稱代名詞，這種縮寫形式用得比較多。例如：

▶ **We're not** eating in the dining room tonight.
我們今晚不在餐廳吃飯。

▶ "**I'm not** against the principle of cosmetic surgery," he said.
「我原則上並不反對整容外科手術。」他說。

no否定 ▷

除了not否定以外，英語中有很多詞彙表示否定形式，包括no，nobody，no one，none，nothing，nowhere，never，neither，nor 等。例如：

▶ I have **no** sympathy for her because I am totally opposed to the kind of money game she plays.
我一點都不同情她，因為我完全反對她玩這種金錢遊戲。

▶ He had **no one** to turn to, no one with whom to share his misery and offer consolation.
他沒有任何人可以依靠，沒有一個人替他分擔痛苦並提供安慰。

▶ You will have **nothing** to fear, or to be agitated about.
沒有任何事情讓你害怕或焦慮不安。

▶ There was **nobody** in the kitchen but herself and Victoria.
廚房裡除了她自己和維多利亞沒有其他人。

▶There was **nowhere** for us to put our belongings.
我們沒有地方放行李。

▶Just 38 percent of black children lived with both parents in 2000; almost one in 10 lived with **neither** parent.
2000年時只有38%的黑人孩子和父母住在一起，幾乎十個孩子裡面就有一個沒有和父母雙方中任何一方住在一起。

上面這些句子都可以轉化成not否定的形式。例如：

▶I **haven't any** sympathy for her because I am totally opposed to the kind of money game she plays.

▶He **didn't** have **anyone** to turn to, no one with whom to share his misery and offer consolation.

▶You will **not** have **anything** to fear, or to be agitated about.

▶There **wasn't anybody** in the kitchen but herself and Victoria.

▶There **wasn't anywhere** for us to put our belongings.

▶Just 38 percent of black children lived with both parents in 2000; almost one in 10 **didn't** live with **either** parent.

換句話說，這些否定詞彙的對應形式如下：

● no — not any
● nowhere — not anywhere
● nobody — not anybody
● never — not ever
● no one — not anyone
● neither — not either
● none — not any
● nor — and not
● nothing — not anything

在實際語言使用中，no否定形式出現的頻率遠遠小於not否定形式。not否定形式相對較隨便一些，no形式否定程度更強，更多地用於書面語。nobody和no one都表示「沒有人」的意思，但是nobody在口語中更常用，而no one在書面語中更常用。

並不是所有的no否定形式都可以轉化為not否定。如果nothing，nobody等否定詞彙作主詞，句子就不能轉化成not否定。例如：

▶**Nobody** as beautiful as you ever works in this factory.
這個工廠裡還沒有過像你這麼漂亮的人。

有時not否定和no否定之間有細微的語義差別。not否定形式意義中性，純粹表示否定。例如下面例子僅僅表示否定：

▶ He is **not a true fighter**.
　他不是一個真正的戰士。

no否定帶有更多的感情色彩，表示對某人能力或水準的評價。這時一般受no否定的名詞是可以區分等級程度的名詞。例如：no fool，no fan，no salesman，no expert，no beauty等。例如：

▶ Minnie is **no fool**.
　米妮才不傻呢。

▶ Mark Thomas is **no great fan** of The Daily Telegraph.
　馬克‧湯瑪斯不怎麼看《每日電訊報》。

▶ Business is slow, and Ella is **no great saleswoman**, sitting passively six hours a day on the street with the bottles at her slippered feet.
　生意不好，而且艾拉壓根兒就不是個在行的推銷員，每天六個小時她只是被動地坐在街上，瓶子擺在穿著拖鞋的腳邊。

有些固定的搭配比較傾向於用no否定形式。例如存在句中經常使用no chance，no evidence，no reason，no doubt，no need，no point，no sign，no way等。

have 句型中經常使用no choice，no desire，no effect，no intention，no reason，no idea等。例如：

▶ **There is no chance** that any of them would be involved in anything crazy like this.
　他們中的任何一個都沒有機會捲入這樣瘋狂的事情。

▶ **There is no evidence** that terrorists possess the capability to build a bomb.
　沒有任何證據證明恐怖分子有能力製造炸彈。

▶ **There is no point** in my making a speech on crime control to a group of drug addicts.
　我對一群吸毒者講犯罪控制沒有任何意義。

▶ We **have no choice** but to keep trying to demonstrate our good intentions by the way we act and behave.
　我們沒有選擇，只能通過我們行動和行為的方式來盡量表達我們的好意。

▶ Many Americans say the scandal will **have no effect** on their vote.
　許多美國人說醜聞對他們投票沒有任何影響。

▶ You **have no reason** to trust me, and I trust no woman except my sister.
　你沒有理由相信我，我除了我姐姐以外也不相信任何女人。

在口語中no經常用來作為一般疑問句的否定回答。例如：

▶A: Who looks like a baby?
B: Jeanette.
A: **No**, she doesn't.
A：誰看上去像個孩子？
B：珍妮特。
A：不，她不像。

hardly, scarcely, seldom, rarely等詞的否定 ▷

hardly，barely，rarely，scarcely，seldom等副詞有近似於否定的含義。含這些副詞的句子可以看成是弱否定句。例如：

▶We very **rarely** have the radio on, except we have the radio on at breakfast time, listen to the news and the weather forecast.
我們很少打開收音機，只有在早飯時間打開一下收聽新聞和天氣預報。

▶He could **scarcely** believe what he had heard.
他幾乎不相信他所聽到的事實。

▶In Rome, you **seldom** see an Italian drunk unless it's an alcoholic vagrant or a politician.
在羅馬，你很少看到義大利人醉酒，除非是流浪漢酒鬼或者是政客。

little和few也有否定意義。兩者既可以作限定詞也可以作代名詞，little還可以作副詞，都是表示否定含義。例如：

▶It was cold and despite their weariness they slept very **little**.
天氣很冷，儘管他們很疲憊，但是卻沒怎麼睡覺。

▶Like most people he had **little** idea of how television programs are made, let alone sold.
和大多數人一樣，他不清楚電視節目是如何製作的，更不用說賣了。

▶**Few** would question his motives under such circumstances.
在這種情況下很少有人會去質疑他的動機。

▶**Few** would disagree that wisdom in any walk of life is very desirable.
每個行業都需要智慧，這一點很少有人不同意。

否定的範圍 ▷

總體來說，否定的範圍可以分為對整個句子的否定和對句子中某些成分的否定，即完全否定和局部否定或不完全否定（Partial Negation or Local Negation）。

具體來講，在形式上，否定是通過否定詞來實現的，而否定的範圍則是指否定詞所作用的範圍。否定詞對謂語的否定通常稱為一般否定，在意義上是句子否定，而否定詞對句子中的單字、片語等的否定通常稱為局部否定。

🎯 句子否定

句子否定是否定整個句子的命題，否定的範圍從否定詞位置到句末位置。有些狀語隨其在not前後位置不同，而意義有所不同。例如entirely，altogether，completely，quite，all the time等副詞如果出現在not後面，處於否定的範圍之內，表示「不完全……」、「並非完全……」等含義。例如：

▶ Lunch had **not altogether** been a waste of time.
午飯也不完全是浪費時間。

▶ Robbins did **not altogether** abandon his parents' word.
羅賓斯沒有完全忘記他父母的承諾。

▶ The government has **not** shielded Justin **completely** from liability against lawsuits in the event the vaccine were to cause illness.
在疫苗可能引發疾病的情況下，政府並沒有完全保護賈斯汀免受法律的起訴。

▶ He was calm, businesslike, and **not quite** aggressive.
他冷靜而務實，並且不太咄咄逼人。

▶ I think it's more important **not** to focus **all the time** on individual cases.
我認為更重要的是不要一直都關注個別的情況。

如果這些詞出現在否定詞的前面，則不處於否定的範圍之內，表示「完全」、「十分」等含義。例如：

▶ I just **completely don't** get what he meant.
我只是一點也沒有明白他的意思。

🎯 片語否定

片語否定指not否定作用的範圍局限於片語內部。例如下面三個句子中not否定作用的範圍是一個狀語片語，整個句子還是表達肯定的含義：

▶ **Not surprisingly**, they became good friends.
他們成為好朋友一點也不奇怪。

▶ This was a very positive outcome, which the teachers, **not unexpectedly**, were very pleased about in the behavior of pupils.
這是一個非常好的結果，不出所料，教師對學生的表現感到非常高興。

▶ I saw a million-dollar home in Beverly Hills **not long ago**.
不久前我在比佛利山看到了一個價值百萬美元的住所。

not的否定範圍還可以是帶有限定詞all，every的名詞片語。這時整個句子表示部分否定的意義（有的文法書稱之為部分否定或者不完全否定）。例如：

▶"**Not all men** are like you—completely averse to marriage," she pointed out.
「不是所有的人都和你一樣完全反對結婚。」她指出。

▶**Not everyone** was bothered by Honolulu's traffic; it depends where you live.
並不是每個人都受檀香山交通的影響,這取決於你住在哪裡。

上面的例子如果要表達完全否定的意思,用相應的no one,none或nobody。例如:

▶**No one** is like you—completely averse to marriage.

▶**Nobody** was bothered by Honolulu's traffic.

🎯 單詞否定

單詞否定常見於一些固定的習語中。no用於否定其後的名詞。例如:

▶It is **no good** you telling me that the bigger the sample surveyed, the closer to reality the average will become.
你告訴我調查樣本越大,平均數越接近實際。這沒什麼用。

▶Most people **have no idea** that he was a lawyer.
多數人不知道他是個律師。

▶It's **no use** struggling against the inevitable.
與必然發生的事情作抗爭是沒有用的。

▶A: I don't know whether it's convenient to talk to you now?
B: **No problem.**
A:我不知道現在和你談是否方便?
B:沒問題。

其他的一些單詞否定的片語包括in no time,in no way,by no means等。

🎯 否定範圍的轉移

有時雖然否定詞處於主句的位置,但是否定的範圍卻局限在子句內。主要有
以下幾種情況:

1. 謂語動詞是think,believe,guess,fancy,expect,imagine等(hope除外)。
例如:

▶I **don't think** there will be much time for slacking off.
我想我們沒有多少時間可以放鬆。

▶I **don't believe** they will even get a refund on their tickets.
我相信他們甚至連票的退款也拿不到。

當這些詞用於問句的回答時，肯定回答用I hope so, I think so, I guess so等。例如：

▶ A: Is her number in the phone book?

B: Uh, I think so. It should be.

A：她的號碼在電話簿裡嗎？

B：嗯，我想是，應該在。

否定回答有兩種形式。afraid，guess，hope可以直接加not。例如：I'm afraid not，I guess not，I hope not。think可以有兩種形式：I don't think so和I think not，後者更正式一些。例如：

▶ A: Were there any subjects she hated?

B: No, I don't think so.

A：有什麼課程是她討厭的嗎？

B：不，我想沒有。

▶ A: Would you like another cream cake?

B: I think not.

A：你想再要一個奶油蛋糕嗎？

B：不要了。

suppose 兩種形式都可以：I don't suppose so 和I suppose not。

▶ A: You won't try to find her, will you?

B: I don't suppose so.

A：你不會去找她，對嗎？

B：我想不會。

▶ A: We can't throw him out in this kind of weather.

B: No, I suppose not.

A：在這種天氣下我們不可能把他扔出去。

B：是的，我想不會的。

2. 謂語動詞是seem，appear等。例如：

▶ It doesn't seem that they're doing a good job at what Walt Disney was famous for—running an amusement park in the best, safest way.

華特·迪士尼以用最好、最安全的方式經營遊樂園著稱，但他們似乎沒有把這個工作做好。

▶ It doesn't appear that that country can have an election before November.

這個國家看起來不像是能在11月之前進行選舉。

3. 有時對主句動詞的否定會轉移為對動名詞（動詞-ing形式）或子句的否定。例如：

▶ I don't remember having heard anything about his career development at the time.
我記得沒有聽說他的事業在這時有任何發展。

▶ It's not a situation where we can't do something because we don't have the money.
現在的情況不是因為我們沒有錢所以不能做事情。

上面兩個句子中，表面是對主要動詞remember和is的否定，實際是對動名詞having heard anything和because子句的否定。

多重否定

多重否定（Multi-negation）指一個句子中包含兩個或兩個以上的否定要素。在標準英語中，如果一個句子包含兩個否定要素，則表示肯定的意思。

雙重否定表示肯定通常出現在比較正式的文體中（如學術文體）。使用這種格式可以謹慎地表達說話者的觀點或態度。例如：

▶ Even if stockpiles have not been found, I've heard no one argue that Saddam Hussein did not have the capability to work on these weapons.
即使儲備武器沒有被發現，也沒有人爭論說薩達姆·侯賽因沒有能力製造這些武器。

▶ Nobody comes to buy nothing.
沒有人來了什麼都不買。

▶ It is not for nothing that they date back to Babylon.
他們回溯至巴比倫時期不是毫無原因的。

▶ None of us in the political game is without guilt.
在政治遊戲中我們沒有一個人是無罪的。

▶ But I was not uninterested and I have not forgotten my subject.
但是我不是沒有興趣，我沒忘記我的主題。

▶ It's not impossible that they may just close our enterprise altogether.
他們完全關掉我們的企業不是沒有可能。

▶ It is not unusual for him to simply not show up for a scheduled event.
對他來說，不出席安排好的活動是很平常的。

▶ It's not a situation where the company does not have the assets to pay its bills.
現在情況不是這個公司沒有足夠的資產來付帳單。

儘管雙重否定表示肯定，但在形式上是否定句，如果有附加疑問句，用肯定形式。例如：

▶ **No** Democrat has won the White House **without** winning Clark County, **is it**?
任何民主黨人如果不贏得克拉克郡選舉就不能贏得白宮，對嗎？

▶ **No** trip to Brussels is complete **without** going up the Atomium, **is it**?
到了布魯塞爾如果不去原子塔，就不算完整的旅行，是不是？

與否定有關的習慣表達 ▷

英語中有些習慣表達雖然含有否定的形式，但卻表達肯定的意義。這些習慣表達主要有以下幾種：

1. cannot/couldn't wait to do 急於做。例如：

▶ He **cannot wait to** take his son to the park, go swimming, all the things that dads do.
他急於帶孩子去公園，去游泳，去做所有父親該做的事情。

2. cannot/couldn't + too/over/enough 越……越，無論怎樣……也不過分。例如：

▶ I **cannot** sing their praises **too** highly.
我無論怎麼讚揚他們都不為過。

▶ Milan Baros **cannot** recover fitness soon **enough**.
米蘭‧巴羅斯越快恢復健康越好。

▶ I **cannot** recommend this amazing film highly **enough**.
我極力推薦這部精彩的電影。

3. not...until/till 直到……時候才。例如：

▶ I did **not** really look at the electric toothbrush **until** this morning, when I opened a pack of batteries to try it out.
直到今天早上打開一包電池試用了一下，我才仔細地研究這個電動牙刷。

▶ The decision will **not** be formally announced for several days, **until** commissioners finish writing their public statements.
幾天內暫時不正式宣佈這個決定，直到委員們寫完公開聲明才宣佈。

4. no/none other than 恰恰，正是。例如：

▶ The lady in question is **none other than** 37-year-old Hollywood actress Halle Berry.
談到的那個女士正是37歲的好萊塢女星荷莉‧貝瑞。

5. nothing/none/no one but 僅僅，只有。例如：

▶ SONY is **nothing but** persistent in its cruel attempt to replace household pets with robot dogs.
索尼公司只是一直在做一種殘忍的嘗試：用機器狗代替家養寵物。

▶ **None but** the most naive or partisan of observers could possibly call this election free or fair.
只有最幼稚的或者最盲目的觀察員才有可能稱這場選舉是自由公正的。

6 not/no＋比較級。例如：

否定詞和比較級的組合有幾種情況。下面前兩個例子表示最高級的意義，後一個例子表示同級的意義。例如：

▶ I **couldn't agree more** with English as a second language.
我完全同意英語是第二語言的觀點。

▶ **Nothing is more addictive than** cigarettes.
沒有什麼比香菸更讓人上癮的了。

▶ The U.S. is **no safer than** it was before 9/11.
美國現在不比911事件前更安全。

7.習慣用語：more often than not 常常；as likely as not 很可能。例如：

▶ In some cases, true love prevails, but **more often than not**, the questionable relationship crashes and burns—and the fallout can hit the unsuspecting lovers like a truck.
有時真愛終究獲得勝利。但很多時候，戀愛關係出現問題而破裂——這種破裂對沒有準備的雙方造成的傷害不亞於一輛卡車的撞擊。

▶ If there is a greater than 1 percent chance that a worker was **as likely as not** to get cancer from his/her calculated dose, the worker will be compensated.
一個工人如果有超過百分之一的可能，因服用既定劑量而患上癌症，那麼這個工人將會得到補償。

否定疑問句

附加疑問句中，如果前半部分是否定的，則後半部分是肯定的。例如：

▶ You aren't a Rafferty, by any chance, **are you**?
你可能不是一個不講章法的人，對嗎？

附加疑問句中，如果前半部分是肯定的，則後半部分可以是肯定的，也可以是否定的。肯定加肯定格式的附加疑問句表示說話者認為答案可能是肯定的。肯定加否定格式的附加疑問句表示說話者不清楚答案肯定與否。例如：

▶ They liked winning the World Cup, didn't they?
他們想贏得世界盃，不是嗎？

▶ He actually wants to become the bird, doesn't he?
他實際上想變成那只鳥，是不是？

▶ So you went to school, did you?
所以說你去學校了，是嗎？

▶ She's a good friend of yours, is she?
她是你的一個好朋友，是嗎？

　　否定附加疑問句還可以表示祈使，尋求贊同或感嘆等語氣。例如：

▶ Do come back in September, won't you?
9月份一定回來，好嗎？

▶ How sweet it is, isn't it?
真甜，是不是？

▶ How wonderful that story is, isn't it?
那個故事真是棒極了，不是嗎？

　　否定的一般疑問句常用來表示驚異、讚嘆、責備、建議和有禮貌的邀請等。

　　這種疑問句常帶有濃厚的感情色彩，比普通的疑問句富有人情味。否定疑問句的答案需要根據事實來回答。若事實是肯定的，則用Yes來回答；若事實是否定的，則用No來回答。例如：

▶ A: Isn't it amazing that somebody can write that many books about science fiction?
B: Yes, it is.
A：有人能寫這麼多科幻小說，這不是太令人驚嘆了嗎？
B：是的，確實如此。

▶ A: Won't you have a cup of coffee?
B: Yes, I will.
A：你不喝一杯咖啡嗎？
B：好的，我喝。

▶ A: Don't you want Pete to tell you what he thinks?
B: No, I don't.
A：你難道不想彼特告訴你他怎麼想的嗎？
B：不，我不想。

在以why開頭的特殊疑問句中，通常加not，用來間接地向對方提出建議，往往有肯定意味，一般不必回答。例如：

▶**Why** don't you give me a call?
為什麼不給我打電話？

▶**Why** don't you call the police and catch the burglar?
為什麼不打電話叫員警把這個竊賊抓起來？

▶**Why** not just keep quiet?
為什麼不保持安靜？

否定與語篇

🎯 加強否定

有些詞彙經常用於否定句中，用來加強否定的語氣。at all經常用於not否定句中。

例如：

▶He did not like my proposal **at all**.
他一點也不喜歡我的提議。

▶Although you look like a child, you are not really a child **at all** because your mind and your powers of reasoning seem to be fully grown-up.
儘管你看起來像個孩子，但實際上你一點也不是，因為你的思想和邏輯能力完全像一個成人。

▶I'm not concerned about David **at all**.
我一點也不在乎大衛。

whatsoever經常用在no，no one，none，nothing等詞後面以加強否定語氣。例如：

▶He had frankly given no thought **whatsoever** to his child's name; he had not yet thought of him as an identity anyway.
他還從來沒有想過孩子的名字，因為他還沒把孩子當作一個個體。

另外，a bit，a little bit，in the least，the least bit 等也可用來加強語氣。例如：

▶You're not **a bit** like your father.
你一點也不像你父親。

▶"I'm not going to feel **in the least** reasonable while you're forcing me to stay in this house," she warned fiercely.
「你這樣強迫我待在這所房子裡，我覺得這沒任何道理。」她強烈地警告道。

▶Two interest rate increases have not cooled the property market **in the least**.
兩次提高利率一點也沒有讓房地產市場降溫。

否定及委婉詞

　　在否定句中，有些詞經常和not連用用來緩和否定語氣，或者使語氣更加婉轉禮貌。這些委婉詞（Hedging）包括：actually，necessarily，really，very等。而altogether，entirely等副詞處於否定範圍內的時候也有類似的作用。例如：

▶ I **wasn't actually** impressed by what I saw last night.
　　昨天晚上看到的並沒有給我留下多大印象。

▶ You **don't really** notice what's going on around you.
　　你並沒有真正注意到你周圍發生了什麼事情。

▶ I **don't really** read the self-improvement books or things like that.
　　我並不讀自我提升之類的書籍。

　　這些婉轉詞結構還經常用來回答問句。例如：

▶ A: Is he a coach cockier than his players?
　　B: **Not really**. Just confident.
　　A：他是一個比他的運動員還驕傲的教練嗎？
　　B：其實不是，他只是自信而已。

▶ A: Are all these beyond the regulatory power of the federal government?
　　B: **Not necessarily**. The government could ban all uses of a product, such as heroin, if the total ban were essential to maintaining control of that substance, he said.
　　A：所有這些超越了聯邦政府的行政權力嗎？
　　B：不一定。他說，政府可以全面禁止使用某一產品，比如海洛因，如果這種禁令對這種物質的控制是必須的話。

小結 ▷

　　本章主要介紹了一般否定和局部否定這兩種形式以及與其相聯繫的四種否定意義的範圍。否定的主要詞語是not 和no。not 否定通常是對謂語成分的否定，no否定是對名詞成分的否定。

　　另外還有些詞語本身包含有否定的含義。否定的範圍可以是一個單字，也可以是一個片語或者句子。當否定的範圍是帶有all，every 或always 等詞語時，整個句子表達的是部分否定的意思。

　　英語中有時用雙重否定來表達肯定的含義，這一般是基於語體或者語用的原因。否定不但用於肯定句也用於疑問句，並且在實際語言應用中可以用一些副詞來加強或者緩和否定的語氣。

倒裝

倒裝概說 ▷

英語的正常語序是主詞－動詞－受詞,也稱為自然語序。但是在交際過程中,為了強調資訊的重點或表達特殊意義,資訊的傳遞者也可以改變語序。

倒裝是常用的改變語序的語法手段之一。本章主要介紹常見的兩種倒裝的方式:全部倒裝和部分倒裝。

自然語序和倒裝語序

英語中大多句子是採用主詞加謂語的自然語序。例如:

► They love Europe. 他們喜歡歐洲。

有些句式是採用倒裝語序,即採用謂語(或部分謂語)加主詞的語序,例如疑問句大部分都是用倒裝語序,不管是一般疑問句、特殊疑問句、選擇疑問句還是附加疑問句。例如:

► Do you want any tea? 你想喝點茶嗎?

► How do you feel about outsourcing jobs to other countries?
你對把工作外包給其他國家這件事怎麼看?

► Are they the ideal family, or are they the ideal soap opera?
他們是完美的家庭還是完美的肥皂劇?

► She seems happy enough in London, doesn't she? 她在倫敦好像非常開心,是不是?

除了疑問句這種特殊句式要求倒裝語序以外,在陳述句中有時也採用倒裝語序。例如:

► In came Richard, holding out flowers. 理查進來了,捧著鮮花。

全部倒裝和部分倒裝

倒裝可以分為全部倒裝和部分倒裝。全部倒裝(或主詞與謂語倒裝)是整個謂語都提到主詞前面。例如下面例句中的整個謂語comes都提到了主詞前面。例如:

▶There **comes old Sir Archibald Drew and his grandson**.

老阿奇博爾德‧德魯爵士和他的孫子來了。

謂語的一部分提前，即助動詞或情態動詞提前，稱為部分倒裝。例如下面例句中只有謂語的一部分had提到了主詞的前面：

▶Hardly **had my valet** locked the door, when Jim and the captain began to knock.

我的僕從剛把門鎖上，吉姆和船長就開始敲門了。

無論是全部倒裝還是部分倒裝，都是由非主詞成分置於句首引起的。在上面的例子中句首成分分別是there 和hardly。

倒裝的主要目的是為了上下文連貫、突出重點或者加強語氣等。下面詳細介紹兩種倒裝在陳述句中的不同用法和功能。

全部倒裝（主詞與謂語倒裝）

全部倒裝一般用於下列情況：

1. 狀語置於句首，表述句子的背景資訊。一般該狀語中會包含回指成分，回指上文中提到過的內容。

2. 動詞是不及物動詞或連綴動詞，且主詞較長。

地點狀語置於句首

1. 一般地點狀語

有些句子中動詞是不及物動詞，並且主詞較長。可以把地點狀語置於句首，而把主詞放在謂語動詞的後面。地點狀語中通常有定冠詞、人稱代名詞等回指成分。採用倒裝語序一方面可以避免頭重腳輕，一方面可以通過回指成分保持上下文連貫。例如：

▶On the table stood two jellies, one red and one green.

桌子上擺著兩個果凍，一個紅的，一個綠的。

▶Next to him stands the less enthusiastic Michael, a mid-level manager at a private food-processing plant.

他旁邊站著略欠熱情的麥可，一個私人食品加工廠的中層經理。

▶Before them lay the bridges over the River Thames.

展現在他們面前的是泰晤士河上的橋。

▶Opposite me, sat a small, thin man with yellowed teeth who ate in a great hurry.

我對面坐著一個小個子的消瘦男人，他牙齒發黃，急匆匆地吃著東西。

▶Within the monument is a small exhibition space, with interesting and changing exhibits on the city's history.

紀念碑裡面是一個小的展覽空間，展示了這個城市發展歷史上的趣聞和變遷。

2. here 和there置於句首

副詞here和there作地點狀語時，通常置於句首，引發全部倒裝語序。這裡的there是表示地點的狀語，不同於存在句中的there。例如：

▶Here's the good and bad news for us. 消息來了，有好也有壞。

▶Here comes another car. 另一輛車來了。

▶Here comes lunch. 午飯來了。

▶There goes my suggestion. 那就是我的建議。

▶There goes the phone. 電話鈴響了。

3. 副詞小品詞置於句首

表示方向的副詞小品詞（Adverb Particle）置於句首作地點狀語時一般也引起主謂倒裝。常見的這類副詞小品詞有：in，back，off，down，round，away，up，out等。例如：

▶In came the tall large woman, preoccupied with a glass she was carrying.
走進來的又高又壯的女人，拿著一個玻璃杯看入神了。

▶Back went the sisters to the Midlands. 姐妹們返回中部地區去了。

▶Back comes Richard Hill from injury 理查‧希爾受傷回來了。

▶Off roared his career. 他的事業如日中天。

▶Down went Jo's face into the wet handkerchief, and she cried despairingly; for she had kept up bravely till now, and never shed a tear.
喬把臉埋到濕濕的手絹裡，絕望地哭泣著。這之前她一直在勇敢地堅持著，不流一滴淚。

▶Round and round ran the car. 汽車一直在轉圈跑。

時間狀語置於句首

由then，again，first，now等詞作時間狀語置於句首時，通常引起倒裝。這些時間狀語都暗含著和前文的聯繫。例如：

▶Then came the recession in 2001 and a recovery marked by often sluggish job creation. 接下來2001年經濟不景氣，然後是就業機會緩慢增加，代表著經濟恢復。

▶Again came the disembodied voice, clearer now, approaching.
又傳來了不知哪裡發出的聲音，越來越近，愈發清晰。

▶First came MP3, a compression technology that made digital music possible.
先是出現了MP3，一項讓電子音樂成為可能的壓縮技術。

▶Now comes supermarket TV, adding yet more commercial "noise" to our lives.
現在出現了超市TV，給我們的生活增加了更多的商業噪音。

少數介係詞片語充當時間狀語置於句首也能引起倒裝。例如：

▶ **After worship comes** a free breakfast and fellowship time.
做禮拜後是免費的早餐和友情交流時間。

▶ **After Monday comes** Tuesday, and Wednesday follows.
星期一之後是星期二，然後是星期三。

🎯 主詞補語置於句首

下列片語作主詞補語前置會引起倒裝：介係詞片語、表示比較的形容詞片語或受程度副詞so 和especially等修飾的形容詞片語、表示方位的副詞片語，以及動詞-ing形式和-ed形式等。

這些句子的共同特點是主詞補語一般包含承上啟下的資訊，謂語動詞是連綴動詞be，主詞通常較長。

1. 介係詞片語置於句首

▶ **On the other side was** an American flag. 另外一面是美國國旗。

▶ **Around the temple are** many shops which sell incense and other items for worship.
寺廟周圍是許多賣香和其他祭拜用品的商店。

▶ **Among the residents are** Pedro Montanez and Arlene Olmeda, a common-law couple who have been together for 10 years and have three children.
住戶當中有佩德羅‧蒙塔內斯和阿琳‧奧爾梅達這一對事實婚姻的夫妻。他們住在一起十年了，並有三個孩子。

2. 形容詞片語置於句首。

表示比較的形容詞片語作前置主詞補語。例如：

▶ **Higher up grow** hardier plants, with sun-lovers such as sedums and buddleias near the top. 再高一點的地方長著耐寒植物，接近頂部是喜歡陽光的佛甲草和醉魚草。

▶ **Worst of all is** crying in an argument. 最糟糕的是在辯論中大喊大叫。

▶ **Worst of all was** the climate of fear I found everywhere.
最糟的是我發現到處充滿著恐懼的氣息。

▶ **Even more important is** the evidence of growing demand inside Japan for the first time in 15 years. 更為重要的是，有證據證明日本國內15年以來第一次出現需求增長。

受程度副詞so，especially等修飾的形容詞片語作前置主詞補語。例如：

▶ **So bad was** the recent flooding that septic tanks overflowed, and human waste saturated the floodwaters inside and outside the ramshackle houses.
最近一次的洪水來勢非常兇猛，以至於化糞池溢出，搖搖欲墜的房子裡裡外外全是夾雜著糞便的洪水。

▶**So different are** impressions on two different people! 對兩個不同的人印象大不相同！

▶**Especially popular are** the pink fish chowder and other seafood.
特別受歡迎的是粉紅色的魚肉雜燴和其他海鮮食品。

3. 副詞片語置於句首

▶**Nearby are** newly built banks, gas stations and fast food eateries.
附近是新建的銀行、加油站和速食店。

▶**Below is** a list of ongoing or recent auctions.
下面是正在進行或將要進行拍賣的物品的清單。

▶**Below is** a guide to how to look after your teeth on a daily basis—from how to brush and floss correctly to which toothbrush to choose and how often to replace it.
下面是一個如何對你的牙齒進行日常護理的指南──從如何正確刷牙、用潔牙線剔牙到如何選擇牙刷及多長時間更換牙刷。

4. 動詞-ing形式和-ed形式置於句首

動詞-ing形式和-ed形式作主詞補語時相當於形容詞，因此置於句首位置時，也會引起倒裝。

動詞-ing形式置於句首。例如：

▶**Lying on the floor was** a dead man, with a knife in his heart.
地板上躺著一個死人，心臟部位插著一把刀。

▶**Standing at the entrance of the clinic was** Annie, a 4-year-old poodle with a hand-painted sign draped over her torso that read," Thank you blood donors, you saved my life!" 門診入口處站著4歲的長鬃毛狗安妮，身上掛著一塊手寫的標牌，上面寫著：「謝謝獻血者，你們救了我的命！」

▶**Adjoining the palace is** the magnificent temple built in 1564.
與宮殿毗鄰的是那座1564年建成的宏偉寺廟。

▶**Waiting alongside him** was a police car. 等在他身旁的是一輛警車。

動詞-ed形式置於句首。例如：

▶**Seated at a table with a tall glass in front of him was** Hacket.
哈克特坐在桌邊，面前是一個大玻璃杯。

▶**The most widely read among the literature group are** novels and short stories, which are read by 45 percent of Americans, or 93 million people.
文學作品中擁有最廣泛讀者群的是長篇小說和短篇小說，有45%的美國人，也就是9,300萬人，在閱讀。

▶**Enclosed is** a listing of the 90 exhibitions going on throughout the city.
附上的是這個城市正在舉行的全部90個展覽的名單。

▶ **Gone were** the days when she could just get up in the morning, make coffee, leave a note for Mrs. Bennett and go off to the lake with, maybe, the anticipation of quite an exciting day.

在那些日子裡，她可以早上起床，煮咖啡，給貝內特夫人留個紙條後就去湖邊，或許還懷著對精彩一天的期待。這些日子都一去不返了。

直接引語插入語中的全部倒裝

在直接引語後面的插入語中，主詞可以放到表示言說意義的動詞後面。例如：

▶ "Catherine, I'd like you to meet my wife," **said** John.
「凱薩琳，我想讓你認識一下我太太。」約翰説。

▶ "Are you scared?" **whispered** Jack.
「你害怕嗎？」傑克小聲問道。

但在這種情況下，並不一定用倒裝語序。例如：

▶ "Happy Christmas," John **said**.
「聖誕快樂。」約翰説。

在下列幾種情況下傾向於用非倒裝語序。

1. 主詞是代名詞。例如：

▶ "We are thirsty for peace," she **said**.
「我們渴望和平。」她説。

2. 謂語動詞是帶有助動詞的複雜片語。例如：

▶ "My daughter is only six," Judith **had answered**.
「我的女兒只有6歲。」裘蒂絲回答説。

3. 動詞後面有受詞。例如：

▶ "This reminds me of Switzerland," Jim **had told her**.
「這讓我想起了瑞士。」吉姆告訴她。

4. 表示資訊來源的子句位於引語前。例如：

▶ She **said**: " There is no doubt my career is on the line."
她説：「毫無疑問我的事業正處在危險中。」

部分倒裝 ▷

部分倒裝和全部倒裝有以下幾點不同：

1. 部分倒裝可以用於及物動詞也可以用於不及物動詞

2. 引發部分倒裝的成分僅僅局限於少數否定詞（或片語）和程度副詞（或片語）

部分倒裝主要有以下幾種：

🎯 否定詞置於句首

否定副詞，例如neither，nor，never，nowhere，not only，hardly，no sooner，rarely，scarcely，seldom, 或者具有否定意義的限制詞如little，less，only等，位於句首會引起部分倒裝。例如：

▶ **Not before dark night did** the men and women come back to the children.
天黑之前這些男人和女人們沒有回到孩子身邊。

▶ **Never again has** he asked for expensive tennis shoes.
他再也沒有要過昂貴的網球鞋。

▶ **Only in this way will** people be convinced of the value of this new currency.
只有通過這種方式才能讓人們相信新貨幣的價值。

否定成分置於句首加強了否定意義。這種句式多在書面語中出現。不過，nor 和neither引導的倒裝子句在口語中使用較多。（參見本章P391〈連接詞so，nor，neither引起的倒裝〉）

🎯 否定範圍與語序關係

需要指出的一點是，只有當否定範圍是整個句子的時候，否定詞置於句首才引起倒裝。如果否定詞的否定範圍僅局限於一個片語，而整個句子仍然表達肯定的含義，這時全句仍然用正常語序。例如下面的例子是採用正常語序：

▶ **No doubt** Mr. Bragg is proud of his achievement.
毫無疑問，布拉格先生為他的成就感到自豪。

▶ **Not surprisingly**, he doesn't like school.
他不喜歡學校，這不奇怪。

▶ **Not long ago**, $100,000 was the average price of a good-sized, downtown home.
不久前，在市中心買一個大小合適的房子均價是10萬美元。

▶ **In no time** he is a medical student, and then a doctor.
很快他成為了一名醫學系學生，然後就做了醫生。

而下面這些例子中整個句子表達否定的含義，所以都是採用倒裝語序。例如：

▶**At no time did** a doctor step outside the hospital.
一個醫生任何時候都不走出醫院。

▶**At no time did** he tell the women he was infected with the HIV virus.
他從來沒有告訴這些女人他感染了愛滋病病毒。

▶**Under no circumstance would** I have tolerated rude and self-centered people.
任何情況下我都不會容忍粗魯和以自我為中心的人。

▶**At no point did** I insult him or his hometown
我從來沒有侮辱過他或者他的家鄉。

🎯 程度副詞so置於句首

程度副詞so 置於句首時，句子需要倒裝。例如：

▶**So ugly was** Gertrude that she was shunned by the other squirrels and was sadly alone atop a magnolia tree eating lunch.
格特魯德非常醜，以至於其他的松鼠都躲著它，它獨自傷心地在木蘭樹頂上吃午飯。

▶**So correct was** this insight that Swatch, through 160 production centers, now owns about a quarter of the world market for watches.
這一見解非常正確，它使斯沃琪公司通過160個生產中心佔據了全球四分之一的手錶市場。

🎯 假設語氣引起的部分倒裝

在正式書面文體中，某些條件子句的連接詞if經常省略，而用should，had或were開頭，成為部分倒裝語序。例如：

▶**Should they** beat French opposition today, they will meet American team in the semi-finals.
如果他們今天能打敗法國隊，他們將在半決賽中與美國隊對決。

▶**Had he** been charged with the theft of electrical equipment, he could have been jailed if convicted.
如果他被指控偷盜電子儀器，一旦被判有罪就會銀鐺入獄。

▶**Were he** in any other business, it would have made his fortune.
如果他從事其他行業，他會賺大錢的。

以may開頭的表示祝願的句子也用部分倒裝語序。例如：

▶**May your marriage** be blessed with many sons!
祝您婚姻幸福，多子多福！

▶**May your mother** also have a long life!
也祝您的母親長壽！

連接詞so，nor，neither引起的倒裝 ▷

連接詞so，nor，neither引出句子位於句首時，該句子需要倒裝。例如：

▶ If she can implement such rules, **so can I**.
如果她能執行這樣的規則，我也行。

▶ If he can do it, **so can I**.
如果他能做，我也能。

▶ I am devastated, and **so is** my life and my family.
我被毀了，我的生活和我的家庭也被毀了。

這種句式中的so 不同於程度副詞so，它承接上文，表示前一句中謂語所表達的內容。比如上面第一句中的倒裝部分相當於I can implement it, too.。

nor，neither和so 類似，只是承接上文，表達前一句中的否定內容。例如：

▶ I don't want to die, I don't deserve it and **neither** do those women held in the Iraqi prisons.
我不想死，我不該死，那些在伊拉克監獄裡的婦女也不該死。

▶ I never knew his last name, **nor** did he know my last name.
我從來不知道他的姓，他也不知道我的姓。

as和than子句中的倒裝 ▷

在正式語體中由as和than引導的表示比較的子句，如果主詞較長，會採用倒裝語序。例如：

▶ Running is a great way to reduce stress in the same way **as** are yoga, meditation, and deep-breathing exercises.
和瑜伽、冥想、深呼吸一樣，跑步是一種非常好的減輕壓力的方式。

▶ We are retiring more nurses because of age **than** are entering the profession.
我們很多護士因年齡大了而退休，這個數量大於進入這個行業的護士數量。

▶ African Americans are at greater risk for stroke **than** are white Americans.
非洲裔美國人比白種美國人更容易得中風。

as引導的其他子句也會採用倒裝語序。例如：

▶ Her father is a Philadelphia lawyer, **as are two of her three brothers**.
她的父親在費城做律師，她的三個哥哥中有兩個也都是一樣。

▶ The undergarments are of good quality, **as are the stockings**.
這些內衣品質很好，長襪也不錯。

► Taxis are plentiful and inexpensive, **as are public buses**, making it easy to explore this paradise.

計程車多而不貴，公共汽車也是如此，所以要遊覽這個天堂非常容易。

► Paul smiled and tilted his head **as is his trait**.

保羅一笑就歪著頭，這是他的特點。

上面的例子中，as分別相當於so 和which。as引導的讓步副詞子句也有部分謂語提前的倒裝情況。例如：

► **Try as he might**, however, Mr. Levine has not been able to learn much about how this carpenter's tool was transformed into a musical folk instrument.

儘管萊文先生努力了，但他還是沒能明白這個木匠工具是如何變成一個民間樂器的。

► **Try as Levin would** to control himself, he remained morose and silent.

儘管萊文想方設法控制自己，但他還是愁眉苦臉，一聲不響。

但是，並不是所有as引導的讓步副詞子句都是主謂倒裝的語序。在下面的例子中，as引導的讓步副詞子句中只是主詞補語或狀語前置，但as子句中的主詞和謂語順序保持不變。例如：

► **Anxious as she was about the neighbors**, she couldn't help laughing as she hurried downstairs.

儘管她為這些鄰居擔心，但她在匆忙下樓的時候還是忍不住大笑。

► **Tired as she was now**, she didn't pause.

儘管她現在很累，但是卻沒有停下來。

► **Hard as David might try**, he failed to save the dog.

儘管大衛非常努力了，但他還是沒有救得了這隻狗。

小結 ▷

本章主要介紹了倒裝的用法。根據倒裝的不同程度，可以將其分為全部倒裝和部分倒裝。全部倒裝是整個謂語都提到主詞前面的位置。含不及物動詞或者連綴動詞的句子容易使用全部倒裝。在全部倒裝中處於句首位置的成分可以是地點狀語、時間狀語、主詞補語、直接引語等。

部分倒裝是把謂語的一部分，即助動詞，提到或加到主詞前面。否定副詞、程度副詞置於句首位置容易引起部分倒裝。假設語氣，連接詞so，nor，neither和as，than子句中也會使用倒裝。

常用不規則動詞

附錄

不變化的不規則動詞 ▷

原形	過去式	過去分詞
bet	bet	bet
broadcast	broadcast	broadcast
burst	burst	burst
cast	cast	cast
cost	cost	cost
cut	cut	cut
forecast	forecast/forecasted	forecast/forecasted
hit	hit	hit
hurt	hurt	hurt
knit	knit/knitted	knit/knitted
let	let	let
put	put	put
quit	quit/quitted	quit/quitted
read	read	read
rid	rid	rid
set	set	set
shed	shed	shed
shut	shut	shut
split	split	split
spread	spread	spread
upset	upset	upset

其他類型的不規則動詞

原形	過去式	過去分詞
abide	abode/abided	abided
arise	arose	arisen
awake	awoke	awoken
be	was/were	been
bear	bore	borne
beat	beat	beaten
become	became	become
begin	began	begun
behold	beheld	beheld
bend	bent	bent
bind	bound	bound
bid	bade/bid	bid/bidden
bite	bit	bitten
bleed	bled	bled
blow	blew	blown
break	broke	broken
breed	bred	bred
bring	brought	brought
build	built	built
burn	burnt/burned	burnt/burned
buy	bought	bought
catch	caught	caught
choose	chose	chosen
come	came	come
creep	crept	crept
deal	dealt	dealt

dive	dived/dove	dived
dig	dug	dug
do	did	done
draw	drew	drawn
dream	dreamed/dreamt	dreamed/dreamt
dress	dressed	dressed
drink	drank	drunk
drive	drove	driven
dwell	dwelt	dwelt
eat	ate	eaten
fall	fell	fallen
feed	fed	fed
feel	felt	felt
fight	fought	fought
find	found	found
flee	fled	fled
fly	flew	flown
forbid	forbade	forbidden
forget	forgot	forgotten
forgive	forgave	forgiven
foresee	foresaw	foreseen
freeze	froze	frozen
get	got	gotten
give	gave	given
go	went	gone
grind	ground	ground
grow	grew	grown
hang	hung/hanged（絞死）	hung/hanged（絞死）

have	had	had
hear	heard	heard
hide	hid	hidden/hid
hold	held	held
keep	kept	kept
kneel	knelt	knelt
know	knew	known
lay	laid	laid
lead	led	led
lean	leant（英）/leaned	leant（英）/leaned
learn	learnt（英）/learned	learnt（英）/learned
leap	leapt（英）/leaped（美）	leapt（英）/leaped（美）
leave	left	left
lend	lent	lent
lie	lay	lain
light	lighted/lit	lighted/lit
lose	lost	lost
make	made	made
mean	meant	meant
meet	met	met
mislead	misled	misled
misspell	misspelt	misspelt
mistake	mistook	mistaken
misunderstand	misunderstood	misunderstood
outdo	outdid	outdone
outgrow	outgrew	outgrown
outrun	outran	outrun
outshine	outshone	outshone

overcome	overcame	overcome
override	overrode	overridden
oversleep	overslept	overslept
overtake	overtook	overtaken
overthrow	overthrew	overthrown
pay	paid	paid
prove	proved	proved/又作proven（美）
rend	rent	rent
repay	repaid	repaid
retell	retold	retold
ride	rode	ridden
ring	rang	rung
rise	rose	risen
run	ran	run
say	said	said
see	saw	seen
seek	sought	sought
sell	sold	sold
send	sent	sent
shake	shook	shaken
shine	shone	shone
shoot	shot	shot
show	showed	shown/showed
shrink	shrunk	shrunk
sing	sang	sung
sink	sunk	sunk
sit	sat	sat
sleep	slept	slept

slide	slid	slid
sling	slung	slung
smell	smelt（英）/smelled	smelt（英）/smelled
speak	spoke	spoken
spend	spent	spent
spill	spilt（英）/spilled	spilt（英）/spilled
spin	spun	spun
spit	spat	spat
spoil	spoilt（英）/spoiled	spoilt（英）/spoiled
spring	sprang/又作sprung（美）	sprung
stand	stood	stood
steal	stole	stolen
stick	stuck	stuck
sting	stung	stung
stride	strode	stridden
strike	struck	struck
strive	strove/strived	strove/strived
swear	swore	sworn
swim	swam	swum
swing	swung	swung
take	took	taken
teach	taught	taught
tear	tore	torn
tell	told	told
think	thought	thought
thrive	throve/thrived	thrived
throw	threw	thrown
tread	trod/treaded	trodden/trod

undergo	underwent	undergone
underlie	underlay	underlain
underpay	underpaid	underpaid
understand	understood	understood
wake	woke/waked	woken/waked
wear	wore	worn
weep	wept	wept
win	won	won
wind	wound	wound
withdraw	withdrew	withdrawn
withstand	withstood	withstood
write	wrote	written

原來如此 系列 E261

第一本結合劍橋語料庫的**文法大全**：
英文文法基礎概念╳劍橋語料庫╳搭配單字

語言學教授親自解析，一本帶你熟悉英文文法！

作　　者	馬博森、寮菲、何文忠編輯團隊 編著
顧　　問	曾文旭
社　　長	王毓芳
編輯統籌	黃璽宇、耿文國
主　　編	吳靜宜
執行主編	潘妍潔
執行編輯	吳芸蓁、吳欣蓉
美術編輯	王桂芳、張嘉容
法律顧問	北辰著作權事務所　蕭雄淋律師、幸秋妙律師

初　　版	2022年08月
出　　版	捷徑文化出版事業有限公司
電　　話	（02）2752-5618
傳　　真	（02）2752-5619

定　　價	新台幣480元／港幣160元
產品內容	一書

總 經 銷	采舍國際有限公司
地　　址	235新北市中和區中山路二段366巷10號3樓
電　　話	（02）8245-8786
傳　　真	（02）8245-8718

港澳地區經銷商	和平圖書有限公司
地　　址	香港柴灣嘉業街12號百樂門大廈17樓
電　　話	（852）2804-6687
傳　　真	（852）2804-6409

本書圖片由Shutterstock提供

捷徑 Book站

本書如有缺頁、破損或倒裝，
請聯絡捷徑文化出版社。

【版權所有　翻印必究】

國家圖書館出版品預行編目資料

第一本結合劍橋語料庫的文法大全：英文文法基礎概念╳劍橋語料庫╳搭配單字／馬博森、寮菲、何文忠編輯團隊. -- 初版.
-- 臺北市：捷徑文化, 2022.08
　面；　公分（原來如此：E261）
ISBN 978-626-7116-07-4（平裝）

1. CST: 英語　2. CST: 語法

805.16　　　　　　　　　111007629